A Significance Novel

UNDENIABLY CHOSEN

A Significance Novel

UNDENIABLY CHOSEN

SHELLY CRANE

Editing services by Todd Barselow at Auspicious Apparatus Press
Formatting by Tianne Samson with E.M. Tippetts Book Designs

emtippettsbookdesigns.com

Printed in the United States.
10 9 8 7 6 5 4 3 2 1
More information can be found at the author's website
shellycrane.blogspot.com

ISBN-13: 978-1508996392

ISBN-10: 1508996393

SHELLY CRANE

Significance Series
Significance
Accordance
Defiance
Reverance
Independence
Consequence
Undeniably Chosen
Undeniably Fated **(Coming Soon)**

Collide Series
Collide
Uprising
Catalyst
Revolution

Wide Awake Series
Wide Awake
Wide Spaces
Wide Open

Devour Series
Devour
Consume
Altered
Smash Into You

Stolen Hearts Series
Stealing Grace
Taking Faith

For Granddad & Granny
Bill & Sally Register

For always being the place we wanted to go to in the summer. It may have just been a farm, but for us it was a make-believe place where we could play and run and pretend we were anywhere in those bushes and ditches and barns. For making me watch the classic, "old", and musical movies that I now cherish. For raising the good man I call my father who knows the importance of family. For staying together all these years and being an amazing example. The world isn't always easy, but it's those times when we're tested that we're forged in fire.

"The world breaks everyone, and afterward, some are strong at the broken places."
- Ernest Hemingway

CHAPTER ONE

I waited for that day, for that one thing to complete me. To feel someone's heartbeat inside my chest and know that it was reciprocated. To find the one who belonged to me and could be the one to make me whole.

I still waited. I was a sophomore in high school. Graduating and heading off to U of T in a just two years so I could be an architect, just like Grandpa.

We just got back from the last reunification. Mom had taken fire for her new rule about the Visionary being able to work and have a day job rather than just…being the Visionary. They wanted her to be 'accessible' at all times and she warred on that she could be accessible and still work with Daddy at the centers as well. That's what cell phones were for.

So I watched as Dad was being extra nice and attentive by cooking dinner that night since, even though she was the Visionary, it sucked when people were against you and questioned your dedication.

Wanna know what else sucked? Being the Visionary's daughter. And the clan leader's daughter deducted even more points.

I loved my parents, don't get me wrong. They were great. Rodney and I both were pretty grounded. We went to the private school here and he played football while I played volleyball. I'd been working at the learning centers for Daddy for a year now.

I loved it, but planned to go work for Grandpa as soon as I graduated from college. Dad was fine with it. He of all people knew what it was like to want to be something, to have the fire for something.

I was fascinated by the thought that I could create something like that.

We used to travel around with Daddy's job, staying in a place for a couple months before moving on to the next place. It might not sound so appealing, but it really was amazing to live in all those states. We lived in New York, Washington, Illinois, Texas, and about fifteen other states. But, when I was almost in high school, they wanted us to settle down, so we moved back to Tennessee and Daddy bought Mom a big, beautiful red house with a wraparound white porch. Rodney's old fort made from wood slats was still in the backyard, though he hadn't been back there in years.

It was our home and I loved it, but also couldn't wait to leave it. My teenage heart was so fickle. But the one thing it wasn't fickle about was wanting my significant.

So, back to the part where I was waiting. Even though I wasn't of age yet, every reunification brought anxiousness for me. I was fifteen. Mom was only seventeen when she imprinted and since all the rules were being broken, I couldn't help but hope that I would imprint soon.

It was more than just wanting to have somebody, it was like this thing in my body was pulled just a little too tight. Just enough to annoy and bother me, but not enough to be painful. My significant was the only one who could make me feel normal. I knew it.

Dad tossed the noodles with the white sauce—Mom's favorite—and divided it onto four plates as our new puppy Mavis rubbed against my leg. Dad glanced up at me with a smile. "Put ice in some glasses for me, sweetheart?"

"Sure."

"Rodney. Rodney!" he called louder.

Rodney took his earphones out and looked at him. "Yeah?"

"Silverware."

"Why are you cooking again?" he asked. "Mom's a way better cook than you."

"Hey!" Dad laughed and slung a noodle at him. It landed on Rodney's face and hair.

He jumped back like that would save him, but it was too late. "Dude!" he shrieked, his voice cracking with puberty as he swatted at his shagged hair.

"Dude, my hair!"

Dad and I were laughing so hard, we could barely stand up as Rodney went on. Rodney jumped across the counter and stuck his finger in the sauce before holding it out to Dad. "You're gonna get it, old man."

I ducked out of the way, fearful for my own hair, and giggled by the fridge as they fought and wrestled. I felt Mom's hands on my arms and heard her laugh behind me. "Oh, my. Ava, what's going on?"

"Dad pulled the unforgiveable. He got noodles in Rod's hair."

She giggled and came around me with her blue silk robe on and bare feet. "Is all this for me?" she crooned sweetly, looking around at the mess on the counter.

"Mom, totally his fault." Rodney pointed at Dad shamelessly as he laughed.

"Oh, I believe you." She wrapped her arms around Dad's neck and wiped a smudge of sauce from his cheek with her thumb.

"You believe him over me?" Daddy asked, his voice changing like it always did where Mom was concerned.

She laughed, reaching up on her tiptoes and kissed him. "Thank you for cooking dinner. You didn't have to."

"I wanted to," he replied. His voice and eyes held a reverence that I'd always seen and heard about my whole life, but never experienced. "You earned it. You're such a good woman, and I know the reunifications take it out of you."

I had watched my parents for what seemed like centuries. The way they existed so effortlessly in each other's world and space. They could go minutes without looking away from each other. They kissed constantly. They hugged all the time, stole touches and wrapped their fingers around the other's wrist. I knew it was to feel their calm, to be wrapped in the little bit of bliss that their touch provided.

I felt like I was watching a real-life romance novel play out before my eyes.

"I'm okay," she told him and whispered her next words. "Thank you for this. And for earlier. I really needed it."

"Eew. Gross. Stop," Rodney said, hands up. He threw some forks haphazardly on the table. "Don't you see the way my ears are singed?"

Mom laughed. "I was talking about the bubble bath your father made me, you goober." She reached up again, kissing Daddy on the lips, but he reached around her and drew her in even more. I turned to fill the glasses. It

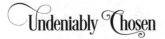

was disgusting; they were my parents after all, but I was also envious. Things were still a little up in the air with the imprints and everything. It seemed that everything had gone back to normal for the most part, except there were no more age limits. You met them when you met them and that was that.

So instead of knowing I'd meet the person I wanted most in a few years while in college, I was forced to spend my days *waiting*.

The only thing a girl in high school—who's never dated anyone before—wants is to find someone to love her. I was breaking out and going my own way, and while I was reinventing myself to become the me I would always be, I was dying to throw my epic love story in the mix.

"I love you, Maggie," I heard behind me.

"I love you more."

"Go sit. I'll bring you a plate." And I waited for it…

The sound of Daddy's palm lightly smacking Mom's butt was my cue that it was okay to turn around. Mom shook her head at Dad as she took a seat. Dad, smug as all get out, brought her plate, kissing her forehead as he sat it in front of her, before setting the rest of the table and playfully yelling at Rodney to sit down and behave like a Jacobson.

They were so predictable. And adorable. And so in love with each other it hurt to look at them.

CHAPTER TWO

Six Years Later

I yawned and got the stink eye from Professor Gracco. I loved and hated my classes, but it was the last week of them before winter break. Every class was a yawn-fest. The teachers knew it, but I think it just made them that much more ornery.

The minutes crawled by and my watch kept winking at me, taunting, begging me to keep looking at it so the time would move even slower.

Only two more years of this and I'd graduate and could go work at the firm with Grandpa. Well, not for very long because he was retiring in a few years. But the chance to work with him at all would be worth it. He was happy that I'd decided to come work with them. A few other family members had taken a cue from Dad and went their own way, running a business that they wanted instead.

But they always seemed to be good businesses. Our kind had a knack for smart ventures and risks that paid off. Businesses that were good for more than just us. Like Daddy with his learning centers and my second cousin, who has a horse farm and had started an equestrian riding school.

When the professor took the little golden bell from his desk and jiggled it in the air at us like it was a catholic school and not a college, we knew the class was over. I packed up my things hurriedly and rushed across campus to the coffee shop. Every Friday I brought the whole staff at the center whatever poison was their favorite beverage.

I was running late. Professor Hubris back there thought that he held our literal futures in his sweaty little hands and it was his duty to teach more than what was outlined in the syllabus.

Like, maybe, how to make someone late for work? It didn't matter that my dad owned the company. That actually made me want to be on time even more—so no one could say that I was just there because my father let me be. I wanted to be a good worker, have ethics and values that people could see on me like a Girl Scout badge.

I wanted to earn what I had, not have things handed to me. No nepotism for me, no sir.

So when I ran into the shop and saw Paul at the counter with a carton of coffee cups, I mouthed a 'Thank you' to him. I got the same exact thing every Friday. One white hot chocolate, one black, one vanilla cappuccino with cream and sugar, and for me, a hazelnut iced coffee. There was a long line today, so I waited in it, pulling out my cell to check messages quickly.

A napkin floated to the floor beside me and I reached absentmindedly to pick it up when someone was next to me doing the same thing. Our fingers almost touched on the napkin and my eyes lifted to see intense blue ones meeting mine. I felt my lips part, not just at his closeness, but at the sheer force of that gaze.

His hair was black and spiked up in the middle in a small fauxhawk. He was tan with a red t-shirt that hugged his neck.

"Thanks," he muttered, his voice as low as gravel. I had to admit that it made me smile for no other reason than the fact that he hadn't taken his eyes off mine yet. He finally, slowly stood.

"No problem," I replied and cleared my throat a little because my voice sounded entirely too affected.

I didn't know what else to say and he just stared, his eyes wandering around my face, before he finally smiled with just one side of his mouth and chuckled a little. "Sorry…you're just really…" He shook his head and stepped back. "Never mind. You go to school here?"

"Yeah. You?"

"Nah," he said, noncommittally. "Just getting some coffee. It was pretty good timing, I guess."

"What was?" I asked, shouldering my bag, refusing to let him go until it was no longer polite to keep him talking.

"Coming here at the same time as you." His smile spoke volumes of things he was thinking that I wasn't privy to. It reminded me of a romance novel…of my parents. I felt a stutter in my chest at what that could mean. "I'm usually here a lot later, but I was early today."

"You're early and I'm late," I said, chagrined that I had forgotten my purpose so easily. I looked over to the counter to see Paul staring an irritated yet intrigued look at my back. I knew he had a little crush on me, but there was no point in pursuing that.

I turned back to blue eyes. He whispered like it was a curse, "Am I keeping you? Do you need to go?"

I stepped off the plank, one hopeful foot in front of the other. "Do you feel that?"

He frowned with his brows, but smiled. "Feel what exactly?"

My spirits fell as fast as they had risen. This was just some college boy checking out girls in the coffee shop. He wasn't Virtuoso, he wasn't a human so intrigued by what was happening to him to press further, and he wasn't someone…that I could go any further with.

I smiled as much as I could, but stepped back. "I really do have to go. I'm really late."

His smile fell and he took a step closer. "Uh…can you stay for one cup of coffee? I'm buying." He tried for a smile again, but I just couldn't let this go any farther.

"I'm late for work already." I turned to give Paul a twenty and told him to keep the change. When I turned back, I expected blue eyes to be gone, done with me, but he wasn't. I smiled and started to move around him toward the side back door.

He called for me to wait a second as he ran back to get his brown bag of whatever he had bought inside from the table, but I kept going. Before I reached the door, his hand gently caught my long sleeve in his fingers. I looked down at his hand first and then at his face. "I'm sorry," he said sincerely. "I'm not trying to be creepy, I just…" He licked his lips.

His red shirt had a fireman symbol on the front with the number 22 in the middle of it. His jeans were dark, worn, and ripped a little at the knee. He

wore black boots and had a brown leather band around his wrist that had the word VIVERE on it.

Wow, this boy was going to be a problem if I didn't get away.

"I know. I wish I had time to talk, I really do, but I really have to go."

"I do feel it," he said in a harsh voice. "I said I didn't feel it before, but I do."

Every movement but breathing stopped. "Feel what?"

"Like…" He moved his hand to my face and I froze in hopeful awe. He swept my hair back behind my ear. "Like we were meant to be here at the same time."

It was when his finger touched the rim of my ear that I felt my life changing before my eyes. He sucked in a huge breath right along with me and immediately I felt his hands on both sides of my face, pulling me in to press his forehead to mine as we watched the scenes play out. I worried about him. He must be a human because I'd never seen him before and was probably freaking out, but all I could do in that second was cling to his shirt with my empty hand, fisting the fabric and hanging on as I watched our future life together.

In one vision, we were lying in the tall grass somewhere. He ran his fingers up and down my arm. I talked and he listened like his life depended on it. The next one was us on terrace rooftop of the palace. Birds were all around us before Seth took off his jacket and laid it down for us to lay on. And then the third came, us in front of a big house. It was a place that looked familiar, but we stood there, older in our years, proud…like we belonged there on the big lawn and grand landscapes that seemed overgrown, but once beautiful. He was kissing my lips so softly.

We eased out of our reverie and his smile wasn't one of a human, it was one of someone who knew exactly what was going on. He moved us gently, pressing my back to the wall by the back door, but kept my face blissfully captive in his warm hands that I just knew were big and hard-worked calloused. "Oh, my g… It can't be," he said, but his smile refuted those words. "It's…really you."

"And I don't even know your name," I whispered in return.

He chuckled a little, deep and heady. "Seth."

"I'm Ava," I answered before he could ask.

"Ava," he repeated and I felt shivers run over me. He smiled, moving a little closer before letting his forehead touch mine once more. "I can't believe this is happening."

"I don't have to wait anymore," I realized happily, my chest humming with new life. Even with school and work and everything going on, I was constantly waiting for this. It consumed a little piece in the back of my brain and I was subconsciously always looking for the one whose touch would bind me to him and also set me free.

His smile faltered a little as he leaned his head back. "So…you're Virtuoso."

I nodded. "How come I've never seen you before?"

"We don't…go to the reunifications," he muttered softly. He looked so nervous and I felt the need to comfort him wash over me.

I still held the carton of coffee in one hand so I un-fisted his shirt and reached for his face. I was utterly shocked at how easily it came to me to be with him already. "Hey. What's the matter?"

"I just…" He shook his head and gulped, covering my hand with his on his cheek, like he wanted to keep it there forever. "I don't want to hurt you. I don't want… Gah, I'm so sorry, Ava."

"For what?" I said, but I saw in his mind for the first time. He was thinking about that house from my last vision. I realized that I remembered it from our histories. Our family taught about that…house…

The coffee cups fell from my hand. It was then the world came back to me and I saw several of the people in the coffee shop staring at us. Even Paul had stopped making coffee and was looking at us, like maybe he wanted to intervene.

I pushed Seth's chest a tiny bit, my hands aching and scolding me for doing so. He went without a fight. "Ava," he reasoned, pleaded.

"I've got to go." I turned to go, my heart banging in my chest.

He grabbed my hand gently, and his calm, the very thing I'd always wanted, shot through me and I couldn't stop the sigh, yet I still yanked my hand away. "Ava, please. Let's just talk for a minute."

I burst through the door and ran to my Volvo parked in front. Seth followed me, but didn't try to stop me. I got in and shut the door, pressing the push-start button, roaring the car to life. He stood outside my window, gripping his hair in his hands as he watched me back out. I heard him in my head as I peeled from the lot.

I'll wait for you however long you need. It's okay. I understand. I'd hate me, too.

I loved his voice. It ran over me like a silk nightgown…and I hated and loved that.

I went straight to the center, blowing through the doors, tears running down my face. Everyone stopped what they were doing and stared, but I looked for Daddy. When I didn't see him with any of the kids, I went right to his office. He was on the phone, but hung up on whoever was on the phone as soon as he saw me.

"Ava—"

"Daddy," I sobbed.

He stood quickly. "What happened?"

"I…imprinted…"

"You did?" He grinned and hugged me to him. "That's amazing, Ava. Where? Who? Why are you crying? Was it—"

"No, Daddy, no." I leaned back.

"What's the matter, baby girl?" he soothed and smoothed my hair like he had done for my entire life. Always comforting, always willing to bust heads if need be to make me happy. But Dad couldn't fix this.

"Daddy, I imprinted…with a Watson."

He squeezed me tighter and then leaned back. I saw his eyes cut to the left. They did that when he was speaking to Mom in his mind.

"Dad, I imprinted with this Seth guy and just ran away. I—" He watched, his eyes filling with sympathy and something else I couldn't put my finger on. When he didn't blow up and start throwing things in rage like I expected, I frowned. "Where's Momma?"

He took my arms in his hands gently. "She's not here yet. She's on the way. We have a lot to talk about."

"Why are you being so calm? It's almost as if you…know something I don't." I tried to pull my arms back, but he held tighter.

"Sit, Ava," he commanded, as my father and my Champion. I sat in his desk chair. He leaned on his desk and crossed his legs and arms. His sigh was enough to push me into a state of annoyance.

"Daddy, oh, my gosh. What is going on?" I hissed.

"Do you remember Ashlyn? From when you were a little girl?"

"Ashlyn?" I whispered. I hadn't heard that name in so long. She was the ghost of a Visionary that used to come to me as a child. But I hadn't seen her in years and no one had brought her up since. "Barely."

"Do you remember her telling you about a boy," he said carefully. I looked up at my father, still so young looking, but a faint crown of greys had started to show making him look a lot like the photos of Grandpa Peter when he was Champion.

"I don't…"

"Maybe we should wait for your mother."

"Dad," I protested.

"I'm here," Mom called from the doorway and rushed to me. She pulled me up and wrapped her arms around me. "Oh, my Ava," she whispered and all at once I was a little girl again. With her rocking me, I could hear them whispering, feel Daddy's hand on my arm and know that my life was about to change. I had waited for this day my entire life, all Virtuoso do, and now my perfect day was being ruined, taken from me. Why?

She sighed and pulled away slightly. "Ava."

The way she said my name made me know right then that they both knew something and had known it for some time.

"Take me home," I said with more force than I believed I had. "And tell me everything."

I expected a fight. This was the Champion, the leader of my clan, and the Visionary, the leader of my race. I got no fight however.

"Come on," she said, taking my hand, and towing me along. I left my car there along with Mom's and rode silently in the back seat of Dad's truck. I watched their clasped hands the entire drive home as if their connection held the answer to everything—the way Daddy's thumb rubbed over her knuckles in their own silent conversation.

I knew their story. I knew how hard they'd had to fight for each other. I knew how the Watsons had tried so hard to destroy them. I knew how Marcus had kidnapped her and how she'd been tortured. How their leaders Sikes and Donald had manipulated the entire clan and used alchemy, experiments, and other means to hurt humans, and even our own kind, to do awful things.

But before Gran had passed away, she made sure to tell us all the good things that had happened, too. How Daddy had gone and searched the woods for Momma when she'd been kidnapped, but ultimately it was Cousin

Rodney who had found her. How Daddy would sneak in her window at night so she would be safe and not wake up in withdrawals, how he had taken her away to California to the beach house to keep her away from the echoling who terrorized her when she closed her eyes, how she had saved his life at a stoplight and that's how they met.

I knew it all.

I also knew that I had my own story now. Right now, Seth was out there freaking out just like I was. I had gotten no ill will from him, nothing but comfort and the need to make sure I was okay in that moment. How could someone who was supposed to be evil be so concerned for me if that were true?

And how was it even possible? Grandpa Haddock was a Watson, making Mamma part Watson, so how could I have imprinted with one? I needed so many answers and I needed them now. I knew that that my body would start rebelling against me soon. It would be begging me to go after Seth, to seek him out, to find him, to touch his skin and find the comfort that only he could give me.

I didn't know what to do. I didn't know what I was *going* to do.

A couple hours later, my heart beat painfully in my chest as I tried to take it all in, tried to keep calm, for I knew that my body was calling the one person to me that I wasn't sure I even wanted here. I had listened to them tell me about Seth, about how he had been an innocent little boy taken from his mother—a woman the Watsons had been doing experiments on. When my parents freed everyone from the compound when I was a child, Seth was the only one that they couldn't find. They ran with him, took him as their own, and though Mom looked for him for a long time, they never found him. Ashlyn told them it was meant to be this way, that Seth was meant to grow up with them, but it didn't stop my parents from looking, from feeling guilty for not making it in time to save him. They showed me the drawings they found at the compound the day they would have rescued him. Mom showed me the vision of Ashlyn as she told us all about Seth and us and the new council. It's why Uncle Bish and Kyle, and Aunt Jen and Lynne were council members now. It's why all of this was happening.

Mom got that look in her eye, the one that said something important and epic was about to happen, but she looked so…pissed. So un-Mom-like in that moment. I looked at Dad and he didn't look much better. They both looked so worried and older in that moment.

She knelt down in front of me. "Ava, I want you to know that we didn't know that Seth was going to be your significant. We knew he'd come back one day and be important, but...not like this."

And so it began. My life was changed with words spoken that could never be taken back as they laid everything out for me, all the things that had happened when I was a child and too little to understand, much less control.

And now, I was no longer a child but an adult who had to face things head on. Whether I knew what those demons looked like or not. Whether the demons looked like my significant or not...

"I don't know if I can even sleep tonight," I muttered and rubbed at my arms. They were restless. "I can already feel myself twitching."

"Tomorrow..." Dad began, but stopped. He sighed forcefully and tightened his fists. "I'll go find him and make him come here if he doesn't come on his own."

"Dad, you didn't see him. He was..." I bit into my lip hard. Just talking about him was making me ache all over. I closed my eyes and tried to breathe.

I heard Mom say, "Baby, I think we need to stop talking about this. It's just making things worse for her."

"I know, but...maybe I should go over there. Maybe I should try to find him and—you know what? No." I looked up to find him looking down at me. "I'm not going to do that. It has to be his choice until it's not. I'll give him until tomorrow to be the good guy. If he doesn't, then I'll go get him and make him. I can tell by looking at you that you want to have faith in him."

"You didn't see him, Dad," I reiterated. "He wanted this. He was worried about me. He'll come. He'll find me." I hoped. "If what you said is true, then he didn't choose any of what happened. He's not a Watson."

"But he's lived with them his whole life," Mom reasoned. "We have no idea the things they've done to him, the things they've made him do. We have to be cautious. *You* have to cautious." She went into the kitchen and I heard a pill bottle shake before she came back. "Here. Take these. They'll help you

sleep tonight. They were Grans," she said softly.

I ached as the pills went down. I heard Rodney coming in the back door loudly. Dad went right to him and put his hand on his chest to stop him. They whispered back and forth and Rodney looked at me over Dad's shoulder. Dad wasn't going to be able to stop him. He didn't know that, but I did.

"Come on, Dad," Rodney said gruffly and looked at him right in his face. "Move."

He pushed his Champion gently in the shoulder and I watched Dad's stunned face as he watched Rodney come and sweep me up in his big brotherly arms on the couch. He said low in my ear, but I knew that they still could hear, "Tell me who I have to hurt. Who is this guy and why isn't he here with you right now?"

I looked at Dad and he looked so amused and bemused all at once. He waved me on and leaned his hip against the counter, pulling Mom into the 'v' of his legs so he could wrap his arms around her from behind, inching his hand under her shirt to make sure his palm was on her skin. I heard her so sigh loud and hated that I was causing them so much distress.

"Seth," I explained. "Seth Watson," I said with as much gumption as I could muster.

His eyes rounded. I told him everything and he tightened his arms on me as he listened.

"Okay," he said and kicked his shoes off the end of the couch. Mom was two seconds from scolding him when he asked, "So where is he? He should be here."

Like fate usually worked, there was a knock on the front door. An insistent knock. Dad shot me a look before taking a loaded breath. I started to shake and stood from the couch quickly. It was him; I knew it like I knew my own name.

"Ava, wait," he told me.

"Dad."

"You, sit," he said in his Champion voice. "I'll answer and let him in. What if the Watsons were planning something and knew you'd run to the door to answer it thinking it was him? We know nothing about him yet. Until we do, we go at this with caution." I sighed. I hated that I had to look at my significant with anything but reverence, but Daddy was right. I mean, I was the one that had run right out of the coffee shop this afternoon. "I mean it, baby girl," he said softly.

Rodney turned me to look at him and held my upper arms in his hands. "If he hurts you, I can't be held accountable for what I do."

"I love you, you know that?" I replied and reached up on my toes to hug him. I tried to smile, but think I failed epically when he put one arm around my shoulders and tugged me keep me there, as if to shield me from whatever or whoever was coming.

Dad had to know I was anxious—he didn't make me wait. He went to the door quickly. I could hear them in the other room with deep, urgent tones. My significant.

And then there he was.

CHAPTER THREE

Ava, I heard in my mind before his mouth said the word out loud. "Ava."

"Well," Dad drawled out—practically growled—and raised an eyebrow at me, letting me know he'd throw him out on his keister if I just gave him the word. It was one of those obviously awkward situations. We all stood in that circle and stared at each other, letting the awkwardness stew and simmer, but all I could do was stare at those blue eyes and wait for him to speak again. "I guess we'll…let you talk for a minute." Dad stepped in front of me to block Seth's view and said in a lower voice, "But we won't be far. At all."

He, Mom, and Rodney stepped to the side of the room to stand at the breakfast bar. I stayed where I was standing in front of the couch and Seth made no move to come closer. He kept his eyes on me and never looked over to my parents. I wondered about that, but not enough to really care.

He stuck his hands in his pockets and licked his lips once before asking, "So you're in college?" I felt a scoffing, silly laugh bubbling up before I could stop it. He smiled just a little. "What?"

"That's what you chose to open with? Of all the opening lines you could have used?" I bit into my lip to stop my smile.

His grin widened and he shrugged. "You're right. That was kind of foolish. How about a do over?" I watched his throat work through a gulp. "I've done nothing but worry about you all afternoon, ever since I watched you leave and I didn't know if I'd ever see you again. I know that this whole..." he swung his hand out between us, "Romeo and Juliet thing we've got working for us is pretty ridiculous, but I'm not going to let that stand in my way. I'm really hoping you aren't going to let it stand in yours. Say that you won't, Ava. Before we go any further, say you're at least going to—"

"Try?" I tried to keep my breathing to a minimum after that speech. My parents were present, after all. What could I say after that turn around? "I'm going to try," I assured and swallowed thickly. "And yes, I'm in college. Architecture," I breathed.

"Architecture," he repeated and smiled. He looked almost—proud. But how could that be when he didn't even know me? "Wow, that's amazing. You have to be smart to handle all the work of that major." I nodded. He took a small step forward. "And dedicated and—I'm sure you know all that. I think that's awesome." I felt my cheeks heat a little. "And you work, too? It's really impressive that you're juggling it all." I felt my brow bunch before I remembered telling him I was late for work at the coffee shop and that's why I had to leave.

"And my grade point average is *way* up there, too." He smiled, seeing where I was going with it.

"Okay, enough grilling you about school." He took another step forward, his hands still in his pockets, but his smile was wide open.

"What about you?" I asked, though I remembered his shirt and the firefighter emblem on it.

"I got my associates degree in business because that's what my family wanted, but I knew I'd never use it. I knew I was going to be a firefighter from the time I turned eight years old."

"Scary job, isn't it?"

He shrugged, bringing one of his hands out of his pocket. His hand caught on the fabric of his shirt in doing so and his shirt rode up his stomach a bit before falling back into place. His thumb rubbed against his lip as he prepared to speak. It was so distracting that I just stared at him doing that while he talked. "It can be. But as long as you know what you're doing and don't get cocky, you'll be fine."

Somehow, I didn't believe him, but believing that he wasn't cocky to some degree was also unbelievable in its own right.

His slight chuckle brought me out of my reverie. I stopped looking at his mouth to find his eyes laughing and bright. He smiled, letting his chin fall a bit. I knew he was laughing at me—in that *caught you looking* kinda way. I finally stopped looking at that mouth and looked at my feet. I felt my own lips lift in a grin.

I managed to say, "I don't believe you."

"What?" he said, completely confused.

"I said, I don't believe you."

"I heard you," he replied with mirth and took a step closer. "I just don't know in what context you mean."

"You said being a fireman was safe like someone would say a trip to the grocery store was fun," he puffed a laugh, "and I know it's not quite as simple as that."

His eyes moved over my face, looking for something, or maybe just learning me as I was trying to learn him—one of us starting on the inside while the other, the outside. We'd trade places soon enough, I was sure of it. They moved to my neck and then back up. I was shocked that he hadn't done a complete once-over. I knew he wanted to. Was it because my parents were still here or because he knew I was watching him do his inspection?

His lip quirked and, oh, it was maddening in the most delicious way.

He said softly, "You don't have to worry about me, if that's what these questions are for." He smiled a little wider. "I have a great team of guys I work with that don't play around…when it comes to the job."

I saw a flash of a big white sheet, him—no shirt, no shoes, laying on the bed, being tossed into the air by big men while in a dead sleep. I jolted a little at seeing something in my mind that didn't belong there. It was a prank…

His interest was piqued, knowing I'd seen it, but how? Significants don't see in each other's minds for quite some time after they bond with each other. The first day? My eyes slid over to my parents to find them talking in the kitchen while Rodney did some schoolwork on his laptop.

Should I ask? I had heard his voice before in my head, but I thought it had been wishful thinking…

Ava.

My eyes flew to his and my lips parted. He smiled again—that devastating smile that made me question how I had existed in this world without it until now. That smile needed to be experienced.

The why's and how's of us being able to speak to each other in our minds and see visions so soon was forgotten.

"No matter what happens—and I know that things aren't going to be easy for us—I'm glad I was early getting my coffee today."

"Running late didn't suck for me either."

He smirked and it slayed the breath in my lungs. His last step was deliberate and final, his eager gaze moved from my hand to my eyes. His eyes weren't really dark at all, they were blue in every sense of the word. So blue. His hair was in a small fauxhawk, which I didn't know when I saw him before but I know now is a Watson 'thing'. They always have their hair done in harsh ways and angles, bangs slashed against their dark hair, making them look so angry all the time. Or maybe that's just their face. Naturally Seth would pick up some of their habits and things living with them all these years. It was a good thing he had black hair or they would never have adopted him, I was sure.

He took my hand in his and must have known that I'd need the extra help to keep standing because when we sighed with the force of our touch, the breath rushing between us, his other hand reached up to grip my elbow gently and bring me into the warmth of his chest. He was almost a full head above me he was so tall.

He murmured against my temple, "I can say with absolute surety that it's nice to meet you, Ava."

"I'm sorry I ran out on you today," I said softly and pushed his chest to lean back enough to see his face. I needed to see him.

He shrugged casually and moved back, but kept my hand in his. "I would have run out, too, if the situation were reversed."

I shook my head. "No, you wouldn't."

He smiled and it was adorable. He smiled almost as if he were caught in something. "Okay. I probably wouldn't. You got me."

He was thinking about joking around and being able to be silly with someone. I got a flash of something then. No…someone.

"Who was that? Who is she?" I asked, a spike of jealousy rushing through my veins like hot anger. It came out of nowhere, but my body knew that this girl wasn't just a nobody. She was young and pretty and she had brought that smile to his face a second ago in that vision…not me.

He seemed surprised. His face ducked and he tried to find my eyes straight on. "You saw Harper just now? In my mind?"

I groaned. I hated her name from his mouth, but not an hour ago I wasn't even sure I wanted *him* at all. I closed my eyes. What was happening to me? I wasn't this girl. I wasn't some jealous, stupid girl.

"It's not stupid." I opened my eyes and found him so close. His lips were parted and his eyes heavy. "It's not stupid. Significants are supposed to be possessive and protective. And even jealous. That's how we keep each other safe and happy. If you saw her in my mind and didn't want to know about her, *I'd be* upset."

I sighed and realized that only then were his fingers on mine drawing off my anxiety. I looked down at them and back up. Before I could say the words, he went on.

"She's nobody that matters to us. She's my cousin, my friend. I was just thinking that it's nice to have someone who jokes around with me like her, who has the same sense of humor."

"She's not actually your cousin though," I said softly, but regretted as soon as it was out. "I'm sorry. I didn't mean—"

"They've always treated me as such." He smiled and rubbed my knuckles with his thumb. "Mostly," he amended. "But Harper has always just been a really good friend. You have nothing to worry about. I've always believed that I would find my significant one day so I've never looked elsewhere."

That thought made me pause. He had to have a reason to believe that, but the Watsons were human so why would he think… "Have you had bonds happening in the Watsons?"

"Of course," he answered and squinted. "Haven't you?"

Oh, God, no. The experiments.

I took a deep breath, knowing we had a long night ahead of us. "We have a lot to talk about."

But first. I pulled him down to hug me, letting my arms wrap around his neck, and sighed really loud and embarrassingly when his arms settled on my lower back, pressing me to him so tightly. "Thank you for finding me," I whispered in his ear and pulled back.

He took my face in his hands, his warm hands holding my cheeks, and leaned in to kiss my forehead. I gripped his shirt in my fist at the assault of tingles that spread through me.

"Wow," he murmured against my skin.

Yeah—wow. I felt like I was losing myself. I pushed him back a little and felt my head swaying with pleasure. "Um…we need to talk."

"Yeah," he agreed too quickly. "There's lots to talk about."

"No, Seth, I mean we need to talk with my parents. There are things that you don't know, things that we need to tell you. We didn't know until tonight and I'm so sorry that all this is just getting dropped on you. There's a lot that's happened. Do you…remember Ashlyn?"

"Ashlyn." He thought and tilted his head even with his squint. "Yeah, she was the ghost of the old Visionary. She used to come visit me when I was kid sometimes."

"Yeah. Me, too."

His head snapped up and then he remembered, just as I had. "Ava…" he muttered my name slowly as he recalled it.

"Yeah. Let's go talk to Mom and she'll explain everything better than I can. There's so much…to say." He seemed less thrilled now and I felt awful. "I'm so sorry, Seth. I just want to say upfront that I never knew about you. I promise. You can read that from my mind and know the truth, but there are some things that may not have been coincidence about us."

He gulped and then came a step closer, taking the ends of my fingers in his. "Things are bound to be weird from now on, right? I just found you, beautiful girl. I'm not giving up on you so easily."

With my heart skidding, I nodded and he followed me into the kitchen.

CHAPTER FOUR

"So, you see, we never meant for any of this to happen. We never meant for you to spend your life with them, the Watsons," my mother said carefully. "We never meant for anyone to get hurt. We're only sorry we didn't make it in time…to save your mother."

Seth stiffened beside me a second before his phone went off. It was a short, sharp, loud ringtone. He apologized and mumbled something about it having to be loud enough to wake him up at night at the fire station as he looked at the text message. I wasn't trying to invade his privacy, but I heard it loud and clear in my mind as he read it over and over in his mind. He stared at it for a few long seconds before shaking his head and then tucking it in his pocket.

Have you finished with her yet?

He looked up with a grimace at my mother and I felt all his emotions at once. Anger, abandonment, happiness, jealousy, sadness, appreciation that they had tried, but they had failed. It wasn't enough. He had lived in a certain kind of hell his whole life and the fact that they had been right there and he was the only one not rescued was like a slap in the face.

I however couldn't stop thinking about that text. *Have you finished with her?* What did that mean and who had sent it? It was obvious it was about me. So he had told his family—the Watsons—about me. And now they were texting wanting to know if he was *finished* with me? What did that even mean?

His warm hand covered mine and I looked up to see him watching my freak out. He looked concerned and shook his head. "It's not what you think. I did tell them and they're really happy for me. For us. They wanted me to bring you to meet everyone tonight."

Everything stopped, especially when Mom's breath caught and the glasses of sweet tea on the coffee table started to shake. Seth leaned back a bit, having his first taste of my mom's powers. Tea sloshed on the table as Dad's hand came up and cupped her cheek. "Baby, everything's okay."

"Caleb," she begged him for something that I didn't understand. Maybe she didn't either. "I didn't understand what it meant until now. She's his significant. That means he's going to take her to—"

"No," Dad argued, and it was evident that he meant it. He looked over at Seth and I started to say something to get him to tame his look, but he went on before I could. "She won't be going to the Watson's with you, Seth. I know they're your family and I know that it's...customary for her to meet the man's family, but with our history with them I don't think it's a good idea."

Seth's jaw tightened. "They didn't think it was a good idea for me to come here either, especially alone. They said it wasn't safe for me, that you'd hold a grudge against them, even after all this time, might try to hurt me. But I had to come. I wasn't going to let Ava suffer because of it."

"That's ridiculous," Mom huffed. "I have a distinct suspicion that what you think happened in the past and what actually happened are two very different things."

Seth stood, taking his hand with him. I felt his absence in my blood like ice. "I didn't have the best life. I'm not going to stand here and pretend that my family is all peaches and cream. They have their problems. We weren't perfect by any means, but they were all I had. They took me in when no one else would and have kept me this whole time—"

"They took you, Seth," Mom told him. "Taking you and *taking care of you* are two different things. You and your mother were...kidnapped and experimented on."

He scoffed and moved away from me around the table. "Now this is just too much." He looked at me, then at Mom before his eyes settled on me once more. "Ava, I know you don't like my family, but you can't expect me to believe

that they—"

"A lot of things happened before we were born," I said softly.

He shook his head, so Mom forged on. "Their powers were taken away." It didn't escape me how she left out the part where *she* had taken their powers. "But even before that, they practiced with potions and blood magic, alchemy, things they had no business messing with. Your Uncle Sikes was the worst of them. He started all this. He made himself a…significant."

"What?" Seth asked.

"He forced an imprint on a human woman, in a sense faking a bond with a potion he gave her. You would never have known. She got the tattoo, they were significants, they healed each other with their touch and he was protective of her. But it was never quite right. When their powers were taken because of the things they were doing, as punishment, they didn't accept that and move on. They did the opposite. They began to practice alchemy even more and…" she shrugged, "we didn't know in time. By the time we found out, it was too late. We've tried to keep a watch on them over the years, but since they fled the compound, we didn't even know where they'd gone to."

"Scattered," Seth muttered, distracted. "We don't live at the compound. It's been abandoned for years. They use it to cellar wine for my cousin's business."

He stared at the floor, looking so dejected and lost. I hated that I was part of the cause of this. "Seth," I whispered.

"I would know," he argued with no one and gritted his teeth. "If my family was doing these unspeakable things you're talking about, I would know. I've lived with them."

I caught a flash of a memory from Seth from when he was a child, something he was trying to remember. A room, a woman, his mother maybe, a table or bed, a bunch of people gathered around her, but when he saw that I saw it, too, he pushed it away and glared at me.

"That doesn't mean that it's what you're talking about!" he yelled, making me jump, my shoulders bunching. He sighed and swallowed. "I'm…I'm sorry. Do you have any idea how hard it was to come here tonight, knowing that you were all going to hate me for my name?" He laughed once with no humor. "And then be completely right?"

"We don't hate you," Mom soothed and stood, but she made no move toward him. I just sat down and stared at my hands. My body ached for him, for his touch, his comfort. Our first day together and we were already fighting and yelling. This wasn't how this was supposed to happen. I felt awful that my significant felt so alienated.

I felt the drop of a warm tear on my hand before I even realized I was crying. I wiped it away and looked up to find Seth had done a complete one-eighty. Apparently, seeing that tear had done him in. With my family there watching, he didn't care a lick. He came and knelt at my feet. His warm hand wrapped around the back of my calf while the other came and went straight to my cheek. I sucked in a short, quick, embarrassing breath when his skin hit mine. He on the other hand let out the tiniest of groans. His thumb swept under my eye twice and he watched his movements as he cleaned up every drop.

"Ava," he said my name under his breath, "this whole time I've selfishly been pouting about how this was affecting me and my family. I'm so sorry. This involves you and your family, too. No matter what happened in the past, that doesn't matter now. I'm sorry I yelled at you." He squinted, as if that caused him pain to think about. It was fascinating to watch. "Can we just move forward, please? We found each other." He looked down and smiled before looked back up. "I found you. And I trust *that* more than I trust anything. So no matter what happens, this is meant to be. You're mine now. So can we just start over and pretend that today never happened?"

I found myself smiling, then I was biting my lip to contain the smile. And then he did the strangest thing. He took his thumb and tugged down, freeing my lip from my teeth.

"You shouldn't ever try to stop that smile," he said softly, his own crooked smile coming through. His thumb moved against my cheek and I felt my eyelids flutter from the pleasure. When I opened my eyes again he looked ready to keel over. He crawled closer, which was almost impossible with mere inches between us. "Ava," he whispered. His phone buzzed with another text and he remembered the one he'd gotten earlier. The look of awe vanished from his face and I cursed whoever it was who was texting him. He leaned back a little. "Ava, we really do need to talk before—"

The back door slammed open, revealing several dark-haired men who rammed their way in before I could even think. Seth had stood and thrown me behind him on instinct, but then he realized who it was. "Uncle Gaston."

The tall, slender man stared at me over Seth's shoulder like a prize and had the audacity to smile. "Seth, you've done marvelous. We'll take it from here."

My heart stopped. Seth's hand tightened on my wrist, but he didn't turn around to look at me. He spoke to his uncle again. "Gaston," Seth said calmly, which was doing nothing to make me feel better about things, "what are you doing here?"

"It's okay, Seth," he soothed and smiled at him. "You did good, son."

"What do you…?" Seth peeked back at me, squinting, and then looked back at his uncle. "You thought I couldn't handle this? You thought they'd hurt me? Gaston, I told you they wouldn't. She's my significant. The family feud between you has to stop."

"We're here now. You don't have to keep this up." I felt my heart tug painfully at his words. Seth gripped my wrist tighter to keep me from running.

"Gaston, what are you doing?" he growled in a voice I'd never heard from my significant's lips.

Gaston pulled a bottle from his inside jacket pocket and held it up in front of his face. He kissed it and then grinned as he tossed it toward his Visionary. She gasped and tried to use her power to stop it, holding her hands out in front of her. But it didn't work. She seemed surprised, her mouth parting and holding open in a silent scream as she awaited the fate of that bottle. Daddy gripped her arm and swung her behind him just as it smashed into his chest.

Gaston growled, angry—either that it hadn't hit her or that it wasn't doing what he thought it was going to do. She screamed just as I did. Seth's tight grip held steady on my arm to keep me safely behind him even as he barked at his uncle angrily, asking him what was going on.

"It's like I've always told you, Seth," he told him calmly, but I wasn't watching him. I was looking at my father as he watched a hole in his shirt eat away and then the skin under it started to turn black. He looked up to Gaston for an answer, who just stared blankly. He returned his gaze to Seth and sighed. "The Watsons led a hard life because of the people in this room. We were never meant to scrounge and beg like humans. Virtuoso are a powerful people with powerful blood in our veins." He looked at my mother. "Did you really think we'd just lie down and accept your punishment?"

Seth jerked and looked at my mother, but she kept her gaze on Gaston. Dad didn't look good and I worried about him. There was so much going on, I didn't know what I should be focusing on.

Seth whispered, "Her? She attacked you at the palace that day?"

"Seth, son," Dad groaned, struggling to remain conscience as he bent to lean on the arm of the chair. Mom whimpered and could no longer keep up the pretenses of the strong leader in charge of things. She caved and rushed to lean down to him, never stopped touching him, but still kept looking back at Gaston as if he'd attack at any moment. I'd never seen my family so helpless. We were always the strong ones, the leaders, the ones all the other clans looked up to. And now the Watsons show up, supposedly with no powers at all, and are able to lay flat my family with one vial?

Dad continued. "I doubt you have the whole story, in truth and in full. Remember that you only know what they've told you, what they want you to know." Gaston growled in warning, but Dad pressed on. "There's a reason that you bonded with my daughter. Remember that."

Seth looked at me over his shoulder and I saw something different in his eyes. It wasn't reverence or the beginnings of love or wonder. It was suspicion. I felt as if he himself had reached up and slapped me. It was *his* family that had come in and attacked my family. I saw him flinch with that thought. It was *his* family that sent him a suspicious text earlier asking if he was 'done with me yet'. He flinched again, seeing where I was going with this. It was *his* family who hurt my father, *his* family who barged in here as if on a mission, and *his* family who were now watching him like they were waiting for something. I backed away a little, pulling my arm from his grasp. His lips moved, saying he word 'no' but no sound left his lips. His eyes begged me as he finally understood the gravity of his actions, of his family's actions. Whether he understood what was going on or not, he was taking a side right now. And it was ripping me in two that he wasn't choosing mine.

Gaston looked at Seth and nodded. Seth shook his head as if he understood what he wanted but he didn't want to do it. It was then I finally understood that my significant came here to betray me. A gut wrenchingly painful breath burst through my chest and out of my throat. The moan stopped Seth dead in his tracks and he moved to come to me, but I put my hand up to stop him.

"How could you?" I asked him with as much conviction as I could, but it came out a pathetic whimper.

He seemed to get it then and straightened. He seemed shocked and shook his head. He glanced back at his uncle and then back to me. "No, Ava. No. This isn't what it looks like. Uncle Gaston came here to make sure I was okay. He…he was worried that your family was going to hurt me. I would never betray you this way," he said angrily. "My family would never do that—the way you're thinking—when they know that we've imprinted. They'd know what that would do to me."

"Seth," Gaston implored in an exasperated tone, "we need to be going. No more stalling."

"Gaston," he growled. "What are you doing?"

I felt his confusion, his anger, his need to protect me, but also his will and want to protect his family. I backed away another step away as his back was turned.

A member of his family that had fallen in the back of the room was getting up. Things were getting worse for us by the second. When Seth heard the noise behind him, he turned and lunged my way. I covered my head on instinct at the roar that erupted from him and the way he came at me. But nothing ever came. I opened my eyes to find Seth's back in my line of sight. I peeked around him and saw the man glaring at him, his arm twisted in Seth's grasp.

"Don't ever touch her," Seth told him in that voice I had heard before. I was so confused I didn't know what to do or think. Was he with me or against me?

I felt arms go around my waist and gasped, but Rodney shushed me. "Come on," he whispered into my hair, but Seth had already turned and started to lunge.

I held up my hand and he stopped immediately. He sighed seeing it was Rodney and then sighed again when he saw me back away another step. "Ava," he begged. For what, I didn't know. What did he want me to do in this situation?

Then his eyes rounded and his mouth opened to speak, but it was too late. I heard Rodney's grunt and then he fell to the floor behind me as Mom screamed. I was yanked roughly by my hair as Gaston dragged me away from Seth who came for us.

"Uh, uh, uh, nephew." He held something over my head. Seth's eyes glued to it as he stopped. "I see that you've let the bonding and intensity of the situation get to you and that presents a problem for us."

"She's my significant," Seth argued. "What did you expect? Would you let someone take Aunt Amy from you?"

He smiled. "You're missing the point. You haven't been with Ava. You don't know her, you haven't slept with her, you haven't fallen in love with her, and my significant isn't the daughter of the woman who destroyed our family," he finished loudly. I couldn't help but flinch. He pulled a little tighter on my hair, but it didn't escape my notice how he made sure not to touch my skin. "This is it. This is our chance, what we've always talked about." Seth paled—actually paled at his uncle's words. "We've always said that when the time came we'd return the favor to the ones who destroyed us. You're bonded with the Visionary's daughter." He grinned. "I see no more fitting restitution than that."

"And what about me?" Seth asked calmly and seemed to throw a wall up in his mind. I got nothing from him. "While you're torturing and doing whatever you plan to do to her, what about me? I'll feel that, have to…deal with that." He gulped, but kept looking at his uncle.

I looked away from him, completely disgusted. Even if he hadn't come here to purposely ambush me, they had talked about 'the family' who had ruined his family all those years ago and apparently that trumped our bond. He was going to let them ruin us.

"Don't worry, Seth," his uncle was saying. "We have our ways of getting around the bond. We even have ways of creating a bond itself." Seth seemed surprised by that, apparently having forgotten what we talked about before… or so it seemed, but who knew what was real anymore. "We'll take care of you. In the meantime, she'll be at your disposal. Whenever you need her, or want her," he tacked on with a grin, "she'll be there."

Seth gulped again and nodded. "That's great, Gaston."

Rodney woke up with a groan and scrambled up at seeing the scene, remembering where he was. His face was red with anger as he cursed and braced himself on the back of the couch. I tried to look at him, but couldn't. Gaston turned us toward my parents and I could practically hear the smile on his face as he began to spew propaganda at them. I didn't hear a word of it as my world crumbled around me. I just stood and tried not to crumble with it.

Rodney's phone dinged with a text. He ignored it. It dinged again, and then again without waiting. He sighed and pulled it out, to turn it off I presumed, but then he stopped and looked at it. Then he started to text back. My mouth fell open and if I could have smacked him in the back of the head, I would have. Only my brother would be texting his buddies back in the middle of a Watson/Jacobson clan battle. What a jerk.

He slipped his phone back in his pocket and looked at me. He looked beyond angry, but there was something else. His eyes shifted left once before he mouthed for me to duck. I didn't wait or think, I just trusted my brother. I yanked out of Gaston's grip as fast and hard as I could. He had been holding me for so long that he has gotten careless and comfortable. I went easily, falling to the floor in a heap, my chin smashing into my knee. I hissed in pain, but before I knew it, Seth was smashing into his uncle from behind, toppling them over the coffee table to the floor. He punched his uncle just once and that was all it took for him to be out cold.

I heard some scuffling behind me, but couldn't look away from Seth as he rushed to me on his knees across the floor.

"You're hurt," he breathed and took my chin in his fingers. His calm didn't seep in, and I wondered if our bond had been severed because my heart was broken. I pushed him away before I could find out or think too hard about it.

He sighed. "Let me help you."

"You chose, didn't you?" I asked softly.

"Ava, please. I need to get them out of here. Let me give you my touch before I have to leave."

"Or you just want my touch for yourself before you go," I said, but didn't look up at him. I felt his fingers under my chin, but it was as if he knew exactly where to press to not hurt where it was aching. He lifted my face gently to make me face him. He was so close that our noses almost touched.

"Do you really believe that?" he asked, his voice gravelly and filled with unchecked emotion. I couldn't answer him. Not only did I not have the answer, but I was afraid of being wrong and afraid of being right. Finally I felt his touch begin to sink into my skin. I was relieved and…so many emotions at once. I wanted him, but was it all chemical? Was it all something in my body that made me want him? What if he didn't want me and I was stuck wanting someone who just wanted to use me? I sighed, letting his touch comfort me for now and heard his responding one, like he was waiting for me to accept his touch before he let himself accept it. "I have to leave, take care of some things," he told me, pressing his forehead to mine. "I *will* be back. I'm so sorry for…" He leaned away and looked like there was a million things he wanted to say. Instead he leaned forward and kissed my forehead. I drew in an embarrassed breath that I'm sure he enjoyed at my expense. "Don't give up on me, Ava."

With that, I watched him pick up his uncle from the ground and heft him over his shoulder. Rodney was dragging someone from the room and I realized the room was clear of everyone but us. My brother was outside with them and I felt a moment of panic before he came in the kitchen door and shut it. Or tried. The hinge was destroyed and wouldn't latch. He gave up and put a chair in front of it to keep it closed and then gave me my phone. "Why do you—"

"Seth had it. Must have picked it up from the table at some point. He was the one texting me. He planned that little…move we pulled."

I gasped and covered my mouth. "What?"

He slid down beside me on the wall. We looked over at Dad and Mom. Dad was already looking better so the poison apparently wasn't deadly or permanent, but Mom had to stay with him. He was asleep with his head in her lap and she looked at us worriedly, listening, splitting her focus between us and Dad. Dad was going to be so pissed when he woke up. He hated when Mom had to take over. He wanted to protect her, always. It was in the Virtuoso man's blood to.

Rodney sighed. "He got your phone off the table sometime during the night, texted me from it, and told me to take out his cousin behind him so he could take his uncle and you wouldn't get hurt in the process. I don't know what happened. I don't know what was going on, what he knew and didn't know, okay? But I do know that he didn't want to hurt you. He wanted to keep you safe."

"How can you say that when—"

"He defied his family, who obviously thought he was going to be on board with his uncle's plan, which was a bust. What do you think they're going to do to him when they wake up?" I groaned and sucked in a breath without even realizing it at the thought. Oh, God… Would they hurt him? He covered my hand on my knee. "I'm just saying, he was ambushed as much as we were. He knew the Watsons and Jacobsons had beef, but he didn't know that Mom was the one who took their powers. They left that important little tidbit out apparently. Why? I don't know. He just thought he was going to have to be overcoming a little tiff, he never imagined he was going to have to deal with all that."

I licked my lips. "He blocked his mind from me. Why would he do that unless he was guilty?"

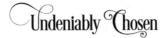

"Maybe he didn't want you to know what his plan was and give it away? I don't know. I just know what he did, and what he did was defy his family and save you. They were planning on taking you away from us, Ava. Do you understand that?" he finished, his words slow and telling.

"Yes," I said quickly.

"Turn on your phone," he said and yawned as he put his head on my shoulder. "Lover boy said to tell you to open your text messages."

I did as he said and there, in a message to no one, was an unsent text. It read: **Don't give up on me, Ava. Please…**

I could do nothing but cry and let Rodney wrap me in his arms.

CHAPTER FIVE

I knew I was dreaming. It was one of those dreams that you knew it was a dream, but you couldn't wake up. I wouldn't have wanted to even if I could have. Seth was here.

I stood in the coffee shop. The other patrons stood as statues, unmoving. He approached me slowly, as if testing me and my reaction. I giggled, unable to stop myself. He was being so funny and adorable. What was he doing?

"Are you okay?" he asked me so softly that I barely heard him.

"Yes. Are you?" I reached out shyly and took his hand. "You're acting so strangely."

He sighed. "Of course. I'm fine, I just…I didn't want to change you. That's not what I was trying to do." He shook his head." His brow furrowed. "What do you remember, Ava?"

"I remember you." His fingers laced with mine and my breath hitched. It was like everything was intensified here, but it really wasn't. His calm wasn't actually seeping into me; I knew that. It was just in my mind, but that didn't make it any less exquisite.

He shook his head and seemed torn. "I don't know if I can…" He looked up. "Will you hate me tomorrow?" he whispered and moved the hair from my temple to behind my ear.

"Why would you say that, Seth?"

He turned his head a little. "I love to hear my name from your mouth. It does something to my insides." He leaned back and looked at me with renewed vigor. "Okay. I'll deal with the consequences tomorrow. Tonight, I just want you to myself, just like this. I want to get to know you, to learn you. If that makes me a bastard, then so be it."

I looked outside. "It's daytime though." I shook my head and grinned. "You're being kind of weird."

"For *today*, can we just pretend that I'm not and enjoy this?"

"What are we going to do? I have to work, don't I?"

"Nope. And neither do I. Look around. Time doesn't matter here." I did and saw all the people as they stood still, time stuck in its place. "We can do anything you want to do. Go anywhere you want." He took my face in his hands and I sighed just because I *had* to and wanted to, not because my body made me from his touch. It was a revelation that I needed more than anything in that moment. I didn't need him…I wanted him. "Where does my significant want to go most in the world?"

I thought about it and pondered it. I'm sure he thought I'd pick the beach or the mountains or some extravagant place, but truly, I could only think of one location.

His eyebrows rose in question.

"You said you never went to reunifications…"

"Yes," he answered hesitantly.

"Then you've never seen the rooftop of the palace in London where we have them. And that's a travesty."

His lip quirked, but he kept his smile in check. "Show me."

He pressed my forehead to his and I imagined what the rooftops looked like, transferring the memory to him. The terrace and the landing, the stars. When I opened my eyes again, I was standing on the terrace under the London sky and it was no longer a memory.

I laughed happily and looked around in a circle. "Wow. This is the best dream. It's so real." I looked up at the London sky, the stars winking back down at me before I came back to him and touched his face. "You feel so real to me. I can even feel your stubble."

He looked at the ground as his arm went slowly around my waist. "The fact that you want me to be real is good enough."

I blinked up at him and wondered why my dream was so strange. It was as if I could hear Maroon 5 in the background and the temperature was perfect, the stars were brighter than they should be, his hands gripping the small of my back were the right amount of pressure and warmth to drive me absolutely insane, but not enough to make me actually do anything about it. Yet. The birds on the terrace were my favorite—robins—because they sing all through the night in London. It was as if it were all orchestrated for me, designed to be perfection.

Seth moved away a little and ticked his head for me to follow him. "Wow," he muttered. "That's London," he mused.

"That's London," I answered as the robins began their song. I smiled and closed my eyes for a second. "It's prettiest at night, I think."

He still had my hand and when his thumb ran down my middle finger, I shivered. He turned and looked at me. He started to take his jacket off.

"I'm okay. I'm…not cold, but thanks."

His tongue touched his lip when he tried to hold back his smile. "I know." He spread it out on the cold stone. "Why don't we use it to lie down?"

He didn't wait for me. He lay down on the brick floor next to the jacket, tucking his arms under his head. I followed him down and felt his hand immediately on mine.

I gasped. "My vision…" I smiled and looked over at him. He was giving me a very cute confused smile in return. "This is one of my imprinting visions. This—right now."

He seemed so happy about that. "Wow. That's awesome."

I gave him my best coy smile. "Are you going to tell me what you saw, Seth?"

He shook his head. "Even I know that's not how it works, little lady."

I smiled and settled back in.

He paused for a few minutes before he spoke again. "Someday, Ava, I want you to bring me here for real," his gruff voice said. He didn't look at me even though I found myself looking over, wondering where the rough emotion was coming from. "I want to see these stars with you and know that everything that was wrong is right. That we made everything better."

Was it the vision talk or was it me? "Seth, I don't—"

"I know, sweetheart," he breathed his words and rolled toward me. He propped up on his elbow and let his eyes roam my face, as if the answers to all his questions were right there for him. "I don't know why you get a reset here and I don't care right now. It must be nice." Again he kept his smile in check, just barely letting it skim the surface.

The birds hopped closer on the terrace wall and we both looked up at them, listening to them sing. "I love listening to them. When I was a kid, I used to pretend that I was one of those little birds because I wanted to sing and fly and get away from everything. If they want to leave, they leave. If they want to sing, they start the most beautiful song. If they want to start a family, they find a boy bird."

He cracked the first barely-there smile and half-snorted.

I moved my fingers to glide across the bottom of his lip. "Why won't you smile? Did something happen today?"

"I'm afraid if I do, then the illusion will fade. That you'll realize this is a dream and it'll all be yanked back into place where it belongs."

"I don't belong here?" I whispered, starting to feel the edges of my skin grow cold.

"You do, little bird," he assured and let his palm coast down my arm and back up to soothe and warm me. "You always belong with me and you're always safe with me. But, Ava, there are things beyond my control, and I hope to God you can remember this tomorrow, because me? I'm just like embers that get caught in the wind. I don't know whether to fall soundlessly and burn out or bide my time, waiting, letting everything think I've died out only to start another fire. I don't know what my true path should be right now. I don't know who to trust." He sighed roughly. "Ava, have you ever had something told to you, every day, like a psalm, like a prayer, like a mantra, and without it you don't know what to do with yourself?"

I shook my head, but then recanted. "Well, yes. I was told every day that I would find you." He sighed and let his hand push higher on my arm to my cheek. "And I was told every day that I would ascend and get my power and," I let my eyes fall so to his neck as I said the next part, "live happily ever after."

He sighed again, harder, meaningfully. "And I was told the Jacobsons would be the people I would avenge someday."

My breath turned shallow, but my heartbeat remained steady. It was as if this dream world was the perfect place...for him to confess such a thing.

"But why?"

"Because of what your mother did. I didn't know. I never actually planned to go through with it. I honestly thought it was just something to keep them busy. In their minds your mother ruined them—no, not in their minds, Ava. Your mother *did* ruin them. She took their power, their very reason for being," he said softly, almost like a scold.

"You don't know the whole story."

"I'm sure more now than ever that I don't. And I'm sure that you're going to tell me." His thumb made a pass over my cheekbone. "And your parents. I don't know if they'll be letting us spend too much time alone now because they don't trust me. This place, well, it will be just for the two of us, little bird."

I felt my scowl, but couldn't stop it. "Seth," I breathed and he closed his eyes.

"I'll never get tired of that. No one warned me what this would feel like."

"Do they…really love their significants?"

His eyes opened slowly, as if clinging to the feeling, rebelling against reality. "I thought so, but after watching your parents together and feeling… this, I'm beginning to wonder if it's the same as others of our kind."

He moved that thumb again and I realized that though I was loving his touch—like, it was amazing—I wasn't getting his calm.

"Seth," I began again, "this isn't real, is it?"

It all started to settle over me. I was okay with it. I was inspired to get to know him more, though I didn't really understand why.

His lips gave me a barely-there smile and he answered, "Yes and no. But I'm proud at how long you lasted." He leaned forward and kissed my forehead. I gasped a little at the closeness and the sweet gesture. I couldn't help but imagine a more intimate gesture on the horizon soon. I looked at him from under my lashes. He smirked at me. It was the first one of the night and I had missed it. He seemed so forlorn tonight and I hated that his heart was so heavy. I knew it was my fault even as I knew there was nothing I could do to change it. I didn't know how I knew. I just knew it was so. His smirk morphed into a smile. "You're a smart girl. Don't worry about me. Just being here with you tonight was enough to ease the ache for me. I'll figure this out for us, Ava. Somehow, I have to figure this out for us."

"Don't go just yet." I wrapped one of my arms around his neck and tugged him closer. His palm slammed into the concrete next to my head to keep from falling as he pressed into me.

"Ava," he begged into my hair as he leaned down on his elbows. "Ava,

you feel like this now because I brought you here. Please remember this," he mumbled under his breath. "Please." He lifted up and looked down at me, hovering just out of reach but still close enough for me to feel his breath on my neck. "Don't give up on me, Ava."

I jolted, feeling a strange sense of déjà vu. He took his thumb and dragged it across the corner of my mouth—rough and calloused—I tried to image him as he dragged hoses and put out fires with those hands. I tried to picture him as he slammed through doors and buildings and carried someone to safety. He would be brave, I knew it.

He shook his head and I could feel and hear his thoughts so clearly as he thought that I was adorably trusting, but he didn't know why. "How can you believe in me so clearly in one area and be completely the opposite in the other?"

I shivered from the way his thumb caressed my skin and felt the skin of my neck burn a hot pink. He smiled, forgetting his question. "You're blushing," he said obviously. "It's so pretty on you. I can't remember ever making a girl blush before."

"Now I know that's a lie," I called him on it and licked my lip with a smile.

"I've waited for you my entire life," he replied, the conviction stealing my very breath, as if that one statement explained everything I'd ever questioned. In a way, I guess it did. "Plus, I spend a lot of time at the fire station with a bunch of guys anyway so." He smiled and I noticed for the first time a little scar on the underside of his chin.

"Well, you certainly know how to make a girl feel significantly exceptional, don't you?"

He chuckled huskily. "You can wax poetic like nobody I know."

I giggled, but before I could say anything in return, a shimmering to my right jolted both of our attentions toward it. "It's because she's an old soul," a soft, feminine, *familiar* voice rang through the light haze before fading away to reveal...

"Ashlyn?" I asked, though I knew the answer.

"Don't tell me you've forgotten me already?" she asked, but she was shimmering. No, that wasn't really the right word. More like coming in and out of focus like on a bad frequency. Seth lifted off me and helped me stand. He seemed to be more about his wits than I was, and I was glad, because I was so stunned to be looking at my childhood friend in the flesh that all I could do was stand there and gawk at her. "Ava, it's all right," she soothed.

"But…it's been so long."

"You grew up." Her gaze settled on Seth. "And so did you. Into a right fine gentleman, I might add. You may not be able to see me, children, but I've been keeping watch over you. You've both made me so proud."

She wiped a tear from the corner of her eye and I was shocked at her emotion for us.

Seth's hand squeezed mine and I realized that he had never let it go. I heard breath leave his lips and realized that he was waiting for something. I looked over at him. And then it hit me. She said she had watched us both… Was he waiting for her to say something about his past that he didn't want me to know?

"How can that be true?" he breathed. "I've…"

He let his sentence die and his sigh die with it. She smiled in her cryptic way and said, "Everything is as it should be. You all need to start believing in the way our lives are laid out. Do you really think that Ava was put in your path by accident?"

"No," he growled, and my heart sang at the protectiveness in it even though I barely knew him. "She belongs with me."

She moved around us. "Then trust it. Trust that beating in your chest that belongs to her and know that everything happens for a reason. You are where you're supposed to be. Anything worth having is worth fighting for."

He scoffed angrily and shook his head as we stood. He tugged me protectively behind me, keeping my hand in his, and I wondered why he felt the need to protect me even from Ashlyn. "I've done nothing but fight my entire life it seems. This one thing," he looked back at me, "this one time in my life, I wanted it to just come like it should."

"Oh, boo hoo," Ashlyn sneered angrily and shimmered in and out even more, fighting to stay visible. Her face contorted into an angry frown as her eyes bounced from his face to mine. "You have it easy! You have no idea what it's like to not be able to touch your significant, and then go mad from it. To be in pain every day from the loss of it. So don't talk to me about having it hard."

"I didn't know—" Seth immediately tried to fix his blunder because he *didn't* know, but Ashlyn was having none of it.

"You just hold your significant's hand and be thankful during this time that, though it may not be ideal, you have each other." She shimmered so bright I squinted. Seth covered his eyes a little and then I gasped as she was suddenly right in our faces. "You never forget that. Especially you," she said hard to me. "Don't forget that you have each other and nothing is worth losing that. Nothing. What happened in the past is just that. The past. Our families have great influence over us and so does things that we don't know, things that alter our perception. Don't let others make your decisions for you. War is coming and you need to be strong. Don't let them destroy you."

Seth's air puffed through his lips from his throat like he was affected greatly by her words. "Do you know something, Ashlyn?"

"All I know is what I've seen, but all that can change. You have to do the work. You have to be willing to accept that life isn't a burning ember waiting to snuff out. You have to control your life and direct it where it's going."

Seth pulled me to him, surprising me as he brought me to his chest, cupping my face with his big take-charge hands. I stared up at him and looked at my future, at everything I'd ever wanted staring right back at me. "I won't let them snuff us out, Ava. I know you won't remember this tomorrow, but I promise you that I'll fix this for us."

I felt this overwhelming need for him to kiss me. For him to show me in some physical way how much he needed me in that moment. He leaned forward and I pulled in a quick, unstable breath in anticipation. He maneuvered his lips just before he reached mine to brush my cheek. He stayed there, pressing them softly to my skin, for a long time. Though it felt heavenly it wasn't the same.

Disappointment washed over me. I didn't understand why my significant wouldn't want to kiss me. That didn't make any sense to me. His mind was a fog that I couldn't sift through.

"Ava," he said softly, that little growl tacked on for good measure as he leaned back, holding my cheek in his palm, "you won't remember this tomorrow. And when I kiss you, I definitely want you to remember."

"I won't remember…because this isn't real," I stated. "It's a dream?"

"It's real," he assured. "It's real to me." He pressed his head to mine. "Come find me when you wake up. Please, Ava. Please," he begged and his voice begging through my very soul was as beautiful as it was agonizing.

"I will. I'll try," I amended and gripped his shirtfront. "Thank you for bringing me here—to my favorite place."

"I'll see you here again," he promised and kissed my forehead. "Tomorrow night?" he said, as if asking permission, and that made me fall for him a tiny bit because he would do such a thing—ask for something, care for my feelings so much, when it was obvious to us both that I wouldn't remember his asking after this moment.

I bit into my lip to contain my smile. "Yes. I'll give you the tour."

He looked down as if he didn't understand why I'd be so happy about seeing him. "Okay, little bird. It's a date." He leaned forward and whispered into my ear, "Wake up, Ava."

We all slept in the living room together that night. I wrapped a blanket around Mom and Dad and put a pillow behind Mom's head. She was as docile as I'd ever seen her—the Visionary, the leader of our people, the wife of our Champion, our mom, mother to Rodney who was always getting into trouble for something, the woman who was so frustrated that she could hear everyone else's thoughts but ours because something about her blood blocks it. So Rodney and I were off limits. It was a blessing in disguise in my eyes, but in hers, she saw it as some sort of motherly punishment. I would said, "Mom, it would be like you reading my diary every day, without my permission."

She would say, "No it wouldn't. I would just peek every once in a while to make sure you were happy and being safe and not getting into—"

"Here's a thought, Mom," Rodney would butt in. "You could ask us." Then he'd bite into whatever he was eating because *Rodney* was always eating.

"But you wouldn't tell me the truth," she'd say saucily and swat him with a towel. "You'd cunningly run around the truth through your handsome Jacobson teeth and think you're getting away with something."

Rodney would grin and say, "Because I usually am."

I would roll my eyes and the convo would start again. The only other people Mom couldn't hear was the Watsons. I didn't like being lumped with them, but if it got me my privacy then I'd take it.

Now, as I looked at Mom and Dad still sleeping on the couch, I realized that there was no way that she had been able to hear Seth's thoughts yesterday either. The Watsons must have given him Mom's blood at some point for that very reason, whether he knew it or not. I *hoped* not, but would I ever really know? Probably not, truly.

I was achy. Seth had left late last night, almost midnight, but my body didn't care if that was only seven short hours ago. It wanted him and I had no idea when I was going to see him again. Or even if I was ever going to see him again. And then I remembered what he told me and what he reiterated with his text on my phone.

Don't give up on me, Ava.

I tried to turn the situation around. I tried to see it from his point of view. He was a boy when he was taken and had been told only what they wanted him to know from that point on. He seemed to be fine, mentally and physically, so I didn't think they had abused him. On the contrary, it seemed as if they raised him as one of their own. Loved him. So he in turn would love them as well, as a family, just as I loved my family. He believed that my mother destroyed his family when in actuality that's exactly what happened. He just didn't have all the facts.

Yes, he said that he wished he had been rescued with the rest of the people all those years ago from the compound, so it apparently hasn't been all sunshine in the land of Watson, but family is family. And that fact should give me some comfort that he thinks so highly of family that he'd go to such great lengths to protect it.

Even if it is the Watsons.

I swallowed against the tightness in my throat and tried to think about what I would have done if I had been in his place. Could I have been so strong? Would I have stood up to my parents and still tried to reassure my significant, to calm the situation until I figured out what was truly going on? Would I?

I shook my head. I shuddered to think about it. And I shuddered to think about the consequences of last night.

Rodney stirred beside me and I went to make some coffee, lumbering through my aches and pains. Eventually I gave up and went to my room to get dressed for the day. I was supposed to work at Dad's office today, but couldn't imagine it with what my body was going through. Every step lumbered, every breath pulled, every move ached.

I always heard it felt like the flu. They weren't kidding. But I wasn't going to sit around here and sulk all day. I refused. I knew Mom would baby me and

Dad was going to go all Champion and wanna bust someone's head. I didn't really want to sit and listen to the play-by-play of last night all day long so I made myself get dressed and then snuck out the back door when no one was looking.

When I woke this morning, it was obvious Dad was going to be fine. His color was back to normal and from the way he was clutching Mom in his sleep, I was sure if they had been in their room instead, frisky business would have been had.

I drove carefully and pretended not to notice the way my fingers shook as they gripped the steering wheel. I took deep breaths. My phone dinged, but I ignored it. I knew it was probably Rodney or Mom mad that I left. I didn't even know where I was going. I just needed to get away.

So I kept driving until eventually I couldn't drive anymore. I pulled over somewhere and laid my head against the steering wheel. My head pounded. My phone rang this time and I reached to grab it, but it fell between the seat and the middle console with my fumbling fingers.

"Fudge," I muttered and moved to wiggle my hand in between the small slit to grab it. After a few minutes of careful maneuvering and moving the seat back and forth, up and down, I finally freed the phone, almost giving up entirely in the process.

When I returned upright, I screamed at the face suddenly in my window. Seth swiftly moved to open my door and leaned down on his haunches next to me. He didn't take my touch like I thought he would, he waited, though I could tell he was in as much pain as I was. My hand still gripped my shirt at my chest from where he scared me, my breaths rushed from me, but I just watched him as he watched me.

"Sorry. I went to your house, but Rodney said you weren't there. It wasn't hard to find you with your heartbeat." His brow lowered, the skin around his blue eyes crinkled a little as he thought about something. It was so totally adorable that it pissed me off because I wanted to be angry with him.

"What?" I asked.

"What are you doing here?" He rubbed his chin, looking uncomfortable. I realized then that he was trying to hide a smile.

Why...

I looked up to see that I had pulled over across the street from the fire station. There was a large gold embossed '22' on the front of the old bricks and I remembered that from the shirt he was wearing in the coffee shop that day. I would never be able to forget that.

"I thought you wouldn't want anything to do with me and then you come *here*?"

"I didn't realize I had," I answered softly. I shivered.

"Please, Ava," he said and when I looked back at him, he was looking right at me. In me, through me, to me. "I know you doubt me and I'm sorry for that. I'll spend as long as it takes proving that I want to be worthy of you one day. You can doubt me all you want, just let me help you. Please," he practically growled and that's how I knew he was for real. He sounded just like Daddy did when it came to Mom and her safety.

The one thing I seemed to forget in this was that no matter what, yes he was a Watson, but we were still imprinted, still bonded. That wasn't fake. It was real.

I barely moved my hand in his direction and he was gripping my fingers in both of his warm hands. I was slammed with calm, a cloud of warmth and need and morphine-like haze everywhere. I felt unhinged. And then he was pulling me towards him before I even realized it, unbuckling me, pulling me down from the car seat into his lap on the ground. He leaned on the car door and held me against his chest.

His breaths raged and I got little glimpses from him. How he was so happy to have me in his arms, no matter how small the time was, how he was surprised that I hadn't hit him for being so bold, how finding me in front of his fire station had brought him so much delicious pain in his chest. Even if I hadn't known or meant to go there, my subconscious still wanted him and that was good enough for him, for now. He was hell bent on figuring this all out, on making this work, on proving himself. He knew he had a lot of work ahead of him and he was up to the challenge.

I leaned back and shivered when my nose grazed his chin. He smiled. "I won't bite."

I scoffed, but bit my lip so I wouldn't smile back. "I don't have any proof of that."

"You'll have to take my word for it."

I looked down, unable to continue to play like nothing had happened. "What now?"

"Well," he said and ran the backs of his fingers down my arm, "we have a lot to talk about." His pause was telling. "My place or yours?"

I yanked my gaze back up. "I'm not going to—"

He pointed across the road. "That's where I live most of the time, but I have my own apartment a couple blocks from here. I live alone."

"Oh. Um…" I licked my lips and would be lying if I said the way his eyes immediately moved to watch it didn't thrill me all over. "Your place. Mine is a little crowded."

He chuckled. I barely stopped my groan. Good Lord, that laugh. He looked at me as if he knew exactly what I was thinking. Maybe he did. His lips quirked. I sighed.

"But how? We aren't supposed to be able hear each other like this yet. It's not…copacetic to our ways. It doesn't makes sense."

"Maybe someone knew we'd need the extra help," he said, as if he knew the answer to that already.

I nodded slowly. "Maybe so."

He helped me stand and held my hand for a couple seconds longer than needed. His eyes met mine just before he released it and I knew he could tell that I wasn't ready for all this yet and that the *only* reason he was giving me the space I needed. His uncle had tried to kidnap me for goodness sake.

His mouth quirked again and I balked at the fact that he thought his uncle trying to kidnap me—

"No," he rushed to explain, "no." He put his hand just below my elbow and gave me a look that dared me to tell him to move it. "*Copacetic to our ways? Goodness sake?* I was thinking…that you wax poetic like nobody I know." He stared at me hard, waiting, but with a little smile, and seemed to be keeping his mind closed in a sense. I wondered what it was about, but was hung up on the "wax poetic" part.

"My grandpa always says that exact same thing about me."

"Your Grandpa Peter?"

I nodded, but felt my eyebrows lower. "How do you know that?"

"They told me a lot of the Jacobson history." He looked down, embarrassed. "Sorry." I could hear the little fuzzy strings of knowledge coming from his mind to mine, how he knew that his family was wrong, but he didn't really know who my family was either. He was so confused. All he knew for certain was that I was his and he had to keep me safe. He knew that our families were going to cause problems for us, on both sides.

He was so much better at the mind reading thing than I was. Everything came to me in fuzzy patches while he seemed to be able to read me so easily. I wondered why that was. Why it was so easy for him.

"I think it's intent, Ava," he muttered under his breath, so low I barely heard him. He looked back up, his blue intense eyes meeting mine so fiercely that I felt as though I'd been physically touched. I rocked back a little and a warm hand on the small of my back stopped me. "I think that I want to know you so completely and it's working in my favor." His smile was a little condescending, but I didn't hold it against him. "One day you'll get up to speed with me. I can hope, right?"

Even that playful, adorable grin that was making my insides shake with all sorts of emotions I didn't want to acknowledge couldn't erase the events that happened last night. The weird texts he kept getting. His family showing up and acting as if there had been some plan. Him leaving with them and just coming to see me today as if nothing had transpired. I knew he was torn, but I needed answers, and as much as it pained me, I needed space because my significant's skin was the most distracting thing I'd ever encountered.

I knew he had heard everything in my head because his blue eyes dulled painfully. It took a lot not to reach out and brush my knuckles against his chin, for my own benefit as much as his, but I couldn't. Right now, he was just a stranger who held my heart, and who also happened to be my enemy.

He jerked as if I'd slapped him. I wondered if Romeo and Juliet had been brought to life if this is what they would have felt. Betrayed, torn, confused, alone even when the person you're supposed to be with is right in front of you.

"Don't say that," he groaned, his hands on my elbows tightening. It was then that I was smacked with the realization that I was still on his lap. I could feel the hot pink racing up the column of my neck. "You're never alone. I promise you, if nothing else, you'll never be alone, Ava."

"Seth." I begged him to release me, hating the way my voice quivered.

His hands released me slowly, painfully, and I stood up, waiting for him to stand, too, so I could close my car door and make use of my shaking fists.

"Want to get some coffee or breakfast before we go to my place?" he asked gruffly and then cleared his throat, realizing how off it sounded. "I don't keep much there because I'm not there much myself."

"Yeah, I do," I answered with as much smile in my voice I could muster and reached for my door. He stopped me with a hand on my mine. I looked up at him and he looked comically torn again. It was obvious he wanted to drive, but was fearful of pushing me too far. "You want to drive?"

His eyebrows shot up. "You're going to let me?" He tacked on a small satisfied grin.

"Don't get smug," I couldn't help but say. "You live close, right? Can we walk?"

He perked up even more at that. "Absolutely. I missed my run the past couple of days, so that's a great idea."

"You run?"

"Fireman have to keep fit somehow. The gym and weights and all that aren't for me. Running is right up my alley, however." He took the keys from my hand and locked my doors before handing them back to me. He swung his arm out. "Shall we?"

I eyed him and lead the way for about two point two seconds before he was right next to me again. "Thanks."

He continued on as if nothing had interrupted. "Running helps me clear my head, helps me think. With my kind of work, your head gets pretty scrambled from the long hours and the things we see sometimes."

"I can imagine," I replied softly. I stopped when he put his hand out in front of me before we looked to cross the street. We waited for the cars to go and I eyed him the entire time. He had to feel the heat from my gaze, but he never looked over. The protectiveness was so endearing…but I needed to be objective right now. And he was making it so hard. "Where are you taking me?"

He looked over a little alarmed, like I thought he was kidnapping me. I laughed once and said, "For breakfast."

The corners of his mouth barely pulled up and it made it evident how much this was affecting him. He hated that he didn't have my trust. I prayed one day that he would. That it would be earned and true and valid.

That my mind and my heart would be on the same page of this book that had just been opened for us.

CHAPTER SIX

"Wow, this has to be the best omelet I've ever had."

He smiled at me over his coffee cup and downed the rest of it. "I knew you'd like it. This grease bucket is a place the fireman love to come to. It has good, plain, strong coffee for people like me and then frou-frou nutty coffee for people like you."

"It's hazelnut!" I laughed.

He smiled as he continued. "It's one of those places that's always open, always serves breakfast or dinner, so we can get whatever we're in the mood for. It's good for people who have no life and work around a schedule like mine."

"Have no life?" I asked and felt my eyebrow raise.

He swallowed and leaned back in his side of the red booth. "Other than my family and the firehouse, I don't have much else to do."

I smirked. Well, what I imagined was a smirk. "Sounds like me. If I'm not in school or working, I'm…" I shrugged. "I'm doing nothing." And then I did what I imagined was a grimace. "That sounds incredibly lame."

His foot touched mine under the table and I couldn't tell if it was a coincidence or not. "Don't your friends from school want you to go out?"

"Don't your friends from the firehouse want you to?" I countered.

He laughed under his breath and mumbled, "Spitfire," before saying fully, "Yeah, they do sometimes. Most of them are married though, so they spend an exorbitant amount of time trying to fix me up with every single girl they have in their entire list of family and friends."

"Same," I muttered. "Except I got the surprise blind dates with frat boys when I went out. They meant well, but the guys they fixed me up with would have never been my type anyway." I laughed softly. "Usually drunk and grabby and way over confident—" I saw Seth's jaw muscle tick. "So I just stopped going out with my friends altogether."

I bit into the side of my lip and looked down at the table. I could feel the tension in his body from across the table, somehow, the way we were now so connected. My body was being taken over by this boy. I hated that we seemed to be letting each other down so soon.

Since I was already grating his nerves with my 'boy talk', I dove right into the one thing I needed to know most of all. "What happened after you went home last night?"

I let my eyes lift slowly from the off-white tabletop to look at his face. His face showed no emotion, but his eyes showed fear—the one thing I hoped I wouldn't see. I sighed. But of course he would be scared. He thought I hated him already.

"You don't?" he whispered.

"Seth," I said quietly, refocusing him. He blew a small breath from his lips and I noticed how his eyes closed a little too long. I squinted, a hint of déjà vu washing over my skin as if there was something I should remember. Something on the edge that I wasn't grasping, but should.

His eyes opened fully at that and he watched me, his lips parted for a few seconds. When I just stared back, he looked away, disappointment all over his face, and signaled the waitress.

I didn't know what I had done to earn that look of disappointment, but it stung nonetheless.

He shook his head at me and took out his wallet before asking the waitress to bring us two of our coffees to-go. "It's not you. It's...me."

I didn't fight him on the check. I knew there was no point. I saw his smirk in his profile as he stood shaking his head. We met her at the counter and grabbed our coffee cups. He balanced the cups in one hand and held the door for me before handing mine to me once we were out on the street.

"Thanks," I said, trying so hard to not fall head-over-feet for the sweet gestures he kept piling up in his favor.

"My apartment is just around the corner," he said just before his phone dinged. He pulled it out and sighed. "Daggumit."

"What is it?" I said as casually as I could.

"Uh…" he stalled and looked over quickly before looking back at his phone, "my uh…Harper is at my place. She says she needs to talk to me."

"Harper," I heard myself say quietly. "The girl I saw in your mind last night."

"She's not a *girl*. She's family. She knew I was seeing you today so she wouldn't have come unless it was important."

Him defending this Harper hit me in the chest like a dirty brick. It must have been like what he felt when I talked about those guys my friends made me go out with. Maybe I was overreacting, but they weren't family—not really. I took a deep breath and just looked out at the street as we walked. Maybe we'd get there and I'd see that there was nothing to worry about, but in my gut, that's not what I felt.

As soon as we turned the corner, I felt the hot poker of jealousy stab me in the gut. As soon as she saw him, she jumped from the steps leading to what I assumed was his apartment and ran toward us in all her porcelain skin, long-legged, dark-haired glory. He left me in my stupor to meet her halfway, though I gave him credit for not galloping after her like she was him.

"Oh, Seth," she whispered miserably into his neck as she wrapped her arms around his head. Her entire body was pressed against his, knee to cheek. I could barely breathe watching the exchange, but I couldn't have looked away if my life depended in it. "Seth, everything is just awful. It's all falling apart."

"It's going to be okay," he soothed and tried to lean back, but she held on tight.

"It won't!" she argued. "Dad is losing it. Everything we worked so hard for, to keep our family together, and now it's all slipping away. Why did this have to happen this way?" Her eyes finally looked up and locked on mine. I waited, hoping I was wrong, but when her lips lifted into a grin, I knew that the Watsons were still up to no good. Even as she continued to spout her pitiful words to him, she made sure I saw her satisfied smile—loving that she had ruined our day, knowing that this was the day we would have been trying to make up, or explain or…understand what was going on between us. "Why is the world playing these cruel tricks on us when all we want is to be happy? When all I want is for you to be happy and now you're just going to be in danger. It's not fair."

He sighed, shifting on his feet. "I'm fine. It doesn't seem like it now, but everything is supposed to happen this way."

"How can you say that when it's destroying our family?"

"It'll work out, Harp. I know it. It'll be okay, all right?"

Harp. He had a nickname for her. His cousin who wasn't really his cousin who was shooting daggers into me that he couldn't see, and he obviously thought she hung the moon. And she thought he did, too, and wanted *so much more* than to be his friend.

I was no longer just the uncomfortable third wheel here. I wanted to away run as fast as I could. I turned to face the other way, no longer able to look at them. I knew that by doing so, I was letting her win. A Watson, with her hands all over my significant. Every bone in my body told me to make her stop, to make him see what was true, but I knew he'd just think it was jealousy. I had only been bonded to him for a day and a half and my claim to him was so strong yet so feeble all at once.

My breaths came hard as my eyes searched around me. My brain couldn't make the decision. I didn't know what to do. I'd never felt so vulnerable in my life. Before I knew it, a hand was touching my wrist. I didn't jolt and that seemed to surprise him. He was breathing harder, too, and his eyes were bunched around the edges. "I'm sorry," he said gruffly and simply.

"She's fine, Seth," I heard behind me, clearly irritated that she wasn't winning this round. "We need to talk about what we're going to do about the family."

"Later," he said not removing his eyes from mine.

"But—" she shrieked.

"Harper," he said harder and looked back at her. He guided me along with his hand on the small of my back. "I'll call you later and we'll talk."

She scoffed as we passed and he guided me up the stairs, his warm hand ever-present on my back.

"Why don't you just come by later when you're done here?" she suggested in a cheery voice. But I wasn't fooled.

"I don't think so," he said and turned to look back at her when we reached a door. "I plan to be busy for a while. We'll work it out, okay? But this is

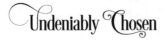

important. I need you all to understand that, but you most of all."

She swallowed and then put on a convincing smile. "Of course, Seth. I'm sorry. I didn't mean to—"

"I know. See you later."

"Have fun," she said suggestively and wiggled a shoulder like she actually meant it.

He laughed once. "Bye, Harper."

"Bye, Seth." The longing in her voice was enough to make me turn for one last look. So Watsons *did* have real feelings. How was Seth so completely naïve to it?

"I know they aren't my blood family, but they're all I've ever known." He shut the door and put his keys on a hook by the door before turning back. "She's the daughter of someone I have looked at as my uncle for all intents and purposes my whole life. I do not now, nor have I ever, had any kind of feelings for Harper. She is family and that's that."

I didn't want to talk about her anymore. I was sure we'd talk about her plenty before it was all said and done. Tonight, I needed to talk about what happened last night after he left my house.

I turned to find a bachelor pad in full swing. And there were drawings littering the place. I felt him as he automatically felt apprehension, wishing he had put those away before he had brought me over, but then he took a deep breath and tried to be okay with it. It wasn't that he didn't want to see, it was the opposite. He wanted me to see, he wanted me to love them. He was afraid that I wouldn't, he was afraid that I would judge him or let my dislike of the situation and his family carry over to that part of things.

I tried not to look at them, really. He was so sensitive about them. But there were so many of them, like he spent all his free time doing it. The bar that separated the kitchen and den had stacks of papers and drawings on it. I sucked on my lip a little as I tried to casually glance at them. The one on top was an old man with a suit and cane, his leg kicked out, his dog by his side as they sat on a bench.

"I drew him at the firehouse one day," I heard next to my ear. I turned to find him so close that his nose brushed my cheek. I inhaled sharply, but didn't move away. Neither did he. "He sat on the bench outside of the firehouse. He comes and walks his dog every day and wears a three piece suit. No idea why. But it's fascinating."

I picked them up and started to leaf through slowly, but then I reached one of—you guessed it—Harper. My heart actually hurt as I looked at that picture. It didn't matter how many others I had passed. Other girls. He drew anything and everything that interested him; literally, art was art to him. He didn't discriminate. But finding Harper drawn so beautifully in the mix hurt me. He had drawn other women the same way. Older woman, younger woman. His mother was one of them, I assumed. Cooking, sitting on porches, fishing. He loved to draw people. That was apparently his *thing*.

Harper was driving. And she was beautiful.

He sighed. "Harper *is* beautiful," I closed my eyes, "but she's just a person," he said and took the picture from me, turning it over on top of the stack so all the pictures were hidden from me. "You're making out like the fact that I drew her makes her more important to me somehow or more...*more*. She's not. Just like that guy with the suit and the dog. Art is art. I drew her just like I draw anyone. I'll draw you someday, too."

I heard a funny tone to his voice and looked at him, but he looked away and even shut his mind to me. I didn't know what that was about.

The bachelor pad was made complete with a street sign over the kitchen bar that said "Easy Street". I looked at him with a raised brow.

He shrugged and said, "The firemen think I have it easy because I don't have a family to take care of and can go out whenever I want, date whoever I want." He gave a wry grin. "Little do they know."

The rest was pretty simple, but it was clean. Like he said, he was barely there. I guess he was right. His couch faced the TV. There were no pictures on the walls except a couple of drawings, both black and white. One of the firehouse and one of the river downtown, the old buildings in the background. There were beautiful and unsigned. I wondered who did them.

He also had a couple awards, but they weren't displayed proudly on the wall. They were laid on the top of the mantle of the fireplace so haphazardly and I almost missed them.

"Bravery Award? Tot Finder Award?" I read aloud. His face was next to mine over my shoulder. I didn't look at him, just looked at the picture of him in his formal fireman's attire as he shook hands with someone higher in rank than him and accepted his award. "You don't look very happy to be receiving this," I mused.

One of his hands leaned on the mantle next to me.

"My captain made me accept it. I didn't want to. People died in that fire and I—" Another wall was slammed shut between us. I was barely able to read him as it was and he was continuing to push me out. I took a deep breath and heard him do the same. "I don't let anyone in there. It's not just you." His sigh was harsh. "I was hurt in that fire and so were others..."

"Is that where you got that scar on your chin?" I asked, treading softly.

"No," he tensed and replied harder, letting me know that scar on his chin wasn't up for discussion.

"Sorry," I whispered.

He sighed again and I felt bad for bringing it up. "All right, we can delve into this another time, if that's okay." He pulled away and leaned on the arm of the couch. He looked so uncomfortable. "We can go ahead and delve headfirst into that other subject I'm so happy to get started on."

Sarcasm. I loved sarcasm. But right now, it was a defense mechanism and I wondered why he was so hell bent on trying to deflect. My faith seemed to be plummeting by the minute that this was ever going to work out, truly.

I turned fully and leaned against the cool wall with my back, biting my lip. The walls were painted white, like he hadn't touched anything when he moved in, just stuck his stuff here. I wondered if his family helped him move. I wondered if they had big dinners. Had Christmas. I wondered how they treated him as a kid. If they tucked him in at night.

If our idea of love would ever be the same.

I finally let my gaze fall on him, knowing I was the one stalling this time.

The way he watched me, his face full of awe and a sense of protection that hit him in the gut, reminded me of the way I'd watched my family be with each other.

He tilted his head a little, the side of his lip raising. "You do this thing with your...never mind," he said and turned away, but not before I saw the insane smile on his face. He was pressing my buttons on purpose.

I felt the sigh bubbling up in my gut, but couldn't stop it. "Don't be coy, Seth," I spouted and crossed my arms. "What were you saying? I do something with my what?"

His smile told me I'd fallen precisely into his trap. Trying to avoid conversation with him was like a Driver's Ed student trying to avoid an orange cone on the first day. Always failed.

He approached slowly, like he knew *I knew* this was a mistake now. He licked his lips slowly and then smiled, the stubble on his jaw so enticing as he looked down at me. He was only inches from me. I could smell him again, feel his warmth. My body begged me reach out and touch him, grab his skin and let his comfort and touch course through my veins like it was destined to.

I held perfectly still except the heaving of my chest, which I couldn't stop for anything.

"I said," he almost whispered he spoke so low, "you do this thing with your lip that's so adorable, it takes all I have not to reach out and..." His eyes searched my face.

"What thing?" I asked, so enraptured with what he was saying. "What thing do I do?"

"You nibble on the side of the bottom of your lip when you're thinking. Or nervous. I'm not exactly sure, but I'm going to find out. One day I'm going to know all those little things about you, Ava. All those little things that make you *you*, makes you tick, makes you gorgeous and beautiful and aggravating as all get out. I'm going to know everything there is."

I was about to bawl my eyes out. I dug my fingernails into my palm to keep it in. "You could just read it from my mind—"

"No. I'm not going to take it from you. I want you to *give* me those things because you want me to have them, Ava."

"Seth," I pleaded, but it was nothing but breath.

He plowed on, leaning down into my space. I turned my face away and his nose brushed my temple. We both sighed at the small rush of calm it provided since we hadn't touched in so long.

"My last name may be Watson, but I'm not the monster you think I am."

Sweet, agonizing guilt built in my gut. Was it unfounded? I didn't know. I just knew that this whole situation sucked. Why couldn't I have my fairy tale, the one I always dreamed about? The one I was promised?

I felt one awful, betraying tear slip from my eye as I looked even further away from him. I heard his breath catch as he saw and reached up to brush it away with his thumb.

"Ava," he breathed and I felt his guilt with every second that went by. His thumb continued to swipe my cheek, for his comfort or for mine, it didn't matter. I sighed and closed my eyes. "I'm...sorry. I'm not the victim here and I'm sorry I—"

"But you are," I squeaked and opened my eyes. "And so am I. You don't feel cheated?" His eyes widened a little at that, but he stayed right where he was. Another swipe of that thumb almost rendered me speechless. Almost. "You don't feel like everything in the universe wants us to hate each other?"

He visibly relaxed, sighing so hard that it blew the hair at my neck. I realized that he thought "cheated" meant that I was cheated by getting him and not someone else.

"Didn't I promise I would fix this for us?" he said low and held my gaze.

I felt it in my very being that he had, that those words had left those lips, but I couldn't remember him actually saying them. I bit my lip and squinted up at him. He smiled and brought his thumb down to tug against my lip instead to free it from my teeth. I flushed, but smiled slightly. He was right. I did that a lot.

"I will fix this for us," he repeated. "I promise you. I will find a way to make this right. For us," he said again and I recognized he was telling me that he meant for me and him, not right for his family. I appreciated that.

"Okay," I agreed. "I just want to get everything out in the open. I have questions. I'm sure you do, too. Let's just…"

"Yeah," he granted and leaned away. "Ladies pick of the palace." He waved his arm at the room for me to pick a seat. I saw his wrist tattoo when he did it. It was just a small black lightning rod with nothing else.

My phone dinged. It had been dinging all morning and I knew it was Mom again. I opened it to find several all caps texts from Mom. I texted her that I was with Seth and I was fine. She said she figured that he had found me because he had been by the house and was sure he had followed my heartbeat but I was getting a very stern talking to when I got home. If I didn't walk through the door in two hours, she was coming after me. I rolled my eyes, but understood. Leaving the house the way I did was pretty not cool of me after what happened last night.

I took my now lukewarm coffee and went to the end of the cracked brown leather couch. The club chair was my first choice, but I didn't want him to think I was purposely not sitting near him if he chose to. Plus, I was interested to see where he was going to sit, see how far he was planning to push me.

He came toward me, took my coffee cup from my fingers, and warmed it in the microwave for a minute before bringing it back. He walked over and plugged, what I assumed, was his phone into a stereo system before music began to play. *Baddest Man Alive* by The Black Keys began to play, but he chuckled and cleared his throat, muttering something under his breath about "the irony".

"Uh, I'll just, uh..." He changed it quickly to *Work It Out* by Knox Hamilton. It subtly floated to us as he settled himself on the opposite far end of the couch. I kicked off my blue Chucks and turned to face him, putting my knees up. He seemed amused by the move, but said nothing.

"Your tattoo," I began and nodded my chin toward it. "I've never seen a clan tattoo like that."

He was already shaking his head. "When your mom took their power, their tattoos disappeared." I felt my eyebrows lift. That was surprising. We hadn't known that. "So, during our *training*, we all get the tattoo, but it's always the same one. They don't do the significant's name around the edge anymore. I've heard about those." He rubbed his mark a little roughly, almost as if...he wanted to remove it. "And I saw your parents' wrist last night. That was the first ones I've seen that were real, that came from...God, or whatever or whoever gives us our significants." He smiled. "It was neat how God just put their names on their wrists like that."

I showed him mine. "It's just the family crest." He kept on smiling as he tentatively touched it. That magical *For now* sitting there between us so heavy.

But then his smile morphed into a frown as he realized that playtime was over and he drew his hand back.

"After we left your house last night, I went back to Uncle Gaston's house with them to find out what was going on."

My fist tightened automatically.

He went on, though his eyes flicked from my face to my fist and then back before settling on the ceiling as he leaned his head back on the couch, as if defeated already.

"They knew about us, obviously. I went and told them as soon as it happened. But they weren't as happy as I thought they'd be." I kept watching him and knew he hated this. He was learning me so well, so I studied him, too. His fingers played with the ragged string on his pant leg. "I thought they'd look past it, the history, all the bull and the things that shouldn't matter anymore. I don't see the family as much as I used to. I'm so busy with work and all." His eyes cut over for a split second and I heard the shaky lie there. He had been *avoiding* them. "But the first thing out of Gaston's mouth was that this was our chance, our shot at finally getting back at the Jacobsons." He

shook his head before looking over fully.

I rubbed my chin on my knee. "And what did you say to that?"

"That I wasn't a pawn in their game anymore. That the game had changed completely. How could he even think that when you were my significant?" He scoffed. "He said he had it all worked out, that I didn't need to worry about that, that he could fix everything for me."

I felt a stab in my gut. "Why are you telling me all this?" I dropped my eyes to stare at the scratched leather of his couch, because I wasn't sure I could stand to see his eyes when he answered. "I know you still have loyalty to your family, that you're confused, that you don't know who to trust. I know that you don't fully trust me and my family, even though you want *my* trust. It's got to be hard for you to spill your guts like this about your family trying to sabotage us."

He scooted closer, the couch dipping under his weight, and though I knew it was coming, I still hissed with pleasure through my parted lips when his calloused fingers lifted my chin. "That's just it. You're my family, too. The tug of war is getting easier, even from yesterday." He sighed deep and let his hand fall from my face to my hand. He took it and brought it to his knee, as if that casual act wasn't a statement. "I told them that I wanted no part in any of their schemes. When I was a teenager, I did anything to fit in." His eyes took on a longing look. I'd seen it at the centers before in the kids. The ones who came after school because they needed somewhere to go, someone to look after them.

His eyes met mine. "I was *always* made aware that they weren't my birth family, but…they still treated me like I should be with them. I did everything I could to try to prove I could be one of them. So when they said it was my destiny to be the one to bring down the Jacobsons one day, I accepted the challenge with gusto." He shook his head. "I was only eight when they started "training" me." He made air quotes with his fingers when he said "training". "Which was essentially them all just sitting around talking about how much they hated the Jacobsons."

"Who raised you?"

"My parents," he said sarcastically. I rolled my eyes and he gave me a sideways grin. "Linda and Marvin Watson. They are pretty mellow. Gaston is the one who took over once I…peaked, I guess you could say. He and his family lived next door to us."

I saw her again, just a flash but it was enough. "Harper. Harper lived next door to you?"

"All my young life," he said carefully. "Our families used to do everything together. Training, dinners, Christmas. We went to school together. She would even come and sneak in my window when her parents were fighting sometimes."

I swallowed down my jealousy, fought to just listen and take it all in, no matter how much the thought of her crawling in his bedroom window made me hurt. "Her parents fought?" I asked and finally met his eyes again. He was watching me intently. He let my reaction go and answered me.

"Yeah. A lot."

"That's strange. Were they not imprinted?"

"No, they were."

I squinted. "Bonded couples wouldn't fight all the time like that."

He chuckled. "Uh, maybe the Jacobsons are happy-go-lucky people, but the Watsons fight like it's the last day on earth and arguing is the only thing that will save them."

Maybe I should have given him a courtesy laugh, but I was wound so tightly. "No, Seth. It's not just the Jacobsons. All the clans are that way. It's not just a clan, it's us, our people, our kind, our…our bodies wouldn't let us act that way to each other."

"What are you talking about?" He leaned back, taking his hand with him. "You're saying that your family never fights? That if I wanted to fight with you, I couldn't? I know that's not true because you've fought me tooth and nail since you met me. You ran out on me not two minutes after meeting me." He was angry, the angriest I'd ever seen him with the exception of when his uncle came to kidnap me. I went to speak and he went on, speaking over me. "Just because people fight doesn't mean they don't love each other. It looks like we're doing a pretty good job of fighting right now, little bird, now doesn't it? And that doesn't mean anything. It doesn't mean that I don't want you. It doesn't mean that you don't belong to me."

I took a deep breath and looked at him, waiting, seeing if he was done. When he just stared back, I went on, surprised by how husky my voice was.

"That's not what I meant." He seemed surprised by how husky my voice was, too. He sighed through his nose and closed his eyes. Hearing him say I belonged to him was like all icing and no cake—the best part.

Little bird…little bird. That sounded so familiar…

"Ava," he rumbled and when I looked up to meet his eyes he once again looked on the verge of a strange happiness that I couldn't grasp. "Something on your mind?"

"No, I just feel déjà vu or something." He swallowed loudly and I watched his throat. He watched me watch him. Ah, it was unnerving and…way too much sexy for this small apartment and my sworn enemy who was so pissed at me all of a sudden.

"Is there something…you want to ask me? You can just get whatever you want out of my head, you know. What's mine is yours. Dig around until you're satisfied that I'm not the Devil." He smirked, but it wasn't the sexy kind; it was the bitter kind. I wanted the sexy kind back, even if I was confused.

I used his own words on him. "No. I'm not going to take those things from you, Seth. I want you to give those things to me because you want me to have them."

His smirk disappeared. He leaned forward and put his elbows on his knees, his head fell forward as he let out a breath. "Ava, we can't keep doing this. This is getting us nowhere."

"Agreed," I whispered.

"So let's call a ceasefire." He turned to face me as he set his coffee on the table, but stayed a safe distance. I knew he was giving me my space, letting me feel comfortable in the bubble of calm I had created—however fragile or false it may have been. "No matter what you think of me, I didn't plan this. I'll start at the beginning, okay?" he suggested quietly and waited for me to agree.

I nodded.

But as soon as he opened his mouth, his phone rang.

Let it ring. Let it ring.

"I can't, Ava," he muttered as he looked down at the name on the screen, clearly hearing my begging. He glanced up and pleaded with me with that gaze. "I know that we need to do this. But my family…needs me, too. Especially after Harper was here earlier and I sent her away. Gaston will be angry. I…" He growled—like an actual growl that if I wasn't bonded to the boy, would have scared me. "I don't know what the hell to do. I'm being pulled in two directions."

I shouldn't have. It wasn't the right thing, but I did it anyway. "What do you feel is the right thing right now?"

Making him choose so early. Wrong move.

"I'm sorry, Ava. My uncle, he…" He sighed as the ringing stopped. "I have to figure out a way to make this right and the only way to do that is to be there and talk to them, make them see that they don't have to hold this grudge anymore. That us bonding is a sign, a reason to stop this. I'm trying to protect you."

He phone dinged again, but this time, he seemed surprised by the text. I tried not to be angry and I purposely avoided reading it.

I leaned up and began putting my shoes on. "Okay."

"We made some progress today. Please don't leave angry."

"I'm not angry," I remarked flatly and stood. "I'll walk to my car. It's not far."

"I'll walk with you."

"No, it's fine," I said harder. Softer I said, "I'm fine. Thanks. You go take care of the things you need to. I'm going to go home and see my family, too. Probably a good thing. I need to check on my parents and see how they're doing with all this—make sure Dad's still okay after what happened last night."

He winced. "I'm still really sorry about that."

"I don't want you to be sorry, Seth," I said and realized in my very soul that my next words were true, "I want you to be on my side."

My words crushed him, I could see. But I couldn't move as I turned to go. He didn't make me beg to be released; he kindly showed me mercy.

He softly rumbled, "I'll see you later. Go ahead and go, check on your dad. Everything will be fine."

If he wasn't with me he was against me, and my saying so obviously meant that I thought he wasn't. He wanted to stop me, but after the last time I accused him of wanting to take my touch for himself instead of give it to me, he wasn't going to dare say it, what with our already shaky foundation crumbling where we stood.

I was surprised that he was going to just let me go and surprised that Mom hadn't gone ballistic and come after me. I stopped before the door, my feet itched, torn between running away and running to the boy who held my heartbeat in his chest.

With soft, whispering pleadings in my head, I turned back and came to him as he stood perfectly still. He opened his arms and accepted me with a deep, contented sigh. I pressed my forehead to his chin, closing my eyes and

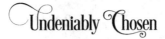

letting our touch carry me away to a second's worth of bliss. It was worth every bit of agony and embarrassment and torment. His palm coasted up the back of my arm before settling on the back of my neck. His thumb came around under my chin to tilt my head back. He stared, so close to my face. He could have kissed me, and, who knew, I might have let him in that moment. I was so blissed out and unencumbered in the moment and situation.

He murmured quietly, "Can I see you later?"

He wanted to see my eyes when he asked me that question. That's why he tilted my head back. He didn't want to come if I didn't truly want him there. He was begging me not to give up on him.

"Why don't you just wait and see how it goes. I'd hate for you make plans, them not work out, and you feel guilty."

He licked his lip a little in thought. "Can I see you later?" he repeated as though nothing else had been spoken between us.

I let my breath go slowly. "Yeah," I whispered.

CHAPTER SEVEN

So it turned out that Mom sent my cousin Drake to "escort" me home and had texted Seth to let him know. That's why neither Seth nor my mom had a problem with me leaving and roaming around town by myself. Pfft. I felt so cheated. I actually thought I had freedom. Silly, naïve, little Ava. Drake met me at the door when I emerged Seth's apartment and all the Legos fell into place. He saw it all happen on my face, too, and apologized.

"Sorry, cuz. From what I hear, things aren't working out so well. Want to me kick his—"

"No," I laughed and looped my arm through his. I put my head on his shoulder, sighing. "Let's just go home and then you can have Mom make you something yummy for being her lap dog. And I can reap the benefits."

He laughed. "Being her lap dag does have its good sides. The woman can cook." When I didn't say anything in return as we crossed the street he stopped. "Hey." I lifted my head, but it took me a minute to look at him. "*It happened,*" he said excitedly for me. "It may not be perfect yet, but it will be."

"You think?"

I turned to look across the street to find Seth watching me go. He was leaning back against his truck door, his legs and arms crossed. He looked so sad in that moment, like he wasn't sure if he'd ever see me again, or he wasn't sure if I ever *wanted to see him* again. Drake looked back at him, too.

"This is your last chance," he joked. "I'll do it. I'll take care of the problem right now."

I laughed, but felt this need to make him sure he knew.

Come tonight. I smiled, biting my lip. *When you're done with...your family. Come see me.*

His lips immediately rose into a smile that had my stomach doing flips. He pushed off his truck and hopped inside, speeding away quickly.

Drake chuckled. "Was it something I said?"

I laughed under my breath. "No," I breathed. "Hopefully, it was something *I said* and he's trying to hurry back."

He grinned. "Who knew you would be the biggest sap." He put his fingers under his chin and spoke in his highest falsetto. "Oh, Seth." I punched his arm, but he kept going. "You're the strongest brute of them all!"

He followed me back to my house in his big truck where Mom had homemade sweet rolls ready. She wrapped some up for him and sent him on his merry way. Pretty sad when bodyguards can happily be paid in baked goods.

That night, I told them how I went to Seth's apartment after he found me at the firehouse. And then it began. The infamous roll fight, which Rodney always started. And lost.

Rodney tossed a little piece of roll into Dad's plate. Dad looked at me and I shook my head. Dad grinned, knowing the culprit. He then took a roll and tossed the entire thing at Rodney's face and made it stop right before it smacked. Rodney's eyes, wide as lemons, stared cross-eyed at it before plucking it out of the air and tossing it back at Dad.

"You just started a wa-aaar," Mom sang.

"Mamma's right," Dad growled and chucked another roll at him, borrowing Mom's ability and slamming the roll into Rod's shoulder.

"Ow, Dad!" he groaned and leaned his head back on his chair. "How could you hit your son?" he said to the ceiling dramatically.

Mom laughed as we waited for Rodney's retaliation. It came in the form of a roll flying up from Rod's hand under the table, up and over the table, over the light fixture, and into Dad's waiting hand.

He smirked. "Amateur."

He wasn't ready for Rod's other roll to come barreling at him as he preened and gloated. It smacked into his forehead. *His forehead*. Rodney and Mom were laughing so hard, Rodney almost fell off of his chair. Dad hadn't been bested at roll retaliation in…ever.

"Yes!" Both hands in the air was the only way Rod handled his gloating. "He shoots, he scores, he wins, folks!" Rodney yelled and high-fived Mom. "Dad, that was epic. Can we do an instant replay so I can put this on my YouTube channel?"

Dad quickly flicked his fingers of both hands up, making Rodney's shirt go up over his head and then wrap around, twisting and trapping him.

"Dude! Payback will be swift, old man!" he yelled from his cocoon.

I laughed at my family and sat back watching, soaking it in. Thinking how close I was to losing all this. It was upwards of the eight o'clock hour and still no Seth. Mom had even postponed dinner to see if he'd make it. I hadn't told her he was coming, but she could apparently tell with all my pacing. We never ate dinner at eight o'clock at night.

I felt Mom kissing my hair and hadn't even seen her get up I was so dazed. I smiled at her, but knew I was failing at showing them I was fine. I got up to help her clear plates, the tinkling of the china barely heard over Rodney and Dad's grunting as they wrestled on the living room floor.

Mom laughed. "Caleb," she sang, "don't be mad when Rodney puts your feet over your head and puts the proof on Instagram again."

"Classic," Rodney managed to wheeze from under him.

"Whose side are you on, woman!" Dad laughed and gave her a look. I rolled my eyes, knowing that look was nothing if not bedroom-driven.

Rodney finally got his head loose. "I'll call child protective services."

"Ha!" Dad scoffed and noogied Rodney's head. "They'd crack you like the FBI. Rookie."

Mom and I laughed and finished up the dishes. There were hardly any.

"I'll call Grandpa!" Rodney yelled as he finally got the upper hand on Dad and slammed him to the floor.

He 'oomphed' and shook his head in mock shame. "I bet you would, traitor."

I barely heard my phone ding over the commotion, but I did. Mom did, too, and gave me a reassuring smile and a head nod. When I didn't run for it like she thought I would she scowled at me and flung her hand. My phone raced through the air stopping abruptly before it would have smashed into

my chest with force. I didn't even flinch, used to her antics. I gave her a look as Dad and Rodney kept at it, oblivious to anything else going on.

'Talk to him,' she mouthed. And then she said loudly over the ruckus. "That yuckiness in your gut, that unease and worry about what's going on, it won't go away until you talk to him."

I smiled as best I could and nodded. I sat in my dining room chair and opened the text.

I'm so sorry. There was a family emergency. I won't be able to come tonight and I hate that you were right about me breaking my promise. I'll be there first thing in the morning, no matter what. Nothing, no family emergency, NOTHING, could keep me away. I'll be there. I'm so sorry. Don't give up on me, Ava.

I stared at it for a minute before looking up.

"He's not coming," I told her and stood. "I'm going to bed."

She intercepted me as I tried to scoot from the room. "Not so fast." She wrapped her arms around me and spoke softly, but firmly. I knew it was my mother talking, not the leader of her race, not the woman who had endured the wrath of many, not the woman who held the fate of so many on her shoulders. This was just the woman who had been in love herself and wanted to comfort her daughter. "This stage sucks. The not-knowing-what's-going-to-happen stage. Even the strongest of relationships go through it." She leaned back. "I know that it's hard to be one of *those couples*. The ones that seem to be fated for something greater." My breath caught in my throat. "Your dad and I were one of those because we were the first imprint in so many years, and then the Visionary stuff happened, and every one spent so much time focusing on us that it was hard for *us* to focus on us sometimes. There *is* a reason for this, sweetheart. I promise you. It doesn't seem like it now, and it hurts and it sucks. But the universe doesn't hand out blank cards to play. You will know your hand soon enough."

"Mom," I could barely get the word out. She wiped my cheek clear of tears before a shadow filled the doorframe and looked at us.

Dad sighed one of those long sighs which you could tell that he was angry and hurt and wanted to bust heads and hold me and do all sorts of things all at once. "Come here, baby girl," he finally said.

His arms were so tight. When I was a little girl, I used to joke about him squeezing all my stuffing out because his hugs were so hard. He said he couldn't help it, that he needed to hug me as hard and as long as he could because one day somebody would come and take me away from him to marry me. I'd say *gross*, over the years it changed to *eww*, then *maybe*, then *when*, then *why not now*, then it happened…and *it was a Watson*.

"I'm okay, Daddy."

"No, you're not." He leaned me back and took my face in his hands. It was the same move that Seth had made, but the meaning was completely different. Both were meant to soothe me, both were meant to show me love of some degree, both were meant to make me see them dead on and know that they meant what they were saying. In that moment, I appreciated them both for it. "You're not okay, Ave, but you will be."

"I hope you're right."

He put an arm around me and another out for Mom to come into. "My girls," he mused and kissed my hair. "I know I'm right, Ava, because I saw Seth last night. I was worried before, and I still am, but not about him. I'm worried about his family. He won't hurt you—well, not on purpose."

I shrugged. "I don't know. He's in pretty deep with his family. You guys haven't seen him with them or heard him talk about them. His cousin, Harper, was at his apartment when we got there yesterday." Dad tensed, but I smoothed his shirt. "It was fine; it was just her. She tried to get him to come…" I almost said home. But that wasn't his home. I shook my head. "She wanted him to go with her to her family's house. Something about family problems. But when he saw how upset I was, he stayed."

"See?" Mom said and rubbed my arm. "That means something."

"But as soon as he got a text from them later on—when we were about to talk about his family and how he was adopted by them, he told me he had to go. And then he didn't come tonight when he said he would because of a *family emergency*."

"That could be them, though," Dad suspected. "I bet his family knew he was supposed to come here and threw something at him so he couldn't come. We have to remember there are more dynamics at play here than just a boy meeting a girl. These families have been fighting since before even my father was born. That isn't going to stop just because you two bonded. No matter how much we want it."

My chest fell, deflated. He noticed. "I hoped that they might call a ceasefire of some sorts, at least for a little while—maybe even some pretense of it, but it

doesn't look as if that's the case. They are and will always be our enemy. Seth, unfortunately, will have to choose a side."

"Why can't it just be easy…like when you guys bonded?"

They looked at each and laughed. Mom whispered, looking at Dad, "If that was easy, then I don't want to know what hard looks like."

"But you know what I mean," I forged on. "At least you knew Dad loved you. At least you didn't have to wonder if it was all a plot."

"Neither do you," Dad said low and looked away from Mom. "I knew that your mom was mine from the moment I took her hand and nothing and no one would have stood in my way. If Grandpa and Gran and the entire Jacobson clan decided they hated her, we would have run off together the second she agreed to it. That's not because of who I am, that's because I'm Virtuoso, and no one is going to keep my woman from me. Seth looked at you the way I look at your mom. That isn't something you can fake, especially after only knowing you just one day. That's something *in you*, something in your guts and soul, *imprinted on you,* something written on your heart from that first touch that doesn't go away."

My lips were parted in shock. I glanced at Mom and she was in a similar state. "Dad," I squeaked.

He smiled. "I have my moments."

I slipped a little bit back into the darkness. "But the Watsons aren't like the rest of the Virtuoso. They don't care about their women like everyone else."

"Ava," he said slowly, "Seth is *not* a Watson."

It was then that it all crashed down on me. I felt the first little bit of happiness smack me and I smiled, giving Daddy what I knew he wanted and needed. "Thank you, Daddy."

"What am I? Chop suey?"

I smiled at Mom and gripped her tightly around her neck. "Thank you, Momma."

"Aww, you haven't called me 'Mamma' in years." She rubbed my back and smoothed my hair as I continued to hold on.

"Today, you reminded me why you're Mom, not the Visionary. And you're really good at it." I tightened my grip. "I know you're both, but sometimes, Mom needs to trump the other—even if it could cause a Virtuoso worldwide incident."

Dad chuckled, as Mom squeezed me tighter. "You guys always come before my duties." I nodded. "Just like I know you'll come before any drama and obstacles with his family. He'll get there, Ava. He's just confused. His entire world just crumbled and came together all in the same day. Remember that."

I hadn't thought of it that way. Wow. A heavy helping of guilt swept over me. And I had spent the entire time just trying to get him to accept that they weren't his family at all, instead of realizing that in essence…he had gained me, but lost his family all in one day. Wow, what a tradeoff…

"I can see your wheels turning." She shook her head. "Don't be too hard on yourself. Go to bed. We'll talk more in the morning."

"He'll be here," Dad said from behind me. I turned to tell him that he texted to say he'd be here in the morning, but who knew if he would show, but from the look on Dad's face I understood. He wasn't asking a question. He was telling me that Seth would be here, that he had no doubts.

"How do you know?"

He smiled. "Guarantee you, he'll be here first thing, sitting in the driveway waiting for you. It's what I would have done."

We'll see. "Night."

They said their goodnights, too, and I turned the corner, but waited. When I peeked back around I knew what I'd find but their predictability was still endearing. Dad pushing Mom by her stomach to the wall, her tugging him down by his collar. Dad was right—the way he looked at Mom was so different than any other way a man looked at a woman. And Seth looked at me that way. With so much want and requirement in his eyes.

I turned away, scrunching my nose, when Dad when in for the kill shot. He never lasted long before he was completely consumed.

As I lay down, I hoped Daddy was right. I hoped Seth wanted me in all ways, and I hoped it was enough.

"Ava," someone whispered in my ear.

I turned to find the voice. It had to be Seth. Had to be. "Seth?" I called and found his face right next to mine. I smiled and sat up quickly. "Seth."

He sat on the edge of my bed and looked as though the weight of the world was on his shoulders. Before I could ask why, he looked up and took my hand in his. "I told you I'd see you tonight, didn't I? See, I kept my promise."

I tried to remember. "Um…"

"It's okay," he soothed in his deep voice and scooted closer to me. My knee was up against my chest so it pressed against his as well, our only barrier as he palmed my cheek. "I know you get a reset here. I shouldn't have said anything."

"Reset?" But then I remembered… "The rooftop."

He looked relieved. "So you remember each visit, each time, just not what goes on in your real life," he muttered to himself. "Okay, I can work with that."

"What do you—"

"Listen," he commanded softly, "there are forces at work against us. This is the only time we have to just be…together. Can we do that, Ava?"

I smiled. I couldn't help it. "I really like the way you say my name." I gripped the wrist of the hand gently holding my face and tried to push whatever calm I could muster into my words since I knew my calming touch wouldn't work here. "I don't know what's going on, but I can see that you're upset. What can I do to help?"

He seemed so confused and…flabbergasted. "So this is what you'd be like if we'd met without all my family drama. This is what you're like when you're happy." His thumb moved against my cheek and my eye lashes fluttered.

"I *am* happy."

"You're not always," he said in a foreboding tone. "I make you unhappy… in another life."

"That's not possible," I muttered and hated the way his eyes shone with truth.

"I don't do it on purpose, but some things are out of our control."

"You wouldn't hurt me," I said with conviction.

His lips opened for a few seconds before the words spilled out. "You actually believe that."

I let that go. "You said before that this was like a dream?" He seemed hesitant. I tilted my head. "What?"

"I need this, little bird." His thumb moved on my cheekbone again and I actually groaned a little, embarrassingly. "You may not want me or think I care, but I need this more than anything right now. Everything is so screwed up with my family and I… If I explain it, it might all go away. And then I'll only be with the you that hates but wants me and doesn't want to." He brought me an inch closer. "And I want this girl. The one that looks at me like I might be worth the effort."

My heart was breaking for him. Why would the other me be so cruel? Why would I be the girl that was breaking his heart his way? I had to have a good reason, I would never do that otherwise, but I couldn't imagine it.

"I like old movies," I blurted. "And the new slapstick comedies."

"Okay," he said with a little smile.

"And the girl who doesn't give you any slack likes them, too." He got my meaning. "And she likes hazelnut coffee and blueberry bagels with blueberry cream cheese. And don't even get her started on fifties and sixties music, particularly Etta James and The Flamingos. You play "*I Only Have Eyes For You*" and she'll swoon big time. She likes poetry. She loves Alfredo, but she loves chili-dogs just as much. She loves rocky road ice cream. And she *loves* her Converse Chucks."

"Thank you, Ava," he said sincerely.

"Well, I don't want you to strike out with her." I grinned and bit into my bottom lip. "If it helps, let me know and I help you."

He laughed once. "You're unreal."

"Take me somewhere," I said suddenly.

Before I could think, we were back at the palace terrace. "You said you would give me the tour," he reminded me.

"I'd love to."

I took his arm, his warm, strong arm grazing side as we walked into the door leading down into the palace. Since this was a dream, no one should be there, right? I led him down into the gold ball room. He looked around, in awe of the sites.

"Wow," he finally muttered.

"Yeah, it's something."

"It's incredible."

"It's gaudy."

He grinned. "Someone who has seen it every year of their life would say that."

"You'll see it soon enough."

His gaze jerked to mine. "What do you mean?"

"The reunification is coming in a few months."

He paused, making me wonder what he was thinking about. "And I'll be expected at this reunification, right?"

"I would say so. Don't you want to go?"

"Go to a room full of people who want to kill me?" He smiled. "No thanks, sweetheart."

"They won't all want to kill you," I assured. "Just most of them."

He laughed. "You're so funny here. And calm. And…happy. I wish I could keep you here forever."

"But it's not *really* real, is it? We're real, but not this. This place?"

He grimaced. "No. It's not real."

"Don't you want the real me to be this happy?"

His sigh was harsh. "I'd kill for it."

"Keep at it. I'll come around; I know it. There's no way you can look at me with those eyes and I won't melt."

He laughed and stopped dead in front of me, looking down at my face. "It's kind of not fair. I feel like I'm getting a behind-the-curtains peek of Ava and you're the tour.'"

"You are getting a tour," I whispered and leaned closer, getting in his space. "And it's not fair. But all's fair in love and war, right?"

"I think whoever said that had never been in love."

"Obviously," I quipped.

"Gah, you're adorable." He looked at me and smoothed that thumb once more, causing my undoing. "I hope you can forgive me. I just wanted to know you. Just wanted to spend time with you and learn you. Wanted you to *see me*. Without the glimmer of my family tainting me, without the mirage of the drama. I just wanted us to have our best chance. If that makes me bad, then so be it. It would be worth it to spend this time with you like this." I felt the breath shudder through me as I listened to his words. "With you so happy and unguarded. When you look so free and easy like this, it's worth almost anything."

"I'll forgive you. I have a feeling it may take some coaxing on your part, but I'll forgive you. Truly. How can I not?" I whispered and stared up, at him with all the awe I felt in my guts. I hoped it shined through. I hoped he understood that I knew he was having a tough time right now, but I knew he was going through to be with me. He was risking everything. He came here, knowing there was a chance that I'd hate him at the end of all this, just so he could get to know me, just so I could get to know him. How could I be upset about that? Look what he was doing for me.

"I hope you're right."

"I am," I said with as much conviction as I could muster into my voice. "Look what you did for me—what you're *doing* for me. If she can't see that? If she can't see what you've gone through to get to know her, to learn all her nooks and crannies? Then she doesn't deserve you."

His hand on my cheek smoothed while his face looked down on me in wonder. "Ava, you're…"

"Come on." I took his hand from my cheek and held it in mine. "I'll show you around." I grinned, feeling cheeky. "You'd totally get lost without me."

"Good thing you're here," he said quietly and let me tug him everywhere, showing him what I deemed important. I showed him the kitchen, the dorm rooms. I took him up to the library and told him the story of how my parents had seen Ashlyn on their visits there, how she led them around in visions and they found out about them keeping her locked up in there. That was why her spirit never rested. That was why she was able to speak to us in the way she was.

He was quiet. I had expected that. It was, again, a strange thing to learn that your family had done something awful when you had expected something different from them.

Then I showed him our names on the wall, just like Dad and Mom had told me they'd be there. I sighed, feeling so many things churning in my guts.

"What are you thinking?" I asked when he was quiet, staring at the wall for so long. "I know I won't remember tomorrow, but I still want to know."

He let a breath loose, the kind that held agony that was too much for your body to handle.

"I can't believe our names are on this wall. Right here, together, years ago, by the Visionary of our race, for all to see that would just open their eyes and look." He scoffed softly. "I just can't believe that it's actually here. The one situation in my life I didn't need any proof of and I have more than enough." He turned to look at me in the dark of the barely lit room. "What do you think this means? Our names up here on this wall together like that?"

"Ashlyn told Mom that it meant we were going to be on the council together one day. That we were…special, going to change things."

His hand reached up to touch his name first and then my name. He made that soft scoffing noise again and it was so endearingly sexy. "Me? A council member of the Virtuoso? Yeah right," he muttered under his breath.

"She also said that we'd find you again one day." He looked over. Blue collided with brown.

His hand slid slowly from the wall to his side as he came toward me. I knew this would be different than the other times. I moved backward until I felt the wall at my back, which wound up only being a couple of steps. I somehow knew I'd need it for support. He stalked right up until his nose was touching my cheek. I sucked in an intoxicating breath, pleasure spiking in my veins. Whether the calm of his touch was there or not, it was pleasure nonetheless.

"And are you pleased, Ava?" his gravelly voice asked. My hand reached out, pressing a palm to his chest. Not to keep him away, but just to touch him. My breaths were ragged as I chased them. "Can you say you're happy with the outcome of finding me?"

He was trying to goad me. He was angry again, with himself, with the situation, with his family, with mine. He wanted me to say that I didn't know or...I wasn't really sure what he wanted me to say. But I was sure that he wanted a fight.

"I only wish we'd found you sooner," I said honestly. Softly. Gently. I closed my eyes and tried to remember my parents that day. They left me there with Nana and Grammy. They came back and I remembered Mom being so upset, even all these years later. I remember finding the drawing in Dad's pocket and talking to Ashlyn about it. I didn't remember it until Dad and Mom said Ashlyn had something to do with it. But now I remembered... It was his. They'd found it at the compound and Mom had been distraught over not getting to him in time.

"Open your eyes, Ave," he commanded just as softly, and when I did, he was no longer angry. No, we were reaching the other end of the spectrum. And it was just as scary in my opinion.

"Ave?"

His mouth quirked on the side. "I'm trying it out. You like?" I opened my mouth to tell him that I wouldn't remember tomorrow, but he cut me off. "I'll surprise you with it tomorrow if you like it." I found myself smiling up at him. He was so tall that I had to crane my neck, but he bent his head to see me, so we would be close.

I nodded. "My dad calls me that sometimes."

His smile was small, but he said, "I'll keep surprising you with these things, these pieces of you that I've discovered… until you can't help but see that I'm here for you most of all."

"Most of all," I mused. "As opposed to?"

"The other you thinks I choose my family over you."

"Do you?" I asked, my voice betraying me.

He swallowed, his hand coming up to rub my elbow. "I don't try to." He squinted. "What's the last thing you remember?"

I tried to think back, pushed my mind and tried to remember. "Um…I don't…I just remember you." I squinted, looking around. "Why can't I remember?"

"Okay," he calmed. "It's okay. You get a reset. Remember?" He gulped again, looking so guilty. I took his shirt in my fist and tugged it a little. "I did this to you. I shouldn't come back—"

"No."

"You're only saying that 'cause I brought you here and you're happy now. But it's…" He looked in my eyes and I saw it. He was about to take it all away. "It's not right." He sighed harshly and angrily. He leaned away, taking my fingers from his shirt and turned away. "It's not right, Ava, and I know I'll probably lose you, but I can't do this to you—"

"No!" He turned back and looked startled at my outburst. "Don't you dare give up on me." My words did something to him.

"Give up on you? No, that's not what—"

"Then what do you call it?" I pushed away from the wall and came right up to his chest, looking up at him, craning my neck high to see the boy who literally held my heart. "I want you to come here every night and fight." I found my chin quivering and realized how true those words were. If what he said was true about what was going on when I was awake, then my dream of finding my significant and living happily ever after was crumbling. "I want you to fight for me."

He groaned and took my face in his hands, smoothing my cheeks with his thumbs as he put his forehead to mine. "Ah, Ava. How could you think for a second that I would just let you go? Of course I'm going to fight for you. I just…" He leaned back a little so I could see his face. "Do you think you'll

forgive me for this? Is it too much? Too far? I never wanted to hurt you. I just wanted to be with you."

I thought honestly about it. If Seth came and told me what he'd done, would I be able to forgive him. It was all for love. I was here. It wasn't an invasion of privacy because *I was here*. I was here the entire time, giving him permission. It wasn't like he was poking around in my head when I was asleep. He was here *with me*.

I smiled. "Fight for me, Seth."

He sighed in such a relieved way and pressed his lips to my forehead. "Thank God. I don't know what I would have done without having this time with you."

"Are you sleeping?" I asked, my eyes closed, my breath speeding up.

"Not fully, it's not deep, but I'll sleep later." He kissed my forehead and I blew out a quiet breath. "It's worth all the missed sleep in the world to see you every night."

"So you'll come? Every night?" I asked hopefully, twisting my fists into his shirt further even as I twisted my soul into his.

"If you'll allow me."

I opened my eyes, finding him close, and couldn't stop my grin. "I can show you so many places."

"And I can show you a few, too. You're really truly with this?"

He chuckled. "Truly. I'd miss you if you weren't here." His breath was loud. "And I'd know," I assured him. "I know you think it wouldn't matter, but I'd know that you weren't here. Trust me; this is right. I have a feeling that I might remember all this one day or…maybe something will come of it. But even if I didn't, just being here with you like this is enough for now. Please don't take that away from me."

"I won't," he promised in a rumble and swiped a palm down my arm. "Not with you looking at me like that."

I felt my face burn hot, but couldn't turn away from him as he watched me.

"How can you do this? The dreams?"

"I've been able to do them since I was a boy." He took my hand and played with my fingers between us. "I don't really know how. I shouldn't be able to. I haven't ascended yet. My Uncle Sikes was an echoling, but I never met him. He died before I was before I was…brought into the family."

"I remember my parents talking about him."

"Only one member of the family can have the same gift at the same time, right?" I nodded. "He died somehow..." He shook his head. "I don't know. I wasn't born Virtuoso—unless somehow someone in my family was. I was eight when I had my first echo dream."

"Does your family know you can do it?"

"No," he answered quickly and looked down at me. "Honestly?" I nodded. "I would never tell the other you this, but I'm scared to tell my family that I can do it. Because I'm afraid that they'll make me do things that I don't want to do."

"Why don't you want to tell the other me this?"

"Because, she hates my family. And I...don't want her to be right about them."

I cupped his face and lifted it. He was so vulnerable. I hated that I wasn't able to be the person he needed when I was awake. But I had to have a reason. "I'm..." I licked my lips and tried to think of something, "sorry that I'm not what you need when we're outside of this place. I wish I was. I don't...know what else to do. I feel like I'm failing you."

I felt like crying.

"No," he shook his head, "no, little bird." He wrapped his arms around me and drew me close. "She has her reasons for doubting me. Don't be harsh with her for that. Things happened. I have her and I have you. For now, that's all I need. The yin and the yang. You're going to help me." He leaned back and smiled. "You're going to help me make her see that her life isn't the disaster she thinks. That it's right on track. That *I'm* what she was meant to find. Right?"

I nodded vehemently, feeling that urge to cry bubble up again. "Yeah. Seth?"

"Yeah, sweetheart?"

My heart beat hard. He felt it, pressing his hand over his chest and letting out a groaning breath. "Thank you."

"What for?"

"For not giving up on me."

His smile was one of pure happiness. "Return the favor? Don't give up on me, Ava."

CHAPTER EIGHT

My alarm clock woke me early. I had classes today, which I didn't want to go to. I lay in bed, looking at the ceiling and tried not to groan at the ache in my body and my heart. He hadn't come last night. He'd chosen his family over me and I know that he must have thought it was really important. I get that. They must have made it seem really important for him not to come. But still…he chose.

And he chose wrong.

I felt the first tear crawl across my cheek and reached up to wipe it away. I shook my head, feeling the tug and pull in my back and arms as my body protested. I refused to sit here and feel sorry for myself. This was my life now. I may as well get over it, right?

If the universe wanted me to be the Juliet to his Romeo, then fine. I'd take his touch when I could and live my life the rest of the time. We needed to figure out what his family was up to because they were definitely up to something. The summit was coming in a week and a half. I'd bet my right hand they were planning something.

I rolled out of bed and wasn't able to stop the groan this time. It wasn't better the second day. Not even close. It was worse, in fact. Way worse. Probably because I hadn't seen him since yesterday afternoon. I scoffed as I moved about the room, slamming drawers as I dressed as quickly as I could. If he wasn't here like he promised me, I'd drive to his house and...

He was here. I just knew it. I could feel him.

That made me move even quicker, moving through my routine in the sloppiest and most uncoordinated I'd ever done it, but the job was done. But then I rethought some things when I looked in the mirror, seeing my handy work. Why would he even *want* to come back when this was the picture I was giving him?

But then I gritted my teeth and shook my head. That was such bull and I scolded myself for even thinking it. He doesn't get to jerk me around and then dictate how I dress myself on top of that! No, no, no.

With my hair piled in my messy bun, the way I was definitely leaving it, but *never* wore it to school, my jeans, Chucks, and a tight-fitting green long-sleeve thin thermal shirt, a little make up, and a lot of anxiety sitting in my belly, I made my way as fast as I could out into the living room to grab my school bag.

"Whoa," I heard. I turned to find my family sitting at the breakfast table and Rodney on the verge of laughter. "Someone's high strung."

"Leave her alone, Rod," Dad ordered and look at me, his eyes softening. "You okay?"

"I'm fine." No one believed me, not even me. My voice shook.

"He's in the driveway," Mom said and smiled. "He's been there since four in the morning, just sitting in his truck." She lifted her eyebrows.

"I told you he'd come," Dad told me and tilted his head.

"He's a little late," I muttered and scuffed my shoe.

"Hear him out," Mom said. "In the meantime, I want you to be careful. Don't go anywhere without your phone. If he's not going to drive you to school, then I want Rodney to. Or text Drake or Jordan—"

"Mom—"

"Do you not remember what happened here the other night?" she said harder. "Good," she spouted, not waiting for me to answer. "Then I don't want to have to worry about you. He may not know it, but the Watsons are planning something. *I know* it. They aren't going to just give up because he said so." That's what I had said, too. "We need to be extra careful. If you want to bring him in, I'll explain that to him."

"No. It's fine," I said quickly.

"I thought so." She smiled. I rubbed my neck, my breath puffed from my lips painfully. "What are you doing, Ava?"

"Stalling," I whispered and turned to look out the window at his truck. Just seeing him out there made my ache even worse, knowing he was in withdrawals, too. I groaned a little.

"I know. But why?"

"Because I'm afraid he'll disappoint me. I'm afraid that he's not what I think he is. Most of all, I'm afraid he's *exactly* what I think he is."

I felt her hands on the tops of my arms. "You've waited for this your whole life, Ava. And now that it's here, you can't run from it just because it's not exactly what you expected. Life never is. If you run from a challenge, then you'll always be running. Look at Seth. From the first day, he has faced this. He came here, to this house full of strangers, who he knew were going to probably hate him—and he did that for you. He's out there now *for you*. Don't give up on him, Ava."

I gasped a little, the breath getting caught in my throat.

Don't give up on me, Ava…

I waited a few beats to catch my breath.

"Thanks, Mom."

I hoisted my bag up and left without another word or a look back. I heard Rodney call out over his cereal. "Is that really what you're wearing?"

"Bye, Rod!" I yelled with a laugh.

I barely made it two steps out my front door when he was opening his door and stepping out of his big Dodge truck. He didn't look so good either. I mean…he looked *amazing*. If men were edible, he would be breakfast. He was scruffy and I determined right then that I liked scruff. He hadn't shaved last night, obviously if he slept in his truck…for me…and his jeans and fire station '22' t-shirt looked a little unkempt, but he looked so good that way. But he also looked as if a regular person, like Rodney, would call him on it for looking a little rough.

His eyes went up and down me a couple times. "Wow, you look…" Okay, maybe Rodney was right… "Really good. Even in the mornings, when this withdrawal thing really sucks."

Oh. He was just being nice.

"I'm not just being nice."

"Will you stop?" I whispered. "It's too early for you to…be in my head."

"I'm not," he promised and smiled. "It's all over your face." He smiled wider. "I brought breakfast. Somehow I knew you wouldn't eat."

I hadn't noticed the coffee and bag in his hands. We may as well go ahead and get this over with. It was going to be awkward no matter what, right? He knew I was angry. I knew he was sorry, but there was nothing he could say to make it better. He chose when I asked him to choose me. So I may as well take the breakfast, take his touch, and then go to school. We could hash this out later.

I reached forward, feeling the painful tug in my back when I did it. I groaned a little and saw his face watch my every move as I let my palm slide against his neck. The second his skin hit mine, it was like a wave of calm settled over me, a shocking ease and fog that crawled through my veins. I felt his sigh in my hair as his arms reached around me. The bag crumpled in his grasp.

"I'm so sorry about last night. I know I hurt you and I wish that there was a way that it could have been different. It seems it's destined to be hard for us."

"Why does it have to be?" My arms were trapped between us and I gripped his neck in my hand, but I surprisingly didn't mind as much. My anger was there, but it had tamed some. It was corralled now, understandably. My pain made my anger and frustration worse. Now that it was gone, I could focus on how I actually felt. Right this second? I just wanted to be near him. I just wanted to stay like this. "Why can't we just keep our promises?"

He leaned back and licked his lip. "My mom—the woman who raised me—had a heart attack last night."

My heart jumped painfully for him. "But...why didn't you just tell me that? I would have—"

"You would have tried to come," he confirmed.

I realized he was right. There was no way I could have laid there all night, knowing he was hurting like that and not gone to comfort him. My significant body wouldn't have let me. I let my eyes fall to his neck, but his used his finger under my chin of the hand holding the coffee to bring it back up.

"And I would have loved you for it." I gasped a little. "But I was with her at the hospital and you would have been waiting for me sometimes. A lot probably. And...as much as it pains me to admit it, I...don't think you should be around my family alone. Not like that. Not yet. I'm sorry. I know you thought I was just blowing you off, or picking them over you, but." He left it at that.

"I did think that," I admitted and felt guilty. Even Mom said I should have faith in him, have more faith in the process that finding my significant is what I was meant to do. Why would I wait an entire lifetime for him and then throw him away the second I find him? I wouldn't. "I'm sorry. You told me not to give up on you and I won't. Let's just…" I pushed him back a little and laughed a little awkwardly, "take things as they come, okay?"

He let a powerful breath go and smiled that smile that knocked the breath from me. "That's the best thing I think I've ever heard you say."

I laughed and squinted. "Um, okay."

He shook his head, getting that I didn't understand. "That you're not giving up on me."

I nodded, biting my lip shyly, just as his phone dinged with a message. I said he could get it and he opened it smiling, but the smile quickly drained away.

I had so much fun last night, S. I've missed you. Don't worry about anything. Everything's going to be okay. Love you. – Harp

"Fun? *Last* night?"

Had I said that out loud?

He exhaled harshly. "You don't want to get inside my head, but you'll read every text message that comes through, no problem," he said angrily.

I looked up at him, clearly shocked. What a one-eighty…

His face fell and he closed his eyes for a few seconds. "I'm angry because it looks like I was lying, but I wasn't. It always looks like I'm lying or have something to hide with you and it's…" he gritted his teeth, "driving me crazy!" He put the breakfast down on the bench by my mom's flowerbed and paced. "I don't know what the hell is going on," he barked. "It feels like I'm being sabotaged."

"Maybe you are," I said under my breath.

He turned, though I don't know how he heard me. "What?"

I changed directions. "What did she mean? What fun did you have?"

"The family all went over to my mom's house. We…played video games and stuff, as a family."

The Watsons play games?

"Is that something you always do?"

"No. Never. I think they were trying to say they were sorry for what they did, trying to smooth things over. Everybody was there. Everybody was being really awesome."

I couldn't help it…couldn't stop it. "And Harper?"

"Yeah. She was there, too. She's my family, Ava. Anyway, then my mom just started having chest pains, right at the time I was supposed to leave to come see you." He grimaced.

"At the time you were supposed to leave…"

"They can't make someone have a heart attack, Ave." I jolted. He tilted his head and smiled a little. "What? You don't like it?"

He gives me a nickname while we're in the middle of talking about Harper? *Harp?*

He deflated so fast.

"I'm going to be late for school," I said softly.

"Can I take you?" he asked hopefully, but the look on his face held no real confidence.

"Yeah." His eyebrows rose to his hairline. "My parents don't want me to be alone right now."

"Ah. My family," he realized. "So it was either me or Rodney, right?"

"Pretty much."

He grabbed the breakfast off the bench and started for the truck. "Well, even though you're pissed at me, I'll take being the lesser of two evils to be able to drive you."

He wasn't smiling when he said it. He wasn't angry either. I didn't know what he was.

I didn't know what *we* were.

I climbed into the truck, not easily I might add, and shut the door. He turned on the heat and radio immediately and I realized he had a serious thing for music. As Vega 4's *Life Is Beautiful* started to play through the truck cab, I felt a hard hit in my chest as I listened to the lyrics.

Life is beautiful, but it's complicated.

Would he eventually not want to keep fighting for me? Would I eventually just not be worth the effort anymore?

"No."

I looked over sharply, not realizing how hard I was breathing. "What?" I barely whispered.

"No." He stared stoically. "That will never happen." He put the truck in

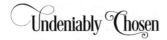

reverse, putting his hand on the headrest behind my head, and backed up from my driveway. "Eat your breakfast, Ava," he told me softly and smiled a little as he pulled onto the highway.

I caved, if for no other reason to give me something to do, taking the cup from the cup holder. I noticed he had one in his also. I took a big gulp, knowing it wasn't still hot after all that time wasting in my driveway.

Hazelnut.

I looked over at him and noticed the little smile he was wearing. So he remembered how I took my coffee.

Okay.

I opened the bag and was hit with a waft of blueberries. I may have groaned a little out loud. I didn't look over to see if his smile grew or not. I reached inside to find a wrapped blueberry bagel with…blueberry cream cheese. I whipped my gaze over to find his smile still small and knowing. "I thought you said you weren't going to dig around in my head?" I accused softly.

"I didn't."

"Then how—"

"You look like a blueberries kind of girl," he said innocently. "Seems I got lucky."

I continued to stare at him. I would have known if he'd been in my head. I would have felt him. Unless he snuck over while I was sleeping and if that was the case, why not just take my touch, too, to keep from being in withdrawal? No, it wasn't that. That was just too ridiculous. He really guessed my favorite bagel?

"We're supposed to be able to figure each other out, right?" His eyes swung over, hitting their mark, right on point and staying there a few seconds, before going back to the road. "Isn't that what we should be doing?"

I nibbled the blueberries, not answering him. "How's your mom? I meant to ask before, but you kind of blindsided me. Sorry."

"She's okay now. It was a minor heart attack. Kind of freaky, really. She's never had any problems before and now she seems to be doing just fine. They're releasing her today."

"Are you and your mom close?"

"Um…" He rubbed his neck. It pulled his arms in his leather jacket *so* the right way, but I couldn't even enjoy that because I heard it. The tone. The one I was learning faster than I had picked up angles and lines—something I loved from the moment we did it in class, and I knew then that I'd work with Grandpa and not Daddy that day. I knew I'd be an architect and I knew that Dad would be okay with that. "I mean, not really, but we're not *not* close, you know? Her and my dad are just not really the touchy feely type."

"What about grandparents?"

He cleared his throat. "Donald would have been my grandfather." He looked over for just a second. "I hear he was a…real winner." That surprised me. So far he'd been so gracious of his family. He chuckled a little. "He's kind of seen as the one who 'failed them'." He smiled a little like it was funny, but I couldn't even think in that moment, couldn't even breath. I tried not to project my thought, my feelings, my epiphany so he wouldn't get wind of it. I knew it would just make him feel conflicted, but it was no use. I didn't know how to do this yet, how to be this side of me, and it blared through even as I turned to look at the window.

He said 'them'. Not 'us'. The one who failed *them*.

I heard his breathing as he tried to keep it steady, in and out, but I could tell it was all an act, a façade of calm. And then his thoughts hit me for the first time full-on without me trying to read him, and I was sure without him trying to push it to me.

What the hell did I just do?

I'd only ever heard one word. *Ava*. My name. That's all I've ever heard that was his voice in my head. Everything else has been flashes and visions, pictures, feelings, thoughts, intuition. But his voice…

His voice in my head was like a punch to the very thing inside me that makes me who I am. Even though the words he'd spoken were in anger and he was probably seething over in his seat, I couldn't help but be in a completely different world over in mine with my revelation. His voice—soothing like music, deep as if tied right to his soul, dark like his coffee, calm like an embrace. His voice…was made for me. He was made for me.

I smiled as I felt a warm tear escape and wiped it away with a curled middle finger. I shook my head at myself. When did I become such a sappy girl? Oh, yeah…

I looked over at him then, unable to do anything but in that moment. What if the situation were reversed? Would I be able to just give Mom and Dad up so easily? What I was asking him to do in a day was something I

wouldn't do myself. And I felt like the worst kind of scum for being so callous.

I noticed his fist shaking on his thigh, the leather "Vivere" bracelet sitting there. I could see the dark mark on his middle finger near his fingernail from his pencils from drawing. It was probably permanent by now. My shoulders shrunk even lower as I realized how angry he really was. I opened my mouth to try to apologize somehow, but he stopped me, lifting that fist. He opened his hand, his fingers white, finally getting pinker as the blood returned. He kept looking between me and the road as we neared the school.

"Once you opened your mind's gate, I guess it was hard to shut."

I didn't understand…until I did. He had heard everything.

I opened my mouth to explain, to tell him…what? It wasn't that I didn't mean it, I just hadn't meant for him to hear it. He chuckled once. "You can still hear me," I declared, knowing it was true.

Adorable.

"It's okay," he promised and tried not to smile, but failed epically. "I won't hold anything I hear against you." His smile grew when he saw me tilt my head at that.

Freaking adorable.

My lips parted at hearing him, not knowing if he'd meant for me to or not. Though now that he knew how much I thoroughly enjoyed it, I could guess I'd hear it all the time.

"Thanks for asking." He took my hand slowly, as if he thought I wouldn't let him, and held it on the seat between us. "About my mom."

With practically a mile of seat between us and both of our arms spread wide to reach the other's hand, that was all we needed right then. And probably all I could take. But it was enough for now.

"Of course. But next time, don't shut me out." I turned on the seat so he could see my face if he wanted to while I said it. "I know that our families are going to be problems for us, but it's up to us how we handle it, how we let that interfere with us. If you have something going on with your family, I might not like it, but instead of being left in dark and wondering what's going on, I'd rather just know. The dark just makes things worse." I looked down at our hands near my knee on the seat. "Your mind runs in the dark."

The truck stopped and I thought he had pulled over at first, but he had pulled into the back of the lot of school. Putting it in park, he mimicked my stance, turning in his seat and looking down at our hands.

"I didn't know what to do. I hate being stuck in the middle like this."

"I get it." I kept his hands in mine but let the fingers of my other hand move up to touch the leather band on his wrist. "What does *Vivere* mean?"

"Uh…" He squinted. "It means *to live* in Latin."

"Did you take Latin in college?"

He smiled, looking down at our hands before swinging his blue eyes up to mine. It was like I'd been hit in the chest that gaze was so powerful. "No. When I used to dream, sometimes that word would stick in my mind. So I looked it up and thought that was a pretty good motto. I figured there had to be a reason I was dreaming about it. At the time I thought it was about my life, becoming a fireman, doing what…needed to be done." He looked at me closely, his thumb sweeping over my mine. "Dreams are kind of important to me so. Vivere. To live."

"That's…truly beautiful, Seth," I whispered. "And powerful. Who else has a story like that? A testimony to back up the whys of the way they do things?"

He shrugged, like it wasn't that big of a deal, but I could see it in his eyes. He didn't know why, but he cherished it. "Thanks. My family didn't get it. They thought it was—"

He stopped, not wanting me to have more ammo against them.

"Do you really think anything will ever change?" I asked softly, with any hope that was left in me.

"It has to." He looked up and begged me to do the same. "I will fix this for us, Ava."

I felt a shiver go down my back. Looking into those eyes and hearing those words…

"You all right?" he asked, his voice deeper than before.

"Yeah. I just…nothing." I glanced out the side window to see all the students heading to class, parking their cars, being so normal. "I better go."

"I can pick you up. What time?"

I thought about it. "You'll have to drop me off at Daddy's center. I'm working there tonight."

He didn't miss a beat. "No problem."

I let out a small sigh, not sure what else to do. "Two."

"I'll be here at two."

"What about work?"

"I've worked so many overtime hours for them for sick babies and

recitals and basketball games. They owe me." He smiled. "I'm the single guy, remember?"

He handed me my coffee that I still had yet to drink and I bagged up the rest of my breakfast.

"Thanks for this." I lifted the bag.

"No sweat. Be careful, uh…getting out."

That's not what he was going to say. He was going to say to watch out for myself today. But that would mean he'd be admitting there might be a threat and he wasn't ready to. I let it go.

I started to get out, but stopped. "You be careful. Don't win anymore awards today, okay. No playing hero."

He grinned, full wattage, heart stopping. "You got it. Just for today." He winked. *Winked*. "I'll see you later. Go fill that pretty head with all sorts of knowledge."

I laughed as I took the door in my hand and stepped out. "Yeah. Bye."

"Bye, sweetheart," he said gently and put the truck in gear, but he stopped me. "Wait." I looked at him and he had a little embarrassed smile on his face. "Uh…I can't leave."

That made me feel…kinda awesome. It was the first time he needed me to release him and not the other way around. "Really?"

He smiled and shook his head. "You're really enjoying this, aren't you?"

"Yep." He laughed, his smile…pretty sexy. "We'll see each other in just a little bit. I promise," I finished so softly, it sucked all the playfulness out of the truck and turned it into something else entirely. We stared at each other. "I'll go this way. You go that way." I tried to smile. "See you later?"

He nodded. "You got it, sweetheart."

As I watched him pull away, I felt an arm swoop through mine, tugging me roughly through the parking lot.

CHAPTER NINE

"Um, tell all, right now!"

I watched Lilith tug her earbuds out and look at me expectantly. We were the exact same height, dark hair, even the same brown eyes. Except she dated anyone and everyone that looked good in a pair of jeans or could play a sport they could brag about. She was studying to be an engineer so we were in a lot of the same classes and had been from the beginning.

We'd met freshman year and she kind of latched herself onto me. But I was okay with that. She was one of those people that pretended they were loners, but they really weren't. They acted like they didn't really like people, but they talked all the time and knew someone everywhere they went. Why she wanted to be my friend, I still didn't know. She was always there, always awesome, always laughing. She was a slice of normal pie.

I never got too attached to people because I knew that they'd want to know things. I knew about Mom's best friend. How things had gone terribly wrong. Dad and his friends had eventually drifted apart because they just can't know about us. Even his best friend Vic. It killed Dad to it, but it's our life. So I just kept all my friends on a very long leash and never got too chummy.

When I went off to college, it was more like *we'll text you sometime* and that's how I wanted it. We never texted though. And that was sad, but okay.

It was safer for them. *Better* for them. Yeah, I'd been friends with Lilith for almost four years now, but it was still so casual. We never hung out much outside of school. Well…much. Yeah, we had a ton of classes together and yeah, we had lunch together just about every day. We even met up with Rodney at lunch sometimes and he had such a crush on her back when he was a freshman…it was so hilarious…and adorably pointless.

I looked over at her. She raised an eyebrow and quirked her lip. "Waiting, *miss I don't date and yet I just jumped out of mister hottie's truck.*"

I snorted. "He's…"

"Oh, boy!" she squealed and tugged me further along with her arm in mine. "You've got it bad!"

"What," I said breathlessly.

"That dot, dot, dot that was implied just now means you've got it bad. I am so glad that you decided to take the chastity belt off—"

"Whoa!" I glared at her. "Nobody is debelting."

That eyebrow got back to work. "Where did you meet?"

"The coffee shop. I was late, he was early." I couldn't help but smile remembering that conversation.

"And he drove you to school. In his truck. That he owns. And I bet he doesn't live with his parents either." I shook my head. "Have you been on a date yet?"

"No. And before you start all your matchmaking crap, we're taking things slow. Like lava slow. There's some things that need to be worked out—family stuff."

She rolled her eyes. "Where does hottie work?"

I sighed, knowing what was coming. "He's…a fireman."

Her mouth opened a full fifteen seconds before words escaped. "You're killing me, Smalls!"

The day dragged. I knew why and it irked me that I had become *that girl.* Or maybe it just pained me that I was surrendering to something without all the facts. It didn't feel right to be so easy with Seth when there were so many unanswered questions with his family still.

I got my work for the day done, ate lunch with Lilith and the rest of my *friends*, and before I knew it, it was time for him to come get me. I was content to sit and wait alone in the courtyard, reading my book, drinking my coffee. I was content to wait alone a lot of the time. Not having many friends was part of the package of being one of my kind.

"Stay gold, Ponyboy, stay gold," a deep voice read from behind me.

I jerked around to find him over my shoulder. He was smiling. "Seth."

His eyebrows shot up. "Expecting someone else?"

"No. I just thought you'd…"

He smiled and chuckled. "Pull up and honk?"

I laughed a little and shook my head. "Uh…yeah, I guess."

He offered his hand as he straightened. I took it, loving the small hiss his breath made when our skin connected. "I'm not the pull-up-and-honk type, Ava. That won't happen. Sorry."

I didn't speak for a while, just soaked up his touch. "I'm not complaining," I finally muttered.

It was like I could hear that song playing in my head again, Vega 4's *"Life Is Beautiful"*.

This is ours just for the moment.

"Ava," he interrupted.

"Yeah."

"Let's go." His smile was one of someone who knew what was up, but wasn't going to say anything. He nodded his head the way of the truck.

You wax poetic even in your head.

I jerked my gaze to his in surprise. He didn't look at me, but his upturned lips stayed put.

I thought you said it was cute.

He laughed out loud, surprised, putting his hand on my back to direct me around the cars. "Oh, it's cute," he rumbled.

I melted under his touch and his laugh. If this was how it was going to be, how was I supposed to survive it? Let alone go as slow as lava?

When we reached the truck he sighed. "We have company again. One of yours, I'm assuming?"

I looked where he nodded his head and saw one of my cousins, Jordan, leaning against his truck. He gave a small wave with a sad smile before getting

in and waiting for us. Dad and Mom had been sending my cousins out to watch me. I looked over to explain or... I shrugged. "I—"

"They don't trust me yet. Why would they?" Seth rubbed the side of his head with his knuckles, a sad smile sitting on his lips. "Look what's happened since I met you? I get it."

I pressed my lips together. "That's Jordan. And my cousin from the other night was Drake. I'll tell my parents to back off—"

"They're just watching out for you." He looked at me closely. "They're just making sure you're safe. I appreciate them for that." My heart pounded. He ticked his head toward his truck. "Come on."

I stared at the glass doors of the center, all covered with pictures of colored art shapes and drawings from the middle school class. I was stalling; not ready to leave.

"I'll come by tonight, okay?" He inched his hand toward mine on the seat slowly. I showed him mercy and took his hand in mine, accepting the hit of calm that shot through my veins like lightning. I closed my eyes for a second and just *felt*. I was so glad that Momma never tried to describe this to me. If I had known, I would never have been so good at waiting.

Though I was awful at waiting anyway.

I could tell he was doing the same thing as me—just soaking in my touch before I left, experiencing everything as it came, in the moment, in *this* moment.

I never got much from him, from his mind, and I wondered why. He seemed to be reading me constantly, but he said it wasn't him, it was me. Like I was broadcasting. But why couldn't I pick him up as easily? I opened myself up and tried to just listen, feel for him. It wasn't hard to get a read on him. I just had to want to.

He was thinking how much he loved my skin, the way it felt against his. He loved the way I was so independent. He loved that about me, but he also loved that I accepted his help, like a hand up from a bench when he offered it. He wanted someone who could stand on her own two feet, but would admit she needed help if she did, in fact, need it. And he wanted me to need it sometimes because he was going to need me sometimes. He wanted us to need each other.

I yanked my mind away and found myself breathing a little harder as I stared into space. I looked over and found him looking at me. His face held a small smile before it morphed into a disappointed frown.

"Your, uh, father is waiting." He pointed out the window.

I waved to him to let him know I was coming, but he continued to wait. I sighed and rolled my eyes a little. All the men in my life were like watch dogs.

"You'll come tonight?" I asked and dared to look hopeful so he'd see how much I wanted him to. "I'll tell Mom to make something really good for dinner."

He smiled gratefully. "At this point, I'm scared to make any promises. And I know that makes me a complete...tool, but I..." He banged his fist lightly on the steering wheel looking out the window before swinging his determined gaze back to me. "I'll try. I want to be there." He smiled, letting my hand go to grip my chin in his fingers gently. "I will try, Ava. Maybe I'll see you in your dreams."

I scoffed. "That's a little presumptuous." He smirked. "But I don't want to see you in my dreams." His look changed to disappointment so fast it startled me for a second before I could go on. "I want to see you for real, in my mother's kitchen, being interrogated by my little brother, okay?"

He seemed relieved and leaned in a little. "Agreed. That sounds like a great night, and I hope that I can make that happen."

"Don't hope." I put my hand over his on my face. "Just...say it's going to happen. We'll plan for it."

He licked his lip. "I'll see you tonight then."

"Tonight."

"Bye, sweetheart."

I groaned as I slid from the truck, taking his touch as I went. "Why do you have to be so dreamy when you say that?"

He chuckled as he put the truck in drive. "Then we're even."

I rolled my eyes dramatically. "How so?"

"Because you can be so freaking adorable sometimes, it physically hurts."

My chest jumped violently, but I still managed to say, "Now you're just showing off."

He winked and smiled widely as I shut the door. I watched him drive away until he was gone, waving at Jordan as he drove by, before turning to Daddy. He was smiling at me in that way that said I was about to be ribbed all night for the goofy look on my face. "Just don't, Dad."

He laughed and swung his arm for me to enter as he opened the door. "I didn't say a word."

"The evil look in your eyes said it for you."

"You're going to chop right through the counter, Ava Winifred!" I scowled at my mother and continued to chop. "He said he was coming. Calm down."

"He said he was coming last night, too."

"There is no way he'd stand you up two nights in a row."

"Not if the boy wants to keep his arms intact." I looked at Daddy as he stood at the counter next to Mom and helped her marinate the steaks. I couldn't help but smile at him. "I am not joking."

I rolled my eyes. "Let's let him mess up before we starting breaking limbs, Daddy."

His lips quirked as he tilted his head. "I think you need to turn that little speech around on yourself. You're the one that's about to ruin your Mamma's kitchen because you think he's going to blow you off."

I tossed the knife into the sink. "There. I just won't help."

"Will you go sit," Mom ordered and laughed, shaking her head as she looked down at the chopping board. "You obliterated that poor cucumber into something inedible anyway."

There were barely tiny slivers left. My scowl deepened as Daddy came around the counter and put his arms around me.

"I saw you two today. I know that it's more than just the bond now. You're..." he squinted, "getting closer. He'll come."

I laughed. "You sound less than thrilled about that." I leaned closer. "Why do you look like you smell bad sushi?"

He chuckled and squeezed me tighter, pulling my head onto his shoulder. "Gah, Ava. I know it's supposed to happen this way, but...he's taking you away from me."

I pushed him back and gave him a stern look. Or what I could only assume was one. "Dad, that won't happen—"

"It will." He smiled sadly. "But it's okay. I'll get over it. And you'll come visit me all the time," he ordered.

"Of course we will, Daddy."

"Knock, knock!" My heart got excited before the door slammed behind her and Ember came in with Maria in tow. "Hey, Aunt Mags." She kissed her cheek and stole a bite of whatever Mom was making over there. I didn't know and didn't care. I was too sulky to notice. Daddy hugged me hard one last time and left me to go back to helping Mom.

"What are you girls up to?" he asked as he picked back up the knife.

"You don't even want to know, Uncle Caleb," Maria laughed and hugged him around his middle. "It involves boys," she whispered conspiratorially. "Or at least I hope it does."

Daddy laughed. "Oh, yeah? And what does Dawson have to say about that?"

The door opened again, causing my heart to erupt in gallops. I glared at Dawson, causing him to put his hands up in mock surrender as he sent me a small smile. "Dawson says she can have all the men she wants," he laughed.

He came and hugged me, patting my back. I rolled my eyes and spoke low into my ear. "I'm guessing by that sympathy pat you've heard?"

He leaned back and grimaced. "You really think Aunt Mags is going to keep to herself the fact that her daughter found a significant? And that he's a Watson?" He hissed like it was painful. "Sorry, cuz." He kissed my forehead. "I got some news to cheer you up though."

"What?" Dad barked and looked at Dawson and then at Maria over his shoulder. "You two better start talking."

They grinned at each other before Dawson left me and went to her, cupping her cheek and giving her that smile that told her and anybody that was looking that she hung the frigging moon.

"Oh, my gosh," I whispered, totally getting it.

Mom gasped next, but Dad and Rodney were clueless.

"M." Dad turned all tense. "Come on now, you're scaring me."

"I'm pregnant, Uncle Caleb."

He sighed, setting his knife down. He chuckled with another sigh and hugged her. "I bet your mom is over the moon."

"She is."

"Well, it took you two long enough."

Dawson laughed and accepted Mom's hug while we both rolled our eyes at each other over her shoulder.

They hadn't gotten pregnant right away like most significants do. They wanted to wait until they got their traveling done. They both worked for Daddy. They did the architectural side of the business and went to set up the new centers, designing them, Daddy had even branched into international territory and they traveled all over putting up centers. Just like Mamma and Daddy had been the rebels who went against the family business, Maria had been the rebel who had waited to have kids.

Dawson was human. They met at college. The first person that Maria ran home to tell was Daddy. She and Daddy have always been close, even though she had Uncle Bish. Daddy and Maria had something different, special.

And Dawson was such a sweetheart. He had no family except a grandfather, Bill, who he took care of so it was like God picked him. And he loved Maria. And he loved our family. And we loved him.

Ember bumped arms with me as she leaned on the counter next to me. "You ready to be an aunt?"

"I've been ready," she said loudly. Then softly she said, "Anything to distract myself from the fact that I haven't found my significant."

I twisted my mouth in sympathy and looped my arm in hers. "Trust me, it's not all it's cracked up to be. It's not all perfect like your parents or lovey-dovey like Mom and Dad's."

She squinted. "You want to spill? Or do I have to ply you with chocolate to get it out of you?"

I noticed that everyone had stopped and was listening. Dawson and Maria especially were glued to what I was going to say next. "Definitely chocolate."

She sighed sadly. "Ave—"

But then the back door opened. I'd given up on letting my heart get fluttery, so I turned expecting Rodney or another cousin, but it wasn't. It *so* wasn't.

My lips parted and my chest dipped with a painful breath.

Everyone must have noticed my reaction because they all turned at the same time to look at him. Seth seemed a little blindsided to find so many

Jacobsons staring him down, but he recovered quickly. His smile came out swinging as he closed the door gently.

"Sorry, I knocked on the front door, but no one heard."

Mom grinned. "That's okay. Come on in. We're backdoor kind of folks anyway." He walked over to my mother first to give her a small hug, which she returned with gusto. I was glad, fearful that she might make things weird for him.

"Mrs. Jacobson."

"Call me Maggie, please," she said and turned to go back to chopping, but not without sending me a big smile.

He. Came.

He shook Dad's hand as Dad said gruffly, "You can call me Mr. Jacobson." Seth's eyes widened. I giggled unable to stop it just as Daddy grinned. "I'm just kidding. Caleb will do." He patted him, maybe a little too roughly, on the back.

Everyone laughed as Ember chimed in. "Uncle Caleb is the Champion of our Clan. Though he's probably the funniest one this clan has ever seen."

"And the most magnanimous," Mom said over-graciously and bowed dramatically, knife in one hand and cucumber in the other.

Everyone laughed loudly, Dad rolling his eyes and crossing his arms with a smile. Seth waved at everyone else slightly before coming to me. I watched his face the entire time. I knew an embarrassing, awkward moment was eminent. The dance—do we hug, do we half-hug, do we shake hands, do we kiss the cheek?

But he stunned me even further. He smiled so easily, like he was genuinely happy to see me.

"Hey," he muttered low, right before he pulled me into his chest, letting his cheek connect with my forehead. We both sighed a little.

There was no awkward dance and I felt stupid for even thinking there would be. We hadn't seen each other in hours. Of course he'd hug me. And Seth didn't seem to be intimidated very easily so the fact that my family was there might be fazing him, but he wasn't showing it.

I let my arms hang on his hips for a few seconds before pulling back.

"Hey," I finally said, but couldn't help but smile because I was so happy that he was there.

He swung around to my side and put his arm around my back, asking with his eyes if it was okay. I bit into my lip to stop my stupid grin, but remembered what he said about trying to stop my smile with my teeth. I smirked instead and shook my head.

He smirked in return, looking pleased.

I smiled wider.

"Uhum."

I swung my head to look at Ember. "I know we practically don't exist right now," Dawson chuckled in the background as she continued, "but can you at least introduce us?"

I felt my neck blare past pink and go straight to fire engine. Seth rubbed my arm. My mouth opened for a full ten seconds before words came out. "I'm sorry. Uh…this is Seth. Sorry. Um, he's my…"

"We got it." Ember giggled and came forward to shake his hand. "Ember. Nice to meet you."

When they touched hands, for a split second, I imagined him bonding with her instead and nightmares ensued. I sighed loudly. "And this is Dawson and Maria. Some of my cousins."

"Nice to meet you," he said politely and continued to rub my shoulder in a small back and forth pattern with his thumb.

"So what's on the agenda tonight?" Maria asked with a little smirk.

"You're staying?" I asked and made sure to give her a little evil-eye where Seth couldn't see.

"Are you kidding?" She grinned and looped her arm through Mom's. "I've missed you guys. I wouldn't miss dinner tonight if you paid me to leave."

I shook my head and gave up, knowing her and Ember would never leave with the opportunity for swoonage and new significants within fifty yards. They *lived* for it.

Ember winked at me with a grin and went to stand next to her gossiping sister. Dawson came and leaned next to me on the counter. "As soon as your mom called and did her rounds with the family letting them know, it's all I've heard—getting over here to see you."

I smiled. "Your wife is a pain in the a—" I looked at Seth and he was smirking at me, daring me. "Butt," I finished. He laughed so loudly and everyone looked to see what was so funny, but we both just stood there grinning. Even Dawson didn't know what was that funny.

"Yeah," Dawson kept moving along, "but she's my pain in the butt." His grin was adorable. "And she's a beautiful pain in the butt. And she—"

"Oh, my gosh. I get it."

He chuckled. "You opened that can."

"I guess I did. So, you're going to be a father," I mused. "A good one."

He looked down at the floor and shook his head. Dawson was one of those guys that grew up with no parents. His grandfather, Bill, raised him so he had old school principles and morals, thank God. More people should. He was polite, he held the door open for women and paid for dinner. Not because they were the lesser class or couldn't do it themselves, but because it was the respectful thing to do, because women were precious, women were to be praised, women were to be shown that a woman with a good heart would be rewarded with a man with a respectful soul for her. Dawson had told me that once. That's what his grandfather had taught him, brought him up to believe, and he was such a good man for it.

His grandfather passed the same year that Gran did. It was a hard time for our family. We loved his grandfather and had brought him into the family fold. Though he hadn't known about our secrets, he had been part of our family nonetheless.

Now two of the greats were gone and people looked to Grandpa Peter and Nana to be the new greats. They were doing a pretty great job of it, too.

"Where did you go?"

I looked up. "What?"

Maria's head was cocked. "Where did you go? You looked happy and sad at the same time."

"I bet *Seth knows* where she went," Ember needled.

Seth didn't skip a beat. "She was thinking about an older man and woman."

Ember's jaw dropped. "Wait. I was kidding! You're not supposed to be able to do that yet!"

I looked up at Seth and he pressed his lips in a tight line, sighing from his nose.

Damn.

We could play it off. His eyes popped wide. *We could pretend that you were just trying to act like you knew.*

I doubt that will work now.

Why?

Because one, they're all staring at us. They know we're talking right now.

I looked and it was true. *And two, you're actually talking to me like this, so normally.* He smiled. *There's no way I'm going to stop now.*

"All right, lovebirds. Spill."

I glared at Ember and mumbled, "You really know how to kill a moment."

She laughed. "How the hell can you do that already?"

"It's just like your mom and I." Dad looked back at Mom. "Baby, will you just…" He waved his hand at the cucumbers.

She gave up with a sigh and dropped the knife in the air, but it didn't fall. "I like to have some sense of normalcy sometimes."

"I know, baby," he soothed as the knife hovered in the air and starting slicing the cucumbers into perfect portions and then another knife came out of the knife block beside us and hovered across the room to the counter to start chopping the lettuce. Seth's eyes followed it, wide as the plates we were about to eat on. I rubbed his chest and he jumped a little.

It's okay.

Okay? That's frigging amazing.

I smiled and loved the way his arm tugged me closer into his chest. I took some initiative and wrapped one of my arms around him, too. He was so tall that my arm sat on his hips. That seemed to bolster him. He put one of his hands on the back of my neck and let it rest there, just let our skin hum and be happy.

It was all I could do not to moan and close my eyes in the middle of our family.

Then I realized that I'd said 'our family' and I hadn't gotten any ill feelings from him. He shrugged.

They are my family. They're pretty awesome, too, from what I've seen so far.

Mom had gotten a glass of tea and then went into Daddy's arms. He would always lean against the counter and she would come and lay on him, put herself in the 'V' his legs made. That was her spot. He would wrap his arms around her and then usually we'd had to look away many times during the convo because he'd be whispering or nibbling on her neck or ear or whatever. Tonight, I'm sure they'd be civil. Probably.

"Now," Dad started, "your mom and I were like that. We could hear each other really quickly, too. Why didn't you say anything?"

"We didn't think it was a big deal," I rushed to say.

"There's a reason that you would be given those certain abilities this way,"

Mom said and shivered. Dad squeezed her and rubbed his chin on her hair. "We needed it for the fight we had coming, for all the things we had to deal with. I pray that that's not why it was given to you, too."

"Well, this is getting heavy," Maria muttered and winked at me. I smiled graciously. "Want to really freak out Seth, Aunt Mags? Break out your crystal ball."

Seth looked at me with a cocked brow and everyone laughed. "No," I said and shook my head.

He half-sighed, half-laughed.

Dawson picked Maria up and set her on the counter. "Take a load off, prego." He started to rub her legs and calves. She groaned. "It's not good for you to stand around anymore."

"Dawson, baby, I'm pregnant not dying." She kissed him and put her arms on his shoulders.

"Well, being the seventh wheel sucks," Ember sulked, but I knew her. She wanted to find her significant so badly. I remembered those days, not too long ago. I looked up at Seth. But now those days were gone.

And then his phone dinged with a text.

His face morphed completely from happy to worried. Scared even.

Don't look at it. Just don't look at it.

Ava.

Did they know you were coming?

No. I haven't spoken to anyone today.

But they had to know that you would be coming here every night, right? Obviously you'd be coming to your significant's house every night.

He pulled it out and closed his eyes as soon as he read it.

Come home. Family meeting. Emergency.

"I'm sorry."

"Me, too."

"I've got to go. Family emergency, but it was nice to meet you all." It wasn't hard to see how upset he was, but I couldn't feel bad for him. No...I wouldn't. Nope. Nuhuh. He was choosing to leave, wasn't he? He'd only been there for fifteen minutes and now he was leaving, again, because of his family. They always stopped us from seeing each other and he still wanted to find good in them.

"Nice to meet you, too," Ember called. "Don't be a stranger!"

He smiled and waved as he went out the door.

I didn't want to walk him outside, I was angry, but it was the only way I was going to get a second of privacy.

"I'll see you in a bit." I squinted and he amended. "Tomorrow."

"Yeah, tomorrow," I muttered.

His sigh was so forlorn and downtrodden. "I am sorry, sweetheart. I wish—I wish your mother did have a crystal ball. I would give anything to use it right now."

"Well, there aren't any crystal balls, Seth. You have to go with your gut, with what you believe in." I could feel myself tearing up because I felt like he didn't believe in me—in us—as much as *them*. "You have to trust in what you know is the right thing." He closed his eyes and let a breath go. "I can't tell you what that is. That's something you have to figure out for yourself."

I didn't waste any more time. I did not want to burst into tears in front of him over his family. I went to him and grabbed his hand, hearing his hiss, loving it and hating it in that moment, too. I held on as long as I could and then turned to go.

"Ava," he called, his voice told me how badly he was hurting, how he was being pulled in two.

I didn't turn. "Yeah?"

"Don't give up on me," he begged. "I believe in us. I do. But if there's even a sliver of something left of my family, I have to see if I can find it. I have to do this to protect you, to keep you safe."

I could hold it in no longer and let the tears come. I went back to him, not because I needed comfort but because he did. I hugged him around his middle and his arms went around my shoulders. I understood this would probably be our norm since he was so tall. I moved to press my face to his neck to make sure we were touching, pushing his jacket collar haphazardly out of the way.

I'll come drive you to school in the morning.

Okay.

Tomorrow night is my last free night. After that, I'm on at the fire station for forty-eight hours.

I sat up and looked at him.

He nodded. "Yeah. It's going to suck for a while there, but we'll figure it out. I just won't sleep." He chuckled.

I didn't laugh. This relationship was starting to feel like nothing but touches to keep from being in withdrawal and that was never what I wanted. I wanted a *real* relationship with love and laughter and happiness and trust and…butterflies and goosebumps.

So far it was a failed kidnapping, distrust, a whole lot of touches before one of us had to leave, and sure, a few butterflies. My eyes hurt from holding the tears back. I looked up to find him so affected by my thoughts he looked like he'd throw up.

"I'm sorry," I told him before I tried to leave, but couldn't. "Release me, please."

He opened his mouth a couple times before finally saying softly, "Go on into the house, Ava, and get warm. I'll be back in the morning. *I promise you.*"

I turned and went into the house and didn't look back. Whether it was for his sake or mine I didn't know.

Chapter Ten

"**S**eth!" I smiled and bit my lip as I leapt into his arms, wrapping them around his neck. I was in my pajamas again, but somehow it didn't matter. He was so warm, even if this was just a dream. I could feel him, feel everything about him.

Seth hugged me back for just a second before setting me away from him. He wasn't his normal self tonight and I knew right away.

"Oh, no. What did she—I do?"

He smiled sadly. "Nothing I didn't deserve."

"Oh, Seth. What's going on?"

He took my hand and we walked along the rooftop for a little bit before he finally said. "She hates me. She thinks our relationship is nothing but a thing to keep us from being in withdrawal. She doesn't think it goes beyond that."

"Seth," I implored softly, "that can't be true. I'm her." I pulled him to a stop so he'd look at me. "Don't you get it? I'm her, she's me. This wouldn't all be happening if not for a reason—the fact that you can bring me here and dream walk and all. I feel things…" I stopped and noticed the way his mouth curled up on one side. "If I can feel things for you then she can and does, too. She's just confused. Maybe she thinks that that's all you think the relationship is."

He shook his head. "No. There's no way she can think that I think that."

"I can be stubborn," I offered. "Maybe you need to lay it out for her exactly how you feel, what you want."

He swallowed. "It won't scare her?"

"Maybe. But maybe she needs to be scared."

"We had so much fun yesterday…for about ten minutes." He smiled and I knew he was thinking about her. About me. "I felt like things might actually be okay and then my family had to go and ruin it again."

"What happened?"l

"I think you were right, the other you. I think they're trying to sabotage us. And I hate it. I don't want to admit that. I don't want to give up my family. I don't want to be thrown away so easily. I don't want to be so expendable." He pursed his lips angrily. "But it looks like that's probably the case. The thing they called me away for yesterday was bogus. And Harper has been coming by my house every day and I've had to send her away. If the other you knew that, she'd go ballistic."

"Harper?" I asked and felt all my bones tense.

"She's my cousin," he said and smiled. "You and the other Ava are more alike than I thought."

"If she's your cousin then why does it matter?"

"Because she's not really my cousin, it's just how I see her. They're my family, but not by blood." He sighed and I could tell he had something he didn't want to say. I nodded so he'd go on. "When I turned twenty, my Uncle Gaston came and asked if I wanted to be bonded to Harper, his daughter. They can force an imprint."

I just stared, feeling my heart hurt. He took my face in his hands. "She was and has always been my cousin to me. I told them that, told them it was disgusting for them to even think that I'd want to, and to never bring it up again. Harper was never in on the idea. I think it was all her dad. We've always been friends. Really good friends." He let his hands fall and took my hand again as we started walking. "But I've never, ever thought of her beyond that. I don't know why Uncle Gaston thought I'd go for it. He knew I was waiting for my significant. I'd told him that before."

Something clicked.

"Wait a minute. They force their imprints with alchemy, they don't get them naturally." He squinted. "They thought you weren't going to bond the natural way. They thought they were going to have to force one with you, too."

I gasped. "You're human. You shouldn't even have imprinted in the first place. It's really rare for humans to imprint. But they were trying to force you to at an earlier age with Harper, who is a Virtuoso."

"Yeah," he said, whether he was following or not.

"So you didn't know that you were human. You've always thought you were Virtuoso and that your mother died," I said softly, "and that the Watsons took you in. That the world is a normal place of humans, but the Watsons were special and you've always known it."

"Yeah, pretty much. I just always thought I was one of them until your mom told me otherwise." He looked down and then back up slowly. "They still don't know that I know what they did. It's hard to be around them and act natural. I'm trying so hard to see if I can find something good in them. And honestly, I'm keeping an eye on them."

"For her," I realized.

For *me*.

He nodded. "I don't want to tell her, but I keep going back to them because I need to make sure they aren't planning something else, planning another attack or something. But even if they were, I don't think they'd tell me or talk about it around me."

I sucked in a quick breath. "You could pretend you're in a fight."

He swung his head over. "What?"

"Pretend you're fighting with her and the family."

He thought. "Well, I am about to be on for a couple days at the fire station, so I wasn't going to be able to go see her anyway. It might work. Maybe I could fool them enough to trust me."

"Go ahead," I goaded and grinned, swinging my shoulders left and right.

"What's that, gorgeous?" he asked, his smile wide.

"Say it."

He laughed. "I'm not sure what you want me to say exactly, but you're a genius. An adorable little evil genius."

"That'll do." I pulled him down to me, hugging him around his neck, and kissed his cheek. His arms around my back tightened and he stayed close, looking like he wanted to do so much more in that tenacious moment growing between us. I pushed his hair that had fallen over his forehead back, loving the way his eyes seemed to roll when I did it. "Have you kissed her yet?"

He shook his head. "No," he said gruffly.

"Why?" My breaths started to turn ragged. "Don't you want to kiss me?"

"More than I've ever wanted anything else," he said with delicious conviction and let his fingers comb my hair back, "I want to know what you taste like."

I closed my eyes for a second and then looked at him, needing to know. "Why haven't you?"

"I'm waiting for her to look at me like you do, like you are right now."

My heart galloped. "Seth, I—"

He cupped my face fully with both hands. "It's okay." He moved forward and I closed my eyes, anticipating those lips I'd been waiting on. I felt the warmth of his breath and then his forehead touched mine, but that was as far as he got.

I opened my eyes to find his eyes closed, him just soaking me in. But that wasn't enough. "Kiss me," I whispered. "Seth."

"I want the first time to be with her." He leaned back and made sure I was listening. "I'm sorry... That's what we're fighting for, right? For Ava, for me and her, for us, for all of us. To see if she can love me like I love her."

I gasped and Seth's eyes went wide before he smiled in that *caught* way. He squinted and cocked his head. "You think that I'm crazy? How can I love someone who obviously hates my guts, who I've known such a short period of time?" He shook his head. "Maybe I am crazy. But I'm falling in love with Ava Jacobson. I just want to be worthy of her, to be worthy of her falling in love with me, too. I hope...one day she sees that I am."

When he looked back up he was surprised to find me crying. "Sweetheart... I'm sorry." He seemed at a loss for a few seconds before he leaned away. "I'll go. I shouldn't have said that—"

"Come here."

He sighed. "Ava, you don't have to—"

"Seth, come here." He came towards me and I wiped under my eye before wrapping my arms around his neck. "Can I just hold you for a minute?"

"No," he exhaled his words and smiled, "but I'll hold you." He sat on the bricks and leaned against the stone wall with me in his lap. I pressed my face into his neck, inhaling and soaking in this small piece of heaven. He did this little chuckle-sigh thing. "Heaven is right," he whispered into my hair. Had I said that out loud? "You smell so good."

"Don't make me crazy, Seth." I pushed his chest a little.

He laughed at that. "Join the club, little bird."

I pulled my knees up, leaning them on his thigh, and put my hands on his chest. "She'll come around. I know it. She won't be able to resist forever. We'll just keep working, keep doing what we're doing, you keep making her fall in love with you, and one day she will."

He swallowed. "I hope you're right."

"I am."

He pulled my head back into the crook of his neck. "Let me hold you a little longer before I have to go back."

With my face against his neck, he took my hand and laced our fingers over and over on his chest. I shivered and he smiled, I felt it against my forehead. "Goosebumps," he mused. "Check."

"What?"

"Nothing," he whispered and trailed his fingers down the goosebumps on my arm. "Something the other you said. She said she hadn't gotten goosebumps with me yet. There was a little list of things she said we were lacking. I'm making it my mission to obliterate that list as soon as my rotation at the fire house is done."

"How can she not like you? Truly-?" I laid my head back down snuggly in the valley of his neck. "You're so…likeable."

He tucked me into his body tighter and sighed. "We'll figure this out, Ava. I'll figure this out for us."

"She loves pancakes." I felt him turn to look down at me. "*I* love pancakes. And I love art and music. And I love overly-dramatic displays of heroism and chivalry." He cocked his brow with a confused smile. "Opening doors, opening pickle jars, slaying dragons."

His smile was adorable. He nodded and laid his forehead to mine. "Okay. I'll remember."

"How long are we going to have to keep her and me separated?"

He rubbed his nose against mine, just once, causing my heart to riot in my chest. "You tell me, little bird."

"He's here already!" Mom called up the stairs.

"He is?"

My phone chimed. I picked it up and looked at the text, knowing it was him.

Thought we could get breakfast before school if you wanted.

I pressed my lips together. He wasn't really giving me a choice, was he?

Coming.

I quickly put on my coat and my scarf. It was freaking cold out. Even though it had snowed last night, I still slipped my Chucks on. I left my hair down today in the brown waves my mom loved so much. Sleep waves she called them. Long, natural, soft, God-given curls that came from rolling around in my sleep, no curling iron needed. Thank you, because I had not the time nor patience to deal with it today anyway. Sometime my curls were awesome and today was definitely one of those days that I was thankful.

"Mom, Seth wants to take me to breakfast," I said as I grabbed my bag and made my way sluggishly toward the door as my back pulled and my arms ached.

"Remember what we said about being alone."

"I will. Promise." I gave her a look. "Not like I'm ever alone anyway with Jordan and Drake lurking about in the background."

She gave me a look in return. "What did you expect your father to do after what happened? Love you, baby."

I stopped at the door and looked at her. "Love you, Momma. I'll see you later."

When I stepped out the door, Seth stepped out of his. I wanted to roll my eyes. He could have just waited. I would be there inside the truck with him in a minute. I saw him look at the ground and forgot he always heard everything I thought. I squinted, hard.

"Sorry," I muttered.

"It's all right. I deserved it after last night, I guess."

When I was almost to him, my Chucks betrayed me and slipped on the

snow covered patio bricks in front of the mailbox. I would have been sent airborne and then on my backside if not for Seth, who gripped my arm tightly to catch me.

"You all right?"

"Yeah."

"Where's your boots?"

I huffed. "I like my Chucks."

He smiled and then tried to cover it with a cough. "Uh…yeah. I can see that." I stared at him with an open mouth, but before I could say anything he reached up and closed my mouth with his gloved-finger under my chin. "Let's go get breakfast. Here, let me help."

"I've got it." I pulled away, but the tugging in my back reminding me that I needed his touch. I held out my hand for his and he watched my face as he took his gloves off and took it slowly.

When our skin touched, even I couldn't stop the hiss. I fell into his chest and let all the aches and pains drain away. And the irritation, too. Most of it.

I reached up and touched his neck, my fingers painting lines of pleasure across his skin with every movement. I longed for the same, but knew we couldn't. When he groaned, and copped my cheek, I opened my eyes to see him completely blissed out. It jolted me awake, aware. I pulled away and crossed my arms, unable to handle not touching him. Unable to handle the weird vibe of our relationship. I just wanted it to be normal. I just wanted to be loved for me, not for my touch. I just wanted him to want me, but I wasn't sure that was the case. I wasn't sure if Seth wanted me or wanted the thought of me and what I represented. I thought he was disappointed, that he had waited this whole time to find his significant and I was what he got stuck with.

He was breathing heavier than usual and when our gazes collided he seemed angry. I leaned away, surprised, but he gripped my arm gently to stop me.

"Don't fall. Come on. Let me buy you breakfast," his mouth said, but his face was anything but looking like he wanted to buy me food right then.

He helped me into the passenger side and then walked to the front of the truck. He stopped and put his hands on the hood, as if he needed time, needed a minute before getting inside. Great. We were just pissing each other off left and right. I looked out my window and waited. A few seconds later, he got in and put it in reverse without waiting or saying another word. When he reached over to put his hand on the head rest, I inhaled at the possibility that he might touch me. It looked like a flinch though, I was sure, and he seemed surprised by it, naturally. He sighed through his nose, looking even angrier, and drove without a word.

He took me to a pancake house. My favorite pancake house to be exact. "I love this place."

He looked over stoically and exhaled. "Well, I was bound to get something right at some point."

He got out and I sat, wondering what we were doing to each other. He opened my door and I started to get out, but he helped me down by gripping my waist and easing me gently to the pavement. My breath halted with our faces so close. "I'd hate to see you eat it with those Chucks on."

Though his words were playful, his face was anything but.

"Thanks," I told him and followed him in to the restaurant since he released me as soon as my feet touched the ground. We sat and I ordered a short stack. He ordered a double. We both ordered coffee and waited quietly for it to come. It was an awkward silence, but it was expected, and that was a comfort in a strange way.

I poured the creamer in, stirring before taking a hesitant sip. "Wow, that's really good."

He looked up, surprised that I had talked. "You've never had their coffee? At your favorite pancake house?"

"I don't usually drink coffee black." He smirked. "What?"

"There's so much cream in that coffee you could make a pie. That's not black."

I sat stunned. Was he just stating a fact or playing with me and being a smartass?

He shook his head, licking his lip. "There's that word again." A smile finally made an appearance.

"What word?" I asked and smiled a little. "Smart?"

He chuckled just as she brought the food.

Yeah. Smart.

He winked as she set it down in front of us. I had just started to feel a little better when his phone chimed and it all came crashing down.

His phone was going to ruin us.

He sighed and then banged his fist loudly on the table next to his plate of pancakes, causing me to jump. It was so loud that the waitress looked over and lifted her eyebrows at me as if to see if I needed help or something. I waved her off and looked at Seth, watched him to see what he was going to do.

He pulled his phone out, without looking at me at all, and he read the text aloud, since he knew that I could read it through him anyway I assumed.

S, I'll stop by while you're on the nightshift and bring you those earbuds Daddy bought me. I know you'll like 'em since they're pitch black & you used to have a pair just like them. See you then! – Harp

I swallowed down the bite of pancakes I had which had suddenly turn to concrete in my mouth. He let his eyes move up and nothing else. We stared at each other.

"Does she come up and hang out at the station with you often?"

He shook his head. "Not anymore she won't."

I don't know why that answer made me crack inside, but it did. He was trying so hard, it was obvious.

"Why don't I start at the beginning? I never got to explain everything to you that day in my apartment." I nodded. "And you'll listen and not use this against me? You'll wait until I'm completely done and not call your mother to go and bomb every family member I have with her Visionary powers or… whatever the hell it is she can do?"

I nodded again and pushed my plate away. As he spoke, I watched the little scar on his chin as it moved with his jaw with every word and I listened to him tell the tale of how he thought things happened from way back when he was a child. A family took him in and cared for him as best they could. No family is perfect. A boy that came from nothing and was brought in to a family like that should be happy to have something at all. At least that's what Seth believed.

So the little pieces of weirdness and strange things he saw over the years, he dismissed and discounted them as that. They were none of his business and besides, he came from a magical family so there were bound to be some strange things going on.

He couldn't remember his mother at all. He was made to believe all sorts of things about her—that they had found a drug addict wandering in the woods with a small boy and when they confronted her, she ran and left him there, but it was on the news later that night that she had died. If they hadn't come along, he would have died, too.

I knew that wasn't the story, but didn't want to try to hash any of that out right now. I'd have to let Mom do that.

There were a lot of things from his childhood he would have changed, he explained, but a lot of things he was grateful for. I felt so bad for him. He was doing a bang-up job of trying to find the good in them at all cost.

"Let's go," I begged.

He deflated and rubbed his hair. "Okay, Ava."

"No, no, not to school." He looked at me with the first spark I'd seen all day. "Take me somewhere."

"I'll take you anywhere," he said almost sadly. "Where do you want to go?"

I took a big sip of my coffee. "Surprise me."

He grinned and then stood, offering me his hand. "Then let's go."

He took me to this art gallery that was nothing but music inspired art pieces. Lyrics, notes, musicians, old, new, jazzy, classical, alternative. It was amazing to see it all smashed together, a smorgasbord of beautiful music and pictures. It was on the outside of town, near the river. When we passed a canvas of Etta James's *At Last* that someone did for her lyrics, I thought I was going to keel over and die right there. We probably stood there for fifteen minutes staring at it.

"How did you know this was here? Better yet," I asked without waiting, "how did you know I would love this?"

"Do you? Love it?" he asked innocently.

I squinted and shook my head. "You're too good at this. It's not fair."

He chuckled and walked closer, taking my hand in his easily, massaging my fingers as if each one was priceless and precious.

"Is this okay?" he asked quietly as we walked.

"Which part? The part where you're totally sweet and hold my hand or the part where you completely ruin me by somehow knowing all my favorite things and make me crazy?"

My breathing was a little rapid at this point, but for some reason this seemed to please him.

He leaned in, inspecting me, and cupped my cheek gently, letting his thumb sweep over my cheek back and forth. "Both of those things sound pretty good to me." His smile was the sweetest smile I'd ever seen. "Come on, little bird. I've got something else to show you."

Little bird…

He took me to this awesome food truck at the river and got us some sweet tea and the most amazing shrimp tacos I'd ever had before taking us out to the mountains. We moved to the back of the truck where he laid out a blanket first and then helped me up into the bed of it by getting in first and giving me a hand up.

We sat back there and ate, watching the waterfalls and the mountain, just enjoying the quiet and the life that Tennessee had to offer. When I was done, he leaned back inside his truck window and got some pencils and paper. "What's this?"

"What do you think?" he explained hesitantly. A little sheepishly. "It's your turn."

"You're going to draw me?" My heart practically sang out loud at those words.

"I'm no Picasso. Keep that I mind."

"I hope not," I scrunched my nose. "Picasso stunk. And he's dead, so."

He laughed and tucked my hair behind my ear, causing me to bite me lip. "You like art, but do you like to draw? Or sing? Play the piano? Anything?"

"No," I answered and tried to see what he was drawing. He pulled it back and smiled, shaking his head. I sat back, giving up. "No, I'm not good at anything. I just have to admire other's work. My uncle can make you good at things with his ability, but I never had any interest in learning that way. It's cheating." I smirked.

"I've always loved to draw. It used to get me into trouble in school." I watched his deft fingers as they worked. And kept watching in silence for the next fifteen minutes until he was done. "It's just your face," he said and cleared his throat, seeming to be nervous.

"I'm sure I'll love it."

He rolled his eyes. "Yeah, you'll have to because you're my—you know. It's like when a mom can't say that a kid's picture is ugly because it's her kid's."

I raised an eyebrow. "It's not really the same thing."

"And we just went through the daggum art gallery. Now you're going to be comparing it to—"

I took it. "Will you just give it to me?" I turned it over slowly and watched his face. He was actually nervous. I looked at it and felt all the air leave my body in a painful burst. It hurt from not breathing. "Seth."

He gripped my forearm. "Ava."

"Oh, my gosh."

"What?"

"It's…" I met his eyes and hoped my face looked like a smile. "I look so… pretty. My hair is so… Blowing in the wind like that, it's so lifelike. And my lips. Is that really what my lips looks like?"

"Absolutely," he growled.

I looked up to find his eyes hooded, and I would have given anything for him to reach over and kiss me right then. It was the first time I really, truly wanted him to kiss me. And it scared the crap out of me.

"It's beautiful. Can I keep it?"

He nodded and kind of smirked a little as he looked down. "I might have a one or two already."

"You do?"

"Of course I do. You're mine, Ava. I dream about you."

I gasped a little and felt that statement all the way to my toes. "I think…I dream about you, too."

His smile never changed. "I think so." I bit into my lip and watched him watch me. He closed his eyes for a second before he said, "Here. Give me your foot." I put my blue Converse in his lap and he pulled a sharpie out of his front shirt pocket. On my shoes that I loved so much, I watched as he made them even better, immortalizing not only our relationship, but my favorite song and singer as he drew in a beautiful script "At Last" on one shoe top and "My Love" on the other.

I wanted to cry, just burst.

Instead I scooted up next to him, looped my arm through his, and we watched the falls for a while and waited until it was time to go in silence. Nothing but the sounds of the water and the beats of our hearts together in his chest to keep us company.

But that was the best kind of music.

I was stalling again. Tonight would be another test. I knew it. He would say he was coming and there would be a chance he would fail and I…

I looked over at him. He was waiting patiently for me, but I could tell by the look on his face that he knew I was right. We were all being tested. His family was being tested, too. If they truly were up to no good, then they wouldn't keep stopping him from seeing me. They wouldn't keep coming up with "emergencies" and things that needed to be done in order for him to not see me.

He licked his lip and furrowed his brow. It was in anger, but not at me.

"Touché," he rumbled and reached across the seat slowly, rubbing his pinky against mine.

It was his capitulation.

It was the first time I'd seen him admit that something was amiss with his family. It broke my heart for him. Though we'd spent all afternoon in an almost-fight about his family, I couldn't stand the thought that his world was crumbling around him. What that realization must feel like inside was ripping me from the inside out. I slid across the seat, noticing the way his eyes widened as I turned to put my back to the steering wheel and my knees to the seat, and curled myself against him. Laying my head against his chin I wrapped one arm around his neck as best I could while taking his arm in mine and putting it around my leg on my calf since he seemed so stunned he didn't move, or was afraid to. I then flushed so hot at why I had done that. But it felt so heavenly. I didn't look up at him, just continued to stare at his neck and chin, breathing in his scent and shirt so close to me. His hair was right near my fingers on the back of his neck. *No,* I told them, *no, God, please, no.*

"Mmmm," he groaned as my fingers dug in and tugged a little. That sound…

That sound could cure what ailed you.

I kept moving them, scratching lightly and tugging, trying to be soothing, trying to push my calm through with my every thought and movement. That was the whole point of this. It didn't matter if we had fought, it didn't matter what had happened. Just like I had told him before. Our kind doesn't fight. He said his aunt and uncle fought so bad every night that Harper had to sneak out and go somewhere else. That just doesn't fit the bill. Once one or the other got that upset, they should be trying to comfort each other. He said his whole family fought—it just isn't the way of our kind.

We work things out. We talk, and argue, and go back and forth, and compromise. We don't *fight*.

I needed to remember that. What we had been doing wasn't fighting. We were gently arguing to the point of working things out.

"I'm sorry, Seth," I whispered and tugged us closer, closing my eyes and pressing us together, physically and in every other way. In that moment, I just wanted to take away all his ache. "I wish there was something I could do."

His fingers went under my chin and he lifted, an expression on his face that confused me. He looked almost angry, but more confused than anything.

"How can you not see what you're doing?" I squinted, thinking I was being scolded, but his hard fingers loosened and that thumb that had tortured me on several occasions already started sweeping across the arc of my jaw. I felt my eyes getting heavy and could see why girls in books could fall so easily for a guy who worked with his hands. Those hands meant something. They worked for something, saved lives, and touched me with meaning—not just for personal pleasure or gain. He was so close that another inch and our noses would have touched. That thumb that was my undoing swept over the curve of my jaw again and I shivered, unable to hold it in. The look of absolute satisfaction and happiness was expected, but different. It didn't come in the form I thought. No smirk emerged, no chuckle, no laugh, no smile. Just utter elation. Absolute joy. He was happy, but didn't want to joke or rub my face in it—he was just happy that he could elicit a response from my body, that I wanted him for more than just his calming touch, and that all he needed to know.

For now.

He moved on with no fanfare and I was grateful. "How can you not see how you're helping me by just being here?" The palm on my calf squeezed. "*This* is what I need. You. Like this," he said, leaning his head back on the seat, his voice fading away in exhaustion. "God, help me, I don't know what to do anymore." His eyes followed the cars that drove past us, like they carried the answers away. "I know you think I'm a fool for believing in them." It wasn't a question. I put my hand on his chest, right on the '22' for his fire station. I gulped, feeling the pain of his words dig into my chest as he felt them, and just clung to the feel of his fingers on the skin of my jaw. "I just wanted to have it all. A family. A great job. A wif—a significant," he corrected.

I looked down at our hands on his chest. But I would be his wife one day. That was a fact. And that didn't scare me as badly as it once had. He brought my face back up with that same torturous thumb. He seemed to be pulling one of my moves. *Stalling.*

He sighed and finally whispered, "Wife," correcting himself once more.

I hadn't realized I was holding my breath until it came rushing out and my eyelids fluttered in a rush with it. The lightheadedness made him seem almost ethereal as I looked at him, a little haze around him. I shook my head and licked my lips.

"You do have a family. I'm sorry that we may not have made you feel as welcome as we should have in the beginning. I'm really sorry about that." I lowered my head shamefully, remembering that first night… He raised it, not letting me get away with it for a second. His thumb brushed side to side across my chin, giving me strength and forgiveness whether I deserved it or not as our breaths picked up speed between us. "But you have family here. You have all the things on your list," I whispered.

His surprised breath was loud. "Ava."

"You do," I insisted, pressing my hand up higher on his chest. "And the fact that you felt like you were not only about to lose your only family, but were about to be inducted into a family that hated you on top of it is…" I shook my head. "We completely dropped the ball. I'm so sorry." I pushed his hand away and took his face in between my hands. His eyes lowered as he emitted a small sound, but I steamed on. "If the situation had been reversed, you would have made sure I felt safe. You would have made sure that I knew that you and your family were there for me. My parents haven't even spoken to you since that first night. I should have…I should have made them go and talk to you—"

"Your father spoke with me," he blurted out.

"What?" I whispered, shocked.

He pulled my hands down gently and held them between in between his own firmly, but gently, with clear intent that he wasn't letting them go.

"This morning when I pulled into your yard," he chuckled in an embarrassed way, "at four a.m., your father came outside to speak with me.

He came out and sat on the bench next to your mom's bushes and waited. I got out and we sat in the dark for a while, not saying anything. And then he started to tell me about your mom, about how he used to sneak in her window at night because her father was human and that was the only way they could be together in the mornings. That he would have done anything to make sure she wasn't hurting," he finished, his voice low and telling. "That they had faced obstacles just like we had to and that it—" He stopped.

"What?" I asked—begged—in a whisper.

"He basically asked me if I thought it was worth it to stick it out. If I thought you were worth all the trouble. That he knew my family has ways of removing my imprint if I wished it. I could even get a new significant." I groaned painfully, hating that statement with every fiber of my being. His fingers swept over mine in apology. "He basically wanted to know why I was still bonded to you, why I still kept coming back, when I had every reason not to and every resource at my disposal. And then he wanted to know if I thought it was worth it, was I going to fight for you with everything in me, with all I have, all I've got, every breath, every beat."

I couldn't breathe.

He didn't make me wait long. He pulled me a half inch closer as he laced our fingers with one hand and put them over his chest.

"No one is taking you away from me," he promised, his voice low and ominous was strangely exactly what I needed in that moment to finish falling over the edge for him. "Are you worth it?" he asked as if it were ludicrous. "Is *this* worth it? Have I waited my entire life for it? Will I give it up just because it's hard? Just because it's not given to me so easily?" He shook his head so slowly and leaned forward, pressing his lips to my hair. "Ah, little bird, you are so worth it," he whispered.

I licked my lips as my breaths raged between them in confusion. *Little bird. Little bird...*

He pulled back and looked at my face. "Yeah," he sighed and smiled. "Little bird." He gulped and searched my face and he took my cheeks in his hands. "You like?"

I nodded. "I like."

He looked down and back up, looking like he wanted to say a million and one things. "Ava."

"That's not the first time you've called me 'little bird', is it? Or the second,

or even third," I whispered in awe. There was something going on, humming at the edges of understanding, but strangely, I wasn't afraid. It was Seth and I knew now, without a shadow of a doubt, that he was on Team Ava. This was a catalyst for the rest of our lives and I didn't know what was going to happen, but I did know that I trusted him—wholly, completely, with my entire beating heart.

"No, sweetheart, it's not," he whispered back. His fingers played with the curls at my ear and I wanted to close my eyes and soak it in, but I focused. I made myself focus. "I don't want you to hate me, Ava."

I smiled, even as he said those words. "I could never hate you."

He tugged me even closer, my hand between us on his heart—our hearts—the only thing separating us. "I wanna…" He growled.

My mouth popped open at that and I found myself giggling. He scoffed. "What?" He chuckled despite himself and shook his head. "My misery is funny to you?"

"You growled." I kept my smirk in place inches from his mouth.

"Yeah," he relented, his eyes hooding a little further, "I growled." Funny how his voice seemed a little bit more growly when he said that.

"But why did you growl?"

"Well it'll just seem stupid now," he pouted. I could have bitten into that lip right then. Nibbled it like a peanut. He made a breathy, growly noise. "So not helping." He leaned up and pressed his mouth to my ear, causing me to moan pretty embarrassingly. "I can hear everything you're thinking like a foghorn, little bird. You've gotta stop."

My hand wrapped in his collar wasn't pushing him away, it was tugging him closer. I fought for air as it raged in my lungs. The scruff of his chin rasped against my cheekbone as he moved.

"What did you want?" I asked, my voice ridiculously breathy.

"What?" He moved his chin and mouth back and forth over my skin.

"You said, 'I wanna.'"

"Growled it, remember?" He grinned against my skin.

I shook my head and laughed as best as my over-charged mind could handle. "You wanna what?"

I gasped when he actually—finally—kissed my skin, the highest point of my cheekbone. My lips were envious at that torturous moment. And then he licked his lips, adding fuel to the already blazing fire—I could feel his tongue sneak out to taste his lip. I groaned. "Seth," I begged.

"You can't hear my mind right now? Really?" he asked. "I can hear everything from you. I don't know why that is, but if you could hear me you'd know that what I wanted, what I was growling about," he said low in my ear, "is that I don't think I can go another night without kissing you, without knowing what your lips feel like. And I know it's only been a few days but, Ava, it feels like an entire lifetime that I've known you." He pulled back to look at my face, holding my cheek so gently in his palm, letting his thumb sweep across my skin as if that act itself was showing me love. "I know it's hard for you to understand, but there is so much more between us than just a few days' worth of hanging out and riding in my truck." I squinted, not understanding him, but also…believing him. I felt the truth of those words in my bones somehow. "The pain of not knowing what your lips feel like isn't something I can deal with for one more night." He leaned forward, tilting his head a little, but stopping, his eyes never leaving mine. "End my misery, Ava—"

I fell the last inch, let the space fall away between us as my mouth touched his for the first time, effectively ending his plea.

How was I supposed to respond to that other than lean forward and let him devour me from the inside out?

His lips were so warm, and warmer still as he groaned against my mouth, sending a warm puff of surprised, happy air to my lips. I pressed my lips harder to his and then tilted my head, slanting them against his, opening mine a little, feeling his open just a little, too.

His hand on my cheek never stopped moving. It caressed, sending calming shivers down my arms and neck. I pulled my knees in tighter to my chest so I could press in closer to him.

Oh, God, thank you…I had waited for this—my first kiss—and it was flawless. I could feel his scruff scratching against my cheek and it did wondrous things to me. His fingers pushed past my face, tunneling into my hair, massaging lightly, tugging gently, always moving, always doing something to have me on the edge of losing my breath.

I had worried that I wouldn't know what to do. That I'd be so nervous it wouldn't be fun. That I would fail epically. That I would be bad at it.

I heard Seth's small chuckle in my mind and then his sigh. *You're so freaking adorable, Ava.*

So far he had let me control things. He hadn't kissed me until I moved

in to do so. He had practically begged me to kiss him and I realized that he wasn't going to until I moved first. Now that I had, it was game on as he bit into my bottom lip, thinking about nibbling peanuts the entire time, making me lose my mind.

Feel my heartbeat right now and ask me if you're bad at this.

He pressed my hand, which was still holding his over his heart harder, and I could feel it. And then his heartbeat worked its way into my own chest because we were in each other's minds and I could feel it beating so hard. I gasped, my mouth opening wider against his at the feel of it banging away so harshly against my own. My eyes opened wide to find him already watching me. He released my hand only to cup the other side of my face and bring me back to him, taking my bottom lip first between his own before opening my mouth gently with his.

An entire world waited there.

When his tongue touched mine, his small growl wasn't all I heard. I heard mine as well. And was surprised by it. Where had that come from? Where had this *girl* come from?

I was getting bits and pieces from Seth. How he was losing his mind. He never thought I would taste this good. He'd never get tired of needing me this way. He was falling so fast for me.

I gripped his shirt in my fists tight and tried to soak all that in. I had to stop listening to him or *I'd* lose *my* mind.

Crap, I had to go to work.

Call in sick.

I smiled against his mouth. *Daddy knows I'm not sick. He knows I'm with you.*

It's so adorable that you call your father 'Daddy'.

I pulled back and licked my lips, loving how he watched the movement. "You think everything is adorable."

He grinned. "Yeah." He leaned in close again. "Call. In. Sick. I'm not ready for this end yet."

"Not ending," I promised. I looked at the center doors and back at him thoughtfully. "You...want to come with me?"

His eyebrows rose. "You want me to walk you inside?"

"No. Come to work with me tonight. Come see what I do with the kids. What my dad does."

"Eh. I'm not sure if I want to get my ass kicked today."

I laughed and hit his chest with the side of my fist. "The kids aren't that bad. Your ass will be perfectly fine."

"I was talking about your dad kicking my ass for showing up unannounced," he muttered and swiped my lip with his thumb. "And since when do you say 'ass'? Good girls don't say 'ass'."

"Who said I was a good girl?"

He groaned, which turned into a laugh, which I eventually joined him in. "I guess I assumed that, now didn't I?"

"Which means..." I sang, "when you assume..."

He grinned at my smirk, shaking his head. "That I have a cute ass?"

"That, too," I conceded.

He sobered and took my face in his hands again, letting his nimble fingers memorize my flesh as his eyes did the same.

"I know things aren't perfect and we still have a lot to talk about, but I hope that after today you at least know that I'm not going anywhere." He leaned in, pressing his lips to my ear. "You're mine, little bird. And no one, family, friend, or foe, will take you from me. You're absolutely safe with me and I will figure this out for us, Ava."

Today, more than any other day, it *mattered* when he said it. And it hit home. And it punctured my heart in all the right ways. I felt the first tear threaten as my throat threatened to clog with tears. He leaned back and his eyes opened a little wider. I grabbed his wrists and smiled as best I could to explain.

"I'm just happy."

"One day everything will be like it's supposed to be," he promised softly.

"And you'll be here."

"You're daggum right," he growled gently. He tugged me to him, pressing my mouth to his, and spoke his words against my lips. "Now, let me get my fill before we go inside."

I sighed and licked my lips in between breaths. "Your fill?" He brought me back to him.

"Yeah. Of you. Your mouth." He chuckled against my lips. "It's not working, not even a little. I don't think there is such a thing. I don't think I'll ever get filled of *this*."

Those words broke me in the best way. I would never get my fill either. As

I clung to the warmth and calm that was everything he was, he pulled back easily.

"Okay. Show me your kids. Just promise me you'll save me from your father if he decides to rip into me."

I grinned. "I may let him so you better behave."

CHAPTER ELEVEN

"**H**ey, guys!"

They all turned away from Daddy and the helpers and rushed us. "Ava!"

Daddy eyed me curiously, but seeing that I was seemingly happy, there was no famous Jacobson scowl to be seen.

"I brought a new helper for the day."

"Dude," one of the boys said, "you're a giant."

Seth chuckled and rubbed his head in an embarrassed way. "Uh, nah. One day you'll be as tall as me, buddy."

He gasped. "And he knows my name! A giant that can read minds!"

I looked at Seth and we smiled. The boy wasn't far off. We could read each other's minds.

"Tony, lots of people call each other buddy. Your mom isn't the first person to do that."

He eyed me suspiciously. "How did you know my mom calls me 'buddy'? Can you read minds, too?"

I laughed and rubbed his head playfully, tempted to give him a noogie if he kept this up. "Lucky guess. This is Seth," I introduced. "He's a fireman,"

I sang, knowing I was throwing him under the bus. And he knew it, too, as soon as it left my lips. He turned to me and opened his mouth, but the sing-song begging of the children had already begun.

"Oh, my gosh! So cool. Where do you keep all those hoses? In one big hose keeper in the backyard?"

"Have you ever been burned?"

"Have you ever saved anyone?"

"Do you have a Dalmatian?"

"What's that symbol on your shirt mean?"

I walked over to Daddy and watched them crowd around him. This was the middle school session so he was pretty much in it deep for the next two hours. He looked over at me with an I-see-what-you-did-there smirk. I winked. His eyes rolled a little and closed for a second.

Don't start that where it can't be finished.

I sat up straighter. *Seth—*

I was going to say Seth Watson. Like playful scolding, but I just couldn't do it. I realized, I would never be able to say it. I felt awful for that. I looked back up, expecting him to be angry again, but he was dividing his attention between the kids and me somehow smoothly. He smiled a little.

It's okay, Ave. My middle name is Cameron. You can use that to scold me.

I'm sorry. I made everything go back to the way it was, didn't I?

No. No way. I looked up at him. *We're never going back, no matter what. Promise me. We have to stick together if we're ever going to survive this.*

I nodded. *My middle name is... Winifred.*

His eyebrows shot up. *Really?*

Truly. It was my Gran's name.

Ava Winifred. He smiled. *I like it. And I'll use it to scold you, too.*

I bit my lip and heard him groan in my mind, making me giggle in my mind.

All right, you.

We're going to have to work on that, he pointed at me with a smile, *in public.*

He went back to the kids as if nothing was going on. He was insane. Daddy made me jump when he bumped my arm. He'd been leaning against the table top with me the entire time. I felt my neck turn that pink that was becoming a permanent color and rolled my eyes.

"You didn't even know I was here," he said and I could tell he was grinning.

"Daddy, stop."

"I don't know what happened today, but I'm glad that you two seemed to have worked things out. I was thinking I was going to have to start looking for a burial plot in the backyard."

I snorted. "I skipped school today," I admitted and shot him a sideways look.

He sighed and twisted his lips. "I figured. How else could you have worked things out in a car ride's time if you hadn't?"

"He's scared, Dad. He's starting to realize that's something's not right with the Watsons. He won't tell me though."

"He doesn't want you to be disappointed in him. And he wants to take care of it. It's his mess, in his mind. He brought all this here to our doorstep. He didn't," he insisted. "We've been fighting with the Watsons for a long time, but that's how he sees it, I'm sure." He sighed loudly and turned to face me where Seth couldn't see. "Shut your mind for a second."

I gave him a look, but made sure that my mind was closed off to Seth and nodded slightly. He went on. "I'm going to send some boys out to the Watson compound to look around."

"Seth said it was abandoned."

"I know."

I gave him another look. "Dad."

"Maybe he just doesn't know. Maybe they haven't given him all the info or let him in on things."

"You trust him, don't you?"

"Yes, I do. And that's *why* I want to send people. I could just use him, Ava. We have a spy in the Watson family now. Do you realize that? But I'd never do that to you or him. We need to find out what they're planning because it's obvious that they *are* planning something. And I don't think they have Seth's best interests at heart."

"Have you heard something?" His eyes crinkled. "Daddy."

"Your mom had a vision last night."

My breath stuck in my throat. "What?"

"It was the room she was held in when she was kidnapped, and someone was in it."

I covered my mouth with my hands to stop the gasp, but that couldn't stop my heart.

Dad grimaced. "Calm down, Ave." But it was too late.

Seth told the kids he'd be back and came rushing over, his hand on his chest. "What's wrong?" He grabbed my arms gently and leaned down to see my face. "Ava?"

"Nothing, I'm fine." I looked at Daddy and shook my head. I wasn't going to be able to do this. I wasn't going to be able to keep things from Seth like this. It wasn't the way our kind did things.

Daddy couldn't hear me, but he still got my meaning. His face scrunched and I could tell he felt guilty for even asking me to do it.

Seth's shoulders sagged as he stood up straight. "So we are going back to that?" he asked softly.

"No," I gripped his sides, "we aren't." I looked at Daddy. "We either trust him completely or we don't. They are his family, yes, but they were our rivals long before that. And I don't think he would have a problem with us checking into things." Seth's brow was now bunched into multiple levels of confusion. "Daddy wants to send some of our people to check out the Watsons." Seth's face straightened a little. "Mom had a vision, not a good one, and we just want to see if we can—"

"Yes."

"What?" Dad asked a little too loudly. He cleared his throat. "What?" he asked quieter, watching the helpers take over with the kids.

"They don't tell me things anymore," Seth explained, his brow furrowed. "They don't leave me alone like they used to. They're always around, always calling and texting, always trying to get me to come over. It's weird." He sighed, his head falling a little. I moved in and hugged him to give him a little comfort if I could. He smiled. "What did I tell you about that?" he said softly, not even caring that my dad was there. "This is what I need," he told me and pulled me as close as I could get, putting his arms around my hips, slipping his thumb just under the hem of my shirt to touch my skin. I tried not to hiss when he touched me, but failed miserably. Then he carried on as if nothing had transpired. I looked up at Daddy to see him shaking his head, all cocked-browed. "I think it's a good idea. They think they have me right where they want me." I jerked my gaze up to meet his. He looked so sad. "I hate to admit that, but they're using me. I know it. Ever since I botched their plan at your house to take you, they haven't been the same. They sabotage every time I try to see you. For what purpose, I haven't figured out yet. But I will. We will."

I'm sorry.

It's not your fault.

I feel like it kinda is.

How?

Because I'm a Jacobson. If you had bonded with anyone else, they probably would have just been happy for you. As happy as a Watson can be anyway.

His face twisted, but he couldn't argue with me. "I'm sorry."

"Me, too."

That night when he dropped me off at the house, as we stood in my yard, he pulled his cell out and texted Harper back.

No thanks. I have everything I need already.

"Thank you."

"There's something I need to tell you about Harper," he hedged carefully and I felt my heart burst a little. He cupped my cheek. "No, no, it's not that. Well, not exactly that."

"Will you just spit it out? Because your preface is killing me," I whispered with my eyes closed, scared to face what he might be about to say.

They had actually been a couple once. He did have feelings for her that were now void. She had been promised to him in some twisted family ritual that involved lamb's blood and goat's milk.

He laughed in a small breath. "Baby, stop. Look at me."

I lifted my face. He called me 'baby'.

"I'm still testing out nicknames. You like?"

"I think you could call you anything and I'd like it. You could call me 'Francine' and I'd practically swoon at your feet."

"Francine?" He laughed.

"Swoonsville," I whispered and tried to smile for him.

His smile was one that showed all his feelings, or at least I hoped it did, because that smile was one of love and adoration. It morphed to seriousness and I was loathe to see it go away.

"I just want to start by saying that Harper and I had nothing to do with it." I tried not to make a face, but wound up gritting my teeth instead. He took my face in his hands. "I know that you don't like Harper, but…she's been my friend for as long as I can remember. We grew up together. She…wouldn't hurt me. If there's some plot they're planning, she's not a part of it."

I pressed my lips together and looked down. Though I didn't like her, he obviously had some strong connection with her. I didn't want to shatter that, but that was exactly what I was about to do with what I saw.

"What?" I met his eyes. "What did you see?"

I stalled. It was my way. Maybe I should have just never said anything. Maybe I should have just let him see it all the day it all happened and been done with it.

"What, Ava?" he said harder.

My eyes burned. I let him see on my face how much I didn't want to show him before I pulled him down to press my head to his. I showed him what happened the day he took me to his apartment and Harper was waiting for us, when she hugged him and grinned so evilly behind his back at me like she was winning, she then fixed her expression when he pulled back. I showed him how she gave me the same look when we made our way inside. And then I showed him how I saw it, a girl would see it, when he was leaving and she looked at him so longingly.

He yanked away, almost slipping in the snow, and paced a few feet away before turning back to face me. "This entire time, you've listened to me defend her..."

"Your whole world was crumbling, Seth." I looked at the ground because I didn't know what else to do. "You kept clinging to her. I didn't know why, but I... I felt like you needed to keep her if that's what you wanted."

"Ava," he said with a sigh, "Uncle Gaston tried to get me to bond with Harper a couple years ago."

I yanked my head up, breathing the cold air painfully, pulling my shoulders tight to myself. "What?" I barely whispered.

"I always thought it was just him, that she didn't want to just like I didn't. It felt...wrong." He shook his head. "We were always family in my mind. Always. Even if we're not blood. And when he brought it up...Harper was there. I started to protest and she jumped in, too. I just assumed that she was just as adamant as I was, but she was just following my lead," he realized. "She wanted to bond to me."

"You were the one they chose to force the imprint with." He was already nodding, figuring it out, too.

"Gah, Harper, why?" he said to the air.

It wasn't hard for me to see why. "I'm so sorry."

He looked at me like I was crazy. "What the hell, Ava? Don't be sorry for her, or them, or any of it. I got you out of this." He came to me, stalking really, so slowly that my breathing had picked up by the time he reached me. "I'd live all this all over again if it meant I got you in the end."

"Stop," I pleaded as he took my face in his big, calloused hands.

"I'm not gonna stop."

I felt my eyes watering in the cold air. "Seth," I begged him. He'd been through so much. He did not deserve this. He did not deserve some psycho girl trying to pick him out of the line-up just because she decided she wanted him, because he was the only one in her family that she could have because he wasn't blood related to her. Though I knew that wasn't all true. I'd seen the way she looked at him. She could have fallen in love with Seth all on her own even if they'd met somewhere else. It wasn't hard to fall in love with him. I'd done it in a mere week.

He puffed a harsh breath against my cheek, listening to my internal rant. "Ava."

"I'm not sorry that all those things led you to me. I'm just sorry that you had to go through them for it *to* lead you to me." I closed the foot of distance between us, the snow crunching under our feet on my front lawn. I wrapped my arms around his neck as best I could with his height. He helped me, widening his legs to make himself shorter. "If you had stayed with your mom and had a normal life, do you think we still would have found each other?"

"I would have found you anywhere," he rumbled, squeezing his fingers on my hips.

"I believe you."

"You need to go inside," he said and gulped down his dislike of that, of us separating for the night. "It's too cold to be out here like this."

"Yes, it is."

We both turned to find Dad coming out the front door with a cup of something steaming in his hand. Seth straightened and sighed a little in aggravation.

"I'll...come in the morning, I guess. But I won't see you tomorrow night. I'm on for forty-eight hours and I have to sleep at the station."

"Come inside, Seth," Dad ordered, using his Champion voice. "You, too, Ava. It's freezing out here."

"Sir," Seth started, but I put a hand on his chest.

"Stay with me tonight," I said softly.

His eyes bugged a little before he looked at Dad and then back at me. "Your parents won't mind?" he whispered.

"No." I chuckled. He cocked his head a little. I took his hand and knew I had some explaining to do on the way our kind handled things. "We'll just be sleeping, right?" I asked coyly.

He looked at Dad in the porch light and answered loudly. "Of *course*."

Dad laughed and slapped his back hard as we passed him. "Oh, Seth. Don't worry, son. We'll have *the talk* after dinner to make sure you know *exactly* what sleeping entails."

I giggled and Seth shot me a raised brow. I shook my head and rolled my eyes as I took his hand and laced his fingers with mine, dragging him into the living room. When Mom saw us I thought she was going to burst right out of her skin with happiness.

Rodney had been at school so much that he missed a lot and was pretty shocked to see the civil and, dare I say even, lovey version of us. He was still skeptical, I think, and kept eyeing Seth sideways. It was going to be a process with him. But that was okay. We had time.

Dinner was okay. We talked, we laughed, we were normal, and that was more than I could ask for these days.

Dad took Seth off to the living room for a few minutes to talk and when he brought him back, it was pretty comical the look on his face.

"You okay?"

"Of course," he soothed and waved to my mom. "Thanks for dinner, Mrs. Jacobson."

"Maggie, please," she pleaded.

"Maggie," he said and it sounded so strange coming from his mouth. He looked at the clock on the wall and then at me. "Ready?"

"Yeah." I nodded.

"Night, all," he called.

"Night," I said and couldn't help but feel a little twinge of weirdness at heading upstairs with my boyfriend.

"Oh, don't worry," he said and chuckled, placing his hand on the small of my back as he guided me upstairs. "There will be nothing but sleeping going on, trust me. Not after that talk with dear old Dad."

I smiled as I looked back at him. "Um, sorry?"

"It's okay. He's your father," he reasoned and pressed up against my back. "Which one's your room?"

"This one. What about your clothes?" I looked at him over my shoulder.

His nose brushed my cheek. "I'll go home in the morning, shower and change before work."

Work clothes... The thought of him in his fireman clothes made me smile. And my neck turn pink.

He laughed under his breath. "We don't wear the garb all day. Only if there's a fire," he whispered conspiratorially and kissed my cheek over my shoulder.

I smiled and opened the door, letting him in first, watching him as he took in the room. I turned on the music in the corner. "*I Feel It All*" by Feist came blaring through the speakers so I turned it down a little and turned to face him. He went to the radio and messed with it, turning the songs, one after another, until I heard "*I Only Have Eyes For You*" come singing through my speakers.

I opened my mouth a couple times before I finally said. "How did you know I loved The Flamingos?" But it came out only breath as their voices slid over us. He didn't answer me, only slowly came to me and pulled me against his chest, hugging me to him by my waist, nuzzling his face into my hair. I sighed and gripped his upper arms.

"Seth."

Neither of us said a word as he walked me backward to the bed and laid me down on top of the covers, following me down, laying on his side and cupping my face, letting that thumb cause me heart palpitations, but he stayed right there, out of reach. "Seth," I complained again through ragged breaths.

"What it is, sweetheart?" he asked, like he had no clue. But he knew.

"Why won't you kiss me?"

He let a breath go through his bitten lip. "After that talk I just had with your father—your father the Champion—I just..."

"You just what? There's nothing wrong with kissing me. I'm your significant. Daddy has no room to talk. He used to sneak in Mom's window and I know they didn't sit in there and play Scrabble all night."

He sighed again. "I feel like your mom is watching or something."

"She can't. She can't see anyone that has her blood. Meaning me. And since you're a Watson, they gave you her blood, because she can't read you

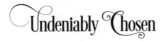

either."

"What?"

I nodded. "All the Watsons have my Mom's blood so she can't read their minds. Something they figured out a long time ago. They must have given it to you because she can't read your mind."

He scrunched his nose. "They gave me your Mom's blood?"

I ran my hand down his face. "Don't think about that right now." I bit my lip.

He looked at my mouth and I saw the change come over him as his eyes hooded a little. "Ava," he said.

It sounded like a scold. It was kind of hot the way he kept saying my name and nothing else, as if that was enough.

"Seth." I leaned in, taking his collar in my fist, pressing my forehead to his. I pushed to find out what my father had said. He was thinking about how my father had told him that he knew we needed to sleep together, that sleeping apart was dumb and unproductive if it just meant I would be hurting in the morning, but he expected Seth to be respectful of me and this house, of the rules set forth in it. That he expected us to sleep on top of the comforter and I was the boss at all times. That he wasn't an idiot and knew we'd be…doing things any *significant* couple would, but that Seth better be careful with me. But the laws and rules of our kind still applied. That with everything going on with the Watsons and the Jacobsons, all Dad cared about was keeping me safe. Seth agreed.

Before I could think, his mouth was covering mine, just once. He breathed against my lips and smiled. "You're gonna get my ass kicked."

I giggled and pulled him closer. "I'll protect your ass."

He rumbled a laughed before rolling over, letting his arm brace above my head to hover over me slightly, but not enough to really count because he wasn't touching me anywhere else. He was using that space as a barrier.

I let my hands grip and tug at his short, dark hair and collar as his lips claimed mine again—his lips eager, his tongue commanding, his hand never leaving the pillow, not once.

His legs were restless at the other end of the bed, but I realized he was kicking his shoes off, so I kicked mine off, too. I rubbed my socked feet against his, letting my calf wrangle between his. His feet were so much larger than mine and that fact made me want to giggle for some reason.

We kept at it for a while, but before long, he rolled over on his back and beckoned me to him. I put my face in his neck and curled against his side. He took our hands and laced them on his chest. When he sighed, I sighed too, out of sheer necessity. And then I fell asleep so easily.

Safe.

Warm.

Happy.

Significant in someone's world.

"I kissed her, Ava."

I looked at him with a smile a mile wide. "I…I'm so happy. I can't believe it. What did she say? What did she do? What happened?"

He laughed, happier than I'd ever seen him. "She kissed me back."

I laughed, but it slowly drained away. "Wait…if you kissed her, then everything is right as rain, right? All is well in la-la land?"

He smirked. "Yeah. Yeah, my little poet, right as rain."

"Then why are you here? Why *am I* still here? Why are she and I still separated? Is something still going on?"

"No," he comforted and came across the terrace toward me. He took my hand and smoothed my hair back that the wind was whipping around. "No, I think everything will be okay on that front."

"So you can kiss me, then?" He looked unsure. "We're the same person. If you've kissed her, then you can kiss me."

He shook his head side to side with a small grin. "You're so much like her. She asked me to kiss her tonight, too."

"I *am* her," I whispered and tilted my head.

He moved forward and I held my breath. He took my face in his big, warm, take-charge hands and brought me up to meet his lips. I closed my eyes, a little disappointed in him and thrilled all at once. But at the last moment, he turned and kissed my cheek, so close to my mouth. He whispered, "Soon, the two of you will merge back together and all of this will just have been a dream. But I can't kiss you. I know you're technically the same person, but

it doesn't feel right to. I wanted to come and say goodbye. To thank you for all you did to bring us to together." I opened my eyes to find him so close. He rubbed his thumb across my chin. "You're the reason I found you. You're the reason I was able to bring Ava home." He palmed his chest, looking so emotional in that moment that I wanted to cry.

I smiled. "I'll miss you."

"No, you won't." He smiled and hugged me hard. "You got me, sweetheart."

"She better realize what she's got."

He laughed and kissed my forehead before leaning back. "I'm with her now." My eyebrows raised. "It's our first night together." They raised higher. "Just sleeping."

I smiled, biting my lip in between my teeth. He shook his head and reached up to release it with his thumb. "She does *that*, too." I gave him a teary smile. I didn't know what else to do. I knew this wasn't goodbye, but it still felt like one. "I'll see you soon, little bird."

I nodded. "And I'll remember everything?"

He nodded. "If not, I'll tell you *everything*. I promise."

I nodded harder. "Okay."

"Thank you. You saved us."

"You saved me."

"Now," he set me away and posed me against the railing, "let me draw you on the terrace with London at your back. This is a memory I want to keep."

I breathed in awe, "You can draw?"

He laughed, shaking his head.

I smacked the alarm and found Seth right where I left him. So it hadn't been a dream. And wow, not waking up in pain and withdrawal was not just awesome, but it rocked. I didn't just feel good, I felt amazing. I felt like I'd been eating vegetables and taking vitamins in my sleep.

I rolled over to face him, feeling not near as bold as I'd been yesterday as I looked down at his scruff. I didn't know why last night had felt different. Maybe being with him all day or something was the difference, but now the shyness was there again, the little edge of awkwardness that hovered when he was near. One day didn't make all that go away.

"As long as you don't go back to hating me." He cracked an eye open and then the other. "How do you feel today?"

I took a deep breath, filling my lungs with the air of a new day. "Pretty marvelous."

He smiled. "Do you…remember?"

I squinted with a confused smile. "Remember that you somehow know that I love the Flamingos?"

His smile shook, but he tried to hold it. "Yeah," he sighed. "We had a great day, right? You remember all that and we aren't going to go back."

That wasn't what he meant, I knew it. There was something he was keeping in the back of his mind, something he didn't want me to see…but he *did* want me to know it. It was like he wanted me to figure it out on my own and was disappointed when I didn't. He looked down at me and watched me work it all out, knowing I was right, but saying nothing.

I laid back down and stared at the ceiling. "I don't understand why you hear *everything* that's in my head. Truly." I focused on blocking him out, but it was an actual effort to do so. It was like I had to sit there and think about it every second to be able to do it. Normal significants only got into each other's head if they tried. It wasn't this way.

"Maybe," he sat up and looked at me, "it has to do with them giving me your mom's…blood or something." He grimaced. "I don't know. Does it bother you that bad?"

"Badly," I corrected absentmindedly and then pressed my lips together, snorting a little.

His face lit, looking pleased for some reason. "I kinda like it. Correction," he leaned a tad closer, "I really like." When his fingers touched my jaw to make me look at him, I wasn't hit with his calm like usual because I'd been absorbing it all night. I felt a little sad that I couldn't experience that buzz his skin could give me. "I like being in that pretty head of yours."

"I don't care if you're in my head," I said truthfully. "I just wish it was the same for me. It's a lot of work to open my mind up to yours all the time and you don't even have to try. All I get are just a couple bits and pieces here or there. It's not fair."

"Maybe that's one of my super powers," he joked and laughed once, but his mind was shut to me. Once again, that thing that he was hiding…

"You can just tell me," I hedged.

His eyes jumped up, surprised that I just blurted it out. He smiled suddenly, surprising me. "You're so much like…"

Her.

He couldn't stop the thought before it was out there. I recoiled, feeling as though he had punched me in the chest. I squeezed my eyes shut, trying to roll over, but he stopped me, cupping my cheeks.

"Look at me, Ava."

"After everything, after you know how I feel about her—" I whispered, my heart literally breaking in my chest.

"I would *never* have said you reminded me of Harper. Not before last night and especially not after it."

"Then who are you talking about, Seth?" I asked, almost hysterically. "Who is *her*?"

He licked his lip, sighing and putting his forehead to mine before pulling back and looking at me for a second. "I told you I dream about you."

I opened my mouth to ask, but he laid his forehead to mine and showed me a clip or scene of us from his dream. We were in my room and he was talking to me, cupping my face on my bed.

It was so vivid and we were so sweet together. I guess it was what he wanted to happen back before it did—when we fighting and he didn't know how to solve it. So he had dreams about us.

I opened my eyes and found him watching, waiting for me to yell and tell him to leave, that I didn't believe him, that I wanted him to go, that he was a liar. "Why would you think I'd do that?" I asked softly.

"It's what my family would do."

"I told you significants don't fight that way."

"Yeah," he nodded and looked down, "but I didn't really believe you. I've seen too much fighting all my life. People can't just be happy all the time, can they?" he said like he'd screwed everything up beyond repair.

I palmed his scruff, lifting his face. "Why not? It's up to you how you react to things. It's up to me how I handle situations. It's up to us how we deal with each other. Each couple is defined by themselves, not by society or any other outside factor…unless they *let* them define them. And once they do, then they no longer have control over their own relationship. And how sad is that? When couples fight about money or sick kids or even silly things to big things, they should be leaning on each other, not being angry at each other when it's out of both of their control. When couples start to get stale, instead of looking to books or movies or other people for their support or romance, they should be coming to each other, ramping things up, making things fun. But they don't. They let things go, let all the blame fall on the other person and say that they didn't make them feel special and sexy, but did they make *them* feel special and sexy?" I was breathing hard at this point, on a roll, unable to stop as he just stared at me. "No, I'm not going to yell at you and leave because not only is that not what significants do, but that's not what real couples do either. What does that accomplish? You can't be worried that every time you screw up I'm going to kick you to the sofa, Seth—and not just because I'd be in withdrawals." His eyes met mine fiercely, blue on brown. "We're going to screw up a lot, we're just getting to know each other, but especially for the environment you grew up in, you're such an amazing, sweet, honorable, prolific man." I gulped. "You make me feel so—"

He cut me off by pulling me up to his mouth.

His mouth—so delicious and addictive. He kept me away from him, his hands only on my face, but his mouth worked overtime to get me breathless. I followed his lead, letting him take me wherever he wanted to go. I opened when he nudged me to, I dueled tongues with him when his fought against mine—my heart was about to beat out of my chest—accepting that kissing was my new favorite pastime, when he bit into my lip.

I appropriately gasped and let slip the little moan that caused him to growl, which set off a new round of deep kisses and we started all over again as he dove in.

Before Rodney walked in—without knocking, but we didn't see him.

Ingrate.

"So this is what I have to look forward to," I heard to my right and gasped, scrambling up to stand beside the bed as he kept going, "when I get myself bonded, huh? Late for school because I'm making out when I *should* be downstairs eating the breakfast my mother cooked with the family that's been waiting for fifteen minutes."

I struggled to get my breathing under control, as Seth did the same, clearing his throat. Seth was taller than Rodney by a good bit.

"Rodney, come on," I complained. "Knock next time."

"I did," he said and made a gross face.

I rolled my eyes and pushed his arm to shoo him. "We'll be down in a minute. Let me change my clothes."

"Whoa!" He turned. "Then Jolly Green Giant needs to come with me."

I opened my mouth to lay into him, but Seth gripped my hand. "I'm going. He's right. Get dressed."

I grumbled, "I would have put you out before I got dressed."

He smirked. "Would you now?"

I giggled.

Rodney rolled his eyes. "God, please, don't ever let me imprint. Keep me celibate."

He padded his big, stupid, judgy feet down the hall and I glared at his back. Seth laughed. I swung my gaze on him. "What are you laughing at?"

"He'll get his," he promised. "He just doesn't know what this," he rubbed his thumb against mine, "feels like."

I swooned in a puddle by my bedroom door. His smile grew. "I'll wait for you downstairs." He gave me a smirk. "You could go fast if you want."

"I will. I'll have mercy. Tell them not to wait for me to eat."

I took care with the fastest shower I'd ever taken and with what I put on. It didn't feel like a t-shirt and jeans day. So I put on my leggings with a crop dress and the infinity scarf Mom and I got in London last year, threw on my boots, left my hair in loose waves, slicked on some light make up and booked it downstairs.

When I entered the kitchen where the breakfast nook was, everyone stopped eating and talking, which made me feel so uncomfortable until Seth stood up so fast that his chair almost tipped over behind him.

He let his out in a slow, low noise before… "Wow."

Mom chuckled and leaned back with a smile, clapping twice. "And that, ladies and gentleman, is how it's done."

My neck was so pink I could feel it, and Seth—realizing he'd just practically fallen at my feet in front of everyone—smiled that smile that tore through me like tissue paper and then turned it on my mother. She sat up straighter and looked at me with wide eyes.

'I know', I mouthed as I moved toward him.

"Eat, Ave," Dad said, knowing what I was doing.

"I'm going to be late. And it's the last day of school before winter break."

"Gee, I wonder why you're late—" Rodney began. I punched his arm.

"I'll just take this." I grabbed a biscuit, stuck a piece of sausage in it, and wrapped it in a napkin. "I'll eat it," I promised.

"I'll make sure she eats," Seth told them. Mom came and hugged him, telling him something in his ear and he nodded. "Thanks, Mrs. Jacobson. I will. I promise."

Dad patted his shoulder and told him to make sure to stop by anytime, no invitation needed. Dad went to the counter and started making me a coffee in a to-go cup. I knew he was doing it, because I saw him pull the Hazelnut creamer from the fridge. But I saw him pull out a second to-go cup…and he made it black. How did he already know that Seth took his coffee black?!

"What is going on here?" I muttered under my breath.

Seth took both of the cups from my dad and guided me with an arm around my back. "Thanks for the coffee and breakfast. Bye, guys."

"Bye, Seth!" Mom called cheerily.

I looked at the snow and the porch as we came outside to make sure that everything was the same, that I hadn't entered an episode of a TV show of some alternate reality or something.

I looked at Seth. "If you tell me your name is *The Doctor*, I'm outta here."

He laughed loudly. "And now you're a "Doctor Who" fan? Freaking adorable," he mumbled under his breath. "Your parents are awesome, Ava." He was so sincere.

"I was worried I was going to have to save you."

"No need." He used his elbow to swipe the snow off of a spot and then set the coffees on his hood. The truck was already cranked so he must have the kind where you do it from the key fob because there were no footprints in the snow. He opened the door, helped me in, and then got the coffees, handing mine to me. "They were awesome about not making me feel weird. Even Rodney wasn't too bad."

He laughed before shutting my door.

My dress wasn't too short, but I did notice how it rose up mid-thigh when I sat down. But the leggings kept the ensemble decent. And warm.

The truck was *so* warm, but I still slid over as soon as he shut my door. When he got in and saw how close I was, his grin was adorable. He got in and turned the heat on even more, looking at my legs and shutting his eyes for a few seconds too long. "You're not too cold with those on?"

"Leggings?" I laughed.

"Is that what they're called?" he half-growled as he backed out and got on the road. "They should be called evil."

"They're just like pants, just thinner. Jeans, just not made of quite the same thing. Jeggings."

He laughed and shook his head. "As long as you're warm, sweetheart, call 'em whatever you want." He looked at my legs again and then away with a little groan. "I'll just call them evil because I can see every inch of your legs in those things."

My heart practically did the Tennessee Waltz behind my ribs. "And that's evil?" I squeaked.

"Evil," he reiterated and smiled.

I boldly took his hand from his leg and held it in between mine on my legs. He tensed and gave me a sidelong look. "Ava."

"You kill me when you say my name like that."

"Like what?" he asked gruffly.

"Anything," I answered truthfully after I thought about it.

He laughed once. "Well then right now, we're even, sweetheart." His eyes brushed over me once more, taking in my legs and making me feel the most beautiful I've ever felt with that look, before looking at the road and keeping his eyes straight ahead the rest of the drive.

When we arrived at the school, I had been preparing a little speech in my head. I was sure he had heard the whole thing, but I wanted to say it anyway. Today, tonight, tomorrow, was going to suck. He had to work and couldn't come. We'd figure it out, all that, we'd get through this together, but he had other plans.

He left the engine running and turned just barely in the seat. He pushed my hair behind my ear and let his eyes rove over my face slowly, thinking how beautiful I was. "Seth."

"Ava." He knew exactly what he doing, now knowing what hearing my name did to me. His smile was genuine as he inched my way slowly and took my mouth so gently, moving his hand to the back of my neck.

I felt a swarm of butterflies attack my gut. When he pulled away, I grunted in dissatisfaction. He seemed pleased by my reaction. "You have to go to class, and I need to go to home and shower."

"Oh, that's helping things," I said coyly.

He gave me a stern look. "You are going to be trouble."

"Not for long. Just until..." I stopped my line of thinking right then and there. Oh, God, help me. I didn't even know what the Watsons did when they bonded. How long they waited until they...

"All right," I started and grabbed my purse, "uh, I'll call you later or something and we'll—"

"Wait." He grabbed my arm to make sure I couldn't leave for good measure. "What's this about? Why are you shutting off your mind? You never do that."

"Nothing. We can talk about it later."

"How long they waited until...they got married?" he guessed and nodded. "Is that what you're talking about? Your dad already laid it all out for me that our kind doesn't have sex until marriage because he didn't know if the Watsons carried on that tradition anymore. They do, by the way. Or, as far as I knew."

"Okay, great," I said softly.

"But we have a long time to worry about that, right?" He laughed. "I'm sure your mom is going to plan some big southern wedding with a million people invited and it'll take her like two years to do it, right? Plus," he hedged and laughed a little, "I kinda have to pop the question first. But I think it's a given."

CHAPTER TWELVE

I just stared. I didn't know what else to do.

I wasn't angry. There wasn't anything to be angry about really, it was just that another piece of my fairytale wasn't happening quite as it should. Everything that Seth and I had to face was going to come head on and full speed into the wall. He didn't get it as he looked at me. And I was a girl, I wanted the perfect story, the perfect thing *for me*. It was awkward. *Hey, I know you barely know me, you like me a whole lot, but it's the custom of our kind to not wait two years, but marry in like two weeks. Wanna?*

His eyes bugged to an impossible size and I realized that I hadn't been blocking him at all in my rant. I apparently turned it all back on and had just scared the bejeezus out of him.

I leaned back a little. "Don't worry about it. I'll text you later or something. I'm…sorry."

He just sat there. I tried to go, but couldn't. I sighed. He had to release me. I opened my mouth to beg him, but once again he showed me mercy that I wasn't sure he even wanted to show me. At least not in that moment anyway.

"Go on," he whispered. "Go and learn something. I'll see you later," he finished so quietly I barely heard him. I wondered if that would be enough to release me. I hoped.

I took my bag again and got out, without taking his touch, but I had been filled with it all morning. It still felt wrong to leave without touching him.

I turned and shut the door easily, making sure not to slam it so he wouldn't think I was angry. I walked a little bit away onto the sidewalk and looked back at him. He was watching me, that same expression on his face. Then he put the truck in drive and slowly drove away.

Was the thought of marrying me so awful? So debilitating? Did he feel like I was taking his life away or something? I didn't know what to think. I just knew everything was fine until that one word came up and now, everything wasn't fine.

"Hey, girl."

I looked up to find Lilith draped around some rugby player. "Hey."

It was then I realized that I forgot my coffee in his truck. I looked at my biscuit and sighed. Lilith called my name and asked if I was okay.

"Yeah. Just…" I looked up to find her worried and the rugby player looked bored out of his skull. "I'm good. See you later, okay? Lunch, maybe? The deli."

"Lunch at the deli!" She called over her shoulder as she was dragged away."

I went to class and tried not to think. I tried not to let my heart hurt because I didn't want Seth to think he needed to come rescue me. For one, I knew that he didn't want to come right now. He was upset with me. And I didn't want him to come because he had to, I wanted him to come because he wanted to, to see me. So I just pushed it all away and tried my best to focus on my classes. I was really good with my classes. I didn't have trouble keeping up or doing the work. I only had a few months left and I was done altogether.

At lunchtime, Lilith sat across from me at one of the outside tables, making jokes and being her normal self. Then she jumped up and said she forgot she had a paper due at the end of the day and needed to go work in the library. It sounded like a total line, but I let it go. I was just about to leave, not wanting to sit out there by myself, when not ten seconds later, I felt him.

I turned to see Seth behind me, walking slowly toward me, a coffee cup in his hand from the place where we met. I felt a breath shudder in my throat.

"Hey," he ventured as soon as he reached me. He was so good at that—not letting things get awkward and weird.

"Hey."

"You left your coffee in my truck this morning so I got you a new one. I'm on my way in to the station."

"Forty-eight hours," I mused.

He nodded. "Forty-eight hours."

I bit my lip and looked down at the ground. I don't know why I felt guilty. I didn't do anything wrong. I had always known that whoever I met I'd marry right away, but if he had been a normal human, he wouldn't know about our kind, would he? And I wouldn't be pushing him to marry me right away, would I? I'd understand. I *expected* him to understand because he was from our world…but he really wasn't, was he?

I expected too much from him. Not just in this, but in a lot of things. I had to look at him differently.

"No, you don't." I startled when I realized he was right up against me, his chin was almost touching my forehead. "I never said I didn't want to marry you, Ava. I just never thought I'd never get to ask the girl." A noise emerged from the back of my throat. I closed my eyes. I heard him sigh. "I'm not saying this right. I'm not trying to make you feel bad; I'm just trying to explain."

"I get it." I opened my eyes, almost wishing he would go at this point. He obviously wanted to. He hadn't even touched me. I saw him wince with that statement. "I'm sorry. I'm sorry for this whole…thing."

"Ava—"

"Miss Jacobson, you're going to be late for my class." I looked away from Seth's blue, intense eyes to see my professor walking past. "I'm almost late, so you're almost late, too. Let's go."

I heard an aggravated noise leave my throat as he walked around me and I let my gaze settle back on my significant. "I better go," I whispered.

"Yeah, it's too cold out here." He eyed me up and down and I couldn't help but notice the shiver that went through him. "You shouldn't be sitting out here with those on anyway."

The tights.

I wanted so much to smile, to smirk, to go back to the playful banter we were so good at this morning, but all I could have done in this moment was burst into tears. Even though he was mad at me—or whatever he was—he still cared enough to worry. But was it because of the bond, or *me*? A few hours ago, I thought I knew.

"Yeah," I said softly. "Bye."

I turned so he wouldn't see my face crumple, but it must not have mattered. My heart was in his chest and he could feel it breaking. He grabbed my coat-covered arm. "Ava," he begged, for what I didn't know.

I wiped under my eyes, but didn't turn. "You're going to be late. And so am I."

"That doesn't matter," he mumbled, but was thinking about getting reamed from his chief for being late and all the extra duties around the firehouse for it. And he was thinking that he needed me to release him when we were done talking. He could feel it already. His legs wouldn't move. I sighed a little.

"I'm fine. I'll see you later. We'll figure it out. Go."

He wanted to give me his touch. He knew that these next couple days were going to be tricky, he hated the thought of me being in withdrawals later, but he backed away instead and walked back to his truck.

I stood there for a minute, just thinking, listening to the quiet of the quad and snow and noise of the bustle of students. And then walked swiftly to class.

Dad picked me up from school and took me to work. I ate supper and then retreated to my room, already feeling the day of not seeing Seth eat away at my body and soul.

He left me so easily today. Or had he? Was I making things too hard? Being too difficult? Was I being that person that I had talked about this morning on my bed—the one who wants to be desired but doesn't do the desiring? Was I leaving everything to Seth and not doing enough to make this work? Was I telling him to fight for me, to not give us on me, but not doing the same?

I wasn't fighting for us.

I sat up. He had come here in the beginning and faced my family even when he thought we'd all hate him. He kept coming back for me, over and over again, even when I didn't want him to, even when he knew I was angry with him. He always found me and made sure I was taken care of.

It was time to return the favor.

I put on my coat and told no one that I was going to the fire station to see Seth. They wouldn't have let me go this late at night and I didn't feel like a debate to be honest, so I just snuck out as quietly as I could.

I pulled out of the driveway and went straight to the coffee shop and got two coffees. One black, one Hazelnut.

"Haven't seen you in here, lately," Paul told me, a little puppy-dog-eye coming through. "I was beginning to worry a little about you."

"Oh, no, everything's fine. Thanks."

"Wait!" He leaned on the counter. "How are you? I haven't seen you in here since that day with that weird guy."

"Uh…that *weird guy* and I are actually dating. Kinda." I wrinkled my nose.

He leaned away from me, disgust evident on his face. "What?"

"Ten years from now, you can say that you knew us back *when*." I smiled as cheerfully as I could muster and hoped that was true.

"Yeah," he mumbled and tossed my receipt in the trash before crossing his arms. He muttered sarcastically, "I hope it works out. See ya."

"Thanks."

I couldn't have stopped the little snort of happiness as I left if I tried. It was short lived, however, as I got back in my car and made the short drive to the fire station. Would he be angry at me for stopping by like this? I looked at the clock on the dash. It was almost nine already. Maybe he would be asleep by now. I pulled across the street where I had parked before and took a deep breath, exhaling all my fears.

I tried to.

I tried to be the woman he deserved. I'd never been in a relationship, but I had watched them all my life. And his heart was in my chest if I *let it be*. I focused, opening up my senses, my mind, and my heart to his. Within seconds, I felt a slow, steady beating beside mine.

I didn't gasp. I covered my chest with both hands, as if to keep it safe, to keep it *mine*. Because he was mine. I didn't know what was going on. I didn't know why our connection didn't seem as…normal as everyone else's. It felt like there was something in the way, something blocking us, something keeping my connection fuzzy, but I was going to figure out what that was and obliterate it. Nothing was coming between us. He had fought for me and I was done being a weak girl who stood by and *waited* to be fought for.

I smiled. I was going to get my man.

With his heart still beating slow, steady but strong, next to mine, I pulled my little purse from the seat and slung it across my shoulder before taking the two coffees and getting out.

With deep breaths pulling from my lungs, I crossed the street. The bay doors were open and the lights were on. There were some guys standing around the truck bumper, talking and laughing. They saw me coming and stopped talking, all turning to look at me. One of them came forward. He was really young, like me. He grinned and held his hands up like he was praying. "Please be here to see me."

I smiled. "Is Seth here?"

One of them whistled. "Our boy Seth is popular tonight." My blood ran cold. Harper, I knew it. Even after he told her not to come. Though, after today…who knew what had happened. It must have been on my face. He cleared his throat. "He's upstairs in the back with Harper—in the kitchen."

They knew her name she was up there so often.

"I'll show you the way," the young guy said.

"Don't "get lost" and steal her on the way there," one of them said and they laughed.

I tried to chuckle and smile for them, but didn't know if I was pulling it off or not. He took me up a flight of stairs and pointed.

"End of the hall on the right." He winked.

I laughed and thanked him. I could hear voices and walked toward them. They must not have heard us coming or they would have stopped. I blocked off my mind. It was probably a bad idea, but I wanted to let him know I was there on my own, not because he knew I was there from my jumbled thoughts.

"I don't get it, Seth," Harper whined. "She comes in, just ruins everything, and you think it's all okay? What has she done to you?"

"There are things you don't know, Harper," he said harshly. "And things you do know. Things that our family has done and everyone just acts like it's all just normal."

"We've done what we had to do to survive. What we had to do because of what that woman did to us!" she hissed. "And then you go and drink the Kool-Aid, forget everything, all our plans?"

"I didn't drink the Kool-Aid, I found my soulmate!" he hissed back. "There's a difference, and the fact that you all act like I'm a traitor pisses me off. All I've been trying to do is keep the peace, try to find a way to bridge the gap for all of us, but you guys won't even try."

"Why should we? We can still keep to the plan."

"How, Harper?" he asked in a hard voice. "How would we do that?"

"Will you stop calling me Harper?" she asked softly and I heard rustling. "Since when do you call me by my full name?"

I heard him sigh and I knew right then that I needed to leave. I didn't need to hear this and I didn't want to. I turned to walk back down the stairs and wait for him, but his next words stopped me dead.

"Since I realized that you wanted to force the imprint with me."

She didn't even try to deny it, which I didn't know if that added to her character or took away from it.

"So?" she whispered and I heard more rustling. I realized she was moving, probably toward him. I felt sick. "Would that have been so bad? At least you wouldn't have all of this to deal with."

His pause was too long, too pregnant, too—

"We're family, Harper," he growled and meant it. "There is never, was never, and will never be anything between us but that. And the fact that you and your father tried to—"

I walked away. It was too much. He was letting into her and I didn't want to hear it. I didn't feel sorry for her, but I still didn't want to hear it. I walked back out to the bay and nodded to the big guy. "He's talking still. I'll wait."

"We'll keep you company," the young guy said and wiggled his eyebrows.

I made my way over to them, accepting the tall stool they put out for me with thanks. I looked at eyebrows. "You're *trouble*, aren't you?"

Everyone laughed. He saluted me and said, "Trouble is my middle name, ma'am."

"Well, Trouble, I'm Ava." I saw his eyes light up like he recognized that name. And then he confirmed it.

"Ahh, so you're *her*." He grinned. "Now it makes sense." He stuck his hand out. "Nice to meet you."

I shook his hand and tried not to sound too nonplussed but I was about to crawl out of my skin with the eagerly happy knowledge that Seth had mentioned me. "Nice to meet you."

"Most people call me Landon" He winked. "But you can call me Trouble anytime."

I laughed and the other guys introduced themselves. I knew I'd never remember them all, but Trouble, I'd definitely remember. They kept me thoroughly entertained as I sipped my coffee. It was only about ten minutes and Harper came steaming down the stairs, black hair, red face, anger practically shooting from her eyes. When she saw me perched on my stool, the guys around me, I thought her head was going to explode, steam from the ears and all.

She didn't say a word, just gave me the glare from hell and walked on out of there. One of the guys whistled. "Well, okay then. I guess he's done talking."

"Yeah," I whispered, but didn't move. He probably needed and wanted a minute, and so did I. Me barging in there after his big fight with Harper was *so* not how I wanted our make up to be tonight. I wanted to just go home and start over another day, but no. I was here, I was doing this.

The guys continued to make cracks around me, pulling me into the jokes, trying to make me laugh, obviously knowing that something was going on, but not knowing what.

I hadn't seen Seth since lunch and my body was definitely feeling it. My back was already starting to get achy, to get stiff. My hands ached to hold him. If he showed his face right now, I'm wasn't sure I wouldn't run across the room and—

"Ava?"

I looked up at the rough voice who had said my name. He stood across the bay on the other side of the trucks, looking as wracked as I felt in that moment. Was it because he needed me? Or was it because he was upset that he'd fought with Harper?

He huffed and shook his head a little as he came toward us. I waited for it, for him to grab my arm and haul me up, take me out of the bay area and ask what I was doing there in the first place.

When his arms wrapped around me and tugged me up from the stool, I was shocked. My face pressed into his warm neck and I groaned into him skin as quietly as I could. Heavens above, I missed him, and he smelled so good. That shower he took when he went home made him smell so…dark and manly. I let my arms go where they may and they went around his neck. My legs felt cooler in that moment and I remembered the dress I was wearing.

I let my arms fall back down to his waist, but Seth was already pulling back, looking at my face. "I'm going on a break," he announced, never letting his eyes leave mine.

"You've been on a break all night."

"Hey!" Trouble said and stood. "She's been waiting down here for him forever! You let him have a break with her. Or *I* will." He grinned, but Seth had already turned his gaze on him. "Whoa, buddy!" He laughed hard. "Our boy Seth has it bad."

"Go," the big guy said and I assumed he was the chief, "but I don't want to hear anything more out of you about us old married saps."

Seth shook his head. "I never say anything about married people."

He squinted. "Maybe not. Go."

Seth took my hand and tugged me to follow behind him, but I quickly grabbed his cup of coffee from one of the bumpers before we went up the narrow, musky concrete stairway. He took me up two flights of stairs to a room full of beds. This was where he'd be sleeping tonight. I stopped my inspection and turned, expecting to find him standing there, but instead he was sitting on one of the beds—his bed I assumed—his head in his hands, his elbows on his knees.

I'd never felt so guilty than in that moment.

He looked up sharply. "What? Why would you feel guilty?"

My neck burned pink. Oh…he was upset about Harper, not me. Yikes. I was walking into one spectacular blunder after another. I looked at the floor for a second but quickly remembered my pep talk to myself. I was going to fight for him. Even if he didn't want to be fought for. I remembered what that felt like.

I smiled as best as I could as I lifted his cup. "I brought you a coffee, black."

He shook his head back and forth, looking angry and confused, pissed and just—ornery.

I was failing epically at *operation fight for us*, mission one.

My mouth opened to explain, to apologize, to…something, but he stood and came my way. I got nothing from him, not an emotion, a thought, a fear, anger, nothing. Just that look that made me think that it was a horrible, horrible mistake to come—

His hand wrapped around the back of my neck gently but his mouth slammed on mine so forcefully the coffee fell from my fingers. I heard the splash, felt it on my boots and tights, but had not a care for those things as his lips slanted over mine, his other arm wrapped around my waist so tightly that if I wanted to gasp it wouldn't have been impossible. His thighs were touching mine and his chest was already puffing with reckless breath.

He released my neck to instead tangle his hand in my hair, letting his fingers get caught and tugging a little, before letting them slip down to my shoulder and starting all over again.

And his mouth—wars could be fought and won with it, with all the ways he was conquering me with his tongue and lips. His lips changed my world, they upset the order of everything I knew.

He groaned a little and I realized he was listening to every word. *You're making me insane, Ave.* He breathed out against my lips. *How could you think for one second that any of this was about* her?

He pulled back to get my answer, but I was having none. I turned us and pushed his chest until his back hit the wall a couple feet away. He grunted with the force and, to his credit, I felt his first smile of the night against my kiss.

Daggum, Ava.

With his satisfaction at my aggression pulsing through me, I reached up on my toes, feeling his legs spread apart to make him shorter so I could reach him better, and gripped his hair with both hands as I opened my mouth and tugged him close. The noise he made, I'd never heard him make before. My pulse banged away. I loved knowing that he could feel every beat in his chest, a rhythm just for us, a rhythm no one else could hear.

And since we were so worked up, I could feel his in my chest, too, and didn't even have to try. I soaked all that in as I moved away from his lips, which earned me a protest as he tried to chase my lips, just before I took a trip to the spot under his ear. I'd wondered what it tasted like and now seemed like a good a time as any to find out. Once I kissed that spot, there were no more grunts of protests. He gripped my hips—to keep me there, to keep me still, to keep me from crawling any closer?

"Ava," he breathed, "is this my punishment? Death by torture?"

I smiled against his skin. "Maybe."

I moved under his chin to that little scar there and paused. He tensed a little, but held still for me and then moved his chin toward my mouth in such a minuscule way, I barely noticed. I kissed it just once, not knowing what this scar was, where it came from, but knowing that it meant something to him and I didn't want to go somewhere he wasn't ready to take me yet.

Then I slowly moved down to the hollow of his neck, where I learned he was the softest, and the side of his neck, where I learned he smelled the best.

He moaned and gripped my hips tighter.

"I'm happy to die a tortured man if that's what you want, but if not, then you've got to stop."

I lifted my head and he took my lips in an instant, switching places with me, pressing me to the wall and cupping my face with both hands as he devoured my lips. And then the torture really began when he left my lips, refusing to meet my eyes, and started to kiss every inch of skin from my lips from one ear to the other. His arm banded around my lower back and he crushed me to him. I could do nothing but hold on for the ride and remember.

To.

Breathe.

Which was embarrassingly loud in his ear, I was sure. Finally, I could stand the torture no more and dragged his mouth back to mine by gripping his collar, but could barely breathe at all at that point. He pulled back and laid his forehead against mine, his own breathing out of control. He didn't waste any time.

"I've been in agony, unable to do anything but think about you. I thought I was going to have to grovel, and do a lot of it. I was prepared to, wanted to, whatever it took to get us back to where we *were*. But then you shock the hell out of me by showing up here when I was on my way to come see you." I felt my eyebrows raise and my heartbeat speed up. He took my face in his hands as he smiled just a little to match mine. "When I was on my way to beg you to forgive me for being a jerk."

I shook my head. "No, I—"

"No," he soothed, his thumbs moving on my cheeks. "Let me take this one, Ava."

"Seth, wait. Listen." His brow bunched. "If you had grown up around our kind, other than the Watsons, and knew all our traditions and things, then I could expect you to know things and do them. But you didn't, and I keep expecting you to just…" I threw my hands at my sides a little in exasperation, but he still held my face, refusing to let me go, "know everything. You're so good at this and it makes me forget that you're…human."

He closed his eyes for a few seconds. "Barely."

"But you're my human." His eyes shot to mine. "And I wanted to come here to tell you that I'm sorry that I didn't fight hard enough." He opened his mouth to speak and I put my fingers over them. "You've fought so hard for me, from the very beginning. The very first thing I did was run away from you, and the very first thing *you did* was tell me you'd wait for me as long as it took." He sighed against my fingers, closing his eyes and then opening them. "I'm done, Seth." He stared. "I'm done not fighting for us. I'm done not trusting, I'm done not believing, I'm done with anything that's not right here." I tugged him closer, moving my fingers from his lips before I kissed them.

He tugged me to him hard. I opened up my mind, willing to hear anything he wanted me to. He was truly happy. Utterly contented. So relieved.

He *had* been coming to me, regardless of what his chief said. He would have been coming earlier and he probably would have been at my house before I even had a chance to leave to come see him if Harper hadn't shown up.

Discord with me hurt him so badly, he could barely breathe or think when we were apart.

We parted to breathe and I kept my hand on his neck because the hum of his skin was becoming so addicting.

"I wanted to ask you to marry me," he blurted.

My breath didn't exist anymore but I heard myself mumble, "W-what did you say?"

He smiled, the smug, cute bastard. "I was so blind-sided because I wasn't aware of the tradition. When my family gets married, they usually just do it, go to the justice of the peace or sometimes have a little backyard wedding. It's never a big deal and I never really thought about how much time had passed. I never thought that there was a Virtuoso tradition to hurry things along, but it does make sense." He chuckled. "I just...when I thought about the girl I was going to meet one day, there was always a proposal in the mix. And a big wedding. With how romantic and sappy our kind is, it's just kind of strange to me that they skip that part."

"I'm sorry," I whispered.

"No," he sighed. "I'm sorry, for how poorly I handled things. It was never about you. Never. I just felt like the one thing that I got to do and have control over was taken from me." He quirked his lips in embarrassment. "And then I made you feel like I didn't want to marry you. Of course I want to marry my significant. I was just...pouting I guess." He laughed, embarrassed. "And then when I tried to make it better by bringing you coffee—your mind is constantly running with these questions that have no business being there."

His face hardened a little, his version of trying to look stern, I assumed. "Like do I worry about you because of you or because of the bond? Like just now, was I upset because of you or because of Harper?" His head shook, his eyes hooded. "Nothing has changed." He took my hand and put it over his chest. "Your heart is in here and it's not going anywhere." I felt a whimper begin, but held it back. "I can feel your heartbeat, I can find you if you're hurt or scared and keep you safe, I can give you my touch to make sure you're *right as rain,*" he threw my words back at me and smiled, "but *none* of that can *make* me care about you, none of that can *make* me fall for you." His nose pressed to my cheek. "That's all you, little bird."

The whimper couldn't be contained this time and I gripped his neck to keep me on the ground, sure I was about to float away. He leaned back and used that torturous thumb to wipe away the tear from my cheek.

"I'm not going to stop fighting for you either."

I shook my head, letting my happy tears fall freely. "I know." I smiled through the tears that he wiped away again. "I'm sorry if I ever made you think I doubted it."

"You didn't."

We moved to the bed—his bed, he confirmed—and sat side by side, not ready for our make up night to be over yet. I leaned back against the wall, since there was no headboard, and he was close, turned toward me, his knee up on the bed touching my leg. He was mid-sentence talking about the jobs they have to do at the station, when he stopped.

"You have coffee on your shoes." He scowled as he got up and went to a sink in the corner and grabbed a hand towel. "That's my fault."

"I'll take some coffee on my shoe any day if you want to tackle me like that."

"Tackle, huh?" he said with a smirk as he came back. His walk seemed lighter, freer somehow. Like the weight of the world was somehow not on his shoulders for the moment.

"You won't get in trouble for being on break this long?"

He sat closer than before and laughed. "No. I'm not on break. We don't really have breaks. We have our chores we do and the rest of the time we just wait for a call." He pulled my leg up on his legs, making my breath stutter for a second. His eyes met mine and he smiled, his eyes twinkling with mischievous. "That was just code for *Don't disturb us.*"

After what just happened in this room, I felt a blush race up my neck. I couldn't help but smile along with it. "Well, then I'm glad they listened to you," I mumbled.

He chuckled lightly, looking at me so intently I ducked my head. I should have known he wouldn't let me get away with it. He put his finger under my chin and brought my face back up, letting his thumb rub across it a couple times. He smiled small, genuinely, as if he was happy looking at me in that moment a little bit more than others for some reason.

"You're blushing," he said softly, so softly I almost didn't hear. "It's pretty on you." I felt the blush get hotter. He swallowed and then said, "I can't remember ever making a girl blush before."

I laughed just once. "Now I know that's a lie," I said, and it actually sounded like one. I squinted feeling a weird sense of déjà vu, but not enough to stop me from checking on him. "Is everything okay?"

He smiled wider and nodded. "It is now. I know everything is going to be okay as long as you and I are."

"We're never going back to the way it was," I promised.

He shook his head. "No, never going back."

He leaned down and kissed my lips like it was normal, like it was an everyday thing, like I was his.

"You *are* mine," he growled softly against my lips.

Growled.

I've always heard about a Virtuoso man when it comes to his girl was not to be trifled with, and I've seen my father firsthand when it comes to my mother, but to have that protectiveness directed *at me* was a fierceness that melted every bone in my body on the spot.

He leaned back as if he hadn't heard my inner spiel. Though I knew he had when he smirked as he brought my boot to his lap and began wiping the spilled coffee splatters away.

He cleaned my boot spotless, and then pulled my other leg in his lap and repeated the move on the other boot. It was possibly the sweetest thing I've ever watched. He was so meticulous, getting every nook and seam. Then he squinted and ran his hand up my leg to my knee, causing a burst of breath to leave me. His head whipped up to mine.

"Sorry," he breathed. "You have coffee splattered on your tights, too. Let me…" I just sat there, open-mouthed, as he tried, like a total guy, but a sweet,

amazing, adorable guy, *to clean my tights* with a wet hand towel.

"It's okay. I'll throw them in the wash when I get home."

He tossed the towel aside and put his hands back on my legs, one near my knee, and the other on my calf. "These tights…"

I smiled and shook my head. I stage-whispered, "I have an entire drawer full of tights." He groaned dramatically. "Well, now I know what to use against you in a fight. I'll stop wearing tights." I looked at him with a little coy smile. "Or…maybe I'll wear them every day."

He laughed. "You wouldn't."

"I might."

"Man, I love this side of us." He sighed and moved his hand on my knee, making me shiver. Goosebumps ran down my arm. His eyes followed them and he looked so happy about them. He opened his mouth, but someone yelled upstairs.

"Breaks over, Romeo!"

"Okay!" He yelled back and chuckled, but sobered, his mouth falling into a soft smile. "This was one of my imprinting visions."

I blushed again. "It was?"

His smile was smug. "Not the *whole* thing. Just this—us, on my bed like this at the firehouse. None of my visions confirmed whether we'd be really together or not, we were just…together in them. So I didn't know what to think about it. But now, I kinda like them. I don't know what they mean or why we get the ones we get, but their mine. And now it's yours, too."

"Mine were the same, except for one." I smiled. "I should have known… and trusted. But I'm not telling you. You'll just have to wait 'til it happens and then I'll spill the beans."

He looked so amused. "Deal. And one more thing." He reached in the little drawer beside his bedside stand and tugged out a messy notepad, papers spewing out from each corner. "I guess I half-lied to you that day in my apartment," he hedged. "When I said that I would draw you one day." He opened the notepad to reveal page after page of *me*. Most were just my face. "I really love to draw you, your face. It's my favorite thing. I do a lot of drawing up here with all the spare time we have." I kept leafing through. There were some that weren't me, some landscapes, some of the same old man and dog that I'd seen before, some of the firehouse, but most were of me.

I looked up. "Wow."

He grimaced. "Your mind is pretty blank right now. Is that a good wow or a *yikes he's a psycho—*"

I reached across the papers, feeling some of them float to the floor as I pulled him to me. "I love it. I love them." I pulled back and looked at the ones still in my hands. "They're all so beautiful and different—each one. I love that you think about me when I'm not here."

"I don't have to draw you to think about you." He chuckled.

I leaned in and kissed him. "It's so beautiful. And it's sorta beautiful that you thought you had to hide it from me." I smiled, shaking my head a little.

He scratched his head. "I drew you the first time the first night we met." He waited for my reaction. "You didn't even like me then. I didn't want to freak you out, but you were so…beautiful. I just had to put you on paper."

I gave my head a weighing shake. "Okay, I may not have been so open to the idea, but seeing my face next to Harper's that day in your apartment wouldn't have been so bad." I poked his chest.

"I'll remember that for the next time we bond," he said sarcastically, a little embarrassed, guilty smile on his face. "And I'm sorry that you're going to be hurting in the morning. I'll have to work out something with the schedules. I'll…"

"Figure something out for us," I finished. "I know. I believe you."

"Ah, little bird," he sighed and cupped my cheek, "you're making it so easy."

He stood, picking up all the papers and tossing them back in the drawer before he pulled me up with him. I looked up at him so close to me. "What's that?"

He smiled and I guess he decided to keep his secret because he turned to go. Well, that wasn't flying with me. I didn't know why our minds didn't work the same, why he got to see my every thought and I had to fight to see the tiniest thing in his, but I looked at his retreating form and focused on the one thing I wanted.

The one thought I wanted to know.

He stopped dead still.

Just as he turned I began to feel him all around me, warm and luscious, he was everywhere. His buzz on my skin, his heartbeat in my chest.

He had a layer of things on the outside that were for me: protection, adoration, his care of my feelings.

His thoughts were all a jumble. Nothing was focused or in place or organized. It was almost as if he wasn't thinking of anything, or maybe thinking of too many things at once.

I closed my eyes and focused. I didn't want to know everything, all I wanted was the one thought. It wasn't fair. I could keep no secrets from him. I was an open book whether I wanted to be or not. I just wanted the one thing, the *one* thing. What was I making so easy for him? It was a simple thing and probably silly, but I couldn't leave without having done this with him at least once. We'd never explored each other's minds yet, never even talked about it much, but I just needed it.

And then out of the jumbled mess came one clear thought, one line. He had been thinking that I was making it so easy for him to fall for me, because he was definitely falling, one foot in front of the other.

I opened my eyes slowly to find him right in front of me, watching me as I searched his mind. If I expected him to be angry, I was sorely mistaken.

He looked so in awe, as blissed out as I felt. "We have to do that again. Soon," he said roughly.

The look he was giving me made my toes curl in my shoes. With my neck turning pink, I told him, "We've had so much going on that we've never really talked about—"

"Yeah," he agreed. "And I know that something's not right. I know you have to fight to hear me and feel what I feel." He swallowed. "We'll talk, I promise, and we'll make everything perfect." He lifted his hand to tug my lip from my teeth. I hadn't even realized I was biting my lip. He smiled and leaned down to press him lips against my ear. "But in the meantime, you can come inside my head anytime you want to. Because that felt amazing," he whispered huskily.

I nodded too fast. "Yeah. It did. I thought it was just me."

"No, little bird." He leaned back just enough to see my face, his nose almost touching mine. "Next time, I'll do the digging."

I could only gulp and hope he wasn't kidding.

"Seth?" I whispered in the dark, confused. I knew he was there. I sat up in my bed and scooted closer to him as he sat in my window sill. "Why are you sitting way over there?"

His sigh was tortured, guilty. "I don't know what to do. Why am I here, Ava?"

I reached him and touched his arm, but he pulled back. "What's wrong?"

"Why am I here?" he said harder. "We worked everything out. Everything is fine, more than fine, everything is great." I couldn't see his face in the darkness—only his back in the moonlight. I could imagine what it looked like though as he spoke. Hard, angry, sad, confused. Not happy to see me, but happy in his life with me. With her. And that was okay because she was me.

Gah, it was so confusing.

"Explain how an echoling works." I moved to sit on the bed across from him so he'd feel less threatened. He seemed to feel like she and I were separated, like we were two separate people, but I had a feeling that wasn't the case. And I had a feeling he was about to tell me that as well and blow his little theory of "the other Ava" out of the water.

He leaned back against the window. The cold window pane had to be freezing on his back, but maybe he felt he deserved it. "It's a dream, for all intents and purposes. I can only come to the person when they're sleeping. I can feel when people fall sleep. If I'm trying to reach a person, I just know if that person is asleep, even it's not at night, even if they've just dozed off for a minute."

"That sounds kinda neat."

"It's neat for a person that wouldn't abuse the gift. What good could come from this gift though? So far, I haven't found a use for it except to travel and sightsee. And this," he said softly. "But I don't know why this is still happening. I thought I was supposed to come here so you could help us stop fighting, but we're fine now."

"So what happens to the person when you…echoling them?"

He chuckled in the dark, despite his foul mood. "Nothing. They're asleep. This is your subconscious. And mine."

"So we're not really here, awake. This isn't really my body." It wasn't a question because I was getting it.

"No. Your body is right there." He pointed at the bed behind me. "Safe and sound."

"Could you hurt me in an echoling?" I asked, making sure it was a strong voice.

"I could. Anything that happens to you in an echoling will carry over to the real you. That's why it can be dangerous. That's why I never wanted my family to know I was one," he said angrily, more angry than usual. I wondered why that was. I wondered what had happened to make him so. I thought he was happy? "My uncle…he did awful things as one from what I heard."

"So…if I'm here asleep," I patted the bed behind me, "and this is my subconscious, then how can I be two different people?" I asked quietly. "I'm me. This version of me just doesn't remember everything yet. And the other version of me doesn't remember everything yet either."

"Ave," he said, tiredly. I got it then. He was tired.

"Why aren't you sleeping?" I rushed before he could say anything else.

"I'm working. And…there's some issues with my job and not getting to Ava…*you* on time in the morning. It's a damn mess," he growled and put his head in his hands.

I couldn't help it. I went to the floor in front of him and put my hands on his forearms. He looked up and started to move away, but stopped.

"You're still my significant, Seth. You said I'm in that bed and this is my subconscious. It's still me," I said, feeling tears gathering, not knowing if he could see them in the dark room or not.

He gathered me to his chest in between his knees and sighed in my hair. "I don't know why this is happening."

"I wish I could help you."

He laughed once and squeezed me. "I told you once, but you don't remember, that just being here *is* helping me."

I sighed all the way into my stomach. He hadn't said "the other you."

"I'm glad you're here, I really am, but if you didn't want to come here, why did you?" I said very carefully.

"It's not that I didn't want to." He leaned back and I could make out his face just a little this close. "I want you to remember. I was sitting on my bed, thinking about what I was going to do about the withdrawals, thinking about sneaking out to come see you, when I felt you fall asleep. But I thought since we'd already taken care of everything that I wouldn't feel the pull anymore. I tried to ignore it, but when I drifted off, I ended up here anyway."

"Maybe," I hedged, but closed my mouth.

"What?"

"Never mind. I don't know anything about echolings."

"Ava, you're the smartest girl I know. You know me and you know the world we live in. There's no one else I would trust to give me advice about this. Tell me."

I stared, dumfounded.

"Am I a good kisser?"

His smile was slow and a little smug if you asked me. "Ava—"

"I might not remember anyway, I just want to know for right now."

"You'll remember," he promised. "One day."

"Then tell me so I'll know for sure."

He breathed out. "Breathtaking."

I absorbed that. If I ever wanted to be described in one word, I thought that taking someone's breath was a pretty good daggum description.

"Okay," I moved along, "well, what if what's going on is something else we need to work out? What if you're here because of something that hasn't happened yet and maybe there's a reason for it?"

"We're moving on from kissing, just like that?" He had a little smile.

"I got what I wanted," I quipped.

He laughed softly. "Uh...I don't know. I've never had this happen before. I've gone in people's minds before more than once, but never had the pull before to keep going back. I've never had a pull before at all."

"Well, it *is* an ability. And we have them for a reason." He sat up a little straighter. "There has to be a reason and purpose for this to be happening the way it is and to us, with me."

"No, Ava," he groaned. "I don't even want to think about that."

"It has to be true. Have you done any more digging with your family?"

"I think I burned that bridge completely. Harper came and tried to get me to break my bond with you. Said that I had been promised to her since she was a teenager and all this bull, and I was never supposed to bond with someone else. That I messed everything up. They had been planning on forcing the imprint on me with Harper in a few months when I bonded with you." I groaned painfully, listening to it all. "Sorry," he said and cupped my jaw, bringing my face back up. "She said I wouldn't even miss you when it was done if I would do it and get it done," he whispered and laughed without humor. "They have no idea about love. It's all chemicals and blood to them, just so they can ascend and get their power." I sucked in a small breath, though I hadn't meant to. Love… He hadn't said anything about love since that day. He smiled a little. He let his hand fall to his leg where he took my hand. His thumb caused me serious heart palpitations. "I haven't even see anyone in the family but my mom in days."

"Have I met anyone?"

"You met Harper." I felt my eyebrows raise. "It wasn't on purpose."

"What about your mom and dad?"

"Uh…" He looked down debating, looking uncomfortable. "I don't know if that would be a good idea. My father is hardcore Watson. He's the one who put me in the care of my uncle to train me along with the others for the day that we'd one day," he used quotation marks with his free hand, "*get their revenge.*"

"I'm sorry." And I was.

"I would say I'd figure this out for us, but you'll just make fun of me for it later." He smiled.

"There's an inside joke in there somewhere, isn't there?"

"Yeah." He sighed.

"Well, then *I'll* figure this out for us. There has to be a reason that you need my subconscious and you keep being pulled back here."

"The summit is in a couple days," he muttered, distracted. "I've never been more terrified of a bunch of stuffy people and a pile of pretty bricks before in my life."

"I'll be there with you."

He looked in my eyes. "Yes, you will. Thank you. Thank you for always being there for me," he chuckled once, "even when you're asleep."

"Of course." I swallowed and thought. "And maybe…maybe you can try to get back in with your family before the summit gets here, before the council arrives."

"I'm sure Harper has run me up the river by now. It'll never work."

"You can tell them that we're fighting, that Daddy is trying to get you to be a spy or something. They'll believe that."

He laughed under his breath. "I was a little surprised he didn't ask actually."

"No. He'd never."

"But he is sending some of your people out to scout or something since we know that my family doesn't really trust me anymore."

"Well, I think it would be worth a shot. I'm sure you'd like to see your Mom."

His lips twisted. "My family isn't like yours. They don't... We don't call each other all the time. We don't stop by just for fun. They only ever talk about business, and that business is revenge. My parents have never said 'I love you' or anything like that." I gasped a little. "No, it's fine," he soothed. "I know I'm not their real son—"

"Seth," I scolded, "that shouldn't matter. If they adopted you and you call them 'Mom' and 'Dad' then they are your parents." He looked down as his thumb moved over my knuckles. I loved him doing that and could have just waited, letting him continue to do it, but my significant body needed to soothe him instead of being soothe. I reached up and took his face in my cool hands, loving the feel of his scratchy jaw on my palms. "It doesn't even matter anymore. Whether or not they are your family is now your decision, not theirs. But you are *my* family. And you have a big family now that wants you, no strings, no ultimatums, just *wants you*. Don't ever feel like you don't belong again, because you belong to me."

He swallowed loudly before his lips parted with a harsh breath. I saw his mouth begin to break with a smile before he laid his head to mine and put his arms back around me.

"Okay, little bird, you've got a deal. I'll put our little plan into action, see if anything pans out, and report back to you."

"Be careful." I looked up at him, feeling a smidge of apprehensive. "Promise?"

"Don't worry." He smiled a secret smile. "I won't be a hero, just for today."

The next morning, I woke early and took the firemen coffee and donuts.

It was a nice ploy that they all saw through, but it didn't matter when I was in withdrawals this badly. Watching Seth take the last box of donuts from my hands, toss it unceremoniously on the table, and tell the guys he'd be back in a few minutes, but take my sleeve instead of my hand was confusing. But it wasn't confusing any longer when we reached my car and he pulled me to the trunk and finally reached for my face.

The explosive groan that came from us both as our skin connected would never have been explained away as normal. As it was, we could barely catch our breath as we hung on to each other and let the aches drain away.

"I am mourning the loss of those tights, but I am glad that you're warm today in these jeans. Which you still somehow manage to make look as sinful as those tights. But warmer."

I shook my head. "Tights *are* warm."

He shook his head, not believing me. Then he stood a little straighter and switched gears. "I was going to sneak out last night to come see you, but there was a call. And if I had been gone when the call came in… I barely slept last night. Just sat up thinking what I could do. Someone was always up. At one point, I thought it was worth it to just let it all go and go to you, but if I lose this, then what do I have to take care of you?" He shook his head. "I bet your father is pissed about this, isn't he?"

I looked away. Daddy was, in fact, pretty ticked that Seth couldn't find a way to change shifts or something. He didn't understand how fire stations worked. And if that was the case then quit, Dad had said. I rolled my eyes. Not all families had money like the Jacobsons. He couldn't just quit. He had rent, he had bills. Daddy just grunted and asked was this going to be my life? Was I going to be in withdrawals for half of my lifespan because Seth wanted to be a fireman?

Seth sighed. "I'll figure this—"

"I know."

He squinted thoughtfully. "I thought a lot about this last night. I do have a business degree."

"Seth, you told me you've wanted to be a fireman since you were eight. You said you got the degree and knew you were never going to use it."

His hands still held my face, his thumbs swept across my cheeks. "But we can't live like this." His sigh was harsh. "Just the thought of your being in withdrawals again in the morning because of this, because of me, makes me physically ill."

And he did look ill. His eyes were tired and had sleep-deprived bags under them, and his face was hard as stone.

I had a thought. "The summit's in a few days."

"But this will all start over again when it's done."

"We'll have some time to think. We'll figure this out, Ava," I said, using a deep tone to pretend to be his voice. "I'll figure this out for us."

He laughed once, a small smile barely cracking. "I do not sound like that."

"Yes, you do. And it's adorable." I put my arms around his neck and moved up on my tiptoes. His legs were already spread to give me room and make him shorter. As soon as my lips touched his, Rodney opened the door and hopped out.

"No." He pointed. "I sat through the goo, goo, ga, ga crap and the *I'll figure this out for us*," he mocked, twitched his fingers in the air. "But I will not sit through making out. Nuhuh. Not happening." He crossed his arms and stared for a few seconds and then nodded. "Later, Seth."

"Later," Seth said, bewildered as Rodney hopped back in the car with a slam of the door. "Your brother hates me."

"No, he doesn't. Rodney is so focused on his music and games and the internet. Don't mind him. He's the reason that I... Rodney told me that it was you that had sent him the text and everything that night at the house."

Seth sighed.

Ah, that night.

I smiled. Maybe since we opened up the floodgates, it would stay. I loved his voice in my mind.

He looked up.

I miss you already.

I couldn't have felt more safe or warm or happy than in that moment.

I miss you, too. Be careful today. No awards. Don't be a hero.

He smiled. *Okay. Just for today.*

His fingers dug into the hair behind my ear and pulled me to him as he took my lips. I twisted my fingers into the first thing they could grab and held on. So I wound up fisting his shirtfront with both hands. His smooth, warm lips carried me away for just a minute to where I needed to be.

Home.

But it didn't last nearly long enough.

"Oh, come on!" Rodney said and slammed his palm on the inside of the top of the car. "We talked about this, guys!"

We laughed as we broke apart. He pulled me to him for one more deep pull of my mouth and then took me to my door and opened it for me. "Uh," he said awkwardly as he leaned over the top of the open door, "I'm not supposed to leave when I'm on duty, so."

"I can stop by again later. Want me to bring food? That seems to keep them busy?" I looked at the firemen still chowing down on the donuts. They saw us looking and waved. Trouble blew me a kiss. I laughed and Seth waved him off.

"They never turn away a meal, but I don't want you to feel like you have to. They love to cook around here. We do a lot of cooking."

"Is that right?" Intriguing.

"Yeah," he said and smiled. "In fact, just come and the boys and I will whip up a batch up of five alarm chili."

My eyebrows rose and I laughed loudly. "That sounds dangerous."

"You have no idea."

"It's okay for me to keep stopping by? You won't get in trouble?"

"The chief is pretty lax about visitors since most of the guys are married. We usually have wives in and out, bringing food and stuff." He realized what he said and smirked, but said nothing else.

Knowing it was time for me to go, he slowly leaned over the top of the open car door and kissed me. When I heard the whoops start across the street, I started to pull back, but Seth grabbed my arm.

"Pay them no mind, sweetheart." He swung his arm at them and that just made them even worse as he came back in for another one, this time, making sure to touch my arms with his. The tingles, the calm, the warmth that spread—he was filling me up with his touch, one for the road. I was grateful. It was going to be a long day.

When he pulled back, he started to say something, but a loud bell started to go off. I looked and everybody jumped up from the table.

"Gotta go. Duty calls."

I nodded. "Go, go."

He pecked my cheek and ran across the street. I felt my first sense of real pride as I watched him put on his uniform. Big yellow, rubber looking pants with suspenders, boots, and a jacket. And then a helmet to top it off. It was far enough away and there were people in the way that I couldn't get a perfectly clear view, but it was enough to make my heart soar. And I also got my first sense of real fear.

He was going to a fire.

The truck tore out of the firehouse and as they passed, I heard him.

This is what I do, sweetheart. Everything is fine. It's just a small kitchen fire. I'll let you know when it's all done. Go fill that pretty head with all sorts of knowledge.

Please be careful.

I promise.

I'll see you later. I. Will. See. You. Later.

Be here at five and I'll show you what real cooking is.

"Ave," Rodney said softly as I stood and stared at the building. "I get that you're having an existential crisis of sorts right now, but can you do it while I'm doing calculus? I'm late."

"Oh, yeah." I slid in and buckled. "Sorry. Um."

"I get it. You knew he was a fireman, but you've never seen him actually have to *be a fireman* before. It sucks."

I looked at him with a grimace. "You are weirdly perceptive. Like…you're a freak."

He laughed. "Right on."

I shook my head as I breathed. I dropped him off and went to classes, late myself. Within an hour and a half of me trying to stay calm, Seth was in my head telling me that all was well, and we spent the whole class talking. This could be a problem, I thought to myself, as the professor got all big-headed when he thought I was thoroughly enjoying his lecture—given by my huge smile and his smirk as he stood straighter and the fact that he kept nodding at me in approval.

No, Professor Grimes. This smile is not for you.

I went and had dinner at the fire station that night with the funniest group of guys I'd ever been around. Granted, I'd never been around that many 'groups of guys', but I'd still say they had the market cornered. The guys were making jokes that Seth was a new man since I came around, that he wasn't so broody so I had to stick around. Seth and I just smiled at each other and took their ribbing.

When it was time to go, it sucked, but it was the last night. He would be

back on the off schedule tomorrow and then we'd be going to the summit.

And things would be going back to normal.

I sat up in bed, Seth's heartbeat pounding in my chest so hard I could barely breathe. Something was wrong. My breaths struggled to keep up. I jumped from the bed and threw on the first clothes I could find. Some jeans and Chucks with my jacket. I didn't even think as I ran down the stairs. I vaguely heard my Dad yelling as I jumped in my car, but I hadn't grabbed my purse or phone, just the keys from the countertop.

And I wasn't stopping.

I didn't know what was wrong, I just knew that *something was* wrong. Seth's heartbeat was beating a rhythm in my chest I'd never felt before and it was painful and I was the most scared I'd ever been. And I didn't even know what was going on.

My car drove as if it knew where it was going, my hands turned the wheel as if they knew just where to go. Before I knew it, minutes had passed and I was turning onto a street and sirens could be heard.

"Oh, God, no," I begged.

Then another street and I saw the blazing fire, the huge building that was taking the beating of a lifetime by it, and the fire trucks surrounding it.

And I knew my significant was inside.

I parked across the street, got out, and ran around the people who were standing there looking up at it. They probably lived there. They were probably watching their home go up in smoke. But me? I was feeling my soulmate's heart in my chest and something wasn't right. He'd already been in at least one fire that I knew about and everything was fine. His heart hadn't done this. Something was wrong.

As I looked up at the blazing building, I'd never been more scared in my life of losing something.

Of losing someone.

It was chaos everywhere. Firemen running, yelling, water being sprayed everywhere. Windows breaking. People screaming.

I crossed the sidewalk and heard my name. I looked around until I saw the chief. He had the most confused look on his face.

"What the hell are you doing here?" he yelled over the noise of the trucks and sirens and water being pumped. "Ava?"

"Where's Seth?"

"What are you—"

"Where's Seth?"

He sighed. "Inside with a unit."

My lip quivered, though I told it not to. "He's not okay, is he?"

He looked at the building. "They're sending another truck from another station. But they're twenty minutes out. Seth's unit went in and we lost radio contact. There's no one else to send in until the others get here."

I stared at him, feeling my significant's heartbeat banging away in my chest, scared, hurt maybe, I didn't know, but I didn't say another word. I walked down the sidewalk away from him.

"Ava," he called over the noise, but I kept walking.

I was about to do the dumbest and smartest thing I knew of. And my Champion was going to be so pissed because it could expose us to the humans, but what was I supposed to do? Let my significant die?

I went to the back of the fire truck and waited until I didn't see anyone and then I walked as close to the shrubs in the dark as I could until I reached the side of the building. I took one deep breath, but that's all I got. If Seth couldn't breathe then I wasn't going to either.

I tapped on the handle and felt that it wasn't hot, so I opened it and made my way inside the building, my significant leading me to him without even knowing it.

I went up a flight before the smoke came, two more flights of stairs before I knew I'd reached the floor they were on. Or *he* was on, anyway. I heard the blaze burning, in the distance. The smoke was everywhere. I had pulled my shirt collar over my nose to try to minimize the coughing, but it was starting.

I walked towards the fire because that's where Seth was. I never thought I'd ever do that, but I felt a strange sense of purpose and calm come over me. I needed to do this. I was going to save him or die trying. There was no alternative. There was no sense in freaking out about it. My heart beat like crazy next to Seth's. Yeah, I was scared, but I was scared with purpose.

The ceiling in the hall was ablaze and I crawled to avoid the heat until I passed it. I was getting closer to him. I could feel it.

I went to the end of the dark hall and met another stairwell and another hall. It was dark all except the orange glow from the fire, making it eerie. I felt like he was on this floor. It was crazy and magical how my insides and guts just *knew*. So I crawled all the way to the end of that hall, feeling the fire burning hotter. The stairwell across the hall was completely enveloped. When I turned the corner, my world stopped when I met blue eyes that were as surprised as they were angry to see me.

"Ava?" I started to stand. "Stay down! Get down!" he ordered with an outstretched hand.

I crawled closer. He was across an expanse—a huge hole that had burned out or had given out, one of the two. Either way, they were at the dead end of the hallway and nowhere to go, and the hole was too big to cross or jump. I looked down and saw that at least one of them had already tried to make the jump across, unsuccessfully, as I saw his twisted body at the bottom. I felt my chest convulse with a sob.

"Hey," Seth called and beckoned my gaze to his. "Don't look at that. Look right here." Then he steeled himself. "What the hell are you doing here, Ava?"

I gave him a sad smile. "You know exactly what I'm doing here."

He closed his eyes, looking so agonized in that moment. He cursed and looked at me. "Get out of here."

"I am not leaving."

He shook his head. "Ava Jacobson, you get the hell out of here!" he yelled. He tried to look mean, to look fierce, to look like he was angry, but all I saw was that he was scared for me. "Go! Turn around and go back the way you came as fast as you can."

I said calmly, "I am not leaving. You know why I'm here. Tell me what to do."

"Ava," he growled and gripped his face, his helmet was long gone. The other two had their helmets on. I didn't know why, but right then it didn't matter. I saw that we weren't alone. There were two other firemen behind him, Trouble being one of them. They watched us in wonder. Wondering what in the hell I was doing there, but wanting to live more than ask questions in that moment. He looked at me once more and tried a different tactic. "Please. Please, sweetheart, go. Just—"

"Seth, what do I do?" He stared, helplessly worried about me. "Tell me what to do, baby."

He groaned and grabbed his hair. When he looked back at me, I knew he'd given in. "Find something to go across the expanse. At least nine feet." I nodded. "Be careful, Ava," he ordered and I could see his fist shaking.

I turned to crawl away.

"Ava!" I looked back. "I love you." His eyes were fierce.

He said it out loud. He could have just said it in my mind, but he chose to say it out loud.

"I love you," I said quickly and didn't wait to see what his face would look like. I didn't have time to be girl and process this.

I crawled as fast as my knees would go. I was sweating in my coat, but I figured it might come in handy for some protection later if I needed it so I kept it on. I started opening any doors that would open and the ones that wouldn't, I bypassed for now. This was an apartment building. This place had to have a janitor's closet or something.

When I reached the end of the hall near the hallway I did find a janitor's closet, but it was locked. I just knew there was something in there to help them. Had to be. I banged my fist on my head. Think, think, think. I looked down one hall and then the other. There was the old wooden staircase…

I got up on my feet and ran, ducked low. Near the staircase the fire hadn't reached yet, but it was coming. When I got there, I kicked one of the round, solid wood slats out and ran back to the janitor's closet with it. Crouched down as low as I could go, and still get a good swing, I banged the doorknob over and over and over again. Over and over and over. I began to cry. It wasn't working.

I rammed it harder and harder and harder.

Sweetheart, it's okay. Go.

I am not leaving you here! You're crazy if you think I'm leaving you here!

I kept ramming that doorknob, feeling my guts tighten, my teeth grating with every ram, my bones and muscles hurt with every move.

Go, Ava. I want you to go. It was soft, like a plea. *Please. I wish I could have stopped my heartbeat from calling you here somehow. I wish that more than anything. I prayed that it wouldn't. I prayed so hard. Please go.*

Seth, I love you, I hit it harder than I thought I was capable of, *but shut up.*

I raised the slat up and had had enough of the stupid doorknob. I yelled when I brought it down. And it felt different when it came down this time. I looked up and actually laughed at the hole in the door that was left behind. I wrenched it open and looked inside.

A ladder was against the back wall. I sobbed as I grabbed it and dragged it out with me. I ducked low all the way down the hall, going as fast as I could. The fire was spreading. I could feel it was hotter than it was before. When I turned the corner to Seth, he grabbed his head. The entire ceiling was engulfed now. I went faster.

When I reached the hole, I looked to him for guidance. The others lined up next to Seth and got ready to catch the ladder.

"All right, sweetheart," he soothed, still on his knees, as were they all, "we've only got one shot at this. We need to get the end across to us. So, sit on your end, and extend it as far as it will go by slowing pushing it out towards us, okay?"

I nodded and did what he said. I got up on my knees on the end of it near the end of the hole and started extending it. Please reach, please reach, please reach, I prayed.

Seth kept looking between me and the ladder. When he saw that the ladder was going to reach him, he shook his head just as the other two guys starting laughing and thanking God.

"You're an angel," Trouble said as Seth reached out and took his end of the ladder.

Seth looked at me and said, "She's in trouble."

"No," he said and glared at him. "Leave her alone. Trouble's my name. Now go."

"No, you go. I was the lead. I'm last."

"No—"

"Landon, go," he growled. "Get your rookie butt across that ladder. You're wasting time."

He sighed, but went, crawling over Seth's hands to the ladder rungs over the hole. He went slow but steady. Seth's eyes stayed on mine the entire time over Trouble's head. I just wanted him there, I just wanted to touch him, I just wanted him safe. It felt like the blink of an eye and Trouble was right in front of me, crawling over my hands. I held the ladder so tight, so scared to let go.

"Let me, darlin'," he urged and I scooted out of the way. He took over the ladder holding and yelled, "Let's go!"

The next guy came over. I didn't know his name. I knelt and leaned my back on the wall so I could see. My heart was beating so fast. I tried to calm down so Seth could focus. The other guy made it over and scooted out of the way behind us. I was physically ill with worry as I watched Seth climb on that ladder with one knee. He looked at me before he moved any further.

Everything is fine, sweetheart. I've done this a million times.

I huffed. *Really? This?*

He had the audacity to smile. *Maybe not this exactly.*

Just make it across that ladder.

Seth took a breath, looking up and down once before he started across. I couldn't have torn my eyes away if I wanted to. When he'd made it about five crawls, the ladder shifted some because there was no one holding the other side. I thought my heart was going to burst as I watched him. My breath stopped. He couldn't look back, he had to trust his guys to tell him to keep going. That was all he could do anyway. A couple more crawls and it shifted again. I couldn't stop my whimper. I was helpless. Completely helpless. A few more crawls and he was grabbing Trouble's arm so they could pull him in.

I didn't believe it was real until he crawled straight over to me, soot on his face, his gear still on from the neck down, and kissed me so hard, right there on our knees against that wall. We both groaned loudly—so loudly. Not only were we in the grip of withdrawals, but we'd just been to hell and back—literally.

Then he pulled back and started to unzip my jacket in a frenzy. I wondered why. He tossed it aside before undoing his own. I got it then. "No. What about you?"

"I'm fine. Don't," he said harder when I went to protest. "Your jacket's flammable. You don't have anything on to protect you. You can at least have half of a protective suit."

I nodded and let him put it on me. He was raw. He was angry. He was scared.

When I looked down the smoke-filled hall I got it completely. This was far from over.

The two others were already down the hall, looking for the best way out. He cupped my face, bringing me around to look back at him.

"Stay with me, *right* with me. Don't look at the fire. Don't even think about it. It's going to be worse than when you came in. We may have to fight our way out, but we *are* getting out."

I nodded since he seemed to be waiting for me. I couldn't stop shaking. I was scared—for him, for me, for us, for the guys down there, for how we were going to explain how I just showed up here and knew where to find him, and I was scared of us not making it out at all and it all being in vain.

He shook his head and kissed my forehead quickly. "We are getting out of here, little bird. Let's go. Stay low."

I knew he wanted to sit there and soothe me, but couldn't. I just wanted to get out of there.

I followed right behind him and we reached the others quickly. For a second, I thought they might have been leaving, but they were just scoping which way to go. They still had their masks on, so their voices were a little muffled.

"Which way did you come?"

"Around two more corners," I told them. "And then down three flights, out the side door."

His eyebrows rose. "You actually remember exactly? You weren't just…" He looked at Seth and back to me, "looking for us?"

"Landon, let's go," Seth ordered. "We'll see if that way is still clear."

"This stairwell doesn't look too bad," the other guy nodded his head toward a door and said. "I think we should go for the quickest route to us."

Seth debated, but I didn't care. It wasn't about picking that guy over me. "Doesn't matter. I just want out. Go." I pushed his back.

"Lead the way, rookie," he ordered and we followed. He opened the door and we all stood and started to descend the steps.

I thought we were home free until we reached the next floor and they went to open the door.

"Wait!" Trouble told the other guy. "Rookie, come on." He pointed to the smoke coming out of the bottom of the door and the orange glow adding to it.

"You're a rookie, too, Landon," he grumbled back and pushed him as he turned around and went the other way.

"But I'm not making rookie mistakes."

"All right, you two," Seth groaned and he put me in front of him, the guys making a wall of protection around me as we trekked back up the stairs.

It was hard to see in the dark halls. The only light in the place was the orange glow from the fire above or the emergency lights that were few and far between that barely worked in the old building. Landon led, his small hatchet in his hand. The smoke was getting worse. I tried not to cough. I didn't want Seth to worry about me, but I was beginning to not to be able to hold back and hide it anymore. And he couldn't either. The other guys had helmets on. I didn't know why he had taken his off or where, but he was starting to cough a little, too.

I pulled my shirt over my nose and mouth again and tried to not think about it.

When we got back up to the floor and turned the corner, the entire ceiling was ablaze. I gasped and leaned back into Seth. I shook my head. Now that I didn't have a purpose driving me, I was just scared.

He pressed his mouth to my ear. "I'm not going to let anything happen to you." He moved me until I was behind him. "Look in my eyes." I could feel the heat around us, see the orange haze all around him, but the blue of his eyes took precedence over everything else. I took a deep breath. "That's right. I'll need my hands, so I want you to hold on to my suspenders and don't let go for anything. You just look at my back and don't worry about what's going on around us. We'll get out here. Ava," he said harder. I nodded, figuring that was what he wanted.

"We'll get out of here," I repeated. "I'll hold your suspenders. I won't look." I coughed, my eyes burning. I refused to say 'I love you' again, because then it would just feel like a goodbye.

"You're daggum right it's not goodbye. Let's go, little bird. Hold on tight and stay low." He swiped my chin with his thumb, feeling bad that he was being so gruff with me, but not having a choice in the moment.

What he didn't understand was that fireman Seth, commanding, demanding, gruff and rough, Seth? He was so sexy. Knowing that this side of Seth existed and could come to the surface if the situation called for it was pretty hot.

Though my brain was scrambled and I could barely think, even I could comprehend that right now—I was going to have fun with fireman Seth in the future.

I took hold of his suspenders like he told me to and looked at his back.

Just keep your eyes on my back. I'll guide us out of here.

I did as he said and could see and feel the orange and black and red in my peripheral. The hall was so dark now except for the fire; the emergency lights completely gone.

I could hear them yelling about something ahead, but couldn't make it out as we turned the last corner. We saw the water pouring in from the ceiling near the end of the hall and heard a loud banging.

"They're coming in!" Trouble yelled. "Back-up must be here finally."

"Let's go!" Seth said and tugged me to follow him down the stairs. Trouble came up the rear and the other guy went ahead. In the stairwell, the creaking and banging and loud noises were awful sounding. I covered my ears, but couldn't hang on to Seth, so I just dealt with it.

"Stairs are coming down!" the other guy yelled from the bottom. "Go, go!"

Seth picked up the pace, reaching for my hand. When we reached the second floor, the fire was engulfing the walkway to get to the other side. It was a really old building. The steps were wooden, like tinder on a bonfire.

"Damn," Seth growled. We watched as Trouble jumped and ran through it.

"Let's go," he said and Seth apparently knew what he meant. He looked at me and I got it. We had to go through it, too. I gritted my teeth and tried to be brave. I'd made it this far.

He cupped my cheek. *You* are *brave. I just need you to keep being brave for a few more minutes.* I nodded. *We're going to jump on three, okay?* I nodded again. *One, two...*

I didn't think. When I felt him tug me, I just closed my eyes, gripped his arm, ran and jumped with everything I had. When I jumped, he lifted my feet way off the floor, but I didn't think about it. I didn't look back. I just looked at Seth to make sure he was okay once we landed. Seeing that he was, I looked at his face to see what was next.

"Let's go!" the guy yelled from the next floor. "All clear."

We started to go and meet him, but the smoke was awful. Seth pulled the jacket I was wearing over my head and face and helped me walk down the last flight of stairs. When I hear the door slam open, I knew it was over.

I pulled the jacket off my head as we emerged from the door, coughing and looking a mess I'm sure, and accepted Seth's arms around me as he lifted my feet from the ground, pressing his face into my neck. He walked with us and pushed through the shrubs to an empty parking lot on the other side so no one would walk by and see us.

Trouble and the other guy followed us and took their helmets and masks off and just stood there.

I glanced over at them and the one I didn't know the name of was looking at me funny. When he saw me catch him looking, he looked away. I got it. I was a freak now. I'm sure they were grateful to be alive, but now that it was over, the thrill was no longer in their veins and they wanted answers.

I leaned back a little and had one thought and one thought only.

What the hell do we do now?

CHAPTER THIRTEEN

I'll think of something. I'll tell them I texted you and told you where to come.

My Seth. Already trying to shoulder the blame. He wasn't going to be able to save me on this one.

They saw how angry you were about me coming. They knew you didn't send for me.

I wasn't angry; I was worried.

I didn't argue with him—though he had definitely been angry. He put me down, but continued to look at me, holding me against him. I knew better than to try to move away, not that I wanted to, but this was serious. We almost died and our significant bodies were not going to let us be apart for a while.

But as I thought that, he was thinking that I needed to get away from there.

His grip became painfully tight on me as he felt my heart spike. "Seth," I begged.

Right now, it's only these two. I'll...figure something out with them.

I saw your chief. Or he saw me. He told me you were inside and had lost radio contact.

Ava... He sighed and laid his forehead to mine. He lifted his head. *Doesn't matter. I'll handle it. I know it hurts to leave, but you need to go. He can't know you went in there. It'll be bad for you. I have to protect you—*

"Uh…Seth, buddy."

We both looked at Trouble and seemed to remember they were there. Seth moved to put himself in front of me a little and I felt my breaths rushing in and out.

"Guys," he began, but they didn't let him get very far.

"You're talking to her, aren't you?" the one I didn't know asked. "It seemed so strange when you were on the ladder. You were just staring at each other, not moving, and then you smiled, and just now, you were doing it again. If you had told me four hours ago that this was possible, I would have told you to you've been kicked in the head too many times. But now…I'm alive because of whatever this is." He flung his hand at me.

Seth rubbed his head. "Gibson, listen."

"She came here to a fire that she had no idea where she was going and had no business being at. She came inside, went up three flights of stairs, and found you. She went *right to you*." He stared Seth down. "How are you really going to explain that away, Seth?" I couldn't see his face, but I could feel him shaking. Gibson came towards us and Seth moved to block him. "Come on, man. Move," he said softly.

Seth waited long seconds before scooting over a smidge, but he didn't relinquish my hand. When Gibson put his arms around me, I gasped a little. "My wife and three month old daughter thank you for coming tonight. That was the stupidest and bravest thing I've ever seen." He leaned back. "I don't know why you found us and I don't want to know. Though I have a feeling you wouldn't tell us anyway."

I felt my eyes watering. I didn't know what to say. I had never expected anyone to be with Seth when I got there. I hadn't expected consequences, though it wouldn't have changed the outcome. If Seth hadn't bonded yet, they would have all died in that fire tonight. I groaned and closed my eyes, hanging my head. Gibson's daughter would have been fatherless.

Seth's fingers rubbed over mine and I looked up.

You did good.

You were pissed at me not twenty minutes ago.

I was scared for you.

I 'oomphed' when Trouble slammed into me with a hug, lifting me from the pavement and taking my hand from Seth's.

"Hey," he growled and then sighed when he saw it was a lost cause as Trouble spun me around.

"Girl, I don't know what he did to deserve you, but daggum…dump this guy already and just marry me."

"All right," Seth said roughly. Clearly it was too much for our bodies to handle and what we'd just been through. I patted Trouble's shoulder and smiled.

"Sorry. I'm as taken as they come."

"I can see that. Thank you for what you did. I don't know if you're a fairy or a siren—"

"For all that's holy, Landon!" Seth shouted.

The guy had to go that last step, the last little bit and just say the words that brought us over the line. He couldn't just let the myth lie there. I sighed and gave him a small smile. "You're welcome."

I pulled from his grasp and went back to Seth, who was already reaching for me. He pulled me back into his chest and rubbed his hand down my hair, trying to think of what to do next.

I've got to get you out of here.

"Please, not without you," I murmured.

"What?" Trouble asked and then squinted. "Oh. Wow, you two are really *are* going at it, aren't you?"

"Guys, look…" Seth gulped. "I…"

"She saved our life," Gibson reasoned. "End of discussion. For today anyway." He looked at Trouble for confirmation and he nodded emphatically, winking at me in that way that was going to get him a black eye one day. He patted Seth on the shoulder. "Get her out of here before anyone sees her like that. We'll stall for a few minutes."

Seth nodded gratefully. "Thanks, man." They walked back through the shrubs and then he looked back at me. "Ava, there's something I haven't told you."

I blinked. "And this is a good time for a confession?"

"No, it's not, but I have no choice. I wanted to wait." He swallowed. "But it's going to get you home safely so." He closed his eyes. I waited. He didn't say anything. After about two minutes, he opened his eyes and cupped my face, kissing my lips softly. "Rodney will be here in a few minutes to get you."

I just stared. "How—"

"I'll explain everything, I promise, but right this second, I just need to hold you before he takes you from me."

I shook my head. "No. Come with me."

"I can't, sweetheart," he said and crushed me to his chest, fitting me under his chin. "There was an incident. People got hurt, a fireman was…killed. The police will be here, if they aren't already, family will have to be notified. I can't leave no matter how much it hurts to put you in that car."

"I'm so sorry about your friend," I told him as softly as I knew how to soften the blow, though that was probably stupid. "I…"

"We told him he couldn't make it." He closed his eyes. "He said one of us had to try. I ordered him not to," his head shook and I cupped his neck, "but he had ran and leapt before I could stop him. He said he was the only one who wasn't attached to anyone in this world and so it had to be him. He said he had to do this for…" He stopped and licked his lip. "Do it for our families."

I felt the tears come. "What was his name?"

"John," he whispered.

"I'm so sorry." I felt helpless, wishing there was something I could do—

"You've done enough tonight. And you're helping me so much by just being here right now." He gulped and sighed as he closed his eyes again and tugged me closer. "When are you going to get that through that pretty head of yours?" he said quietly.

My arms wouldn't stop shaking. It wasn't that cold in his big jacket, but I just couldn't…stop…

"Your system overloaded with adrenaline to get you through that. Now that it's all over, you're shaking because you're body doesn't know what else to do with it."

I reached up on my tiptoes and wrapped my arms around his neck. "I'm sorry if I messed everything up for you." I looked into his blue eyes and felt it all come crashing down on me, a wave of misery and worry and happiness and relief. My face crumpled, my chest ached as the sob tore from me. "Your heartbeat—"

"Shhh," he soothed and sat in the grass on the edge of the parking lot. He put his legs out in front of him and pulled me down, turning me to face him. I automatically put one leg on each side of him and let him tug me to him as close as we could get. He pressed me to his chest and put my face against his neck, one of his hands ran from the small of my back to the top of my spine.

I sighed from my soul to my lungs at all the ways he was good at taking care of me. "First things, first," he murmured into the skin near my hairline. "My job isn't more important that you. Second." That hand kept soothing, working its way up and down my spine. Even though it wasn't touching my skin, it was a magic all its own. "I have never been more terrified in my entire life than when I saw you come around that corner." I lifted my head, ready to take more scolding. He cupped my face with both hands and brought me to him for one sweet kiss right in the center of my lips. "And I've never been more proud." I jolted. Proud? "And I've never been more honored and scared in the same moment." My chest shook. "I've never been happy and worried at the same time. I've never wanted to spank you and kiss you both." I smiled through my tears. "And I've never felt more that you are the one put on this earth just for me."

I tried to look down, but he wouldn't let me, bringing my face back up with his fingers. "You were angry."

"I was scared out of mind for you." His thumbs skimmed my cheeks. "My chest ached beyond anything I've ever felt." It was his imprint, whether he knew it or not. "If I could have gotten you to leave, I would have done anything."

"Don't you know that I felt the exact same thing?" I sniffed and felt a tremor in my chest. "If I couldn't have reached you—" A sob tore through me as I continued to shake.

"Okay, okay." He stopped that, feeling what it was doing to me. Finally getting that I felt just as much as he did. "But you did reach me. And you saved the lives of two rookies."

"Yeah," I sighed and sniffed again. "Two rookies who think I'm a siren."

He chuckled a little. "We'll come up with something to handle those two. Don't worry about them."

"They probably think I lured you in with my siren song and that's why you've..."

"What?" He grinned. "Fallen for you so quickly? Keep bringing you around? Maybe you are a siren. If that's what you are then I'm happy to be caught in your snare. As long as you keep me there."

"Very funny," I whispered.

He sobered. "You saved my life, sweetheart. Thank you," he whispered.

I didn't know what to say. "I'd do it all over again," I whispered in return.

His arms twitched a little and that's when I remembered he'd given me his jacket. Gah, how could I have not noticed that!

"Probably because we almost died."

"Put your arms in here to keep warm," I ignored him.

He smiled and made a little noise in the back of his throat. "That's one way to start a fire," he murmured, but followed my instructions as I opened my jacket for him.

His arms wrapped around me on the inside of the jacket, overlapping, bringing us so close, there was literally no space between us. We were pressed together everywhere and I wasn't the only one who was having trouble breathing. Our quick breaths puffed cold fog between us.

We stared at each other, letting the tension build, as his hands caressed and moved on me. He brought his thumb to my lips before letting his hand move up to my cheek as his fingertips grazed my flesh softly, his fingers writing love letters to my skin that no pen and paper could even begin to comprehend.

And then his hungry mouth touched mine. I pressed right back. I was still shaking. I didn't know how to stop, but I just took what he gave me and wrapped my arms around his shoulders to try to keep him warm. That wasn't the only reason, but it was the main one, I told myself.

Mostly.

At this angle, I was a little taller than him and I liked that immensely. I used the leverage, taking the sides of my jacket, making sure they were good and open wide around him, before letting my hand scrub the back of his head, nails and fingers. I opened my mouth wide, needing to get as much of him as possible.

He groaned into my mouth and I didn't think he'd ever kissed me this deeply. Or maybe I was kissing him this way. Either way, I just needed this. I needed to feel him alive and real and safe in my arms. I felt that my cheeks were still wet, or maybe it was new wetness. I didn't know. I was so raw I didn't know what to do with myself at this point. I just knew I needed Seth, that he was the cure for everything wrong in this moment in time.

He brought one of his hands up in the back of the jacket to my neck and ran it into my hair as far as he could reach. I felt my eyes roll a little before he released my neck and went back to hugging and tugging my torso and shirt.

When I couldn't breathe any longer, I kept going, but he pulled back, suspending my desperation. "I'm not going anywhere, Ave. We're safe, okay?"

I sighed, my eyes falling to a close and let him settle my desperate, restless body. He tucked me to his chest and we waited just like that until Dad's car pulled into the lot.

We got up and he opened the door for me. I knew leaving was going to be hard, but it was like my body literally didn't want to go. It was painful. He knew it; he felt the same. He kissed me once more and then physically set me inside on the seat.

He leaned inside. "Rodney, thanks man." Rodney nodded and they shared this look that I knew meant something. It had to do with how Rodney was here. I looked at Seth, but his eyes begged me to ask later. I nodded. "Crank up the heat, will ya?" he asked Rodney.

I started to take the jacket off.

"Keep it on. It's too cold."

"What are you going to say to explain why you don't have it?"

"Baby, it doesn't matter," he said sadly.

I got it. "Seth, no. You love this job."

"I love you more." He got down on his haunches beside the open car door. "You could have died today because you were coming to save me. I'll never be able to go into another burning building knowing that if something happened my heartbeat would call you to me. I was the biggest idiot for not realizing it in the first place."

I felt a tear slide down my hot cheek. "I hate that you have to give this up for me," I whispered, feeling so guilty.

He smiled as he wiped it away. "Ah, sweetheart. I'd do anything for you. Haven't you figured that out yet?"

I hiccupped with my tears miserably and closed my eyes. I felt him lean in and kiss my forehead, but as he leaned away, I gripped his face and brought him back to me, kissing him, thanking him, loving him.

His fingers caressed and loved on my skin in small circles. All our stalling was pathetic, but the loud boom from the building pulled us back to reality.

He sighed as he released me. "Everything's okay. I'll be there as soon as I can." He licked his lips. "Promise."

I nodded, realizing he was releasing me with his words, and held onto his fingers until the last second as he leaned away. The door was slammed and Rodney immediately drove away, probably understanding that he needed to get me away from there, but away from Seth, too, because I wanted nothing more than to wrench that door open and run back to him as I watched him from the window. He didn't move. He watched us go, his chest heaving, puffs of cold air leaving his mouth.

I was leaving him at the very site that I'd found him about to die. The imprint in my chest wasn't happy at all. It was pissed, in fact.

I rolled over to face away from the window as Rodney drove past the fire trucks and building. I shut my eyes and pretended nothing existed right now but Seth and that he was okay.

Rodney gripped my hand. His was so warm. I opened my eyes to look at him and was surprised by the look of worry on his face. He looked between me and the road.

"You scared the hell out of us." Oh, right… I ran out in the middle of the night. Forgot about that little tidbit. "Dad figured it out, that it had to be something to do with Seth. So naturally they thought that the Watson's had kidnapped you or Seth or something and they'd never see again. Little did they know you were just saving your boy from a freaking fire. That's all," he spouted sarcastically, angrily.

Everyone was going to scold me tonight it seemed.

"I had to," I whispered. "He was—"

"I get it." He looked at me and smiled a little. "I changed my mind."

"About what?" I was suddenly exhausted. Not tired. There was no way I could sleep. Just…exhausted, drained, emotionally shattered.

"I do want to find my soulmate." I felt the first of what I knew would be many small sobs wrack into me. "I do want to bond with someone. And one day…she'll need me. And I'll be there, just like you were for Seth tonight."

I let them go, unable to hold them in any longer. He wrapped his arm around my shoulder and used that leverage to tug me closer until I was leaning against him. I held his arm like a vice grip.

Sweetheart…

I'm fine. Just…doing some bonding with Rodney, I promised him. *Please hurry back to me.*

I took a deep breath and tried to calm myself.

"I love you, Rod. Thanks for coming to get me."

"This might sound weird at a time like this, but that guy seriously has a thing for you."

I snorted. "I hope so."

When we pulled in, Dad and Mom were pulling an epic freak out on our porch. Their eyes searched me as we got out of the car and came toward them and they looked so wide-eyed. When Dad saw the fireman's jacket, the pieces started to click and they weren't exactly pulling in Seth's favor.

"Daddy," I said to hopefully calm him as Rodney helped me up the porch stairs.

Daddy snatched me gently to his chest and hugged me hard, in one of those almost-too-hard hugs I used to get as a kid. "Daddy, you're squeezing me," I whispered what I always told him, making me five years old again.

I felt his chest shake once as he pulled back and cupped my cheek. "Ava…" He shook his head. "If I had lost you because of this…"

"Caleb," Mom implored, "baby, she had to." She wiped her eye and came to me, taking me in her arms. "Oh, God, thank you." She looked at Daddy over her shoulder. "We get these gifts for a reason, remember? The same reason I get visions. I don't get them and them not come true half the time. They do come true unless we fight them for a purpose. And we feel our soulmate's heartbeat so we can do something about it if they need us."

Daddy ran his hand through his hair. "What if—" He lifted his hands in surrender. "Baby girl, I'm glad you're okay. Everybody come inside out of the cold."

He went inside, leaving the door wide open.

Mom tugged me inside. "He's been going crazy since you ran out."

"I figured. I'm sorry. There wasn't time to—"

"I know. Your dad has saved me before and I've saved him, both because of our heartbeats over the years. We both know how it works. Your dad is just worried about his only little girl." She started to take Seth's jacket off and I yanked the lapels back into place.

"Sorry. No, Mom, not yet." I couldn't take it off…

"I shouldn't have even tried. Sorry." She smiled softly. "When will he be here?"

"How do you know he's coming here?"

She raised an eyebrow. "Because he's Virtuoso."

I sighed. "He would be here already, but a fireman…died."

She gasped softly. "Oh, no."

"He had to stay behind and give reports or statements or whatever. He couldn't leave because he was there and saw it. He was his friend."

"Oh...poor guy. Poor Seth." She rubbed my arm. "Sometimes your father forgets that we live in a human world and the human world doesn't know or care about our kind and what we need."

That's exactly what I felt. I needed Seth, I needed to comfort him, and he couldn't be here. He watched his fellow fireman die, and I needed to help him somehow.

"What happened, Ava?" she whispered. I didn't answer—couldn't. She must have known. "Just go try to get some sleep. It'll make the time go by faster," she said that part in a hurry when she saw me protesting.

"No. I can't sleep. I'll just wait in my room."

I went toward the stairs, but felt a hand on my arm. "Rodney, not now," I begged, but it was Dad. He had one of his mugs in his hand with hot chocolate.

"Here," he urged gently, and I knew this was his apology. Daddy was so protective of his girls, and when he got heated, he always felt bad after. "It'll help warm you up."

"I was in a fire, Daddy," I said with angry distraction and shook my head back and forth with my frenzy. "I don't need to be warmed up."

"Gah, Ava." He knew, but hearing it was another thing. He gulped. He saw my tears coming. "Come here."

He put his arm around me and took my numb body to the couch in the den, the same den where Seth had come and met my family, the same couch we had sat side-by-side on as we navigated our first day together.

Daddy sat down, setting the cup down on the table next to us, and then pulled me against him. I put my feet up on the couch and turned so I could curl up, putting my head on his chest. He dragged his fingers through my hair. He would get no protest from me.

It was amazing how two men in your life could love you, soothe you, hold you, comfort you, and it be in completely different ways. I wrapped my arms around his arm like it was the only thing connecting me to this world and let him soothe me. Momma came in and picked up my legs so she could sit under them. I was holding Dad's arm hostage so she settled for rubbing his neck, her arm along the back of the couch. They stared at each other.

Caleb and Maggie. Always Caleb and Maggie.

Their love story was what sparked the need and want for my own. It wasn't just because I was a Virtuoso. It *wasn't* just because I knew my soulmate was out there. It *wasn't* just because I had been told it was coming all my life.

It was because of these two people right here.

The way they loved and cared for each other was beyond what our hearts and mind could comprehend—it went straight for the soul, winding around, locking in tight, and putting everything else to shame.

I always hoped I would find my own story, but honestly, didn't think it could measure up to theirs. Like their love story was on a pedestal no one else could reach.

But then I met Seth and I *got it.*

Everyone's love story is epic in its own way. It's up to you how epic you make it. It's up to you how much you love them and how much you fight for them and keep them and wind them around your soul.

I closed my eyes, tried not to fly apart into a million pieces, but failed as the quiet and still finally let it all settle into me.

"Oh, God…" I whispered, breaking the silence. "He almost died, Dad," I cried miserably.

He squeezed me tighter, in true form. "I think I'm finally understanding that." He kissed my ear and whispered, "I'm sorry. Breathe, baby girl. Just breathe."

Mom scooted even closer and I pulled my knees in so we could huddle.

Luckily, since Seth couldn't be there, I had the next best people there holding me together. I cried on Daddy's shirt for a few minutes, but the rest of the next hour we just…*were.* Sometimes you just needed to be together and right then, I needed to just be with them more than anything if Seth couldn't be there.

Rodney had come in and was trying to look like he was texting on his phone, but I knew better.

"I'm fine," I muttered and looked over at him. He was sitting in my favorite big brown and teal club chair with his ankle on his knee. His leg was bouncing like crazy.

"What?" He shrugged his shoulders.

"Thanks for coming to get me." I didn't mention how he knew to because I didn't want to get into it in front of Mom and Dad. He apparently didn't either.

He nodded quickly. "Of course."

Mom patted my leg. "You may not want hot chocolate, but I do."

"I could go for some, actually." I looked at Dad from under my lashes. "Sorry I snapped at you. And wasted perfectly good hot chocolate."

He kissed my forehead. "It's forgotten, baby girl," he whispered.

He must've been really worried about me. He hadn't called me that in a while and now I was going to start counting.

"Ava," Mom called from the kitchen calmly. A weird, too-calm.

Dad tensed and said softly, "Go, Ave."

I got up and walked at an almost run past the living room to the kitchen and stopped at the sight of my mother hugging a dirty, sooty, exhausted, obviously distressed, and very confused version of Seth.

His arms stayed a little out to the sides and I didn't know if that was because he was dirty or just because she was hugging him and he didn't know why.

When he looked up and saw me, his face changed so drastically to one of relief. "Ava."

I'd never felt so loved. Was he really that happy to see me?

He shook his head as he moved forward, my mother long gone as soon as she saw me come in.

He said low, "We're going to have to work on that, little bird."

His long, big arms hadn't even wrapped around me before his mouth was pressed to mine. This was not open-mouthed, tongues, and hands like in the fire station that day. No. It was so much more than that. With just the pressure of his mouth, he was simply saying he needed me and that was so much more than any passionate romp we could have.

As he lifted my feet from the floor and pressed me to him like he'd never let go again, I hoped I was conveying the same thing.

He put my feet down, but didn't release me, just put his forehead to mine. Our breath raged between us.

"I'm sorry," he said, the agony back on his face. As he leaned away, I questioned him with my eyes, but I saw him shift his gaze to my father. I hadn't even realized they had followed us in, but should have guessed. He was next to Mom. Seth gulped. "I'm sorry that I put her in danger. I never meant... I would never have gone in if I thought..." He sighed angrily.

"Seth," Mom tried softly.

"I couldn't stop my heartbeat." He leaned against the counter, keeping me right against him. I could tell he was beyond exhausted. "Couldn't calm down. I tried. I tried everything." He looked down at me. "It was like my body called to you without my permission."

"Your bodies—when we imprint," Dad explained, "that's what it does. It imprints a little piece of you on the other person's soul. If we're ever in trouble, that's why it calls to them. We have no control."

Seth grimaced, his hands shaking with anger on my hip. "She could have died trying to save me!"

"That's not how it works for us," Mom stepped in, leaving Dad's embrace. He seemed loathe to let her go. We were all on edge. She came and leaned on the counter next to us. "For our kind, our gifts are for a reason." She glanced at Dad for a second. We had just had this discussion. "If you're given an ability, it's for a purpose." Seth's arms tensed around me and I didn't know why…or maybe I did. I peeked up at him. He was so exhausted. He had soot on his cheek… No, I wasn't going to grill him about that now. "Our kind believes that these are gifts, not burdens. If you were meant to be saved, then you were. You bonded to my daughter for a reason. You can't look at this like a human would."

Seth scoffed tiredly. "Like a human would? What—rationally?"

Mom smiled. "Remember that I was a human."

Seth squinted. "I didn't know that." She nodded. "The Visionary is a human?" She nodded again and smirked. I shook my head. Mom loved to point that out. "Okay, I understand all that, but you don't understand what happened tonight."

My heartbeat spiked.

Don't mention the humans.

He looked down at me. *Humans,* he scoffed. *What? Why?*

Because it's against the law. For our kind.

He stared. *Oh…you're serious.*

It's a big law that they don't know anything about us.

They won't say anything.

I'm sorry. I know I screwed up, but what was I supposed to do?

He cupped my jaw. *They won't. Say. Anything.*

He looked back at my mom, who was waiting patiently for us to finish. It wasn't the first time she had to wait for a Virtuoso couple to talk amongst themselves and it wouldn't be the last. He sighed, rethinking everything.

"Why didn't you tell me you were on the way here?" I asked.

"He didn't want you to go after him before he could get here," Dad guessed and nodded. He looked at me as he moved toward us. "Which you would have, by the way." I opened my mouth, but stopped. Maybe… "I appreciate that," he told him and held his hand out to Seth. Seth separated from me and looked at his slightly dirty hand, but Dad didn't care as they shook. Then Dad pulled him in for a hug, which surprised the ever-loving mess out of me. "Glad you're okay."

Seth leaned back, looking so exhausted, but was clearly surprised. "Thanks, Mr. Jacobson."

"Caleb. And you don't have to thank me for being glad you're alive. You're my daughter's significant and if something had happened to you, she would be hurting. So you're here to stay, kid." He patted his shoulder, while I went to take Seth's hand. "Now, why don't y'all go on upstairs." It wasn't a request. "We'll talk tomorrow. You both look like you're about ready to fall over."

"Go on," Mom urged and smiled at me. "I'll bring you some tea up in just a second. Do you need anything else? Seth, are you hungry?"

"No, ma'am," he answered so quietly, rubbing his head. I'd never seen anybody this tired before. "Something to drink would be perfect though, thank you. I've got everything else I need."

I put his arm over my shoulder and we started out of the kitchen, with my first real smile of the night on my tired face.

Chapter Fourteen

Seth kicked his boots off at the top of the hallway. It turned into carpet near our bedrooms and he didn't want to get anything on it, he said. I did the same, just in case, looking down, mourning my ruined Chucks that Seth had so lovingly made special.

"Aw, I'm sorry, sweetheart."

I tried to shrug. "They're just shoes, right? Do you want to take a shower?" I asked.

"No," he sighed, "I don't think I could make it through it."

When we got into my room, I realized that Seth had gotten another jacket from somewhere. It was sooty and dirty, too. He took it off, going into the bathroom and laying it across the sink. I followed him in and he reached for my jacket before I could even try. I let him and when the jacket left my body, a huge whoosh left my lips at how much lighter I was. He gave me a small smile.

Turning to get a washcloth from the cabinet was my first look at myself. I stopped. It was hard to breathe and process and think…

Seth was dirty and sooty and exhausted…but so was I.

I had soot on my cheek and my neck. My pants and shirt were ruined from crawling through the building. My chest had scratch marks on it that I could only imagine were from me when I was freaking out about Seth coming across the ladder. My hair was all over the place. My eyes were so red from smoke, from crying…

I looked like a horror film's leading lady.

And then I looked over at Seth to ask him why he hadn't said anything, or why he thought my parents hadn't said anything—I mean I probably ruined the stupid sofa and their clothes—but he was looking at me like there was nothing in the world he'd rather be doing than standing in a bathroom with me, cleaning up, getting ready for bed, knowing that our touch would carry us to sleep, and that we'd wake up, withdrawal free to start a new day together. A day that we would always cherish because we had survived.

And I guessed my stupid soot face didn't matter that much anymore. A tear escaped, but I still turned to get the washcloth.

"Ava, here's the tea, and I added a couple turkey sandwiches, just in case," Mom called out from my room. "Also, I put a stack of clean clothes out here of your Dad's for Seth—sleep clothes and clothes for tomorrow, okay?"

"Thanks, Mom," I called back through the open door, but wet the cloth and didn't look out for her.

When it warmed, I wrung it out and looked up at him. He wiped the tear from my cheek, but smiled and I knew it just smudged the dirt there. I pushed his stomach until he sat on the edge of the tub and then bunched it in my fingers before rubbing the cloth across his forehead. He sighed so loudly. He leaned his head back and closed his eyes, opening his knees for me and tugging me in between them with his hands on the backs of my thighs. Even in his exhaustion, his hands sought me out.

I kept wiping, feeling the relief settle into me more and more the cleaner he got, the more I could see his face clearly. I cleaned his neck next and each arm, leaning over to rinse the cloth in between. I made him stand and when he did, he winced a little, instantly regretting it when I saw.

Everything in me went on high alert again. "Off," I ordered.

"Ava," he soothed.

"Off," I said again and gripped the hem of his shirt.

He pressed his lips together and I knew why. He knew that whatever I was going to find under there I couldn't do anything about. We hadn't ascended yet so I couldn't heal him.

He felt like it was pointless to put myself through it to see it if I could nothing about it.

"If I was hurt, would you want to see?" I countered.

He growled a little under his breath. "That was dirty."

"It's fair actually."

He reached for the hem of his shirt with me and, even though I was exhausted, I opened my mind so I'd know how he truly felt, if he was really in pain or just playing it down for my benefit. I helped him pull it over his head. He made no noise and I knew it pulled a little, but it didn't seem too bad… until he dropped the shirt and stood up straight.

I couldn't even appreciate the fact that he was shirtless and amazing in front of me, and I would always be angry at that fire for taking this first experience from me.

He had a large hand-sized bruise forming over his left ribs. I moved right up against him and barely touched it with my fingertips. "Oh, Seth."

"I caught the railing. It's okay. These things happen sometimes. It'll heal. They're not broken…this time."

"You've broken your ribs before?" I whispered, but couldn't tear my eyes from it.

"Yeah," he said and sighed.

I waited, thinking he was about to give me the list of bodily injuries, but realized that was a stupid thing to think. He would never do that. I let my gaze move to up to meet his blue eyes, but he wasn't looking at me, he was looking at my fingers on his ribs.

"I can't believe you're being like this."

"Like what?"

"Why haven't you asked me yet?" He finally looked up and he looked equal parts scared and curious. "I thought it was going to be the first thing you asked when you got me alone."

He wanted to know why I hadn't asked how he got Rodney there by just closing his eyes.

"You said you wanted to wait, right?" I said carefully. He nodded. "There was a reason for that, I'm sure." He nodded again. "Honestly, after what just happened, I just don't care about anything else right now. I'm too exhausted to process anything else but you being safe."

His hand covered mine on his ribs for a few seconds before he steered me to the sink. He lifted me to sit on it before I could protest. "It's just a bruise. I'm fine," he insisted.

He got a new washcloth and repeated the process with me that I had done with him, washing my face, neck, and arms.

Even in the state I was in, it was hard not to notice how amazingly rugged he was everywhere. I tried not to stare at his chest, but he was at eye level. I almost groaned at his shoulders alone…they were so…hard and strong.

I looked away, feeling bad for looking at him like that after what happened tonight. His friend died, for goodness sake. He didn't want me to gawk—

He took my chin and made me look at him. My belly ached so sweetly at the sweet smile he was trying to give me. "Gosh, you are the most adorable woman I have ever…" He sighed, so tired. "Of course I want my significant to think I look good with my shirt off."

The corners of my mouth lifted as he matched my smile.

Then he lifted me back down and walked out to the stuff Mom had brought and put on the bed. "Your mom is the best," he said softly.

On the tray of food were two glasses of iced tea and two sandwiches cut diagonally down the middle. With the pile of clothes she had even put socks and a new toothbrush on top.

I smiled. "Yeah, she is."

He took his pile into the bathroom and I got dressed quickly in my room. I tossed my destroyed clothes in the small trash can by my door and stared at them as I drank the tea and sat on the bed. I started to open my mind to make sure that Seth was okay, but decided not to. He was going through a lot and I wanted to let him have his peace. I thought maybe he'd sit in there for a while and take a minute.

He didn't take long at all.

He emerged wearing some of Dad's VOLs pants and one of his band t-shirts—The Rocketboys. The pants were a smidge too short, but that did nothing to mar the image. "This is the most adorable you've ever been."

He cracked a small smile as he made his way over. "That's not exactly what a man wants to hear."

"You've been every other step on the spectrum already—adorable was the only one that was left. Rugged, handsome, gorgeous, searing to the point of eye damage."

He chuckled as he sat next to me on the bed and took me in. "Okay. I'll let you have adorable this time," he said softly, his eyelids barely holding themselves up.

"Here," I said, feeling bad for joking. I handed him his tea and then took the tray, setting it on nightstand. Last time he stayed here we just flopped on top of the bed in our clothes. Not this time. He deserved a real night's sleep with comfort and warmth. So I got my favorite big blanket from the window reading nook and spread it out on top of the bed. I turned back to him and he had almost downed the whole tea and had started in on one of the sandwiches.

"You don't have to."

"No," he said and chewed slowly as he moved to look at my room. "Now that I've tasted it, I'm starving. That's a mean turkey sandwich. What the hell is on this?" he said comically.

"Avocado." I smiled. "Mom made it her mission to be a good cook since she was so epically bad at it when she and Dad first got married."

He was looking at my photos; I was looking at his bare feet. Not adorable, my butt.

"You played volleyball?"

"Yeah. And swim team. Come on," I said, seeing that he was done with his sandwich. "Come to bed. You look like you could sleep for two days."

He looked back at the pictures like he didn't want to leave them.

"I feel like it." He put his glass on the tray and climbed on top of the comforter. I went and turned my light off and got beside him, tossing my big blanket over us. "Your bed's going to smell like smoke tomorrow," he whispered as I slid closer to him.

"That doesn't matter. I'll wash the comforter." I let my elbow rest against his chest; I didn't know how much room to give him for his bruise. Frankly, I didn't know how he liked to sleep or if he just wanted some space after everything that happened—

"Ava," he groaned and reached under my elbow to tug me until I was against him on our sides facing each other. "The only thing I need is you," he said simply, tiredly, and with finality.

I sighed. Okay.

"I quit," he said. It was obvious that it was not up for discussion. He was just letting me know. "It's not uncommon when there's a traumatic incident for it to be too much and firemen quit sometimes. No one will think anything of it."

"I'm sorry."

"I did this." He stroked his fingers down my arm. "Now I'm fixing it. I told the chief you knew a classmate in the building and just happened to be there." So he had asked why I was there. "Landon and Gibson didn't say anything. And they kept telling me to tell you 'Thank you.'" He chuckled a little. "And I thought Landon had a crush on you before..." He swallowed, his hand moving to my back just under the hem of my shirt and kept moving small circles. "I don't know what I'm going to do now, but I promise you..."

I kissed him, loving that even in this state he searched me out for more, but then I scooted up a little and wrapped my arms around him, pressing his cheek to my chest, letting him settle into the nooks and crevices our bodies made together. We fit together so well just lying there in the dark as I tried to tell him that everything was going to be all right with every stroke of my fingers through his hair.

He was asleep before I was.

CHAPTER FIFTEEN

I covered my mouth as I looked at him. "What's wrong?"

"There was a fire."

I gasped. "A fire! What—"

"No, I'm a fireman, Ave." He smiled as best he could. "I'm just exhausted. No offense, but I hoped I wouldn't come here tonight. But...as soon as you fell asleep, I felt the pull."

"You're a fireman?" I smiled a little and bit my lip.

He shook his head. "What is it with women and firemen?"

"I'm sorry. What happened?"

He shook his head. "No."

I nodded. "You look exhausted."

"I *am* exhausted."

"I'm so sorry. Is there any way that you can go back?"

"No. Not with you. With everyone else, I can come and go as I please and they always remember when they wake up. You're different. It's like I'm stuck here."

"I'm sorry." I licked my lips, feeling so bad. He obviously needed to sleep and instead he was stuck with me.

I felt his fingers under my chin. I hadn't even seen him move. I pulled my legs to me so he could sit on the bed beside me. He looked so guilty and I didn't understand.

"I'm so sorry. I keep..." He looked down and back up to me. "I keep treating you like you're not the same girl, the same person, but you are. I'm sorry. You're not keeping me from her. I just had a really crummy day and— sorry I took it out on you. It's no excuse for being an ass."

I looked around. "Maybe if you lie down in the dream, you'll get some rest for your real body. Yeah?" I said hopefully.

He smiled, letting his hand fall to grip mine. "Thank you, beautiful girl, but it doesn't work that way. We'll have to find something else to do to bide our time."

"Well," I said coyly, "we do have some plotting to do, don't we?"

His eyebrow rose. "Plotting?"

"Operation get-your-family-to-trust-you-again?"

He laughed once. "Oh, that. I'm not sure it's going to work."

I smirked. "Ye of little faith."

He rubbed my knuckles. "Even your subconscious completely believes in me."

I tilted my head. "That should tell you something."

"It does." His sigh was rough as he leaned forward to cup my face. "It does." He leaned in and kissed my forehead. "Let's get to work."

When I woke, the next morning, I didn't move a muscle. I was so warm and content, and couldn't remember my body being this relaxed in a long time. I glanced over at my clock and saw that it was almost one in the afternoon. I didn't know exactly what time we'd gone to bed last night, but it had to be around two or three. So honestly, for what the guy had been through, it wasn't too bad. I saw that my curtains had been pulled to in my room and knew that Mom had been in to check on us. I had left my door cracked, knowing that she was going to be doing that anyway.

My parents were pros at worrying.

I was content to lay there for as long as he needed, seriously. It was funny to me that we hadn't moved an inch in the night. He was exactly where I'd put him. I stroked his hair so gently. I didn't dare wake him, but I did want to touch him. I almost wanted the hit our calm gave us when we'd been without it for a while. This was amazing, being filled to the brim with him, the buzz of him in my veins, but having a shot of him hit me all at once was also amazing.

I couldn't see his face, but I imagined that it was peaceful. I hoped it was. I laid my hand on his head and left it there just as Mom came in again.

"Hey," she whispered. "You're awake."

"Mom," I said, unable to help myself, and weirdly not caring that my boyfriend was practically laying on top of me. Boyfriend. I smiled. "How is he... How does his face look?" I whispered. She squinted. "I mean, does he look peaceful? Does he look okay?"

She smiled, tilting her head. She even looked like she might cry for a second. I didn't understand that. "He's fine, Ave. He looks like he's right where he wants to be."

"I just didn't want to let him keep sleeping if he was having nightmares or something."

She nodded. "He's going to be okay. And so are you. But for today..." I looked up at that tone. "It was meant to be a surprise, but then all this happened. The family is coming at six for a bar-b-que. To meet Seth."

I grimaced. The good old Jacobson grilling.

They grilled the meat and then they grilled the new significant.

"And of course, everyone is dying to meet Seth because your cousins can't stop blabbing about seeing him at the house that day." I groaned. "They all want to know who this guy is who swooped up our Ava."

I gave her a look, making sure to whisper. "Are you sure they don't want to see the Watson and try to figure out if he's for real or not?"

"I've assured them all that Seth is the real deal. After everything, after seeing you two tonight, I don't know how anyone could doubt it, but that's up to you. If you two aren't up to it, I'll cancel. No worries. I know it's a lot. I just really wanted him to know the family before we went to the summit. It would be better that way. But...I get it if it's too much today."

I nodded.

She turned to go and looked back. "I'm proud of you, Ava."

I felt my eyes burn and fill, my chest ached with surprise. "For what?"

"For being brave enough to do what needed to be done. I don't want to know what happened." She twisted her lips, as if keeping herself in check. "But I can imagine with the way you came home looking what it was like. And you did that for him. Because you love him." I smiled at my mother, feeling the first tear fall. "And one day, he's going to return the favor. I know that my daughter is safe with him. I've seen the way he looks at you when you're not watching, the way his hands fidget when he's not able to touch you, and that's a good feeling—to know that your daughter will not only be happy with the person she's with, but he'll keep her safe. Things won't always be easy for our kind and I have a feeling that things are about to start getting worse." She gulped. "Knowing you're safe with him and that he'll do anything to keep you that way is the best thing in my world right now."

I didn't say anything as she left. I didn't know what *to* say.

I stayed there like that with him for another two hours, stroking his hair sometimes, before I felt him stirring. I didn't move, just let him come out of it on his own. When he lifted his head, he looked at me, our faces so close, his hair spiked cutely from my fingers. I used my fingers again to comb them down, but he still just looked at me.

"Hey," I eventually said.

"Hey," he said, his voice gravelly. He pushed up a bit to reach me, pressing the lightest kiss to my lips. Once, twice, three times. "Thank you, Ava." I was just about to say 'What for?' when he said. "I'll have to start a list." He groaned, sighing with his entire body, and laid back down on my chest. "Ah, I don't remember ever sleeping so well."

"You slept a long time."

He looked up at the clock. "What the—have you been waiting for me to wake up?"

"It's okay. Not for long. You needed the sleep," I told him as I raked his hair back. He pinched his eyes together. "It's okay."

He shook his head. "Crap. Sorry. I didn't mean to…" He looked at me. "Sorry."

"I like lying here with you. It's quiet. It's peaceful. I don't know. I don't mind it. If I had, I could have scooted out," I said wryly. "So, Mom had a surprise for you today."

"Oh, yeah?" he said distractedly, enjoying my ministrations. When I didn't say anything he lifted his head from my chest. "Oh, the kind of surprise where I get my ass kicked."

I laughed loudly and cupped his face. "No. The kind of surprise where… you meet my entire family." His eyes went wide. "The whole Jacobson clan will be here in a couple hours, unless you don't want them to. Mom said it was up to you." He 'pffted'. "Really, if you don't want to because of everything that happened we don't have to. But we do have the summit and it would be better if you knew my family before then."

He stared. "How many Jacobsons are we talking?"

I shrugged. "Fifty."

"Fifty!"

"Or so," I amended. I pulled him closer by his cheeks. "It'll be fine. Unless you don't—"

"I can't back out. That's the first sign of weakness. Besides, I know they all just want to get a good look at the *Watson*. May as well let them get—"

"That is not what's going on. My mom is very convincing. When she tells people things, they listen, and she told them that this is legit, okay? They don't care who you are, they just care that you're mine. My significant," I corrected and smiled. "They just want to meet you. We always have a family together when someone bonds."

"You do?" He smirked. "So I'm not special."

"No, you're not special." I kissed him once more, happy that he seemed to be better today. "Want to take a shower? I'll leave your stuff here and go take one in my parent's room downstairs."

He nodded and sighed as he stretched and rolled over. The white t-shirt rode up and I saw the bottom of his bruise peeking out. I winced and hissed.

"It doesn't hurt that bad," he acknowledged.

I lifted his shirt and felt my eyes bulge. It had more than doubled in color. It was now a deep purple with hints of blue around the edges. I whispered my fingers across it, my pale fingers a stark contrast against the colors. I felt sick looking at it, knowing that in just a few weeks, I'd be able to take it all away with a touch.

He put his hand behind my neck and tugged me down to kiss him. I protested—I was almost laying on his bruise.

"It doesn't really hurt that bad, I said," he told me against my mouth. "Don't even think about it. It'll be gone in a couple days." He pecked my lips once more and released me. When I got up my hand brushed his stomach on the other side where his shirt had been lifted. I felt something there, too. I peeked at it wondering what other on-duty wounds I was going to find.

"That's something from my childhood," he murmured.

It was a long scar across his side. How had I missed that last night? I guess I was so focused on his bruised ribs not much else mattered. But from the tone, I could tell he didn't want to talk about it and I certainly wasn't ready to make him feel bad now. I wanted him to feel good after everything he'd been through yesterday.

"Do you have any more scars?"

He chuckled hotly. "A lot. We'll have to have some time if you want to go through all that, sweetheart."

For some reason, that made my neck hot. I smiled and looked down. He laughed again. "On that note," he leaned up and kissed my forehead, "I'm going to take a shower."

"Okay." I watched him go. "I'll be downstairs somewhere when you're done. Just come find me."

He nodded as he shut the door, a little smile on his lips. I sighed, feeling a million pounds lighter.

Holy to the *crap*. He was about to meet my crazy family.

I went to my closet and ransacked it, looking for adorable-ness, but grown-up-ness in the same ensemble. I decided to go *without* the tights—give poor Seth a break for the day—and went with a long sleeve, scoop neck, canary yellow top with a pair of light jeans. I grabbed my gold bird dangle earrings and ran to Mom's shower. I tried to hurry.

When I got out, I could smell the smoke on my clothes *so* bad. No wonder Dad had freaked out last night.

I decided to put my hair up this time. Instead of going back upstairs, I made do with Mom's makeup, just using her eye shadow and eye liner and forgoing any face powder. Putting in my last earring, I could hear Ember laughing in the kitchen and should have known everyone would be early, so eager to get the grilling started.

In Dad's ridiculously large four car garage, we had a big kitchen in back so we just had our 'in-door bar-b-que' in there when it was too cold. Everyone would set up tables and chairs and still play Cornhole and all their games in there. Dad always wound up playing guitar at some point. It was the loudest, most packed, best smelling, most ridiculous garage bar-b-que you'd ever been

to.

I looked at myself in the mirror. I slicked on a touch of Mom's lipgloss, her favorite thing she wore, and decided that I wasn't going to be intimidated by my family. They were amazing, they meant well, they were just loud and in great numbers. I would protect Seth tonight from them, from their nagging questions, from their inappropriate prodding trying to be funny, and I would make this a good night for him.

I smiled at my reflection. I would get him to understand that this family wanted him, no matter what.

I inched out of the bathroom into the hall, not wanting anyone to know I was there yet. I peeked my head around the corner to find all of Ember's family there with my parents. Uncle Bish and Aunt Jen, Maria and Dawson, Grandpa Peter and Nana Rachel. And Uncle Kyle, Aunt Lynne and their kids, Drake and Laurelyn—named after her mom.

And Seth was right smack in the middle of them.

He beat me out. He was leaned on the back of the couch, his hands in his pockets casually, he listened as Ember was talking about something, but I didn't hear any of the words. I just looked at him.

He was wearing Dad's clothes, but you couldn't tell. The pants reached his big boots and that was good enough. Daddy had always been a big guy, so the shirt fit him pretty good.

Then he laughed at something she said and reached up to rub his arm as he did so. Wow, did that shirt fit him…

And he fit in so well. I had been freaking out about making him feel comfortable today, rescuing him from the crazies, and look at him. He was a genius at it already.

It's all in the eyes.

I looked up to see I'd been caught. He was smiling and maneuvering to look around my mom to see me. Giving away my position.

Traitor.

"Ava!" Ember called, but stopped when she saw me. "Ava, good…Lord." She looked at Mom and back at Seth. "Did they ascend already?"

I knew what she was doing. When you ascend, you get that final spurt of growth and features for your face and body that make you feel and look so mature and just…finished. People look so beautiful and happy after they ascend. They looked that way before, too, but it adds a cherry on top of the sundae. It means everything is complete. That you are truly one and it has all come full circle. Your powers can be united and so much can happen between you now. It's magical.

"Shut up, Ember," I tried, begging she wouldn't keep going, but she pulled my arms out to my sides.

"Baby girl, if this is what bonding does to a body, I need to get myself bonded."

"Cut it out," I hissed and rolled my eyes as she laughed, even slapping my butt as I passed her. She was our wild one. I heard Uncle Bish sigh exasperatingly with a chuckle. We loved her.

I let my smile loose on Seth as I made my way to him. This room was like a tank full of swarming sharks. You couldn't show any fear, couldn't let a drop of blood fall in the water, or they'd start in, piece by piece. They'd love nothing more than to embarrass me, to share a story that would make me cringe, to see us squirm under their scrutiny.

Oh, no, Jacobsons. Not today.

Lesson learned.

Seth had heard my entire pep talk, and even though his face as he looked me over made me want to jump him right there on the living room rug, I casually turned slightly to face him, taking one of his arms hostage to claim him and—even though he obviously didn't need it—hopefully offer him some sense of a shield if he wanted one. He laced our fingers together beside us and I smiled at the gathered masses.

"It appears that Seth beat me out here. I was hoping to spare him the Jacobson ambush—"

"Pfft," Ember scoffed and everybody laughed.

"He was laughing when I came out." I looked up at him and grinned. "That's better than crying in a corner."

He laughed nervously as everyone laughed around us.

Ember yelled, "Dawson totally deserved it!"

Dawson rolled his eyes and came to Seth's side. "I can see right now that I'm going to have to rescue you on more than one occasion. The Jacobson women are a force to be reckoned with." He smiled at me. "Except," he tapped my nose with his finger, "this one right here. You're safe with this one."

"Hey!" Maria said and laughed as she scooted into his arms. "I didn't say a word, buster. Why am I getting thrown under the bus?"

"Because you're the worst one," he said, laughing. "Silent, calculating, waiting in the wings. Ember lets you know she's coming from a mile away, no one could miss her."

"Hey, pal!" Ember said, her mouth full of something that Mom had been passing around.

"Laurelyn's swift and cunning, but sugar-sweet."

"Oh," she laughed, "you think adding the 'sugar' on at the end is going to save you?"

He kept going. "And Maggie is the sweetest one in the bunch, but if you tick her off, all she has to do is look at you and poof—you're gone like yesterday's leftovers."

Mom straightened from giving Grandpa Peter a hug and then shrugged. "True. So watch it, buddy."

Seth's fingers rubbed against mine as he laughed.

You were worried about nothing. Your family is great.

This is just a few of them. And this isn't even the loud ones.

He seemed surprised and Ember said, "See. Told you they could talk already."

I looked to see she was talking to her parents.

"All right," Dad called and swooped in, clapping Seth on the shoulder. "Who wants to come with me and show Seth how to lose at horseshoes?" He pointed. "Mom, you cannot come."

Nana laughed. "Fine." She hooked her arm through mine. "I wanted to talk boys with my granddaughter anyway."

Seth and I looked at each other. I so did not want to leave him yet. No one but us and Mom and Dad knew what had happened last night.

He winked. *I'll be fine, sweetheart.*

Dawson, Dad, Uncle Bish and the rest of the guys took Seth out to the garage while the girls stayed inside to "gab". Which was code for grill me on how a fireman kissed.

Mom rolled her eyes and told them to leave me alone, but there was no satisfying the frenzy that had begun in my living room.

"I don't want Seth to kiss and tell, so why would I?"

"Great answer, babe," Mom said and winked.

"Oh, boo, bad answer. And your avoidance of the question is an answer in itself that he is, in fact, a terrific kisser." I stared at Ember and wondered where her brain got the energy. "You really don't think he's not out there telling everyone that you're an awesome tongue twister?" She thought about it as I lifted an eyebrow. "Okay, you're right. He's probably not out there telling your dad and uncles and granddad how well you kiss. That one took a second to catch up with me. But at the fire station then? I'm sure he tells all."

"Trust me, he doesn't. Can we talk about something else? Like you, Maria?"

"Why me?" she said and glared, giving me a look.

"Duh. Because you're preg..." Oh, she hadn't told the rest of the family. Only her parents. "Prego sauce is...awesome." She winced at my bad attempt to fix it and then laughed when people turned to look at her, completely getting what I had just let spill. "I'm so sorry," I whispered. "I didn't know you hadn't told anyone."

"It's okay," she drawled and came to hug me. "We were just going to wait until after your party. We didn't want to take any of the focus off of you and Seth."

"Please, take our focus. We don't want it."

She laughed. "That's why we didn't want to. This is your only time to be in the spotlight and show him off. Everyone is so happy for you, Ave. Don't run from that. Eat it up and be proud to have found him, for this one day."

I could have cried. "Thanks, M. I *am* sorry."

"No worries." She looked back at the group of women, waiting eagerly for us to finish. "Yes, I'm pregnant," she sang and they exploded with every nice thing someone could say in this scenario.

When we moseyed to the garage, Dad, Uncle Bish, and Uncle Kyle had already started cooking on the grills. I went up behind Dad and hugged him from behind, my chin on his arm. "Hey."

"Hey, there, Ave!" Uncle Kyle called over the fan of the stove as he flipped hotdogs on another grill and saluted me with his tongs. I smiled.

"Why so sad all of a sudden, baby girl?" Dad asked as he moved the ribs around.

"Not sad. Just...I didn't realize that I looked like that last night...when I came in." He patted my hands as I moved back. "That must have been scary, and I was just worried about Seth and..."

He hugged me to him. "You're supposed to worry about him. I'm supposed to worry about you. That's the way of it."

"I'm sorry, Dad."

He chuckled a little. "Between the two of you apologizing there won't be anyone having fun today." I squinted. "He came to me and told me that he doesn't work there anymore. That he'll figure something else out after the summit. And I believe him." He kissed my forehead. "Now go have some fun and stop being sorry."

I smiled. "I love you, Dad."

His smile in return was big. "Never gets old hearing it. I love you, too, baby."

I pointed at the grill as I walked away. "Don't burn those like last time, Champion."

"If one more person brings that up..."

I found Seth by the jukebox that Mom bought Dad for his birthday a few years back. He and Dawson were flipping through, trying to find something to play. I could see they were going to be friends, kindred spirits and all that, outsiders who were now insiders. Humans.

"Whatcha doing?" I sang.

"Nothing," he said quickly, pressing buttons, and turned to face me. "What are you doing?"

"Did you have fun losing at horseshoes?" I smiled to ease the sting.

"How do you know I lost?" He arched his brow as he came toward me. When we connected it was as easy as breathing, like we already had a way of doing things, a rhythm that was so in tune. Our hands sought each other's and we got as close as was proper.

I grinned. "I know my family. They don't lose at horseshoes. It's their game."

"What else do they play?" he said, game-face on.

"Um," it hadn't escaped my notice that practically the entire family was watching. "Darts? There's a pool table upstairs. Cornhole?"

"Cornhole!" He grinned. "Oh, it's go time."

I laughed, but sobered. "Wait, what about your ribs?"

"I'm fine. I can toss a beanbag."

I looked for Uncle Bish to get it set up, when I heard Dawson say, 'Yes' and then the jukebox started to play.

I glanced at him, confused at Seth's smug smile, until I heard "*Til Then*" by The Orioles come over the speakers. I felt my lips part and stared at him, knowing that I was going to get made fun of later for this, but it just didn't seem to matter all that much in that moment.

I heard Ember say from behind me, "He even puts up with her crappy tastes in music. *Wow*, he really is a keeper."

I cracked a smile and ignored her. "Hungry?"

"Starved."

"Come on, Mamma!" Grandpa Peter pulled Grandma Rachel to the middle near us. "Dance with me."

"It's not crappy."

I jerked back to look at him. "What?"

"Your music. It's not crappy. Music is what speaks to your soul, what moves us and makes us feel alive. We find the kind we feel that does that for us and we don't feel ashamed for it."

No one had ever stuck up for me about my music except Dad and Gran. Everybody else thought it was strange for me to love it so much. "I do listen to regular music, also, I just...love the old stuff."

"It speaks to you," he said low and smiled.

"Yeah."

"That's kind of how I feel when I draw. I feel...like I'm doing what I was put here to do. I thought that was fighting fires at one time, but... I think all art does that to people, brings out this piece of you that was hidden or locked away. Makes you *feel*."

I nodded. I heard them laughing behind us and saw a few of them dancing, but the song ended. I looked back at Seth and nodded my head toward the back kitchen. "I think it's time you had a Jacobson rib sandwich."

"Lovebirds go through the line first!" Maria yelled. She rubbed her belly and poked it out. "Hurry up, we're starving."

"You're barely pregnant, M," I said, grabbing a couple plates as Seth followed me. "You can't use that one yet."

"Oh, yes I can!" she sang happily.

I tried not to let the eyes on us deter me from being my normal self with him. He didn't seem to notice everyone as we washed our hands and moved into the kitchen. He watched me get everything ready, watching my fingers and then my face, then my hands again, and my face with interest. When our eyes would meet, he'd smile.

Everyone was so bad at trying to look like they weren't watching us like their favorite soap opera.

When I had the buns on the plate, I took a few of Dad's ribs, cooked to perfection, and pulled the meat from the bone with my fingers. He moved closer, his fingers cupping my elbow. I hissed a breath through my lips and looked over my shoulder to his face—so close. His face was dark, his eyes were hooded, and his lips were pout—almost comically so. It was such a stark contrasting about-face to where he was not two minutes before that I opened my mouth to ask what was wrong. But he stopped me.

I never really got why guys at the station talked about their wives cooking for them and making them lunch. I thought a sandwich and a sweet tea was enough, but seeing you right now…making that for me…

Stop it.

He smiled. *I am completely serious.*

I know and that's why you have to stop. You're making me totally crazy. I shook my head.

His shoulders shook with a silent laugh. "Do we need to keep score on that, *Miss I'll wear tights every day to torture you?*" he said aloud and Dawson laughed into his fist, not knowing what we were talking about, but he was close enough to hear and got the gist.

"No." I smirked. "No, we don't," I said coyly and bit into my lip smartly as I turned.

Uhoh. I started something, didn't I?

I looked at him and he was thoroughly enjoying this.

Baby, you started a war.

He laughed out loud, kissing my temple, and staying right behind me as I finished them. His hand was on the counter next to my arm and I swear, the parts of us that weren't touching were crackling with electricity.

I put another piece of meat on the buns, licking my finger, pretending that I hadn't heard his small groan in my mind, and then reached for Mom's coleslaw. He reached for it, too, since he was taller.

"I've got it," he said in my ear.

"And then you," I explained, as unflustered as I could manage, "top it with a little slaw and you're done once you put your condiments on."

He came next to me and eyed the bottles. He took the mayo and squirted it on both. I just watched. Then he reached for the mustard barbeque sauce…

There's no way that he—

He squirted it on mine and then eyed it. "I guess I can give it a try." Then he squirted it on his as well. He gave me a sideways smile that was filled with happiness and everything I hoped I would see shining through.

"How did you..." I shook my head. "You've got to stop doing this," I barely murmured through my numb lips that wanted nothing more than to drag him away to a dark corner and kiss him until he could no longer breathe.

"Stop doing what?" he whispered back, taking the ends of my fingers in his.

"Knowing me so completely."

CHAPTER SIXTEEN

"Thank you for making him feel at home," I told everyone when Seth was somewhere with Dawson. Getting more marshmallows probably. "I know you all have a grudge against the Watsons, for good reason, and I appreciate it that you didn't take it out on him or hold it against him."

"So…" Uncle Bish asked slowly. And here we go. He looked back to make sure they weren't coming yet. "He still lives with them? Still talks to them? I mean, Maggie told us that he's not really one of them, that he's one of the people that they kept in the compound, but—"

"Uncle Bish," I begged.

He held up his hands. "Okay."

"He's trying so hard to make this an easy transition. His family isn't happy about it. For all intents and purposes, they raised him. They're his family." Everyone looked around and I slung my hand out. "No. No, we're not doing this. For right now. All you have to know is that he's my significant. Okay?" I moved to sit next to Grandpa Peter. "Hey, Gramps. How you doing?"

"Oh, I'm all right," he said, age had taken some of his voice and strength away, but he was still as vibrant as ever. He and Nana were always off doing something, seeing something, going somewhere. He'd spent his whole life working so hard to take care of his family and that's what he'd done. Now it was his turn to have some fun and relax. They still went on gem expeditions once a month or so to keep up the funds. "How are you doing with all this, honey?" he asked softly.

"I'm all right. Seth is amazing, I just…" I looked up into his eyes, just like Daddy's. "I just wish everyone thought of him like I did, instead of as a Watson. I feel like everyone thinks that he might have an agenda…or be used for some plot one day or something. They're being nice, but I can tell they all want to ask."

"Well," he drawled, "you did almost get kidnapped the first night he came to see you." He twisted his lips. I sighed.

There was nothing to say to that except, "He didn't have anything to do with that."

He nodded. "Yeah. He was just a ploy?"

"Gramps."

He covered the tops of my arms with his palms. "Ave, you know I love you, but I used to be the Champion and that doesn't turn off. The Watsons are *not* finished here."

I shivered. "I think they've given up. Seth is their family—"

"No, he isn't. They've had the sting of revenge in their veins long before they stole a little boy to experiment on." I moaned in pain at the thought of him as a kid…I couldn't even think. He looked so stricken. "I'm so sorry, Ava. I wasn't thinking. That was stupid of me." He pulled me to him, rocking me and patting my back. "I'm so sorry, honey." I heard him say for someone to stop looking, that I was fine, so…that was awesome.

I settled after a few minutes and leaned away, telling him I was fine. Grandpa Jim sat down next to me just as Seth was returning with Dawson in the distance laughing at something.

"Hey, Ave. How's things?"

"I'm okay. I haven't seen you and Grammy in a while."

He smiled. "We've been away. She's got the travel bug." He leaned closer and brushed my hair back. "We miss you. And are so happy for you. We just want what's best for you." He looked up and leaned back.

I looked and scooted over on the big log bench around the fire pit to make room for Seth. He had a blanket on his arm and tossed it around us.

"Aww," Ember sighed, but Dawson was passing blankets around to the girls and lifted his arms in a what-am-I-chopped-liver motion as he handed her one. "Oh. Well, whatever. It's still sweet."

He smirked and went to his wife on the lounger. The snow on the ground had mostly melted, but around the fire, it was definitely gone now. We came out here to do the fire and some marshmallows.

But as Seth settled in next to me under the blanket, I could tell something wasn't quite right. As Seth put his arm around me and tugged me to his side so we'd be as warm as possible, I could feel the shift in the air.

I looked up at his face to see if he noticed it, too. He smiled and I realized how close we were. He tugged the edges of the blanket around my neck and his together, making our faces almost touch. "You okay?"

"Yeah," I said, but it came out a whisper. I tried again, but in a low voice so our conversation would be ours and no one else's. "Yeah. Are you having an okay time? Everybody…behaving?"

He chuckled and answered just as low. "Everybody's been great." He was surprised. He expected there to be some discord. "Your family is just so *nice*. Are they being like this for my benefit?"

I turned a little letting my knee sit atop his thigh. "No," I said truthfully, "this is them. They don't really know how to be any other way. Just crazy."

He laughed and looked around at everyone. His face changed and he grimaced. "Crazy's better than fighting and plotting."

I moved my hand to his thigh, his hand covered mine. I thought of what I could say in that moment as he thought about his life, how different things were now, how he remembered his childhood, how he couldn't remember all of it. And then Grandpa Jim spoke and an eerie quite fell over everyone. The only noise that could be heard except his deep timbered voice was the crack of the fire in front of us and the banging of my heart, begging for what was about to happen not to be true.

"So, Seth," he began and smiled, not meeting my eyes, not looking my way, "Caleb tells me you're a fireman, but you have a…business degree that you have no plans to use?"

Seth's brow bunched at the odd line of questioning that seemed to come out of nowhere, but gave an easy smile. "Yeah. My family…" He wished he hadn't said that, but he kept going. "They wanted me to go to college and have a degree of some kind to fall back on, but I wanted to be a fireman."

I looked out at the family. Ember, Dawson, Maria. They all looked as surprised as I was, but who knew…

I looked at Mom and Dad. They looked unreadable as they stared at Grandpa Jim, switching their gaze from him to Seth. I didn't know what to think. I felt the fingers of disappointment and betrayal flicking up my spine.

"Hey, you okay?" Seth whispered and rubbed my knuckles with his thumb. *That thumb.* I nodded, unable to speak, and tucked myself closer, pressing my face into his neck. He seemed happy with the move.

Grandpa went on as if nothing had happened. "And you haven't lived with your family for some time, right?"

"No," Seth answered slowly. "I live alone. I have an apartment near the fire station."

"Where do you think you guys will live after you're married?"

Seth chuckled uncomfortably. "Uh…"

"Grandpa," I complained.

"Okay, okay. How do you feel about the family? So far?" he amended with a smile.

Seth chuckled a little more. "Everyone's been great. I haven't met a Jacobson I didn't like."

"How do you feel about Ava's annoying habit of never wearing the right shoes for snow and ice?"

Seth laughed and looked down at me with a grin. "I've noticed. I'll work on it."

Grandpa thought, his finger to his lip. "Were the Watsons upset about our breaking traditions? Because Ava hasn't gone to be included in your clan and won't ever be doing so?"

Seth just stared, as stunned at the bluntness as I was. Tonight wasn't supposed to be about this.

My eyes searched my family, looking for the ones who were on board with this. There. Uncle Kyle. His face was hard, but he did look sorry when he saw that I'd figured it out. And Uncle Bish, too. They both looked away from me. They were always the ones who felt like they had to do the hard jobs, be the bad guys.

I looked at my lap and tried not to cry as I heard my grandfather ask another question. I was sure there were others who were on board with this, but I just didn't care. It was obvious that this party hadn't just been to welcome my significant into the family; it was to see if he was even worthy of being here in the first place.

Seth was so focused on answering the questions right that he couldn't hear what I was thinking. And I was glad. I hoped he never knew what went on here. I hoped to spare him of how petty my family was being.

But that was a dream that couldn't come true when the next question Grandpa asked was so brutal.

"I feel like I need to ask, at least once. We know that they attempted to take Ava," I sat up straighter, but he held his hand up, "the first time you came to see her, and I know you say you didn't have anything to do with it—"

"I didn't," Seth said, his voice hard, fighting to stay respectful to my grandfather.

Rodney, who had been quiet the whole night, stepped forward and said, "I already told you that he was the one who saved her that night. They *would* have taken her if not for him. He can't help that they took him as a kid. But the fact the he is bonded to my sister changes everything. You guys should know that. I'm not even bonded yet and *even I know* that you can't just throw that away for some revenge plot and pretend it didn't happen. It's stronger than that. Just like our vows say." He looked at Grandpa Peter and he mouthed the words as Rodney said them. "It's bigger than any ocean, deeper than any well, more powerful than any storm. Remember?"

He pushed through someone and went inside. I still sat up, surprised that my brother had defended Seth with so much gusto and more surprised that Seth hadn't gotten up and left, never looking back at this point.

Grandpa Jim sighed and leaned on his elbows. "But we still have to protect Ava. And I think the Watsons might have asked you to do things. You can come in the Champion's house." I stood, unable to listen to another second of it, but he went on. "You can come in the Visionary's house—the Visionary that took their powers away. And you're telling me they never asked you to do them any favors? You're eventually going to love Ava, I get it. But that doesn't mean that you have to love her family. You could be with Ava and still carry out the acts that they want you to do to the rest of the family—"

"Grandpa, no," I begged, letting my chin fall to my chest. I felt a little hysterical. I covered my eyes with my fingers. "You don't know everything. You don't know what you're talking about."

"Then let me ask him, Ava." I looked up and finally he was looking at me. "I just want him to answer me. And then I'll know. We all can go back to being friends and we never have to think about this again."

"But don't you see," I said, my voice cracking, my heart breaking a little. "The damage is done." I hadn't looked at Seth since the questioning began, too afraid of what I'd see there on his face. I knew he was confused. I knew he was angry. "His first memory of this family will be that you thought he was a traitor, a spy," I hissed the word I was so mad. "How could you do that? How could you do that to him and how could you do that to me?" I felt the first tear come and hated that tear with everything in me.

I felt Seth's fingers wrap around my wrist. I was too scared to look at him. *His ability is that he can feel and read your intent. It's lessened over the years and you have to say the answer out loud for him to get a read on it.*

He scoffed in my mind. *That's a neat trick.*

I'm so s—

He didn't let me finish my apology in my mind. He leaned forward with his elbows on his knees and began to tell them whatever they wanted to hear. "Yes, the first few days my family spent a *great deal* of time trying to get me to participate in all sorts of plots and plans. But as Rodney so eloquently put, Ava is my significant and I'm not going to hurt her. Hurting her family would hurt her and I'm not going to do that. They said they could break our imprint." I whimpered and wrapped my arms around myself. Seth stopped for a few seconds before going on. "That they could force an imprint with me and someone else and I would never know the difference. I don't remember much about my childhood, from when I was young, but I do remember growing up after they adopted me. I grew up with them and the others with a certain mindset. Honestly, I never paid much mind to it. I just wanted to get out, go to college, and get a job, be a fireman just like any other teenager does. All that revenge-Jacobson business didn't interest me, it was just something I was fed all the time. And then a few years after I moved…I bonded with one."

Grandpa Jim thought on that and I tried not to glare at him. "What kinds of revenge plans?"

Then I did glare. "Grandpa."

"Sir, I understand that you're worried about me being a spy or something. Did I pass your test, by the way?" It was obvious that Seth was also losing his cool a bit.

Grandpa leaned back a little as everyone looked at him to confirm.

"Yes. I don't feel any ill will at all towards us or Ava from him." There were actually a couple sighs. I glared at the lot of them. "But we need to know what their plans are for the Visionary and the Champion, and he has all but said that they have them."

"Of course they have them, Grandpa. They're the Watsons. We've been fighting since before every single one of us was born," I yelled.

"But if he knows what they're planning—"

Seth sighed and chuckled sadly. "So it's not okay for the Watsons to use me as a spy, but it's okay for the Jacobsons to?"

Everyone stopped.

And that was the kicker. Everyone finally got it. Seth was smack dab in the middle of a war with no side and it sucked. He loved a family that didn't love him back and was now in a family that apparently didn't trust him.

Mom stood and I didn't know what she was going to do. She looked like she wanted to do something, but didn't know what, and at this point, I was unaware of what side she was on.

I threw caution to the wind and hoped he would accept me, hoped he would still want me, even if my family didn't seem to.

I turned, putting my back to the fire and a lot of my family, and faced him. I held my hand out to him and waited. I finally saw his face. He didn't look angry, per se, just…numb. Disappointed, maybe. He took a few seconds to look up at me and when he did he blinked like he wasn't sure what he was seeing.

Ava, you don't have to.

Yes, I do.

You don't have to choose. I'll sit here and take it. It's worth it if makes them—

Come with me, Seth. Please.

He realized that he'd been staring for a while at my hand and didn't want to embarrass me or make it seem like he wasn't choosing me, so he moved and took my fingers in his, towering over me, his normally tan, firm face now lit with fire and a scowl as he thought about everything my grandfather had said. And the implications.

I tugged him to follow me as I moved around Grandpa Jim, not looking him in the eye. No one said a word to us. No one. I looked over at Maria and Dawson on their lounger and saw her shake her head and mouth a 'No'.

No, they hadn't known about the ambush. I tried my best smile and went inside to get my phone.

"Do you have everything?" I asked him.

"Everything for what?"

I was so angry I was shaking. I couldn't even think. "We're going to your place."

He put his hands on my arms. "I know you're mad—"

"I want to leave before someone comes in and—"

The kitchen side door swung open and I groaned.

"It's just me," Mom said. She came to us slowly. "I threatened bodily harm to anyone else that comes inside." She sighed harshly. "Daddy's going to get his. Don't worry."

I was still shaking. I leaned against the counter and as soon as I did I watched my mother take my significant and hug him so hard. My mouth fell open, but not in the surprised way or the shocked way. It was in the way that you do hoping it will help stop the tears, the pain in your chest, when it's too much and you need to release something and don't know how.

I watched Seth over my mother's shoulder and he looked so wracked as she whispered to him.

Then she said out loud so I could hear, "We had no part in that, Ava."

I saw then that he was fighting his emotion. I opened my mind a little, wanting to help him if I could, feeling so guilty for what my family did to him. But it was my mom that was making him feel this way. His mother was never this way with him. He never knew it could be this way and it was so good to feel loved, even with what had just happened out there just now, he could still find so much joy in this moment?

God, I loved this man.

She pulled back and cupped his face hard so he'd listen. "You are my daughter's significant and that's it. You're not a spy. We don't want to use you. We don't want to take advantage of you." I felt my chest get tight and gripped my hands together at my chin. "We don't want to see if there's some ploy where we can get information from you because you're an inside man. No, Seth. We love you because our daughter loves you and because we see how much you love her." A sob slipped through. "Everyone in this family does not believe the same. It may not have seemed like it out there, but more people than not agree with me. And lucky for you, I'm the boss." She smiled and let her hands fall away.

"It's okay, Mrs. J. They had to at least ask, right? I expected it. I'm the enemy's son." He looked at me. "Romeo and Juliet. In fact, I expected it from you, but it never came. It stung," he admitted, looking at the floor, "but I knew at some point it was coming."

"There were better ways—"

"It's okay," he soothed. "It's done."

Then she turned to me and we both walked to each other. "Your father didn't do it either," she promised.

I sighed in relief. "Thank you."

"I don't know what Daddy was thinking, but I'm sure he knew that we'd be against it, or maybe he thought we'd be too attached." She leaned back and we both looked at Seth, leaned on the breakfast nook. "He's right." She grinned. "Come here."

He smiled and came to her other arm. We made an awkward hug, but Mom didn't care. Seth wound his arm around my waist and took advantage of it.

"We're going to get through this. And it's going be hard, but someone told me once that the things that come hard are things that are worth it. I have faith in you two. I know that you're going to be more than just a great couple, but you're....destined to do things." Her eyes lit up. "Actually, let me show you something."

She went into the desk in the den and pulled out a small lockbox from underneath. In it were signed papers and documents. The deed to the house, titles, all sorts of things, and then she pulled out a stack of papers with a drawing on top.

"When we…" She looked up and locked eyes with Seth. "With everything that's happened tonight, I don't know if you want to hear anything else about your family right n—"

"Tell me. I trust you."

"Well, when we raided the Watson compound that day, we found some drawings." She laid it on the stack of papers and Seth picked it up in wonder. He chuckled.

Even back then you were good.

He shook his head. *You don't have to lie to me, sweetheart. I just can't believe she has this. I don't have anything from when I was a kid.*

She shrugged. "There's only two, but they're yours. You drew them. You should have them." Mom seemed sad to let them go.

"Thank you," Seth said, his voice cracking with emotion as he looked at the little boy on a hill holding hands with the woman. "I wonder who the woman is."

"Ashlyn," Mom said softly. "Ava told us when she saw it, after we brought it back with us."

He looked at me. He looked so...awe-filled. "It's so strange to me that we were connected back then in ways and wound up finding each other again all these years later." He looked at the drawing. "Do you remember us and Ashlyn together?" he whispered. He looked at me like this answer was particularly important.

"Yeah, some. I didn't know it was you, until Mom told me it was you. I didn't remember his name, I just remembered that Ashlyn would take me to see a boy and he...was always so happy to see us."

Mom looked at the picture. "We were so upset about not finding you at the compound." She pressed her lips together to stop her tears. To this day she felt guilty. "Ashlyn visited Ava for the last time that night. She said you were supposed to grow up with the Watsons, that by going and saving those people, I had already altered your course and saved you. She told Ava that you would be her friend one day and that when you were ready, you would find us."

Seth's free hand wrapped around my wrist. "I guess I did."

"Take them. They're yours. This one, too." She reached for the one of a boy on a horse and I was pulled into a vision. It yanked me so hard, I could barely breathe.

It was a woman. She was running through the woods. She was captured. She was pregnant. We couldn't see her face as she laid on a cot in a dingy room, but you could tell she'd been mistreated, but she wasn't pregnant anymore. Her arms were bruised at the crook of her elbows from needles. She was only wearing a t-shirt that was too big for her. She was dirty. She was thin. Her hair was matted. And I didn't think any of those things were up to her. She was chained to the bed by her ankle and the way she was rolling and looking around the room made me think she was drugged. Then they came in and I saw the whole situation for what it was. This woman was part of the Watson experiments. I gasped just as she did as they turned her over, but her face was still covered by the person who had come into the room.

"Now, little one, let's see if we can get some use out of you yet." And then he moved to stick something in her arm again. Even in her weak state, she fought him, shouting and trying to scratch at him.

Good for her.

Even though he held her down easily.

I felt myself being pulled out and grabbed the corner of the table to keep myself upright. I felt Seth's hands on my face, pulling me up, asking if I was okay.

"I'm okay," I muttered.

"Answer me, Ava, where I can hear you."

Boy, the fireman in him was coming out. And it was so dang hot. He tried to hide his smirk, but failed. "Ave," he sighed.

"I'm, okay. Sir."

He rolled his eyes.

"You called her 'Ave," Mom said.

His hands fell away and he looked at her. "Will that come true? What you saw?"

"Oh, Seth," she sighed and I heard the tone. "You don't understand. That wasn't the future, it was the past."

"What do you mean?" When she didn't answer him right away, he leaned back some. "You know who that was, don't you?"

"Seth," she began.

"Don't bullcrap me," he whispered. "Not about this."

He knew. In his gut, he knew. Mom sighed. "I'm sorry, Seth."

He shook his head. "They told me they found me in the woods. That she hadn't wanted me, that I was abandoned, but I always wondered if that was the way it actually happened. I can't believe..." He shook his head. He never knew his mother, but it still sucked that they had taken her from him before he had the chance. And that she was tortured and the proof of that was now right there in front of our eyes.

I took Seth's hand in both of mine and looked at my mother, the Visionary. "We're staying at Seth's tonight, okay?"

I saw Seth look at my profile, but I didn't look at him. I stared at my mother who wanted to tell me 'No', but knew she couldn't. I wasn't a teenager. I was a woman who had just fought her family for her significant.

"Just leave your phone on, okay?" she finally said.

"I will." I went and hugged her and whispered. "Thanks for believing in him."

She nodded. "Scarf," she insisted.

I quickly grabbed one that was hanging on the hall tree and wrapped it over my coat collar.

"Bye, Mrs. J," Seth said with a two-finger wave in the air.

"Maggie," she scolded.

"I compromised," he said and sent her that smile that melted her.

"Oh, all right."

I shut the door behind me and wondered what kind of mood Seth was going to be in as he tugged me by my hand through the parked cars to his truck. I felt awful for him after the hell he'd just been through tonight. My family freaking ambushed him and then the vision about his mom. He was probably ready to ditch me and take his family up on their offer.

He moved swiftly until we reached his truck. When we got there, it was already running and the windshield defrosting. He opened my door for me and I kept my head down, wondering what to say. We were finally alone.

One of his warm hands pressed on my left hip, pushing me to lean against the truck seat. His other hand used those expert fingers to lift my face. The open truck door blocked the wind for us. He wasn't smiling, but he looked so intently at my face.

That warm hand on my hip inched around to my lower back. The one on my chin spread out and cupped my face.

"What are you doing?" I said, so confused at why he wasn't angry.

"Falling more in love with you than I thought was possible. Ava, you just fought your family for me."

"Seth…" I smiled, but felt the tears coming. That seemed to be happening a lot lately. "You fought your family for me the very first day you met me."

He remembered then and sighed, his breath puffing in the cold air between us, letting his head fall and almost touching mine. "It's not the same."

"I know. Yours was worse."

He smiled a little. "We're not comparing. I can't believe you just did that."

I felt angry all over again. Enough to start shaking. "I can't believe *they* just did *that*. They completely ambushed you. I wasn't going to let them—"

"I know," he breathed, coming closer, erasing the space between us, warming me with his body and with his presence. His next words were not breath however, they were growled as he moved his lips against my own. He wanted me to *feel them*. "And it was the sexiest, the most amazing thing I've ever seen in my entire life."

And then I *did* feel them. I felt them as he pressed me to into the seat and devoured my mouth. I wrapped my arms around his neck and held on as he showed me what love felt like. As he showed me that a kiss could change your entire world.

I was just as hungry as he was. He moved, putting his arms inside my jacket, so he could feel *me*, we could both feel each other's warmth. He groaned a little when we came back together. I was up on my tiptoes to reach him, and once they got tired and I went back down, he spread his legs like always to make himself shorter. He was always accommodating me.

My cell phone dinged with a text message in my pocket, but I didn't even flinch. Neither did Seth. He kept right on licking his way into my mouth, not a care in the world but what was waiting inside for him.

I felt different, like something had shifted for us. It felt like us against the world now. Like…even my family weren't at our backs. We could only fully trust ourselves. And that wasn't as awful a thing as I thought it would feel like. It felt good to have one person in the world I knew I could trust completely.

I tilted my head a little, giving him the hint I hoped he'd take. He took it and kissed my jaw first, then under it. He pulled my scarf down a bit, but then decided to take it off.

Pulling it gently, it went, and then I felt his lips on my collar bone. I breathed into his hair and gripped it tightly in my fists. The assaults moved to the other side and back up to my mouth with an ease but a ferocity that made me so hot in my veins.

"Don't worry about your family," he finally said, his head to mine, his breaths a little ragged as we tried to calm down. "I can handle your family."

"You shouldn't have to."

His smirk was adorable. "Come on, beautiful, most families despise their in-laws. It's a fact." I shook my head at his attempt to make it all okay. "I expected it, sweetheart."

I looked away, but he brought me back, that thumb on my chin, always commanding in the most sweet and uncommanding way—saying trust me, stay with me, love me, I'll figure this out for us.

I gripped his shirt in my fingers and waited.

"I expected them to ask," he looked down a little and smiled. "Did I expect them to have a guy that could read my intent? No, but that was clever."

"It was underhanded."

"They were protecting you. And themselves. It was smart. They were using what they had at their disposal."

"Seth, don't. Don't make out like what they did was okay."

"They," he began slowly, "maybe could have done it in a more..."

"Tactful way?" I said harshly. "Without the entire family watching? Without making it seem like the whole family was against you? Without making me have to choose you over them like that? And they had to know, right? What did they think I was going to do when they starting asking you all those questions? Did they think I was stupid and wouldn't get it? That I would just watch and let it happen?"

He smoothed his thumb over my chin. "I don't know, sweetheart. And I'm sorry that you had to choose."

I sighed and tugged him closer by his shirt. He 'oomphed' against me as I hugged him. "Let's get out of here. I don't want to be here when they start leaving."

"Whatever you want. You sure you're okay to stay at my place?" he asked, but he looked pretty excited by the idea.

I lifted one shoulder and bit into my lip. "I'm fine."

One side of his mouth lifted. "Ava Jacobson, are you flirting with me?"

"Maybe," I whispered and smiled. "Would flirting get me some coffee?"

His smile grew. "Flirting would have gotten you coffee the first time we met if you had stayed. But you were in a rush to get away from me if I recall."

I smiled and looked down. "What if we were just two normal Virtuoso people and we met. We would have met and been happy, all our families would been happy." I looked back up.

"But you wouldn't be Ava Jacobson then. And that's the girl I'm in love with."

My heart stuttered behind my ribs, painfully, beautifully. He turned me and put his hands on my waist to help my stunned body into the cab of the truck. He ran around and got in, putting his hand on my thigh to tug me so I'd be right against him. "This okay?"

I looked over. "Yeah. Yeah," I said and laughed a little. I needed to get a grip. "Seth?" I whispered, feeling all my emotion bubble to the surface, as I turned and put my hands around his upper arm.

He looked over, our faces only inches apart. "Yeah?"

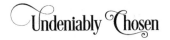

"You wouldn't be Seth Watson either. And that's the guy I'm in love with."

He took a few seconds. He didn't even look like he was breathing really. We just stared at each other. I'd called him 'Watson' and it wasn't with disdain, it was with love. It was his name, whether he or I wanted it to be or not. And I loved him.

He eventually sighed, a little harshly, and then a hand tunneled in my hair, dragging me back to him for the softest kiss I'd ever had. He exhaled, his breath blowing down my neck. "You're killing me in all the ways that matter, little bird."

"You're absolutely killing me," I whispered back. "Truly. Thank you for being so gracious about my family. After what you've been through with the Watsons, they…don't deserve it."

He paused, looking at me for a moment before he said, so softly, like his words would punch through me and he was trying to ease the jolt. "We have to be bigger than the things we suffer."

My chest hurt at how beautiful and painfully true that was.

I leaned in and kissed his mouth once more before putting my hand on his thigh, and licking my lips. I could still taste him there. I closed my eyes for a second before opening to find him watching me.

He shook his head with a heated chuckle as he put the truck in reverse and looked behind us. "Gah, you are going to be trouble."

CHAPTER SEVENTEEN

We got coffee at the place where we met. Paul was none too happy to see us waltzing in, but I honestly couldn't care and was barely paying attention. We found a small booth in the back and decided to sit there and talk for a while.

About nothing. About everything.

I learned that he played football in high school and was the—wait for it—quarterback. With those arms, I couldn't see how not. He said high school was a very strange time because there was no dating and he loved sports so girls were all over the place.

I crinkled my nose, making him laugh. It was cute, thinking about a high school Seth.

But he never dated. He just worked, played sports, and was with his family. Training, plotting, waiting patiently until he could be free.

The drive was short and I almost wished it was longer. His hand stuck between my thighs was comforting, warming, and possessive. I hated that he had to move it.

He got out and then pulled me out the driver's side, his hands on my waist. "Thanks."

His smirk was small. He nodded his head toward his place. "Come on."

The last time I'd been here, Harper was there. I looked around, half expecting her to be here now. "She won't. She's done with me, I promise. And vice versa."

I didn't say anything. I just left it at that.

He unlocked the door and I walked over the worn "Welcome" mat. The darkness didn't scare me, even though it was pitch black inside. I took a few steps inside, maybe to show him that I was okay, that I trusted him and his place. I heard him locking the door behind me and the lights came on.

It was exactly as I remembered.

I set my coffee on the bar by the kitchen and started to take my coat off. He came to help me, placing a quick kiss on the back of my neck as the jacket slid from my arms. He moved away to hang it on the coatrack along with his own.

This visit to his apartment felt so different from last time.

"Well," he began out loud, "last time you were here, you kinda hated me." He smiled, but I could tell he was thinking about that day just like I was.

"I'm sorry."

He shook his head. "It's done. We're not going back, remember?"

I shook my head. "Not going back."

We stared at each other across the room.

"What do you want to do now that you're here?"

I thought about this place. About how last time, I had been so unsure of him, but *wanted* to believe in him so badly. I looked around the room. I remembered it all, all my feelings, all my wanting to touch him and just have everything that was promised to me. I remembered feeling cheated and saying so.

Seth watched me as I worked through it all.

"Why don't we start with the couch?" I finally said.

He didn't move, but I saw his throat work through a loud swallow. "Sweetheart, you're going to have to elaborate on that."

I giggled as I got the implication of my words.

"All the memories here are things I want to forget. When I come here, and I don't know what we're going to do later on and I don't care right now, but I want to think about good memories of this place. So let's take a bad memory and erase it, replace it with a good one." I moved to the couch. "The couch was where we fought, sort of. Let's start here with a new, better memory."

He moved toward me and stopped at the arm of the couch. "What did you have in mind?"

"Do you have any movies?"

"I have Netflix," he said with a grin.

"Do you want to watch a movie with me?" I asked, suddenly shy. It was something so simple. I forgot that we were still learning how to be a couple. I didn't even know what kind of movies he liked.

"Sure." He kicked his shoes off at the end of couch and grabbed a remote, handing it to me. He went to the kitchen and started looking around.

"Want some popcorn? Are you a popcorn or candy person?"

"Popcorn. Though, who turns down candy, seriously?"

I could hear his chuckle over the crinkling of a wrapper and then the noises of a microwave. When he came back in, he had grabbed my coffee off the bar by the kitchen as well as a big bottle of blue Gatorade for himself. "Thanks."

"What are we watching?" he asked as he settled in next to me, propping one ankle on his knee and letting one of his arms come around me. The bowl of popcorn sat in his lap.

I looked at him. "You're letting me pick?"

He shrugged. "If you want."

"Okay," I said casually and let the little boxes jump over until it reached *Steel Magnolias*. "Awesome," I said excitedly. "I haven't watched this in ages."

To his credit he kept a straight face. He leaned back further, settling in and shook his head once, like he was putting on his game face. "*Steel Magnolias*. Love those girls."

I snorted under my breath. "Are you serious?"

"What? I can hang with Clairee and Ouiser now. Those broads are tough."

"Oh, my gosh." I swatted him, though I wasn't sure why. He was spoiling my plan. "You actually *have* watched *Steel Magnolias*!"

He laughed and held up his arm in defense a little. "What? We have limited channels at the station and it gets boring. What can I say? All the firemen of Station 22 have seen *Steel Magnolias*."

I laughed so hard, giggling and falling into him. He laughed into my hair. I sat up and slapped his thigh. "I would never make you watch *Steel Magnolias*. But thank you for being so willing.

"Whatever you want," he said, his smile wide.

"How about a…comedy?" He said 'comedy' the same time I did. I grinned. "Okay." I snuggled in closer under his arm, putting my socked feet up on the coffee table. I clicked through movie after movie. The new stuff was all junk. Nothing was funny nowadays. I missed humor when people were focused on family and finding love. Now people were focused on jobs and finding sex.

I stopped on *Dodgeball* and looked over at him. He grinned and chuckled silently.

"You like *Dodgeball*?"

"It's hilarious." He squinted, looking at me funny. "You don't believe me?" I bit my lip a little. "Go look in my mind for yourself and see if I'm telling the truth." My words were barely breathed and his face changed immediately.

He breathed out. "Ava, I want to, but I don't want it to be in response to your family."

"What?"

He licked his lips and held my chin, which I was learning was becoming his *move*. "When we decide to go there, to do that again, I want it to be because you're happy and ready and… Not because you're at my place, hiding from your family that currently doesn't know if they trust me or not."

"You passed their little test," I sneered. "They trust you."

"Well whatever. That's not how I want this," his fingers moved to graze my temple, "to start." I let my gaze swing up to him, but he was smiling, looking at my skin as he was off in his own world.

"Seth?" I whispered.

"You didn't doubt for a second." His eyes met mine. "When your grandpa was questioning me. You knew that he was about to expose anything and everything and I would have no idea. And yet, not once in your mind, did you have a thought that I might not pass his test." I shook my head. Nope. Not once. I knew he was there for me. "You were just upset that my welcoming party was being ruined at the very end with a heaping of betrayal." He chuckled once without humor. "But it really wasn't betrayal, Ava. They don't know me. They don't owe me anything. But you, trusting me completely, believing in me? Thank you."

"Seth…" I bit into my lip and closed my eyes, trying to make sense of this. Feeling his thumb on my chin to release my lip from my teeth was as welcoming and comforting as a warm blanket. "I wasn't smiling," I reminded him and opened my eyes. He didn't release a smile, he just released my lip.

"You should be," he said, ordered really, and the blood in my veins lit up with crackles as he leaned in. We were already so close as it was. "When you smile, it's like my body can relax. Something inside me, in here," he palmed his chest, "aches when you're not smiling, and the thought of you unhappy at all makes me physically hurt. Tonight, I wanted to stand up and punch someone for making you feel that way. But I knew that doing that would just make you feel worse. Punching that old grandpa wouldn't solve anything, right?" He searched for my gaze and the second he found it, I cracked a smile. "There it is." He palmed his chest and sighed. "All is right with the world again."

What could I say to that?

"Tomorrow night we can watch *Ron Burgundy* if you want?"

He stared. "You do *not* like *Ron Burgundy*."

"Yes, I—"

"Where did you come from? Are you a fembot?" I laughed loudly, my face in his neck. I heard him laughing around me. I lifted up, but he didn't let me get far, wrapping his arms around me. "I'm completely serious. You're not real. No girl watches guy comedies, listens to old music, and stands up to her family without blinking an eye." He finished so softly. He moved in to cup my face with one hand and kissed my lips. "You're not real, but you're sitting right here, aren't you?"

I smiled and we stared, blue colliding with brown in a war that was meant to be lost. He eventually took the remote from my fingers and pressed enter. "*Dodgeball* it is."

Then he stuck his hand between my thighs and looked at me with a smile, remembering what I'd thought about how I felt about that. He leaned in and kissed me once before looking back at the movie.

I snuggled into him, hugging his arm with both of my arms and laying my head on his shoulder.

I wanted someone to take a picture of us like this, because surely this was the happiest I'd ever looked in my life, surely I was glowing, surely my smile had never been more genuine. I wanted a picture because this was the first time in my life that my home and my heart were in the same place, and I wanted someone to capture that for the whole world to see.

Seth wiggled next to me until he got his phone out of his pocket. I grinned as he pressed his thumb on the screen several times until the camera was up. He looked at me with an easy smile.

"Ready?" I nodded. He held his phone in his hand up high above him and said, "Smile, little bird."

Click.

"So, you have to get away from me today at some point and go see your family, before you get ready for the summit. They don't know about the fire, they don't know that you quit the fire station. None of it. You make out like it's all just too much right now, that I don't understand your job, that my family is pressuring you to be a spy for them, just like we said."

He rubbed his hair. "I don't know. Things are really weird. Your family kinda ambushed me." He chuckled and looked up. "Your grandpa—"

I sighed. "Grandpa Jim. Of course."

"Yeah. They started in on me at the bar-b-que and you lost it."

"They did that at the bar-b-que!" I cried. I was livid.

Seth just laughed. "Don't worry. You took care of it. You let them have it, trust me. And I passed your grandpa's test with flying colors."

"Of course you did." I rolled my eyes. "Where are you now?"

"I took you back to my place. We've been staying at your parents because of my family, but your mom didn't argue when you said we were leaving. I think she knew you needed to get out. And she knows I'll protect you."

I smiled, biting my lip a little thinking about it. "What do we do together?"

"Last night we watched our first movie." He raised his eyebrow in challenge. "*Dodgeball.*"

"I *love Dodgeball,*" I squealed. "Did I say half the lines?"

He laughed and quirked his eyebrow instead this time. "No."

"I was just holding back. Don't worry. You'll get to experience that next time."

He laughed again and looked out the window. "It's time. I'll go to my family today. The plan will work. I promise. It has to."

I nodded and hugged him around his middle. "Be careful. Please. See you soon."

"Bye, Ave," he said into my hair.

"Bye, Seth."

I woke in soft, dark sheets in a dark room. I'd fallen asleep on Seth last night and he carried me to bed. I woke as he was laying me down. Talk about swooning. There's nothing like being carried and put to bed.

He gave me a pair of his shorts to put on so I didn't have to wear my jeans with snow and salt on the bottom to bed. His boxers were huge, but the elastic kept them up. I kept my thin yellow shirt on and when I came out, he was just pulling a shirt on.

I missed the show. Mmm.

He looked at me as he settled on the bed. "All right," he said, though I could tell he could laugh at any second. "That's enough out of you."

"I said *not a word*." I smiled as I crawled across the bed to him. I probably could have walked over but… "The thoughts in my head are private. You can't use that against me. It would never stand up in court."

He chuckled and did this growl, groan thing as he reached over to turn off the lamp at the same time.

"Your case is on shaky foundation," he said into my hair as he laid down on his back. His massive frame took up a great deal of the bed. His arm was around my back, tugging me so I just curled up against his side. He yanked a blanket that he had pulled out around us.

With my face in his neck, I could breathe him in all night and didn't even have to try. I moved one of my legs and rubbed it against his cautiously. He sighed a little when I did.

I felt so safe as I slept that night, and now as I woke, I felt just as safe. We never moved in the night. I noticed that before—we always woke in the exact same spot as when we went to sleep. And as if he knew that I was now awake, his eyes popped open and he glanced over at me. His smile was small and immediate, crooked, like I'd put his whole world off its axis but he was somehow okay with that.

"Morning, beautiful," he murmured.

I started to bite my lip, but when his eyes went to my lip, I stopped. He smirked, so smug and cute.

"Good morning, gorgeous." He chuckled, but I moved up on my elbow and poked his chin with my pointer finger. "You don't think you're gorgeous?" He just stared at me, his hand moving up my back.

"I've never been called that before, no."

"What have you been called?"

He thought. "Hoser. Rookie. Roughneck. Hose dragger."

I laughed, letting my forehead fall on his stomach. "Oh, my gosh."

"Whacker."

"Stop!"

"Bulldog. Skater. Doorway dancer. Nozzle jockey."

"Seth!" I fell back on the pillow next to him. "My guts hurts!"

He chuckled as he leaned over me a little. "Can I say something?"

"Always."

His entire body and being sighed at those words. "It may be a tad too soon, but it has to be said," he breathed his words and swallowed as he looked down at my collarbone and neck, and finally my eyes. He leaned down, brushing my hair back behind my ear. It occurred to me that I hadn't even adjusted it when I woke. My eyes went wide. Oh, gosh. There was no telling what he was looking at right now. He smiled and shook his head. "That's what I'm talking about." His fingers combed behind my ear once more. "You are... absolutely edible in the mornings." His eyes roamed around my face while his hand went down to wrap around my neck gently. "No wonder significants run to get married because," his eyes met mine, "this is almost torture."

I felt his hand on my pink neck and his eyes on mine and couldn't find a thing to say that made sense. "I'm sorry?"

His smile grew. "I like to be tortured by you. Waking up to you every day doesn't suck. You keep being edible and I'll keep buying the coffee. Deal?" He leaned in and kissed my stunned lips once before rolling off the bed, grabbing some clothes from the drawers, and leaving the room. Before long I heard the shower turn on in the hall.

I closed my eyes and tried not to think about it.

I got up, making his bed neatly and even picking up his clothes that he'd thrown on the floor last night. When I stood I found a mirror above the dresser. My hair was all tussled, like someone had had their hands in it maybe. My neck was flushed from blushing, my brown eyes stood out with no make up on. My lips were a soft pink against my tan skin.

Edible, huh. I grinned.

I turned to put my jeans back on, finger-combed my hair, and then went to find the coffee pot. His kitchen was small, but packed in and functional. He had a Keurig and I practically jumped when I saw it. Hazelnut or not, I could get down with any coffee that had flavor.

I was looking through the cupboards to see if I could find his cups when he came up behind me and grabbed my hand. "We can get some coffee on the way to your house."

He had his fire station shirt on. I squinted in confusion. He shrugged. "It's just a shirt. Now, I hate to rush you out, but I do have a few things I have to do today."

"Yeah," I replied thoughtfully. "And I'm sure my family will be trying to either apologize or tell me they were right to try or…something. I might as well face that."

He moved until he was right in front of me and took my face in his hands. "Everything is going to be okay, little bird. Thank you for trusting me."

"Of course," I said. There was no other answer.

He looked at me, his eyes searching my face, roaming all the specks of my eyes, my lips, until he settled back on my eyes and I knew that something was different today.

"Is everything okay?" I gripped his wrist.

He smiled at my concern. "Everything's fine." He kissed my forehead and stayed there. "I'm fixing everything for us."

That statement should have made me feel better, but it somehow made me feel a little shift of unease.

I grabbed my bag and he drove me to my house. The whole way there, though I sat up against his side, I felt like there was something wrong. I couldn't put my finger on it. Something just wasn't quite right. I could go digging around in his mind and find what he was doing.

I became suddenly angry.

It wasn't fair that my body didn't let me see his mind the way that he saw mine all the time. It wasn't fair. But he wouldn't want me digging for this. I knew. And he'd know that I was digging and would just shut me out the second I began. It was pointless to even try. Besides, I didn't really want to take things from him, I wanted him to give them to me. If he thought this was something he didn't want me to know, then there had to be a reason.

He parked the truck and turned to me. "Everything is fine," he soothed, feeling how anxious I was. He took my chin captive by that thumb. "I'll be back before you know it."

"Seth."

"Don't worry about anything. I promise. Everything's okay. Just tying up loose ends. I'll see you in a little bit," he said, releasing me. He leaned in and kissed my shaky mouth.

"I don't know what's going on, but please be careful. Don't be a hero."

He smiled a little and looked down, and I knew—something was definitely going on. He looked back up and cupped my face fully with both hands. "I love you, Ava." Neither of us had said it since the fire. "And I'll see you tonight, at this house, all in one piece. I promise you, sweetheart."

I sighed. It was as if I could finally breathe. "I love you more."

He grinned before he laughed softly. "Oh, we're going to play that game?"

"No," I shook my head. "I just win. I love you more." I gripped him around his neck tightly, trying not cry. I wanted to believe him that he would be back in one piece. He seemed so confident. There could only be one place he was going.

His arms went inside my jacket around my sides to crush me to him. His face pressed into that place where my neck and shoulder met and spoke into my hair and skin, his breath warm.

"If you want to battle it out for who loves who more, we can do that, but I just want to know what I get when I win." He sighed. "I've got to go, sweetheart."

I leaned back and kissed him once. If he wanted anything more than that, he had to come back.

He snorted at that.

"I'm coming back," he breathed into my hair. "I promise." He kissed my hair and that was my cue to scoot over and get out. I looked at him through the open door once more before shutting it. He backed out and stopped in the road. He looked at me, that gaze so intense, even that far away.

Everything's fine. Promise.

I'll be here.

Bye, little bird.

Bye...

He drove away and I pivoted on my driveway to face my house.

And Ember, Dawson, Maria, Laurelyn, and Drake, too, apparently. I sighed, my aggravation manifesting in a huge puff of cold smoke in front of my mouth.

"We had nothing to do with that—that—ambush," Ember said and ran down the stairs, almost slipping on the melting snow as she greeted me. "You have to be—"

"I believe you." I rolled my eyes as we made our way into the kitchen. "Did you guys stay the night?"

"We felt terrible." She looked at our cousins. "And so did Daddy. And so did Uncle Kyle. Grandpa was the only one who was still so adamant that it was the right thing to do. But when we all saw your face. And his face." She shook her head and looked down. I balked. Ember looked like she actually might cry.

"Ember," I breathed and went to her, hugging my cousin. Weird, I was comforting her when it was me and my significant who were being pounced on.

"Everything's okay. Seth wasn't even angry." She leaned back in surprise. I shrugged and leaned back against the counter. "He said he understood that my family would want to know his intentions, and he was actually surprised that we hadn't ambushed him already."

"Seth is a freaking saint," Dawson muttered under his breath and shook his head. "If that had been me, I wouldn't have been so calm. The boy was *too* calm." He met my eyes. "I guess he was being good for your benefit so you wouldn't freak." He smirked. "Well, any more than you did anyway."

"From day one Seth has been so levelheaded about things," I said softly. "When we imprinted and both figured out who the other was, he knew I was a Jacobson somehow from his visions just like I knew that he was a Watson from mine, but he didn't know that Mom was the Visionary." I crossed my arms and stared at my shoes on my Mom's grey stone floor. I missed my Chucks. "He told me then that he was sorry, that he understood if I hated him, that he might hate him too if the situation were reversed. That he'd wait for me as long it took."

"Wait for you?" Maria asked, glued to the story, her eyes wide.

I swallowed before I spoke. "I ran. I didn't know what else to do. We were in the coffee shop by my school and I...imprinted with a *Watson*. At first, he was just a boy and I was so happy. So was he. And then the pieces started to fall into place." I shook my head and laughed once without humor. "I didn't know what to do or what *he* might do or… But I never got any ill will from him. I only ever felt like he wanted to help me and was interested in me like a significant should be. He let me go without a fight. And that night, when his family ambushed us, he fought them and saved me."

"The whole thing is so romantic," Laurelyn said and smiled. "Don't worry about what anybody else says. Now you have a great story to tell. A real Romeo and Juliet. Your kids will love it one day."

I smiled, remembering that Seth had called us that once. "I hope so."

"Where did Seth go?" Dawson asked, rubbing Maria's shoulders just as I heard Mom start to bang pots in the kitchen.

"He had a few things to do today. He'll be here tonight."

"Brunch anyone?" Mom poked her head in. "Everybody got a late start so I figured we'd have brunch instead of lunch today. We have the summit tomorrow. The council members will be here tonight, very late. And then tomorrow," she straightened, "the torture begins."

We laughed. The council consisted of Mom, Dad, Aunt Jen, Uncle Bish, Uncle Kyle, Aunt Lynne, and several members of the others clans. Mom tried to explain to them about a vision she'd had, about how the council was supposed to be set up, but they were having none of that. One family to rule the race? No. That wasn't happening. They did, however, stop being so tight with the rules. For instance, they were coming here instead of us going there.

This summit was called because of me. I knew it. No one had outright said it, but I just knew it had to be. Because I had bonded to a Watson and that was in essence, against the law. Members of rival clans weren't supposed to, um, canoodle. Because it just causes more strife between clans and you've all read Shakespeare. It doesn't end well. Now, we hadn't canoodled and we didn't even know that we were rivals before we touched. But imprinting with a rival clan member was a whole other ballpark. I don't think it's ever even happened before. And I'm sure they were coming to see what the Watsons were up to.

So Mom was going to be on Visionary duty while they were here for the next three days. All the family was coming in. The Gemino clan was coming in, too, to help us with security, making sure that the Watsons didn't use this as an opportunity, even though there's no way they would we were even having a summit. Seth passed Grandpa Jim's test, and okay, I got why they felt like they had to do that right before the summit, but everything was fine. We were careful as we always were. Aliases were used, the hotel and conference room where we were having it was being booked under an insurance convention.

It was foolproof. It worked every time. We kept tabs on them. Dad and his guys he sent out had seen them trying to track the summit before, so it wasn't like they weren't looking, they just couldn't figure it out.

We all helped Mom cook brunch and then I went and did some homework while Ember and Laurelyn walked around my room and tried not to distract me. Yeah right.

Eventually I gave up and tossed my books aside. We talked about school, we talked about their family stuff, they wanted to know every detail of my relationship.

"No, I am not telling you what scruff feels like," I said dryly. "Ember, come on."

"I may never feel scruff! Come on, Ava."

"Ember, you're not that much younger than me. It can happen any day now."

"Every day is its own infinity, every hour, its own eternity, every minute, its own forever." I just stared, unable to breathe for a second. She sighed with a smile. "When I finally do meet him, I'll be more ready for him than I've been for anything in my life."

"Ember..." I didn't want to stomp her good mood, but... "Sometimes it doesn't happen the way we want. I mean, look at me."

"Yes," she smiled, "look at you."

I felt immediately chagrined, so put in my place by her words. "You're right. It has definitely worked out for us, after everything we've been through, and I love him so—"

They both gasped, hands to their throats. You would have thought I said the president was chubby or something. "What?"

"You love him? Does he know?"

"Yeah," I breathed. "We both told each other for the first time at the fire. I guess it was wondering if we'd ever—"

"Fire?"

I scoffed. "I thought my mother was the gossiping queen and told you guys everything?"

"She's been busy. So spill. You were in a fire? What the hell? Why wouldn't you have told us about this?"

"It was the night before the bar-b-que. Seth is—was a fireman." I bit my lip for a second. "I could feel his heart beating so hard and I just had to go to him. When I followed it, there was a burning building."

They gasped. "No, Ava."

"Don't worry, I got scolded plenty." I looked down and smiled a little remembering him as he begged to go, how much he tried to protect me, to sacrifice himself. "I had to do it, I had to go inside and find him."

When I looked up they were open-mouthed.

"Oh, my gosh, Ave." Laurelyn wiped under her eye. This is like a freaking romance novel. What happened next?"

So I told them. I told them everything. By the time I was done, we were all crying, but I was smiling through them.

Ember sniffed. "I would have gone in, too." I looked up to meet her gaze. "Into the burning building." She nodded. "I would have gone in after my significant. I mean...at least I think I would."

I tilted my head and sighed. I hoped that Ember would find her soulmate soon. She joked around a lot and she could be loud and fun and silly, but she was also be this loving, caring, passionate spirit. I think that's why she wanted to find her significant so badly; because she was so passionate and loving.

"Scruff feels rough and a little soft at the same time. It feels like...a little bit of pain with a little bit of pleasure mixed in."

She smiled crookedly and we leaned over to hug each other.

"Your significant is coming, Ember," I promised. Mom had taken care of that.

"Thank you. And Ava, everything is going to be okay." She leaned back. "This summit...bullcrap. We're all behind you. Just don't show them any fear."

I nodded and hadn't realized how truly distressed I was about it until she started talking about it. I hugged her hard. I heard Ember say, "Oh, get in here, Lore."

We all laughed and hugged each other, remembering what it was like to grow up together. Maria used to babysit us. We'd watch movies and talk about bonding with our soulmate one day, meeting him, what the visions would be like, what someone's calming touch would be like.

After a while of lounging and TV, I asked what they wanted to do. I should have known they'd pick horseshoes.

We had another Jacobson family get-together coming up tomorrow. We might as well practice.

Ember was the queen of horseshoes, even throwing them behind her back. It was ridiculous. And the gloating…

That was how Seth found us. It had been hours since I'd seen him. It was nearing sunset, in fact. I wondered what he'd been doing all day, but didn't dare actually bring those thoughts to the frontline. There was this part of me, this part of my mind that I just couldn't understand that was at peace with not knowing, with letting him do this. He needed to and for some reason, he couldn't tell me the whys of it yet.

I squinted as that stung, but knew that eventually he *would* tell me. I knew that with certainty.

The girls' widening eyes looked behind me and Ember's eyes moved away to settled back on our game. That should have been my first clue. Ember had reached her limit of all things significant today.

Arms reached around my waist and I smiled as his scruff rubbed against my cheek, forcing a calm-filled, ecstasy-inducing gasp from my lips. But when I heard his sigh, it wasn't just one that was filled of longing from being gone all day. No, this was something else.

I tried to smile as I whispered, "What's wrong?" but he couldn't see my face. The smile was for Laurelyn and Ember's benefit and they'd already gotten the gist.

Laurelyn mouthed, 'We'll go.' She tugged Ember's hand and they went back up to the house.

I tried to turn, but he held me tight. "Just wait," he sighed tiredly. "I just want to feel you like this." He rubbed his cheek against mine.

My heart pounded harder. "Seth, you're scaring me."

"Everything's fine, sweetheart," he assured, but he stayed right there, just holding me, just…being.

I couldn't take it. "Baby," I begged, "please."

He did this half-groan, half-breathe thing that lit every vein in my body on fire as he turned me to face him. He cupped my face. You would think that after so long, after so many times, that his skin on mine, his fingers across my face wouldn't elicit such a delicious response.

I fought it so my eyes didn't roll to the back of my head.

"Ava," he said softly, "I…I wish you could remember." I felt my breath catch. "I want you to remember," he said, almost like it was a command. He looked awful. Like someone who had been through the emotional ringer today. He obviously needed me and whatever the "thing" was that we'd been dancing around, it was eating at him. And he needed me and I couldn't be there for him because I didn't know how to. I'd never felt guilty for something that I couldn't remember. He shook his head quickly, closing his eyes. Gosh, he looked so tired and emotionally beaten. I wondered what they'd done to him today. "Sweetheart, you did nothing wrong. I just wish I knew how to..." He sighed. "I don't want to... I'm afraid that if I go about it the wrong way that I'll hurt you. That's the last thing I want to do."

The wheels began to turn a little. "Seth—"

"Seth. Oh, good, you're back." I rolled my eyes at my mother and turned to look at her. "I need you two to come inside and let's talk about what's going to go on with the summit." I stared. She waved her hand to come inside. "Come on. I made corn nuggets. If you hurry, you can beat your dad to them." She turned, not waiting for answer. Because not only was she my mother, and I respected her, but she was the freaking Visionary.

I sighed and turned to Seth to find him extra smiley. "What are you so smiley about, mister?"

He chuckled at the nickname. "You're adorable." He came to me, slicing the space between us into nothing. "We'll talk, little bird," he promised and kissed my forehead.

Inside Mom force-fed Seth corn nuggets as we sat at the big dining room table and she tried to prepare us for the grilling we would receive. It was all technicality, it was all old rules and traditions, but that's what our entire race and lives were built on, so we couldn't just discount it and act like it didn't matter, Mom said. This had to be handled delicately or else they'd turn on us.

So we would just keep our head down and let Mom do the talking.

"So their plane comes in tonight and then we'll just head over in the morning. We'll get one more night of good sleep at least." She smiled. "Seth, I know this is going to be overwhelming. But this isn't what our reunifications are like. Not really. So please don't be discouraged and try not to be disappointed. Some of the council members lived in the palace almost all their adult life until I became the Visionary and did away with that. So...just try not to be put off by the old ways of our people."

Seth smiled tightly. "Growing up with my family, I don't think there's any risk of me being disappointed by these people."

I squeezed his fingers. What the hell happened today?

He looked at me, our hands on the table between us.

Gah, Ava, sometimes I feel like I've screwed things up beyond repair and then other times, it's the only thing that makes sense to figure all this out. He breathed out his nose angrily. *I don't know what to do.*

I tilted my head, feeling hurt settle in my gut.

You could talk to me about it.

He leaned his head back, raking his free fingers through his hair with his eyes closed tightly. When his head came back down he came straight for me. He pressed his forehead to mine and sighed harshly, his teeth set, his lips open as he struggled with something that I had no idea about, because I didn't know anything. But then two whispered words stopped me, stopped my brain from obsessing, stopped my body from moving.

"I do." He kissed my hair as he got up and stopped, his lips pressed there. "I will figured this out for us, sweetheart. I promise you."

Then he left me there to wonder what the hell all that meant. Mom was long gone. Not a minute later I heard Seth in the kitchen with her making the food for dinner to go along with the corn nuggets.

I do... He does talk to me about it...and he wants me to remember... something. And he was upset when he came home from the Watsons today. Maybe they did something. Maybe there was some plot against me and he was working to stop it. Maybe that was why he wanted to go today and wanted to keep everything secret from me.

Maybe I was just going crazy. Maybe I should talk to Mom...but then she would bring Dad into it and then it would be a big mess of them trying to figure out what's wrong with me. They wouldn't rest until it was done and they wouldn't be rational about it. They'd go straight after the Watsons. They'd start a war at a time that a war couldn't happen.

No. Seth was working on something. I just had to trust that he would figure this out for us, like he always promised.

"Ava," Pablo crooned and hugged me affectionately. "So good to see you."

Pablo was Paolo son's and had stepped in to take his place on the council. Or should I say he was 'voted' in, but it was almost unanimous. In their clan, Paulo's family was like the Jacobsons—they were loved by all and were a fair and just family for the most part. Once the Watsons were gone and they were no longer under the thumb of Donald, they became a pretty thriving clan.

"You, too. This is Seth," I said and stepped back a bit to let them shake hands.

"Good to meet you, sir."

"Likewise, young man." He looked at him closely. "Good strong grip. I like that."

Seth's nervous laugh made an appearance. It really was endearing. "Thank you, sir."

I could tell Seth was nervous still, but not as much as before. Last night we cooked as a family and ate as one. He got a heaping dose of Jacobson culture—how my family interacts with one another on a regular, daily basis. Ember and Laurelyn stayed again and we just showed him how it was in the family. I hoped he was enjoying himself and he seemed to be. We all sat by the fire in the den that night together, drinking hot tea or cocoa, and just told stories about each other. Seth listened, soaking it all in. Anytime there was a story about me, I could physically feel him tense behind me as he perked up to listen.

He and I sat on the big brown and teal club chair together. He sat down and had beckoned me to him, letting me sit next to his legs and lean back against his chest. His hands had coasted up and down my arms all night. When I shivered, I could hear the smile in his voice when he pressed his mouth against my ear and growled, "Goosebumps. Check."

I hadn't known what it was for, but it was *so* hot.

That night, I had been whipped into such a frenzy from his warm palms coasting down my skin and his cryptic messages that when we finally decided to go to bed, there wasn't a whole lot of sleeping going on for a quite a while.

It was a tame make out session, but still hot nonetheless. The way he kept his hands purposely flat on the bed beside my head, as if that would keep me safe.

And this morning had been hectic. When we stood outside the room, I could tell he was nervous. I was nervous for him. But I needed to say something. He was my significant and it was my job to protect him, even if it was from a room of old people with judgy opinions.

"They don't matter in our world," I whispered, getting his attention. He looked over, gripping my fingers tighter. I took his other hand in mine, too, and tugged him to face me so he had nowhere to go, our fingers laced together, our gazes colliding. "Those people in that room," I nodded, "yeah, they're important. They're our people. But in my world," I whispered and got as close as I could get, "it just doesn't matter. Do you understand that?" I looked into his blue eyes and waited for him to really connect. When he sagged a little relaxing, I knew he was with me. "Do you understand that no matter what goes on in that room this weekend that you're mine and that will always be so?"

He let a long breath go as if he'd been holding it, letting his forehead rest against mine. His eyes opened and blue collided with brown once again. I bit my lip, feeling the sting of tears in my eyes. I didn't know what they had planned for him, but I hated that I couldn't protect my significant from this.

He leaned back just a little and looked at me with awe and adoration. "Aww, my little bird." He took my chin with thumb and his fingers, tugging my lip from my teeth, leaning in. "We talked about this. Especially going into this room—people are going to be watching me, right? You can't drive me crazy with that lip, Ava." My mouth fell open with a scoffing laugh. "What?" He grinned. "Don't act like you don't know what you biting that lip does to me."

I arched my brow and felt my teeth automatically reach for the corner of my bottom lip. It was like a security blanket. He gave me a wild look as he watched me release my lip. "See," he said triumphantly.

"Shut up," I said, pushing his stomach. Gosh, it was like pushing two by fours it was so hard. "And just kiss me."

He obliged and then shook his head as he leaned away. "I love every side of you. There isn't a side of you I've met that I haven't fallen in love with."

My heart clenched.

"You're going to be great in there," I told him. "Don't worry about anything. Not only is my mom on our side, but my family is behind us. Regardless of the other night, they're still ready to fight for us. I know you've never had to deal with the council before. Just be respectful. And be yourself. They'll love you in no time. And *I'll* fight them if we have to. I will fight them if it comes to that, to the end, until they understand that they can't take you away from me."

I cupped his face with both hands, loving his scruff on my palms and tried to smile, but I felt a little bit teary. "You just charm them and don't worry about anything. You're this amazing man and I know they'll love you. If it comes to it when they make their decision, then we'll show them what a mistake that is."

The kiss I laid on him was of the slow, torturous variety. He groaned and gripped my back, my shirt slipping and moving under his hands as he tugged me closer and moved me against him since he couldn't reach my face.

"Daggum, Ava," he finally muttered when the both of us could no longer breathe.

Being scolded by Seth was the highest compliment.

And now, as I watched him face a room full of people who were about to judge him for his last name alone, I was so proud of him.

"Yes," Pablo continued in his serious voice. "I hear congratulations are in order."

"Thank you," I said and smiled brightly, taking Seth's arm. "Mom is ecstatic."

He hesitated and I knew this was the start of the judging, the questions, the part where I would have to defend Seth, the part where I was about to get *really* pissed.

"Oh, yeah?" he asked, his accent lilting a little on the crescendo. He still had his smile pasted on, but his questionable eyebrows were now in place. It was like a Mr. Potato Head where he pulled the expression he wanted out of his back pocket and fixed it on perfectly. "Well, to be honest I would have thought she would be a little upset to find her daughter imprinted with a rival clan," he said gently, even going so far as to suck the air through his teeth like you do when you tell someone bad news. "Especially between the Watsons and the Jacobsons. Their rivalry is legendary," he said in a flourish. "We've never had two clans to hate each other so much. So for *this* to happen between these two clans…we never would have even dreamed. So I'm just surprised when you say your mother is happy." He gave me a little sad, smiley, fake, nose-scrunched look. "If she can find happiness in all this mess then that's amazing!"

And there's another expression, pulled right out of his Mr. Potato head butt.

Seth snorted next to me and then coughed into his hand several times and waved off Pablo's concern. I just kept on my fixed small smile, because if I did anything else, I might scream.

I took a deep breath and squeezed Seth's arm in my hands, using him for my strength. Seth reached over and put his hand over mine on his arm, letting his touch soak into my skin. I was so upset that I hissed a little when he touched me. I let my eyes swing up to his and his jaw was set. He was angry, too. His thumb ran over my knuckles. He knew what his thumb did to me. I smiled at him and then looked back to Pablo.

I gave him a small smile. "If she can find happiness in all this mess? Sir...I found my soulmate, just like you did, just like my mom did, just like everyone here did. I walked into a coffee shop and met the person that was intended to be mine. I don't see what a last name has to do with—"

"Now, Ava." He held up his hand and I stopped out of respect. The summit could take up to three days depending on how long they needed, and until the decision was made, I would show respect and make sure that they saw that we were just like any other significants in this room.

"Yes, sir."

"Let's just let Seth go schmooze with everyone and have some lunch, shall we?"

"If that's what you want, sir." He took a breath, standing a little taller, and I could tell that my being so obviously nice while it was *so obvious* that I was angry on the inside was getting to him. "It was nice to see you again."

I tugged Seth away before I had a chance to hurt anyone. I breathed in deep as we walked away. Oh, God, please don't let everyone be so blunt about their disdain for our relationship. I wanted to cry. I looked to the wall to my left so no one would see that I was fighting tears. The way Seth looked at me— it was obvious to anyone within a two mile radius that he adored me, that he had a protective sense for me, that he looked at me like a Virtuoso man looked at his significant woman. So why wasn't that good enough?

I felt Seth's fingers on my jaw, pulling my face to look at him. We had stopped walking. I hadn't even realized. The conference room we were in was impersonal and there wasn't anything in there but a few tables, a bunch of people, and a small stage. It was dimly lit, enough for us all to see each other, but dim enough so that you didn't feel like you were under a spotlight the entire time you walked across the room.

So when Seth's hand palmed my cheek, I didn't think anything of it.

When Seth moved into my space, I didn't think anyone would notice. When Seth pressed his forehead to mine, I didn't think anyone could really see or would be paying attention. When Seth's other hand wrapped around my wrist, his thumb rubbing over my tattoo, and he began to murmur words of love and comfort to me, his breath puffing against my cheek and lips, because his mouth was so close to mine, I pretended like it mattered not a bit in this world.

"Where's your head right now?"

"Firmly on my shoulders."

He laughed and shook his head. "Smartass. Look, you told me before we came in here that no matter what happened in this room that I was yours and always would be. The same goes for you." His thumb moved on my cheek. *That thumb…* "There isn't anything they could say today…nothing," he said harshly. "You're mine, little bird." He closed his eyes and so did I. "*You're mine, Ava.* Nobody, with just a few spoken words, can undo that and take you away from me. You are completely safe with me and completely mine, I promise."

It was the thing I needed to hear. I wanted to feel safe today and I didn't. I felt like I could be ripped away at any moment, but Seth had crushed all that. I opened my eyes slowly to meet his. My hand lifted to his face and I pulled him to my lips. Warm and light, I just wanted to feel him pressed there. I opened my mouth slightly and he followed suit. When he licked the seam of my mouth, I heaved a breath. With one more press of my mouth, I pulled back, already breathless. He lifted my chin so I had to look at him.

He looked into my eyes, his own eyes wild with passion from our kiss and anger from the summit. Blue colliding with brown.

"I love you," he said simply. "I just wanted to make sure you remembered that today."

Despite it all, I did that half-almost-cry, half-smile, thing I was getting so good at, apparently. "I love you, Seth."

He growled a little and laughed. "I love it when you say my name."

I smiled wider. "I know."

"So, Virtuoso," Pablo said loudly over the clinking glasses and forks. We'd just sat down with our food and now came the stuff that my Mother absolutely hated, but they insisted on. And she let them keep it. It was something they had done since the beginning when they had a Visionary, and who was she to take that from them, she said. "Stand for your Visionary."

We all stood as Mom came in, Dad just a couple steps behind her. She fought for that right. She insisted that, even as the Visionary, it was being a significant that made her so powerful and she needed her counterpart. They agreed only if the male of the Visionary was always presented a few steps behind her out of respect and so our people have no question that the Visionary is still the leader of our people.

Like it could be forgotten when it's shoved down our throats. But the Visionary really isn't the leader of our people, she's a symbol for them, a beacon of hope, of the future, more than ever now since the imprints have returned. But the Visionary doesn't rule our people…the council does. And I think they know that and I think they know that the Visionary knows it.

I wondered how long that game could last.

Mom turned her head to invite Dad to join her and he took her hand, giving her that same little smile he'd been giving her for years. They made their way to the head of the Jacobson table just as a couple of my cousins come in behind them. Late. To the summit. Not good. They don't go to their seats, they go straight to Dad. Their Champion.

I get it then. These were the ones Dad sent to the Watson's place to see what was going on. The spies.

I perked up and tried to listen, but Jordan spoke too low in Dad's ear. When he leaned away, he looked at me quickly and I saw it. The sympathy. But why?

Dad looked at us both and stood. Each clan was separated by a table. It had always been that way. We always took our meals together and then reconvened with everyone when we were done. Dad looked at everyone and reached into his pocket. I felt myself grimace and took Seth's hand in mine. This wasn't going to be good, whatever it was.

Dad took out the cog from his pocket and rubbed it in his fingers. Mom covered her mouth with her hands, closing her eyes. I could hear her sucking in a desperate breath.

God help me, what was going on?

And then Dad looked at me and I knew that something had changed in him. His eyes lifted to our family and he held up his hand. "I know that you all just sat down to eat, but this can't wait. I'm afraid we need to have a family meeting and this can't happen here." He nodded his head toward the doors. "Let's do this quickly." He smiled tightly. I recognized it as his "Champion" smile.

Boy, he was pissed about something.

We filed out the double doors to another conference room a short ways down the hall that Jordan had scouted and was standing at the doors waiting. We all filed in. I was gripping Seth's hand so hard. He knew. He didn't know the what's and how's and why's, but he knew it was about the Watsons in some regard, and that circled back around to him somehow.

And he knew that I knew it.

His thumb kept making a pass over my knuckles to soothe me, to comfort me, to prepare me for whatever was coming.

But nothing prepared me for what happened when the last Jacobson filed in and Jordan slammed the door. His partner in crime that had gone with him, Drake, reached for Seth's collar just as Mom reached for me to hold my arms down at my sides, her arms around mine like bands.

"Wait, Ava. Just wait. They have to do this," she hissed into my ear.

Drake, my cousin who I've known my entire life, who used to come to my house and eat s'mores with me at the Jacobson get-togethers, slammed my significant to the wall with his hand around his throat.

Seth didn't meet his eyes, but instead looked at me. "It's all right, sweetheart," he soothed, but when he saw me struggling against my mother still, he said louder, "Baby, stop." He squeezed his eyes for a second and wheezed against my cousin's fingers. I whimpered. "I'm okay. It's all right," he said slowly, speaking to my very core.

He finally looked at my cousin and then my father who was walking slowly to their side. I couldn't believe this was happening. I looked around my family and they all just watched, even Ember, Maria, and Dawson were glued, ready to listen to anything my father had to say. They weren't going to jump on my side on this...and when I looked at Dad I got why. My shoulders sagged as I saw the cog in his fingers. He was the Champion and he had called the meeting to order when he pulled that out of his pocket. In their minds, whatever he had to say was the law and final word. I was about to lose before the war even began.

I looked at Seth as he stared at my father. Dad walked closer to him and tilted his head. He looked so angry his hand was actually shaking. What had happened? What could his spies have seen to make him so angry with Seth? That didn't make any sense...

"Seth, you told me, in my own house, that I should send spies out to the Watson's place because they no longer trusted you, and if we wanted to see what they were up to that might be the only way."

Seth waited a few seconds, obviously knowing that Dad was angry and he was baiting him. "Yes, sir, I did. And I'm assuming that you did that. And your spies found something you didn't like?"

Dad actually made a growly noise as he got in his face. I fought Mom's grasp, but she held tight. I realized when I saw a few blue ribbons in the air she was using her gift on me. I looked at her with a grimace. How could she? I swung my gaze back to Seth and waited for the next step.

"You know what we found," Dad yelled at him. "I trusted you. I let you into my home. I let you take my daughter, my *only daughter*, to your home—"

"Sir, I don't know what they saw or what they think they saw," Seth said in return. He heaved his breaths, understanding they this was serious. My cousins told my father something that he obviously believed. "But you can trust me. I'm your daughter's significant and that hasn't changed."

"Has it?" Dad asked softly, deadly, and the entire temperature of the room changed after that.

Seth didn't move an inch except for his face as he lifted it to stare at my father. "What did you say?" he whispered.

"I said, has it changed? Are you still my daughter's significant—"

"Of course I am!" Seth barked, but Dad just talked over him.

"—or are you planning for that title to change soon?"

Seth's chest heaved. "I don't know what the hell you're talking about."

"We know your family can force an imprint."

"What does that have to do with Ava and me?"

"We also know that the Watsons attempted a kidnapping on my daughter the first night that failed. There hasn't been a peep from them since. Not a mutter or sighting. Weird for them considering that they don't back down."

Seth licked his bottom lip angrily. "Mr. Jacobson."

Dad pointed over at Jordan by the door. "He saw you, and heard you, today before you came here, before you went to *my daughter*—telling the Watsons that we had sent you there as a spy for our family." Mom inhaled sharply behind me. "But that our family had betrayed you and you had had enough." I heard muttering around me and swallowed. My heart pounded as I tried to catch my breath. Seth's eyes looked past Dad to me and he begged me not to believe, to just trust, but just as I felt like I had a foothold, Dad started again. "That she didn't want you to see your family anymore, and you had reconsidered the breaking of your imprint and imprinting with someone else." I couldn't help it. Hearing it—I groaned in agony.

"Ava, don't listen to him," Seth begged me.

"You don't speak to her," Dad cut him off and grabbed his collar. That was it.

There was something in me, something in the back of my mind, the recesses, that just…knew. As Dad went on, talking about how Seth told the Watsons his plan to sabotage us, to keep pretending to be in love with me when he really wasn't so they could come in and finish what they'd started that day, I noticed that Seth wasn't denying it. He just begged me with his eyes…to believe in him.

"Oh, God," he said miserably. "There's no way out of this."

"What?" Dad barked. "So you admit it?" he growled.

"No, not in the way you think. There's no way I could explain that you would believe me. I'm…screwed either way." He looked at me. "I'm so sorry I didn't tell you—"

"No," Dad said and started to drag him from the room. "No more. We have heard all we need to hear."

"Stop!" I yelled. Or rather my mouth did. That part of my brain…it just knew, it couldn't let this happen. I tried to move from Mom's grasp, my eyes latched on Seth's wide ones. She wasn't budging. I looked back at her. "Mom," I whispered. "I need to do this."

She sighed. "It'll just hurt more, Ava."

"Let go, Mom."

She let go without another word and I looked around the room at my quiet family before I made my way to my father and Seth.

"Ava," Dad cautioned, but I held up my hand as I stopped in front of my significant.

"He didn't do it," my mouth said again without my permission, almost.

Seth sagged. "Ava," he said thankfully.

"Your cousins saw him, Ava," Dad said carefully.

"Dad, he didn't do it." I looked at him. "There's gotta be some explanation."

He looked at me with sympathy that I didn't want. "I know you want to believe that—"

"No, I don't want to believe it. It's true." I pushed on Dad's arm. "Let him go," I said harder. "You've got the door blocked. It's not like he can get away."

Dad hesitated, but then released Seth with a sigh and stepped back to put his arm around Mom.

As soon as his arm was free of Seth, I swooped in and hugged his middle. "Ava," he said into my hair. He pulled back and looked to be in the middle of a happy confusion. "Why do you believe me? I haven't even explained myself yet."

"I don't think I need you to," I said weirdly and frowned. "If it weren't for my curiosity and the firing squad." I looked at Dad and he still scowled at us, hearing every word. "I just...believe you. If you say you were there under different circumstances then you were."

He cupped my cheek. "Even with the mounting evidence against me?"

I cupped his cheek in return. "*I believe* you."

He sighed his words." I love you, little bird."

Mom gasped, covering her mouth. I guess they were surprised that he'd told me he loved me. Or maybe that we'd said it already. Or in front of all these people. I let my eyes flick over and saw several wide-eyed people.

"I love you. Explain," I whispered. "Loudly."

He looked around, his scowl settling back into place, one to rival my father's. I took his hand as it fell from my face.

"It was your idea," he told me. "To go to my family and tell them that your family had asked me to be a spy for them."

My lips fell open, but Dad barked, "You're not going to start spouting things to confuse her just so she'll believe you."

"I already believe him, Dad." I looked back and him and gave him a look, begging him to just stop and let me handle this. "I'm not gullible just because

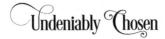

I do. Please," I whispered.

His lips twisted and he actually looked a little guilty. I looked back up at Seth and he gave me a few seconds to catch my breath. I loved that about him. He could read me like a book.

"I should have told you about my ability. I meant to. I'm sorry I didn't, and now they'll never believe me, and maybe you won't either after I tell you everything."

"What the hell are you talking about? What ability?" Jordan yelled.

Everyone knows that we don't have powers yet. We hadn't ascended so… what was Seth talking about? I squinted. The dreams?

He sighed, his eyes bouncing from face to face nervously. His eyes landed back on me again and I knew this was it. I was going to learn everything.

"Remember me telling you that I dream about you at night?" he asked and I immediately knew that it wasn't just a dream. That little piece of my mind was so adamant that he was innocent. It had to be real. I nodded. "They're not just dreams." I shuddered as reality slammed into my bones, into my very existence. I shuddered so violently that he had to grip me around the waist so I wouldn't buckle. My head fell back and I started to see flashes. Seth kept going. "We meet every night, in your room most nights…" I shook against his chest as I saw us there, talking, laughing. I gripped his neck with my hand.

"Stop!" I heard Dad boom and Mom joined in, but she seemed to be calming him down, holding him back, telling him that I needed to hear this from him. I heard my family around me, a chorus of angry words. Some said for someone to stop him, that he was killing me, some said for him to leave me alone, some for *them* to leave *him* alone—that he wasn't hurting me. But Seth held me steadily, not paying them any attention, and put his hand on my cheek to pull my face up.

"Look at me, sweetheart," he begged, his voice filled with agonizing love and patience. I opened my eyes and tried to push away the strange pressure in my chest. It didn't work, but if Seth was looking in my eyes it seemed to dim to a manageable ache. He nodded, realizing it, too. "Keep your eyes right here. I know it's too much right now, but I need for you to hear this. We need to get this all out in the open and then it'll all go away, okay?" I nodded. I'd do anything he wanted if this would stop. His arm banded around my waist tighter, bringing my face even closer to his, our chests pressed so tightly together. I sucked in a breath and felt my eyelids flutter. I leaned in and kissed his mouth, just once, because I *had to*. He smiled a little in spite of the situation.

"Had to, huh?" he asked and chuckled once.

I breathed out. "Haven't you ever just *had to*?"

He nodded, his lips twisted. "With you, often." He glanced over super quickly over at the rabble and then back to me with a small smile. "Now can I get back to my story so I don't get my ass kicked?"

I put my thumb over his lips. "I'll protect your ass," I said, but my voice cracked. Our playful banter had come back around to reality. I was going to fight this with everything in me, but if the Champion and Visionary decided to go against me and not believe me, what could I really do about it? He kissed my thumb and pulled my hand down, keeping it in his.

Keep your eyes on mine.

With my eyes right on his, he started again loudly enough for everyone to hear. If it was weird for anyone that they had to listen to this story while Seth and I stared at each other...I didn't care. They had just tried to take my significant from me and I was quite peeved. "I don't know why I have an ability and I haven't ascended yet. I never told my family and I never told you." He sighed. "I didn't want them to use it to their advantage. And I didn't want you to have more reasons to hate them when I was trying to find reasons to make it work with both families. So I was stalling. I was going to tell you. But ever since I was a little boy I could go into people's dreams. My uncle could do it, too. An—"

"Echoling," Mom said at the same time as him. And no one could mistake the pain in her voice. Or the disgust.

He looked away from me for a second to look at her because it was a shock to hear that in her voice and I buckled against him.

"I'm sorry," he whispered. He spoke to my mother, but looked at me. "I take it you had a bad experience with my uncle."

"He tortured her," Dad explained with a growl. "On several occasions. We had to run away to get away from him. And the fact that you can do the same things that he can is not speaking to your favor, Seth."

Seth sighed. "Just because I can doesn't mean I will. I've been able to do them this entire time, since I was eight, and have I ever come at anyone in this family? I never even told my family I had the gift because I knew what they would make me do with it. Even as a boy, I knew."

"You've been doing them to Ava apparently."

Seth's blood boiled over. He stood taller and looked away from me as he yelled back, almost growling, "Ava is my significant. It's my right to go in her mind if I want to and she gives me permission."

He quickly looked back to me, apologizing.

Dad stood there, stunned. Then he lowered his head a little and sighed. He must have realized that Seth was right; you don't challenge a Virtuoso man's right to his significant, but Dad wasn't happy about it.

"And has she given you permission?"

"Dad, stop," I hissed. "Now you're just reaching. Of course I've given him permission."

"How could you have if you don't even remember these dreams?"

"My mind is his."

"I didn't mean for her to forget," Seth said loudly over us. "It's not supposed to be that way."

"What—"

"The other times I went into someone's mind, they remembered. I could come and go as I pleased and they would remember the next day, but with you, it was different." He swallowed. "With you, I just went the first night to try to talk to you after the kidnapping attempt. I thought maybe if we met that way that it would be better, easier, but you didn't remember anything that had happened. You only remembered that we bonded at the coffee shop. The next morning, I went to see you and you didn't remember the dream—that's never happened before. And then the next night, I felt this amazing pull in my chest to go see you again. So I went to your dream. I can feel it when people go to sleep. That's how an echoling knows that he can go to someone. And when I got there, you remembered our dream from the previous night, but not the day we'd had, nothing from your real life. It was as if you got a reset of some kind and no one I had ever visited ever got that before. So every night, I've gone to you. I tried not to go some nights, but the pull in chest… it won't let me stay away. And every night, you don't remember your real life in your subconscious, and every day, you don't remember that I came to your dream. But it's all real. So the dream you and me came up with a plan to go to my family and tell them that your father asked me to spy for them, that you and I had been fighting, that your family had betrayed me, that it just wasn't working out and I had changed my mind about everything."

"What good would that do?" Dad asked gruffly, but he had calmed down quite a bit.

"Your daughter's genius plan was so I could get back in my family's good graces. Because she felt like my family might try something at the summit." I heard gasps around me. "We thought maybe that was why my ability kept pulling me back to her and she couldn't remember it all, her subconscious was separate. None of it made sense, but it had to be for a reason. And the Visionary kept talking about how abilities were for a purpose," he said harder and it escaped no one's notice, I'm sure, how he called her 'the Visionary'. "So I had to believe it, I had to trust this thing between us. But my family believed me." He smiled at me proudly. "Your plan worked like a charm, but they didn't have anything planned for the summit like we thought. They just wanted me to pull a reverse on you guys. They said I should spy on you instead." He pulled his phone from his pocket. "They even gave me a new phone in case you were tracking my old one." He scoffed a laugh.

"They just have new phones lying around?" Drake asked.

"A family that is always running from people they think are trying to kill them?" Seth raised his eyebrow. "Yeah."

"He's lying," someone said. "His family could be about to attack the summit any minute."

"Why would he warn us if that were true?" I said loudly.

"But he—"

"I want all thoughts that Seth is trying to sabotage us to cease." I could barely talk I was breathing so hard. Seth sighed and rubbed my arm, trying to calm me, trying to fill me with what he could. "If you don't trust him, fine. Trust me. I'm telling you that what he's saying happened."

"You don't remember," someone argued.

"I remember bits and pieces."

"He could be feeding you those memories, making you feel like you're remembering."

I scoffed. "Wow, you guys really want to hate him." I turned away from Seth, feeling the pressure in my chest slam into me, but I had to look them in the eyes. "Why?" I cried. "Were you all just waiting for a reason to turn on... him." I blinked as my eyes began to blur.

Bright lights and spots shined and moved in my vision. Seth's arms wrapped around me tighter from behind. I blinked more rapidly and couldn't believe my eyes as a small bird flew down the high ceiling lights. It looked like he had a halo of lights around him as he descended and landed on the ground in front of me.

"Do you see that?" I whispered, but knew I sounded delirious. "It's just like the ones from the palace."

"What's that, little bird?" Seth asked, his cheek pressed to mine, his voice almost echoed around me as he said it.

Little bird, little bird, little bird…

Everything snapped into place. I gasped and felt Seth's echoing inhalation breath in my ear. The pressure in my chest was gone and so was the bird that no one else had seen but me. I felt a little crazy but I also felt sane for the first time today. I turned to Seth and gave him a little smile.

"Little bird…because of the robins from the palace?"

He huffed a small laugh and nodded. "You remember?"

"No, just…I can't really explain it. You take me there in my dreams, don't you?"

"Sometimes. The rooftop is your favorite place. You told me."

I looked down so I wouldn't cry. "It is. I can't wait to take you there for real."

He sighed through his nose and brought my face back up with his finger. "Do you know how many times you've said those exact words to me?"

"No," I gripped the wrist holding my face, "I don't."

"Champion," Jordan interrupted and crossed his arms. He looked at me and sighed before looking back at Dad. "What do you want us to do?"

Dad looked at me and we locked eyes. I honestly had no idea what he was going to do. There was no proof I could give them. I couldn't show them a vision above my head like Mom could. I couldn't prove anything Seth was saying. Mom couldn't get a vision from Seth because he had her blood…

I gasped, turned to Seth, and locked eyes with him as I reached into his front pocket to get his phone. He gulped, his lips parting with a little breath that blew across my hair. I could have asked him for the phone I guess, but this felt like an emergency, and girls acted in an emergency. We didn't dawdle and worry about things like…reaching in boys pockets and how that made our heart crazy. There wasn't time for that.

He had no idea what was up, given by the bunched brow when I turned, but he said nothing. My family may not be ready to trust me completely, but my significant did. And okay, I was still in college, I had done nothing to prove myself to my family. Granted I had never been given any opportunity to prove myself, but still. Why would they blindly follow me and say, okay, we'll trust the enemy's son because you say so. I got it, but it still stung.

We had to fight at every turn and I wondered if they would ever truly trust him. If every time something came up with the Watsons, because something *always* came up with the Watsons, if they would turn to him and wonder if he had something to do with it. I refused to live that way.

I held the phone out in front of me as I went to Mom. She and Dad watched me solemnly, but Mom clicked before Dad did. She met me halfway and gripped the phone with me, understanding exactly what I wanted from her.

She couldn't get a vision from Seth because he had her blood, but he'd gotten the phone from the Watsons today. Maybe she could get a vision from the object that—

I sucked in a breath that burned my lungs. I heard Dad tell Seth I was okay as I fell into the vision with Mom.

Seth was at a table in a kitchen with several other Watson members. There was about fifteen of them piled into that small kitchen. Someone—a small woman—was cooking something on the stove. It smelled like beef stew.

"—if you were to go and do that, then we'd have our in."

"I could," Seth agreed and leaned back in his chair. He looked comfortable, but also uncomfortable. He looked like he belonged there, like he grew up there, like he'd sat in that chair all his life, but I could tell he wasn't normal. He acted differently with them than he did with me. "Like I said, I'm over it."

A man smiled at him and kicked Seth's boot under the table. "Glad to see you've got your wits about you, boy."

The woman at the stove brought Seth a glass of something and a bowl of the stew. "Thanks, Mom."

"Mmhmm," she hummed back politely, but it was like he said. She didn't even look at him. It was like she had to give him the bowl and that was that. I found I was right when she started serving up everyone in the room. They all thanked her and she gave them the customary 'mmhmm'.

They were civil. Who knew?

I stared at the woman who adopted Seth, who he wanted so badly to love him like a mother but didn't. I wanted to meet her for the sake of nothing else but knowing my significant's mother, but that would never happen. It pained me to know that.

A knock on the door startled me, but whoever it was didn't wait to be let in. Seth's Uncle Gaston came in and I gasped, covering my mouth, forgetting that this was a memory and they couldn't see or hear me. And Harper came in right behind him. A little growly breath left my throat without my permission as I saw her make her way right to Seth. Her lips curled into a victorious smile at seeing him. Like, see, I won after all.

If I had been there in real life, I couldn't have promised anyone that I wouldn't have ripped her hair out in that moment. Though it would have been a lady-like-ripping-out-of-her-hair, of course, but it would have been *done*.

"Seth," Gaston said and smiled, showing teeth and everything. "I'm so happy to see you back here, son."

"Me, too," Seth answered and swallowed his stew.

"We've got big plans. Now that you're on board, just like we always planned, we can do so much with you on the inside."

"Yeah," he said gruffly and took a drink. "I can just keep pretending that I'm happy there and be on the inside, listening, waiting, watching. They'll never suspect a thing."

Harper came while Seth spoke and got behind him, putting her hands on his shoulders. My heart beat painfully. How far was Seth's pretending going to go? But I saw Seth tense and his eyes dull. His family talked around him, not paying him any real attention as they plotted and planned. Harper leaned in and put her mouth on his ear. I stopped breathing as she said, "I knew you'd come back to me."

He leaned forward so fast, his stew bowl spilled on the table and his glass sloshed a little. Everyone looked. He looked back at her over his shoulder.

"Get off me, Harper."

She pressed her lips angrily together. "So, you don't want to ditch that *little girl* and force the bond with me like your Daddy said?" She looked over at him with a glare before looking back at Seth.

"I am ditching the *little girl* eventually. But I never said I was taking you in her place." Harper's mouth opened in a silent gasp. "I don't want anyone that's going to chase me around. No thanks," he said softly. "I'll find someone to take her place, but for now, I'm stuck with her until we finish this. The plan is to keep using her."

She leaned against the wall and crossed her arms. "And what's first? The summit?"

Seth eyed her. "How do you know about the summit?"

"You're not the only spy," she sneered.

Seth gulped before he turned to face his family. "So? What do you wanna do? The summit is here, in this town, so are you going to do something about it?"

"No," Gaston said quickly and held his hand out as someone started to argue. "The Summit is a small fish. There are hardly any families here. There would only be the Jacobsons and one other to hold guard and be witnesses. If we went after the council, we'd want to go to London and take them all out," he growled and slammed his fist on the table, knocking over the salt shaker. "No, we don't go after the summit and tip them off. That would just make them cautious and know that we want them all dead. Right now, they think our beef is just with the Jacobsons and it can stay that way. The reunification is in six months. That's plenty of time to plan a glorious attack. For now, we wait."

"So what do you want me to do right now?"

"Go to the summit," he said harshly. "Be a loving significant, and make them believe it so they don't deunify you and Ava."

Seth paled a little. "Deunify?"

"Rival clans can't mate. But a bond between them has never happened before. I can't imagine that they'd do that to their precious Visionary's daughter, but it wouldn't be the first time they've tortured their Visionary. Now go." Seth got up to leave without looking back, but his uncle wasn't done. "And Seth?" Seth stopped and slowly looked over his shoulder. "Don't fail us again."

Seth left in a hurry all the way to his truck and finally breathed when he got inside. He beat his fist on the steering wheel after he cranked it and sighed harshly. "Ah, Ave. What have we gotten ourselves into?"

Mom yanked us out of the vision and I felt the arms around me for the first time; around my middle and around my shoulders near my neck. Dad's arms were around Mom, too.

I sagged, leaning my head to the side, seeking him, so relieved when he pressed his cheek to mine. I covered his hands with mine. Okay, so the vision worked, he'd gone to his family, I could see how my cousins seeing that could misconstrue that he had flipped his loyalties, but now there was still no way to convince everyone. Mom had seen the vision, but…it still wasn't clear cut. It still looked kind of like Seth had switched sides, didn't it? And even then, it was Mom's word against everyone else's…

I looked up to see that she had projected the vision. Blue ribbons swirled around us and I was grateful that no explanation was to be had, but also the vision was a little damning. Could they interpret it for what it was or was this lynch mob about to get a whole lot more hairy?

I began to shake a little, cold and so ready for this to be over. I felt Seth turning me into his chest, pressing me and soothing me with his arms, his hand going to the back of my neck. I looked up at him and knew that he knew that I saw it all. I wish I could remember, I wish I could remember how we had talked in our dreams, how we planned it all, how our plan was working.

"Me, too," he whispered.

I looked over at my parents, the blue ribbons finally dissipating and crackling away into nothing. Dad and Mom were looking at each other. I knew they were talking, deciding Seth's fate. I looked over at my family and saw some of them talking, chatting and tittering amongst themselves, like they actually deserved to have a say in the life of my significant. Uncle Kyle's and Bish's families just waited, watching. Ember caught my eye and tried for a smile. I tried to smile back, but knew I failed.

Seth took my chin in his fingers and turned me to look at him. "Baby, they had to."

I felt my eyebrows scrunch and looked at him with nothing but disbelief. "What… These are the people who just tried to send you away…and you're defending them?"

He smiled sadly and moved his thumb on my chin. "They were protecting you. Don't you see that? They may have been lynching me, but they don't care about me. Yet. But they love you, Ava, and so do I, and they were protecting the thing that I love."

I opened my mouth, but nothing came out. I closed it, feeling sad and so much all at once bubble in my gut. How could he possibly be so…

"You're so…" I tried, but Mom cut me off.

"Amazing." We both looked over to find her with a tear hanging on her lashes. "When we didn't find you that day at the compound, I've always felt guilty. Ashlyn said that it was supposed to be that way and we'd see you again, that it would all work out like it was supposed to, but I don't know that I actually believed her. Until right. This. Moment." Her chest shook once and I couldn't believe that Mom felt so strongly about this. I'd always known she felt guilty about that day, but she was showing her entire clan this. "For you two to take this upon yourselves, for Seth to risk his life by going in and pretending with his family to make sure that they weren't planning anything for the summit…" She shook her head and then came to us. I moved back just in time before she gripped him tightly to her. Seth looked more than stunned, but recovered quickly as he rubbed her back. "Thank you. I'm completely blind when it comes to the Watsons and we always worry." She leaned back. "We bring in an extra family to do security, but really that just adds more people to get hurt if they decide to do something."

Seth nodded, uncomfortable with the attention he was getting as everyone's eyes were on him. "I just, uh, realized that my family…" He shook his head and looked at the floor. "I wanted to believe that there was something worth saving there with them, but there isn't."

What happened? What changed to make him change his mind? He looked at me and I could see the sadness in his mind.

"They shunned me and said I wasn't welcome back, after Harper ran to them and told them about our conversation. Said I was a traitor, all because I found my soulmate and didn't want to kill her."

Mom covered her mouth as I stared in complete awe. It took me a second to move and take his hand. "Seth," I sighed in agony for him.

He'd lost the only family he'd known. They turned on him, and then the family that should have embraced him fully as their own was accusing him of being a traitor, after they'd already ambushed him once. I felt a tear slide down my cheek. He smiled and shook his head as he moved right up against me and wiped it away with his thumb.

"Sweetheart, I told you. Your family had to protect you."

"From my own significant?" I said loudly, feeling so hurt and ashamed of my family and just sad and…confused. I swung my gaze over to my family. They at least had to the good graces to look embarrassed and some of them even looked guilty as they watched the scene play out. I looked back at him. I got it. I did. They were protecting me, but now it was my turn to protect him. No one else was. Literally everyone in the world but me had turned their back on him. A sob punched my chest at that thought.

He cupped my face. "Ava, stop," he ordered softly. "You're just making yourself upset for nothing."

"How can you be so calm? How can you just…"

"Ava, our lives will always keep moving on whether we want them to or not. Even after tragedy and betrayal, we have to take what's left of the ashes and do something with them."

I stared at him in awe-filled silence along with everyone else.

"Everyone," Dad called, "Seth is innocent. Back to your seats." His Champion voice was one you didn't trifle with. No one questioned him. They all filed out into the hall and back to their seats at the table quickly, and got back to eating. But when I saw Jordan and Drake standing there, I was shocked that they hadn't obeyed their Champion. He was, too, apparently.

His eyebrow shot up and his chin went down. "That means you, too," he said slowly.

"I know," Jordan said slowly, "I just have to say sorry to Ava and Seth—"

"Jordan!" Dad boomed.

"It's okay, Dad," I tried.

"Ava, we can talk to them later. Right now we need to—"

"Dad, if I had made an epic blunder that caused my family to go into an uproar of this size, I'd want to apologize right away, too." Jordan winced, scrunching his nose and rubbing his hair. "Let him."

Dad sighed. "Ava—"

Mom grabbed his shirt front. "Caleb, come on."

Dad threw his hands up. "All my women are just going to gang up on me? Does no one listen to their Champion anymore?" Mom just smiled, knowing we'd won.

"Come eat with me. Let them…" She flitted her hands at us. "*Talk.*"

Dad growled and looked at Jordan and Drake. "Your Visionary saved you. I hope you know that."

"We do," Drake said and couldn't hide his smile, but he was trying. Dad was pretty funny when he was bring "handled" by Mom.

Dad turned back to Mom and put his arms around her waist as he practically dragged her away.

"Gah, you drive me *crazy*, baby," he said in that growly, possessive voice I was so used to with them.

I turned back to Jordan and Drake.

Drake looked beyond sorry. "I'm so sorry. We were sent there to see if we saw anything out of the ordinary and you...talking about coming here and being a spy is out of the ordinary, man."

Seth had his arm around me and his fingers were moving in a soothing rhythm on my back. "I understand. We hadn't really thought that out, I guess. I knew that Mr. Jacobson was sending someone out to scout, I just thought... I don't know what I thought," he said in a rushed breath.

"You thought they might attack the summit," Drake said and clapped him on the shoulder. "So did we. But we couldn't do anything about it but scout things out. We can't just run every time we think they might do something. That's not a life. And that's not in our nature. Thanks for doing that. We're sorry about everything."

"Yeah," Jordan said and kicked his shoe on the floor. "Really sorry."

"Thanks, guys. It's all okay. Promise," Seth assured and turned to me without anything else to them.

They went to sit with the family, but I just wasn't hungry.

"Me either."

I smiled. "I miss your mind. Even though I've never been able to do that and be in your head like you're in mine, I still miss it terribly," I said softly.

His lips twisted, his brow lowered. "I'm sorry. I don't know why—"

"It's not your fault."

"There has to be a reason." His brow went even lower as he thought. "Every couple can hear each other and if you can't hear me, then it's some supernatural...motive."

I groaned softly, putting my head on his chest. "I don't want to think about it."

With my head on his chest like this I could see my family perfectly. They were doing a poor job of eating and trying to look inconspicuous as they did so and not look like they weren't watching my every move. Seth was right. My family had always been that way. They focused on the one who was bonding at the time. They had their famous family bar-b-que to welcome them to the family and "grill" them on all their business. They thought they were so clever on that one.

And they just kept right on doing it until the next person bonded. They texted, they visited, they prepped the wedding, they got all in your business.

It was the Jacobson way. And it was awesome. But this time, the protective Jacobson way had just gone a little too far with the grudges, that was all.

The Watsons and Jacobsons were like oil and water. Everybody knows they don't mix. But what most people don't know is that oil *will* mix with water if you add a little egg yolk. Seth and I were that egg yolk.

And my family had just learned a hard lesson about grudges and about oil and water and egg yolks and the whole bit. And they were feeling pretty guilty if the looks on their faces were any indication.

I looked away just as Pablo came back to the front and cleared his throat. "Well, from what I hear, things certainly have gotten exciting, haven't they? And the excitement isn't over, I'm afraid. The reason the council convened was because two members from opposite clans have fraternized—"

"Not true," I said quietly, but in the vast of the quiet room, I may as well have screamed it. Everyone stopped and looked at me.

Pablo cocked his eyebrow at me. "The accused can come forward and plead their case now."

Plead their case? Is he for real?

"Each accused may bring a member from their family to help them plead their case."

I turned around and shot a glare so hot at Pablo, I didn't see how he didn't light on fire right there in that room. He knew that Seth didn't have any family. We just had this big blowup about his family and he was just going to dig the knife in further?

"It's all right—" Seth began to ease me, but my mother stopped him by putting her hand on his shoulder.

"I'll plead for him."

Pablo smiled like he was dealing with a child, while Seth looked at my mother like she hung the freaking moon.

"Visionary, that's noble, but—"

"He's my family now. Don't you dare tell me he's not."

Pablo actually gulped at her tone and looked away. Dad had come to stand beside me. I gripped his arm with one hand and Seth's with the other. Dad kissed my forehead before I looked to Seth.

"Let's begin," Pablo announced and looked at the council table and then at us. "Let the accused go first."

"I guess that means me?" I said angrily, sarcastically.

"Ava," Dad scolded in a whisper and exhaled.

I looked down, shaking my head, and then looked at the council table. Aunt Jen, Uncle Bish, Uncle Kyle and Aunt Lynne had joined them. "You say that it's against the law for rival clans to *fraternize*, but we didn't. We never even knew each other before we bonded in the coffee shop. So how did we fraternize? God put us together and bonded us. We imprinted. That's how everyone else in this room found their soulmate. So I can't see how that's any different."

I squeezed Seth's hand so I wouldn't scream.

He licked his bottom lip before he got started and if we weren't it this stupid situation I would have thought it was adorable.

"Well, just like Ava said, you say it's rival clans who can't fraternize, but are the Watsons even a clan anymore? They're human, they don't go to reunifications and even if they tried to, would they be welcome? The Watsons used to be a clan of the Virtuoso. But no more. Now they're just an enemy."

The council talked amongst themselves. I looked at Pablo and could see his color rising. Something was amiss. Why did it seem like Pablo wanted this to happen so badly? Why was he so against this?

Dad took out the cog from his pocket and rubbed it in his fingers. "This isn't really official family business, but it should be. Our family has done a grave disservice to Seth in the interest of keeping our Ava safe. We need the opportunity to make it up to my daughter's significant—the significant that was chosen for her, not by us, but by the same thing that chooses all our soulmates." He put the cog back in his pocket and looked at Seth, biting his lip as he thought. "I'm so sorry, son."

Seth shook his head before Dad was even done. "Like I told Ava, you were protecting her and that's all I want to do."

"Okay, all right," Pablo spouted and huffed a little. "We can do that later. We need to do the business now. Visionary." He swung his arm out. "You have the floor."

She gave him a long look before looking out at the council. "I believe that ignorance of the law does not dismiss your responsibility of it. However, in this case, when you're chosen, and a person is imprinted on your heart like we are when our soulmate is found, how is that a crime? It wasn't something they were looking for. They never once broke a law that we have set out for them. The law says no fraternizing and they had never even met before that day. As for fraternizing now that they're soulmates and separating them? I can't even believe that would be up for discussion, and if it is—not just because she's my daughter, if this was any member of my people—you'll see a *brand new* side of me. I can promise you."

The chandelier above us began to shake. Seth gripped my arm, pulling me behind him a little, still not used to Mom's power and still not understanding that it was her that was doing it. Dad slowly made his way over to her.

"Maggie," he whispered. "Breathe."

"I am breathing," she said through gritted teeth, so low no one could hear but us.

He chuckled a little. "No, you're not." He gripped her wrist in his hand and took a deep breath, as if he could breathe for her. "Just breathe, baby." She closed her eyes for a second and then the chandelier stopped its dance. She exhaled and gave him a look. "I know," he soothed and put his forehead against hers, letting his nose rub hers. "Everything will be okay."

I looked over at the council to see how they were taking in all this. They still just tittered away. Seth was looking at my parents like they were aliens. I reached up and pulled his face over to look at me like he had done to me so many times. He looked scared for us and a little slap happy.

"And so in love with you," he added and pulled me to him, his hands on the backs on my hips. "It doesn't matter what they say," he whispered and leaned in. "Remember what I told you? No one—family, friend, or foe—is taking you away from me. If we had to run..." He stopped and waited for my answer to the dot, dot, dot.

"Then we'd be okay," I said quickly, quietly.

He shook his head and laughed once with no humor, at all. "All this for my last name that *they* gave me, because *they kidnapped me* and kept me all these years. A last name that I don't even want anymore."

He hadn't realized how loud he'd gotten until the middle council member stood. She was from the Petrona clan. She looked to her left and then to her right down the line of councilors and then at us before she said, "The accused will not be deunified," my family started shouting and hooting, "or punished in any way. Majority rules. Case closed."

Before I could even turn to face him, Seth was grabbing me, lifting me up and kissing me. This was not a brushing of the lips, no. His arms were tight around my back and his lips made all my aches go away. He swung me around I didn't know how many times. I wasn't counting, I was just focusing on his lips.

"Well," Pablo shouted over the ruckus. "I guess we have it all cinched up, now don't we. Now that this ridiculous business is done, I want to dance with my wife." He clapped his hands. "Everyone get to first position for the Theoli dance."

"The *what* dance?" Seth laughed as he set me back to my feet.

"It's a customary dance we all learned from going to the reunifications every year." I screwed up my lips. "But you wouldn't know that because you've never been. They do all sorts of things at the reunifications that you're probably going to think is a little cuckoo." I laughed a little. "It's really just one big party with folk dances and games, but they're all organized and kinda... weird. But fun."

He watched them as they got into place in the middle of the room. "And you all know these dances. Every single one of you." He smiled at me. "Everyone except me." His smile got sadder, whether he knew it or not. "You know all the games, all the ins and outs of everything and I'll always be a step behind because they took me from my mother." He huffed. "And even if they hadn't taken me from my mother, I still would be a step behind you because I would have grown up completely human, with no knowledge of this world at all." He looked down, his sad little smile in place.

I gripped him around his waist, looking up and catching his gaze. Once we were locked in place I took one of his hands and put it on my side. The other hand, I took in mine, holding it.

"Now we dance," I told him and started to sway back and forth. I bit my lip at the intensity of looking into his eyes. He made a rumbling sound and used the hand on my side to pull me closer. It was so rushed that I gasped a little from the move. His smile morphed into a smirk and I wanted to scream in triumph.

There it is.

What's that, beautiful?

He knew exactly what I meant.

Your smirk that I miss so much.

He chuckled. *You like my smirk? Why's that?*

Because it means that you're the happiest. He tilted his head. *When you're joking and playing, you're so happy. And I want you to always be the happiest.*

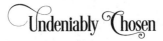

Sweetheart, you have no idea how happy you make me if you think that the only time I'm happy is when I make a stupid gesture with my lips. He pulled me up as he came down and leaned his forehead to mine. *That's the only reason I was worried about our plan not working with my family. Because they'll see how happy I am.*

I sighed, biting my lip, happy for now. *Okay. Just dance with me.*

You stop biting that lip and show me the steps.

He looked at everyone in the middle of the room, doing the Theoli and looked like he could throw up.

I'll show you the steps.

I started to sway my hips again, moving my feet, and put my head on his chest. "See, it's easy."

"No one else is slow dancing, Ave," he stated the obvious.

I lifted my head. "We're oil and water and we're never going to mix with the rest of our kind. We may as well just accept that. They do a jig, oil and water slow dances."

He chuckled into my hair before kissing my hairline. "Thank you," he said gratefully. "But you don't always have to be oil and water for me. Sometimes we can do the jig."

I smiled up at him and bit my lip just for his benefit. "Sometimes we will. But not today."

CHAPTER EIGHTEEN

"So, tonight when I go to sleep, you're going to see me again, my subconscious?"

He rubbed his scruffy chin against my cheekbone as he hummed a, "Mmhmm," and took another gulp of his tea, turning some music on with his phone. "*All You Wanted*" by Sounds Under Radio began to play as I looked up at the stars. The night was so clear it was kind of ridiculous. We sat in one of Mom's big green Adirondack chairs in the backyard. Seth had lit the fire pit— you know, firemen and their fire. He couldn't help himself. And Mom, Dad, and Rodney had come out there and we'd just sat together. Eventually Ember, Drake, Maria, Dawson, Jordan, and Laurelyn made their way over after the summit and we sat out there for hours. Dad eventually broke out the grill and hotdogs, and we made a night of it.

But now, way past midnight, everyone was gone, the night was so still I could feel every breath Seth took, hear every rustle of the leaves, and we just sat there together in the chair with me on his lap as I waited for a shooting star. I was sure that wasn't what Seth was doing, but as I listened to him speak, soaking his voice into my skin as he spoke against my temple, I waited for one. I figured we deserved one after the hell the universe had put us through.

Seth chuckled a little. "In the beginning, you were so different in your dreams. You hated me in real life and in your dreams we had just bonded and that was it. You didn't understand why the real you would be angry with me." I couldn't see his smile, but heard it. "It was strange but amazing to get these two sides of you. And then you started telling me all these things about you." I gasped and looked at him over my shoulder.

"The blueberry bagel with blueberry cream cheese!"

He grinned. "It was her—your idea. I told you I wanted to learn you and you started spouting all these random things about yourself." He chuckled again. "That wasn't really what I had in mind, but you said if it seemed like I was figuring you out, like I was trying, that your stubborn side would smooth over."

I scrunched my nose at him with a smile and laid back down. "I can't believe I would say that about myself."

"The dream you is very rational."

"She sounds like a goody two shoes," I spouted back.

He laughed and squeezed his arms around me tighter. "She learned that from you."

"Pfft," I scoffed and settled in deeper, my eyes never leaving the skies, even in our bantering. "So the coffee, the bagels, the art, the…songs," I realized and whispered. "You learned all that from *me*."

"We wanted us to work," he said into the skin just under my jaw. "You wanted us to work so badly."

I felt my breath stutter in my chest as it fought its way out. "Ahh…"

"What, baby?" He sat up a little, and turned my face over my shoulder so he could see me. "Ava."

"You did all this…for me. You came to my dreams to find me." His brow lowered. "I wouldn't connect to you here, so you went to my dreams hoping that it would somehow be different there, that it would be easier for me."

His lip curled and he shook his head. "Don't give me too much credit, now. I wanted to find you because I needed you. Wanted you."

"You don't think I wanted you, too?" He gave me a disbelieving look. "I did. Even after all that stuff with your uncle at my house. I wanted you, in my veins," I whispered, "in my gut, in my chest. Even if I didn't know why exactly, or want to want you yet. I'm glad you came to my dreams. I'm glad you're an…echoling?" I tested. He smiled and nodded. "It's a gift. You may not think so, but it is."

"I never thought it was a gift until the moment I was able to go to your dreams and have hope of salvaging the train wreck of what was started of us. And then when you didn't remember anything and you wanted to actually spend time with me there—see I thought I was going there to talk, to convince you that I wasn't the monster you thought I was, and instead you wanted me to take you on walks and talk about robins and blueberry bagels." He smiled, but then it drained away. "But I felt like I was cheating somehow, like you were angry with me in real life and you were supposed to be angry with me in the echoling. We were supposed to be working things out, not taking walks and talking about—" He sighed harshly. "But you said it was to learn you and I should trust and not feel guilty."

"And you shouldn't have felt guilty. You were pulled there. I gave you permission. You're my soulmate. You didn't do anything wrong." He still didn't look satisfied.

His eyes looked up to meet mine. "You always begged me to kiss you. You said you were the same person, that it didn't matter, that you wanted me even if the real you didn't."

I felt my lips part a little. "And did you?" I barely heard myself ask.

His hand moved into my hair, bunching and rubbing it in his fingers. "No." I don't know why it mattered, but it did. I was relieved. "No, I told you that I couldn't kiss you in your dreams. That I had to save that for when you were awake, to make sure you remembered." He leaned forward and barely let his lips brush mine. "That was only for this you."

"You really can read my soul like a book, can't you?"

He leaned back a little to see my face full on. His eyes roamed my face and he smiled just enough to make me happy. "Yeah, I think I can, little bird. Is that all right with you?"

"Yeah," I replied and leaned back against him content to settle in for the night, "it's all right with me if I can do the same one day."

"I'm begging for you to," he said into my hair.

He sighed all of a sudden, shifting in the chair slightly. "I forgot, John, the fireman who died?" I nodded. "His funeral is tomorrow."

I rubbed his chest with my curled fingers. "I'm sorry."

"Will you come with me?"

"You don't even have to ask."

I closed my eyes, content to let Seth take me away to another dream, when I heard the door shut to the back door, and turned to see Mom and Dad coming across the back lawn with a couple of thick blankets in hand.

I gave them a curious look as I could. I was sure I didn't have to say anything to get my point across. It was almost one in the morning.

"We're coming with you," Mom explained and let Dad sit down first in the Adirondack next to us before she sat in his lap, mimicking our pose, "in the echoling."

She tossed a blanket over us and then pulled one over her and Dad. She then snuggled against his cheek and held her hand out to me.

"Okay, Seth, take us to la, la land."

"Uh…" Seth looked at me and back to her. "What exactly are you going to do in the echoling with us?"

"I have a theory," she said and left it that. "I'm the Visionary for a reason. Let's go. What does it hurt for you to take us one time, anyway?"

"Yes, ma'am," he muttered and rubbed his head. He looked at our hands as I reached out to take Mom's hand between the chairs and shook his head. "That won't hold. You'll just let go when you fall asleep."

"Oh," Mom said quickly and pulled the scarf from her neck, "I've taken care of that." She leaned forward and tied our wrists together gently with it. Daddy was rubbing her back as she leaned forward and I noticed for the first time how uptight he seemed. "There," she said as she leaned back.

"How did you know you had to be touching?"

"I didn't, but I figured."

"Daddy," I whispered before anybody else could speak or do anything.

He looked at me, knowing I was checking on him. He looked at Seth. "The last time my wife was in an echoling, she was tortured." Seth and Dad stared at each other. "I can't talk her out of this so this is all in your hands."

Seth scoffed just a little. I felt the hurt coming off of him and sat up on his lap enough to turn to him. Daggumit, Daddy. All my family ever managed to do was make Seth feel like crap. I wrapped my hand around Seth's neck, hearing his breath hiss as my calm hit his skin.

He looked at me and rubbed my arm. "Thank you, sweetheart. It's okay." He looked back at my father. "Sir, how many times how I hugged your wife and not given her an offense mark? I understand the want to keep your significant safe and from harm. I *have* one. I think people in your family and mine keep forgetting that. And I think people keep forgetting that I wasn't born a Watson, I never wanted to be one, and I've done things to try to prove myself already that I'm *not* one. So it would be great if everyone would stop treating me like the enemy."

Dad thankfully started doing that lip chewing thing he did when he was thinking things over instead of blowing up, which I would have blown right back up at him. And then Dad started to look a little guilty, thankfully.

"It's in the Virtuoso blood to protect his women, all of them," Dad explained. "You'll understand one day when you have a daughter."

"I can't wait for that day," Seth replied, not skipping a beat, making my heart do the two-step behind my ribs, "but when that day comes and she brings me her significant…I hope I'm more open to the idea that the universe and God might have chosen someone less conventional for her. And I hope I'll understand for both their sakes."

Dad breathed in deep through his nose. "Touché, son." He rubbed his head and looked at Mom, who was already looking at him. "We never really talked about everything that happened at the summit, Seth. We will, all right? And you're right. You're an echoling, that doesn't mean you do the same things that a Watson echoling would do with his ability. I'm sorry."

Seth seemed taken aback that he actually got an apology out of Dad, and so quickly. "It's all right." He cleared his throat and rubbed my arm again. "If everyone is ready, you all have to go to sleep before me."

I leaned in and kissed Seth's lips and then moved slowly to kiss the little scar under his chin. He closed his eyes and accepted that kiss without flinching. I opened my eyes to meet his. He rubbed the backs of his fingers down my cheek; his way to say 'thank you' without making a fuss.

So I lay back down, turning on my side with my torso just a bit to snuggle my face into Seth's neck, knowing that would end any struggle with alertness.

"Goodnight, Ava," he whispered and kissed my temple. "I'll see you in your dreams."

"I'm sorry that I won't remember this."

"One day you will," he promised.

"Seth," I sighed and hurried to him quickly. He wrapped his arms around me and lifted my feet off the floor. "Did it work? Did our plan work?" I asked in rushed whispers.

"Yes. It worked." He put me down, holding my sides in his easy grip. "And better than that, they didn't have anything planned for the summit so there was no plan to thwart. Everyone was safe. And I told the real you about the echolings, all of it. She knows."

I gasped. "What did I say? Did I think it was romantic how you came and did all this for me?"

He laughed. "How did you know?"

I shrugged and put my arms around his shoulders. "I know myself, and I'm a romantic."

"You come to her room every night?" We both turned to find Mom and Dad there. Mom continued, "Of all the places you could go?"

"We've been to the palace also," Seth explained, "but this is where Ava feels comfortable. I'm not trying to use this as a vacation. Not until Ava remembers anyway. Then we'll see. Right now, we're just trying to figure out why Ava's subconscious is separated."

"Seth," I whispered, "why are my parents in my subconscious?"

"Oh," he laughed, "we brought them. Your Mom wanted to come."

"Take us to the palace," Mom said and came my way. "Hey, honey."

"Hey…Mom." I cocked a brow at her.

"So…when's the last time you saw *me*?"

"This morning. When I left for school. Why?" I leaned back. "Why is everyone being so weird… Wait. Oh. Because you told me in my real life, so everyone knows. Now you think *this* me has been like stuck in some dream world motherless for weeks or something?"

She stared and then said, "Yes. Actually."

I laughed. "Mom, this is just my subconscious. To me, this is the same night. I don't feel like any time has really passed. When Seth leaves here, it feels like he was just here a few minutes ago when he leaves and comes back."

"Really," she asked, clearly intrigued.

I could see more questions coming, forming behind her eyes.

"Mom, you said something about the palace? Why?"

"Oh." She glanced at Dad, who was borderline grouchy as he watched the whole thing, and then back to me. "I have a theory."

"What theory?"

She huffed. "I am the Visionary! I don't have to explain myself. Let's go!"

I held up my hands and rolled my eyes when I turned where she couldn't see me. "Okay, yikes." I gripped Seth's forearm. "Too bad we can't feel our calming touch in here because Mom clearly needs at hit," I muttered my words almost into Seth's shirt.

Seth half snorted and then looked at Mom like she might turn him into a toad or something.

"I heard that," she tossed back at us saucily and smirked.

I peeked at her over my shoulder and grinned as Seth put his arm around me and the palace came into view all around us.

I let out a happy sigh as I looked out across the terrace to see the London skyline in the dark. "The last time we were here—"

"I appeared."

We turned, jerked really, to find Ashlyn. "Ashlyn."

"I knew it," Mom said. "See," she said to us, but kept her eyes on the ghostly Visionary, "sometimes I know what I'm talking about." She stepped toward Ashlyn, who was standing near the terrace door. "What's going on with my daughter?"

"That's not the right question."

Mom clamped down on her jaw. "We're not playing this game again. You made me play it with Seth when he was a boy and I was trying to find him. You wouldn't help, you said not to go after him—"

"And he turned out just fine, didn't he?"

Mom was about to boil over. She opened her mouth to lay into her, but Seth's quiet, dangerous tone silenced them both.

"You told her not to go after me?"

I knew that my touch wouldn't help him feel any better, but I touched him anyway. I gripped his forearm with both hands and looked up at him, but he was looking at her.

"And you told her to leave me with them? Knowing that they had kidnapped me? Knowing that they tortured and then killed my mother? You don't know what they did to me, do you?"

I had actually leaned back a little, surprised at the level of his anger and the growled disgust coming from him. He always tried to say he wanted to find the best in them, that he was looking for goodness in them, that they were his family. I'd never seen him admit that they killed his mother before. We had avoided that. I guess *he* had avoided it…for as long as he could.

She didn't answer, just stoically stared at him.

When he saw that I had leaned away, he looked at me, his expression changing. "I'm sorry."

"No," I whispered. "You're okay."

He shook, his head. "No, I'm not." He looked down at me, looking probably the most broken, the most bleak, sad, and dejected he'd ever looked.

I moved swiftly—swifter than I realized—and pulled him to me, even as I pressed against him. I wrapped my arms around his middle, my face in his neck. His arms engulfed me so tightly I could barely breathe. We lived in the small space between us and we existed on the air that was in each other's lungs.

I wrapped my hand around the back of his neck and looked up into his face, my brown eyes colliding with his blue, and tried to convey any sense of calm and love I had to him. I didn't know if it was working. I hated that I couldn't calm him with a touch here.

"I'm sorry," I whispered and refused to look away.

"You didn't make them kidnap me," was his sarcastic response, and his way of making me feel better.

"No," I insisted, "I'm sorry that I can't make you feel better."

"I feel better already," he promised as his arms tugged me closer, in a way of proving his point.

"Don't lie to me," I whispered, scratching the hair at the base of his neck a little.

He sighed, giving up, and looked over at Ashlyn.

I started to feel so…cold. I shivered once with goosebumps.

"I think it's time for the truth, Ashlyn. For everyone."

Her smile wasn't pleasant. "The truth. I don't think even I know exactly what that is anymore."

He huffed. "What—"

"Maybe it's been so changed, so watered down, so burned down into the ashes that there is no truth left. There's only what we perceive of it."

The cold that had begun crept inward, making it impossible to get warm. I began to shiver inside my sweater. Seth noticed and started to rub my arms with his impossibly warm palms. They felt like a balm to a sore, but I was still freezing.

"Ashlyn," Mom begged. "Please."

"It's you," she replied and then surprisingly looked up at me, locking her eyes in on mine. Seth pushed me behind him a little out of protectiveness, but she kept speaking. "You're the one. You're my truth, Ava." She surprised me impossibly further by swiping a tear as it fell from her eye. "I'm not sorry it was you. There could be no one else. I am sorry if it was too much to bear, but it's eased me over the years." She smiled. "How it's made me feel so much lighter." She closed her eyes. "And now that you're all here again, I can finally be free and go."

Seth's hand on my wrist tightened in fear of her ominous message. "Go where? What the hell are you talking about?"

"Where do any of us go, Seth? I'm so sorry that you had to stay." Her face crumpled and I stared, shocked that she would feel so much for him. "I saw it and if you had been rescued, if she had rescued you, you wouldn't have found your way back."

He huffed. "The fact that I was rescued or not doesn't mean anything. We would have still been significants." His anger grew by the second. "We would have been meant for each other regardless. I eventually would have made my way here subconsciously, somehow, to find her, so your argument—"

"No, Seth." She gulped. "I never said you weren't significants. I said you wouldn't have found your way back to Ava." I waited for the punchline. "The foster care system isn't always the prettiest place and sometimes the homes and the centers that the kids are placed in are..." She lowered her head. "You would have never found your way back to Ava..." She paused and I knew why before she even said the words. I gasped and was about to tell her not to say the words. Please, just no, no, no, don't. "...because you weren't there to—"

A noise left my throat. I shook my head. I couldn't hear this. "Stop."

"Stop," Seth commanded at the same time.

"Stop!" Dad yelled. "Can't you see what you're doing to her? You don't tell someone their significant could have died."

"Would have died," she corrected. "And it's better than your significant actually dying, now isn't it?" she finished softly, her eyes drifting off, her mind somewhere else, somewhere I didn't want to think about, but I was sure I knew.

Seth turned me to him, pressing my face gently into his chest.

Don't even think about it. And I would have found my way to you. Nothing would have stopped me.

Mom started in, her Visionary voice that I was sure Ashlyn had used herself before was in full swing.

"Ashlyn, we know your story. We know that they kept you separated from him and that they…" She couldn't say it. She couldn't say out loud that the Watsons killed him. "But what does that have to do with Ava and Seth? What do you mean that Ava is *the one* and…. What does any of this have to do with us? How does all this add up to us being here now?"

Seth was barely listening to my mother as he rubbed my arms vigorously.

Ashlyn watched us, a look passing over her face that I didn't understand. I was so cold that I couldn't even think anymore.

He pulled my chin up and looked at my face. "Look at me, Ava."

"I am," I barely managed as I finally made my eyes roll up to meet him. Something wasn't right. I felt like I was draining away or something. I was so shaky, so cold, so strange. I clung to Seth's shirt, but I didn't need to. He was holding me to him so tightly. I knew he was scared.

I could only imagine the glare he was sending her as he roared over my head, "What the hell did you do to her?"

"You're looking at this all wrong, Seth," she said softly. I turned to see her. I had to. Her voice—something in her voice made me pause. She was looking at Seth with this look in her eyes, and then I realized she was looking at his—

"Your eyes are just like his. So blue, like I'm lost in the ocean, but I don't ever want to be rescued."

Seth tensed beside me, the muscles under his chest hard like stone. "What—"

"Richard was tall, too, like you. He didn't have your hair or your smile or wear those God awful clothes." She laughed at her own joke a little and we all watched in wonder as she walked to the rail and looked out at the city skyline, lost in her reverie, not knowing or not caring that she was dropping bombs on us left and right.

"Ashlyn," I tried, my voice so weak. I didn't understand it. It scared me, the hoarseness of it, and everyone's head jerked to look at me—except her. "Please, Ashlyn—"

"We stood here once." She didn't turn. She ran her hand down the railing, so sad, so lost. "Just once. We looked out at the city." My vision started to blur a little. "I had come up here—snuck really—and he managed to find me. He came and stood as close as was proper." The spots bounced in front of my vision, just like that night at the summit, when I saw the bird that no one else saw. I squeezed my eyes, but it was still there. I vaguely heard and felt Seth's pleas, asking if I was okay, but all I could hear was Ashlyn talking in the background, as clear as a bell. "He told me to look out at the city, to imagine another life, maybe one where I found my significant and lived happily ever after." As she said it, I could see it in my mind; him and her, as they were. Her so shy, him so taken by her to the point that his eyes never left her as he spoke. She turned to look at us. "This was the spot. I could see it in my mind, the way it would have played out if I had let it. This was the very spot where we would have bonded, where he would have touched my hand for the first time and our souls would have reached out, knowing that they belonged to each other." Everyone had stopped whatever protest they had been doing for my safety when she started *that* story." She smiled, but it faded quickly. "But we didn't touch, because back then people didn't touch for no reason, and we weren't alone long enough for us to get up the courage. When he would have, the council had already found us and never let that happen again. It was the one and only time we were ever truly alone. And I regret it every. Single. Day of my existence, that I didn't go with my gut and just reach out…" She stepped forward and my vision cleared a little. She reached us and Seth tugged me and put me behind him. It was a little comical that Seth thought I needed protecting from this little woman and it was also comical that he thought he could protect me from the previous Visionary if she truly wanted to hurt me.

"I don't want to hurt her," she insisted. "That's never what I wanted to do. Or you." I looked around Seth's arm to find them staring at each other, Seth in complete confusion. He glanced at me and then back at her.

"How it that…possible," he finally mumbled.

I didn't know what he was talking about. I tightened my grip on his arm as much as I could to get him to see that I was still here. He looked at me again, but his gaze once again settled on Ashlyn. He leaned in and took her chin in his fingers…the way he'd done me so many times. I took a deep, painful breath, looking away, but he released her just as quickly.

"It's you." He looked at me. "It's you."

"What?" I whispered.

"She has your eyes." He looked back at Ashlyn, suspicion all over him.

"We both have brown eyes—"

"No, Ave. Those are *your* eyes. I'm looking at you when I look at her. I'm looking *right at you*, right into your soul."

I blinked, not understanding, and then her comment about Seth's eyes struck me. *You have his eyes...*

"Oh, God... Ashlyn, what did you do?"

She smiled sadly. "It's not what I did, or what we did. It's what *they* did. We didn't get our happily ever after. Don't you see? We never got our life. When there's so much evil on a life it can't leave this world without leaving a mark, without leaving an *imprint*," she insisted.

"Just like the first imprints were a product of rage—it trickled down from his blood in the well and affected an entire town, and oh, how that one instance, that one moment in time, one ripple, affected an entire world, an entire race of people. One man in a well!" She shook her head, awe on her face.

"Ashlyn," my mother said and we all knew it was about to go down if Ashlyn didn't spill.

"They did this to us, Ava," she said as she looked into my eyes, and for the first time, I got her meaning, as she looked at me so sadly. She didn't mean her and Richard 'us', she meant her and *me* 'us'.

I could barely breathe as understanding smacked into me. "Oh, God."

Seth's arm wound around from behind, but Ashlyn was reaching for me at the same time, both of them trying to keep them in their worlds. No one won the battle. Her hand wrapped around my wrist, around my tattoo, and I saw what she remembered. I could tell that Seth was seeing it, too. Mom ran forward, understanding that we were seeing a vision, or something to that effect, and grabbed my arm, Dad right behind her, and we all tumbled down into it together.

I watched the terrace as Ashlyn's young smiling form bounced on light feet and went to the railing. She was carefree, she was free, she was happy. She closed her eyes and leaned over. I gasped. What was she doing?

She was *letting go.*

The edges around me shimmered and there were spots of light around us that didn't belong. I could still feel Seth's arms tight around my waist, my anchor, and Ashlyn's hand around my wrist. This was just a vision, nothing more.

A door opened behind us and I turned just as Richard passed through us. I gasped, feeling him, his every thought and desire as he passed through me. He had been searching for her for over an hour and a half. He wanted nothing more than to spend time with her and understand this urge to in his heart to be more than her subject. This hadn't been a happy coincidence.

"Fancy meeting you here," he said, smiling and removed his hat.

That scoundrel.

I smiled, despite everything. Ashlyn, wasn't the bitter, used woman she was today—no. She was a prim, proper, shy girl of the day with just a dash of spunk. She glanced at him quickly before looking away and smiling shyly. "Yes. Fancy that. Now what?"

"Well, I…I don't know. I guess we can just look at the city together before going down to supper. Do you mind if I walk you?"

Her cheeks turned so rosy. "I'd like that."

He beamed and I caught a glimpse of his face when he turned a little. I hadn't seen his face since he'd come out here and I found myself pulling away from Seth to see it more full on. He fiddled with his hat as he looked from the dark town below to Ashlyn's face. Seth tried to keep me there, but I *had* to see.

I finally pulled away and went to stand in front of him. It was as if he didn't see me at all. Because he didn't; I wasn't there. This was a memory. Ashlyn's memory.

He was handsome. I could see why Ashlyn or any girl would be taken by him. But it was his eyes that made me want to shatter right there on the bricks under my feet. He looked at Ashlyn behind me, but he was looking right at me, through me. Those ocean blue eyes and the soul inside have looked at me what felt like a thousand times before. I didn't move, I barely breathed.

"Seth," I whispered, not believing what I was seeing.

A robin came and landed on the railing between them. She looked at it and began to spout about how the Robins were her favorite and she loved to come up there to listen at night. When more came, she laughed happily, giggling, and told him that she wanted to be one of those birds.

"No," I heard myself say. "It's not possible."

285

She moved, chasing them further down, and he chased her, a smile on his face that said he would do just about anything she wanted. He went right through me once more before I could move out of the way. I turned, needing to see where this went, needing for this to play out. I finally felt Seth's arms close around me from behind me, but he wasn't trying to stop me or pull me away, he was watching with me—he just needed to touch me. I knew the feeling. I clawed at his arms around my chest to keep him there and felt his mouth press to my ear.

"I'm right here, baby." I took a deep breath, sighing, soaking his presence in, his voice. It didn't matter if his touch wasn't helping me physically, his touch helped me with him just being there. His touch made my soul sing, and if we left here and his calm never seeped into my skin again, that would be okay. I wanted him, not what his touch could give me.

"They like you," Richard was saying to her and made a circle around her. The birds sat on the railing and some sat on the bricks around their feet. He was just flirting, of course. Birds were just being birds. They were hoping they had crumbs to throw out as most tourists in London did, I was sure.

"I really do wish I was a bird sometimes." She leaned down and held her hand out, her finger extended toward one. The birds near her hand flew away as she neared them. She sighed. "They sing their song," she told him, "they can do whatever they want. They're free. If they wanted to leave they could." She looked at him from her bent position. "If they wanted to find someone to be with, they're free to. Everyone doesn't have that luxury," she finished, her words barely breath as they stared at each other.

He came a couple steps closer. "Some of us do have that luxury. Don't you feel that?"

She stared. "I…"

"Ashlyn," he said. Her name, just her name.

I heard Seth make a noise from behind me, realizing as I did that this was more than a memory just for Ashlyn.

Her chest began to move up and down rapidly. "Richard." Then her lips began to lift into a smile.

He cleared his throat and pulled something from his pocket—a folded piece of paper. He unfolded it carefully and showed it to her. "I, uh, did this for you."

We couldn't see what was on it, but she said, "You drew this? Truly?"

SHELLY CRANE

"Ahh," I groaned as Seth gripped me tightly, understanding it all.

"Sweetheart," he whispered and turned me to face him instead, pressing me tightly into his chest, keeping me in the safe place that I loved there. If he felt the tears that were already soaking his shirt, he said nothing. He just kept me there, a hand on the back of my neck and one of the middle of my back and we watched.

We watched knowing our lives were changing, they weren't our own, and we didn't know what the hell to do anymore. We'd thought the Watsons had been our only obstacle. How naïve we'd been.

I shivered again as the cold seeped into me bone-deep and those hazy, ethereal spots in her vision returned. And then it was as if I could feel her, see through her eyes, feel her heart pounding a heavy rhythm in our chests, and I knew that something awful was about to happen...and I was going to feel it all just as Ashlyn had felt it.

He smiled at her and then he held his hand out to help her up. Ashlyn reached for his hand slowly, knowing this was it, that her life would be different, that she'd get everything she ever wanted, that her fairy tale would come true with one touch, just like she was always promised. But a man came rushing through the heavy terrace door, along with other council members, and ruined everything. She never touched her significant that day. If she had known what would have happened, how the council and the man staring her down now would have been so hell bent on keeping them separated, she might have just touched him quickly just to bond, reached out to him, made it happen, but she knew that would have just made things worse. Either way, they would have never let them be together, but at least she would have gotten to see the visions of their life together. It would have been worth it for that.

When they took Richard by the arms and dragged him toward the door, my chest ached so badly I could barely breathe as I realized what was happening. We tried to keep our composure however.

Both Ashlyn and I both asked as one, "What are you doing?"

"Richard and I need to have a chat. That's all. About boundaries. The Visionary is special." He touched her arm. I felt it and shivered, disgust crawling through my veins. Bile seeped up into my throat. I tried not to gag on it. "You keep forgetting how special you are, Visionary. You aren't some Virtuoso that can play house and have rendezvous on rooftops."

His breath brushed against my check he was so close. It was such a strange thing. I felt like I was being ripped in two. I could feel her world, yet I could still feel mine. The disgusting breath on my cheek and Seth's arms still around me, holding me tight. And I wasn't about to lose myself to Ashlyn's world. No. I clung to Seth harder, even digging my nails and fingers into his upper arms. I looked at her as she tried to come up with something to say to him and then looked at Seth. His face was right above mine, waiting. Just waiting for me.

"Don't lose me," I begged him. "Seth, please, don't lose me—"

He cut me off with his lips—just pressing them against mine gently. One of his arms released me and his hand came up to hold my face and smooth my cheek.

He eased away just far enough to say, "I've got you." I could feel his lips move when he said it against mine because he was still so close, breathing life into those words. "I've got you, sweetheart. I promise you won't be lost."

"But," I protested, "I feel…I'm—" I looked at Ashlyn and then up into his eyes. "I feel so lost already."

His handed smoothed my cheek once more. "It's not you. It's her."

The cold came back, blasting through my bones once more. I shivered, my teeth started to hurt from clamping down to keep them from chattering. "I'm being pulled away. I can feel it—Seth."

His jaw was rigid. "I've got you. Ava, look in my eyes. It's me. If you go, I go." He huffed a little and shook his head. "I think we've proved that we're a package deal." He smiled which surprised me in the circumstances. "Significants belong to each other. Our souls belong to each other. I don't care where you go or when or how. I'll come with you," he said hard and loud, almost yelling it, as if he wanted everyone to hear it. "And I'll find you, always. Your heart belongs to me." He took my hand and put it on his chest, his head rested against mine. "Safe. Right beside mine, right where it belongs. You're not lost, little bird, and you won't be."

I shuddered and leaned up, kissing him fervently, worried that this could be the last time. I pulled back, my body aching in more ways than one.

"No one else saves me like you," I whispered. "You bastard." I raised my head, my eyes wide, shocked at what had come out of Ashlyn's mouth. And mine. We turned to look at her.

She was glaring at the carefully orchestrated hand on her arm that wasn't touching any skin, only her jacket. "I can walk. Get your hands off me."

"Our Visionary is obviously suffering from a fit of some sort," he said and nodded to someone. "Hysteria perhaps."

"Where are you taking him?" we asked.

"Locked in his room, of course." He smiled, but it was unlike any smile I wanted to be on the other end of. "Unless we should put him in the only place that he can't get out of."

We gasped. "No."

"Didn't I warn you about meeting him? A girl meeting a boy who isn't her significant. Shame on you."

"He would have been," we said and she turned to look at Richard. His eyes were already on her from his place on his knees. She locked eyes with him and begged. "You didn't give us the opportunity. We hadn't touched yet. If you never let me see anyone then how would I ever touch anyone to bond with them? Please, just let—"

"You aren't here to bond. You're here to lead your people," he dismissed and nodded to the men. They each came and grabbed a sleeved-arm of hers.

She struggled. "No. You don't understand. I felt it. So did he. We would have bonded had we touched. If you'll only let us—"

"All the more reason to keep him locked up. In fact, to the dungeon with him."

"No," we screamed and fell to our knees, grabbing our chest. We were both pulled back up, but in completely different ways—mine was in love and worry, hers was in hate and fury. He was dragged through the door and so was she. Then everything changed so quickly, we couldn't even think, catch our breath or adjust.

We were in the dungeons. It had been a while because the man I saw before me behind those bars wasn't the same man who'd I'd just seen on the rooftop. His hair was longer, curling around his ears, but not in a good way at all. His beard was overgrown, he was so thin. His fingers wrapped around the bars and his eyes begged her to come closer, to just reach out and touch him...but they begged her to go, to get out of there, to never come back.

"Ashlyn, get out of here before they find you."

She smiled; I felt it on my face. "I made it. I actually made it to you."

"And now I want to you to leave," he said as she came down the stairs toward him.

"Richard, tell me what I can—"

She never made it. We watched in horrified wonder as she was overrun.

"Ashlyn!" he screamed. "Don't you dare hurt her."

"No, get your hands off me," we screamed. "Richard." It was so strange saying someone else's name, but it also felt…right in some weird way.

Ashlyn and Richard reached for each other as Ashlyn was pulled away, fighting with everything she had in her. It was the most heartbreaking thing I'd ever seen in my entire life.

"Stop fighting, Ash, you're going to hurt yourself," he said and the way he said it and the way he used her nickname reminded me so much of Seth.

"Richard," she cried, "please don't. I can't live in a world where you aren't there with me." She cried so hard in the guard's arm. He realized that she had stopped fighting and so he stopped struggling with her.

"Yes, you can. Go and change things. Show our people that these monsters aren't who *we are*." The guard chuckled at Richard's dig and wasn't prepared for Ashlyn to snatch away. She ran for the cell. It all happened as if in slow motion for us. For me at least. I knew the outcome. I knew she didn't make it, but still, I waited with bated breath and wanted so much for her to reach him. Once again they stretched their arms out toward each other. Their fingers got the closest they'd ever gotten. The angry guard jerked her back by her arm just as their fingers narrowly missed each other.

"No!" we wailed, knowing this was it, that had been our final shot.

"Vivere, Ashlyn. Remember. Live!" he called, his arms reaching through the bars, just for the sake of reaching. His head rested on the bars, too, to try to see me for as long as he could before I was gone. "Vivere!"

"Oh, my God…" I heard Seth in my ear.

"Amor in aeternum!" Ashlyn and I yelled together, my voice croaking. "I love you," we sobbed as best as we could as we turned the corner, the guard snatching her around carelessly and burning an offense mark on Ashlyn's forearm.

"I love you, Ashlyn!" we heard him yell down the passageway. It didn't echo. It was a solid message, meant to rip through the ripples of time like tissue paper. "I'll find you again."

Just like that we were back on the rooftop. It was such a harsh transition, that I almost fell and had to hold my hands out. But then I saw what this vision was and I wished we had stayed in the dungeon. Richard was on his knees on the bricks, no shirt on. He was still so thin and his beard and hair were scraggily. He had three men around him and this didn't look like a tea party.

This looked like an execution.

"Oh, Richard," the same man said, swiping his fingers over chin. "It didn't have to be this way."

And that's when I knew. This *was* an execution.

"Oh, no," I mumbled.

"You're right," Richard said. But I looked over at Seth...because he had said it, too. I watched as Seth's mouth moved as Richard continued. "It didn't have to be this way. You're choosing this."

The man smiled. "You're right. I am. And as soon as you're gone, she'll finally stop acting like a stupid child and get back to her duties."

"And what's that? Watson family lapdog, Sid?"

Sid...

Sid nodded to the one behind him and he put his hands on either side of Richard's head. It wasn't until Seth hissed that I understood what I was too dense to see before.

"No," I said and shook my head as I took Seth's face in my hands, pulling his face to look at me. His eyes had dulled, and when he looked at me it was like he wasn't seeing me. It was like he was seeing another place. "No. Please."

He started to buckle and I struggled to catch him, finally seeing everything around me. Daddy ran to help me, but Seth fell to his knees. I looked at him helplessly. And then shifted my gaze to Richard to see what was coming next.

The man's hands shook a little beside Richard's head. Richard started to fight, so the other two grabbed his arms and held him down on his knees. I moved back a little, waiting for Seth to start swinging, but he didn't. I cupped his face again.

"Seth, don't get lost," I whispered, telling him the same thing he'd told me. "I'm right here. I've got you. I'm not letting go. You go, I go."

He gasped. "You think you can do this to her?" I turned to look at Richard. He shook his head angrily, even as they held him down, sweat pouring from his brow and chin. "She'll *end you*. She will take care of her people, one way or another. If you think you're going to just get away with this, you really are the most daft, mad man on the planet. She loves me, yes, but she loves her people, too. She's the Visionary, you fool! By getting rid of me, you're solving nothing! She still loves her people." I swung my gaze to Seth and watched his lips—the beautiful words coming from his lips. Even in that moment, as they were about to kill him, he was still fighting for her. My heart could have burst in that moment. "You think you've broken her."

"I have." Sid smirked. "Just like a mare that needs to be broken before she's saddled."

Seth gulped. I was sure that Richard had as well. "You can try to break her, but she'll just be stronger when she comes out on the other side. You're forging her with fire. People who have been broken are fearsome because they know how to stay alive."

The man's hands shook harder and Richard's head began to shake with it at a small, rapid pace that was barely noticeable. He groaned and Seth groaned with him. Richard's nose began to bleed.

"You plead for someone that can't even hear you," Sid said and laughed once, looking down on him as if he pitied him.

"She doesn't need to hear me. I'm not pleading for her. I'm making sure you know that she'll get the last word."

Sid smiled, showing no teeth. "Funny thing about last words—often times you hear them at your back." He nodded once the man. "Goodbye, Richard. Don't worry about our girl," Richard began to struggle against the two men again, but his thin, hungry body was no match, "I'll be taking *very* good care of her. Finish him." Sid turned to go without another glance.

Watching Richard fight against them as the man used his ability and smiled—actually smiled—made me ache in my chest, my imprint actually hurt, as if Richard belonged to me. Blood ran more from his nose, and then from his ear. I gasped and turn to check Seth. He wasn't bleeding, but he was shaking. I wrapped my arms around his head, pressing his head to my chest and whispered that I had him, that he was mine, that he wasn't going anywhere, that if he left, I was going, too.

And since I was watching Richard die in front of my eyes, I was really starting to worry that it might be a possibility.

A loud bang behind us had us all turning to see. A distraught, disheveled Ashlyn came bursting through the door. She was barefoot in a long pale pink nightgown with long sleeves that had been torn and clawed at, it seemed. She was dirty, too. Her hair piled on top of her head in a bun that was falling loose.

"Ashlyn," Richard sighed and coughed, choking on his blood. "Get the hell away from here," he and Seth growled in a voice I'd never heard.

Richard was scared for her, yes, but more than that he didn't want her to watch him die. And that was exactly what was about to happen.

"Oh, God, help me," she whispered as she stopped walking and looked at him.

"Visionary," Sid groaned as he grabbed her upper clothed-arm and swung her around. "Since you are so determined to evade my rules and guards I had placed for you, then you can watch as the blood vessels in your precious Richard's head are expanded until they burst."

"No!" she screamed.

"I tried to protect you from this," he said and gave her a look. What a bastard. Trying to act as if he cared while he killed her significant. "I tried to shield you from this. That's why I placed the guard at the library with you, but you just don't ever listen to me." Richard groaned as the man kept working on him. "You have to start trusting me. If you had, you wouldn't be watching this right now." He nodded his head to the man. "Finish it."

When the groaning and gurgling from Richard, and the screaming from Ashlyn started, I hugged Seth to my chest and looked away completely. I couldn't watch a man die. I just couldn't.

"Vivere, Ashlyn. Amor in aeternum," he and Seth groaned. I looked at Seth's face as he said the explanation, needing to say the final words that Sid didn't understand—they weren't for him. "Live. Forever, my love."

Seth's eyes didn't see me and I knew that he was in that state of dream and memory just like I had been. But what an awful memory to be trapped in. When I heard Ashlyn gasp, I made myself look away from him to see Richard's chest buckled out wide and his arms flung out. I looked back at Seth to make sure he wasn't following suit, but he seemed to be let go at that point.

I sighed harshly, accepting his hug, pressing our foreheads together for just a few seconds, but then I had to see. I had to be there for Ashlyn and see this thing through. Ashlyn had closed her eyes. They let his body fall to the brick under our feet carelessly, like he didn't matter at all, like he wasn't a person, like they hadn't just murdered someone's significant and then they were going to go inside and have dinner with theirs.

Sid let her go. That surprised me. I watched as she ran with all she had to him and knelt down. She finally got to touch him, but it all was all too late. She was sobbing so loud, her mouth wide, not wiping her tears. She landed on her knees hard. The first thing her hand touched was his cheek that was smeared with his blood from his nose, but she didn't even seem to notice the blood—all she saw was him.

"Richard," she whispered, like she was coaxing him awake, "I'm here now. I was just a little bit late." She sobbed again, her chest wracking so hard she could barely catch her breath. "I'm so sorry! I tried to get out. I tried to get to you, but I was too late. I'll never forgive myself for that. I'm so sorry. I ruined everything. I didn't touch you that day on the rooftop. I was scared. I was too scared. I was a fool!" she wailed and leaned down, putting her head on his chest. "Richard, please. I'm sorry. Please don't leave me here."

I felt my chest shaking as I watched it. I'd never been so heartbroken watching something. I felt Seth touch my chin. He seemed pale, but focused.

"Don't watch," he said softly and I fought him to look again.

"I have to."

"No, baby," he whispered in my ear, hugging my head to his chest. "I wouldn't want you to watch if that was me on the ground."

I winced, squeezing my eyes shut. Neither would I. I'd beg him to leave. To run. I let him take me away from that scene, to look at him instead, right in his ocean blue eyes. Oh, God, I prayed that this night would end.

"Enough," Sid said calmly. We both looked over to see him giving her a sympathetic look that would rival any funeral-goer. "I'm sorry about this. I let you say your goodbye. Now we have work to do. It's time to get back to—"

"You know you're going to rot for this, right?"

He stopped and cocked his head. "Excuse me?"

She leaned in, kissing Richard's forehead, getting some of his blood on her jaw in the process. She looked at him once more, smoothing back his hair as she stood on her shaky legs. This was the only time she'd ever gotten to touch him. She stood, her eyes red, her hair wild, her nightgown torn, barefoot, and blood now on her face. She looked like a wild, scorned thing and now, thanks to him, she was one.

"I said, you're going to *rot in Hell*. You'll pay for this, one way or another. All of you will pay for what you've done. And the ones who knew and just stood by and did…nothing."

Sid smirked. "Oh, Visionary. You're here to transcribe scrolls and motivate our people…to do what I say. If only you had that kind of power."

The vision faded and we were left in the dream—my dream—with my parents standing there with Ashlyn. I let out a whoosh of a breath and tried to catch a steady lungful, but couldn't get a good handle on it with the small sob still chasing the breaths in my chest.

"Aw, Ava," Ashlyn soothed, "it truly warms my heart that you would care so much."

"Don't speak to her, Ashlyn," Seth defended and hugged me harder, shielding me from her. "What you just did was—"

"I showed you what you needed to see."

"You blindsided us. There were a thousand ways to tell us...*that* other than showing us that way," he growled in that voice that I realized was a lot like Richard's when he was angry. I squeezed my eyes shut tight against Seth's shirt.

"You needed to see."

"I'm not so sure."

"You did! She did."

"Now you're really losing me. I think she needed to see least of all," Seth said back, but his bite was gone. I looked up at him, at his face. He looked at Ashlyn and I knew—he couldn't be angry with her just like I couldn't be angry with Richard if he was here. He'd just been in Richard's body, spouting his love for her as he died *for* her.

Another spike of gut-wrenching agony slashed across my chest. A noise emerged from my throat and I turned to look at Ashlyn.

"Please, no more games. Just tell us why. Why did you make us watch, and," I gulped, "what connection exactly...do Seth and I have to you and Richard?"

I waited and prayed, begged with everything in me that she wasn't going to say that we were them, that they were us, that we were reincarnated or re-embodiments of them. I just wanted to be myself. I wanted to love Seth and I wanted for my heart and soul to be my own. I didn't want her to say that he only loved me because Richard had loved her and he was just chasing her soul through me.

She looked at my face and for the first time I saw remorse.

"No! That can't be true." I looked at Seth and back at her. "I don't love him just because you love Richard." I felt the tears coming down my face and let them come. I let them fall heavy and loud to the ground like stomps of rebellion. "I love him because he's mine, because he was promised to me, because he's a good person regardless of his environment, because he wanted me even when I didn't want him," I sniffed, remembering, "because he has amazing taste in music, because he looks just as good in his fireman suit as he does barefoot in a pair of jeans and a t-shirt, because he can draw me a picture that takes my breath away, because even when we touches me in the dream where I can't feel his calm or tingles, I still get tingles *because it's him*, because he took the time to find out all my favorite things, and because he came to my dreams to find me when I couldn't be found sitting right next to him."

Seth's mouth was open as he looked at me. He didn't look at her at all. "Is that really how you see me?"

"Oh, my gosh, yes," I mumbled and leaned up, wrapping my hands around the back of his neck. I brought my mouth right up to the place before you kiss someone. "If I never kissed you again, if I never got to feel your calm again, if I never got to wake up with you and look at your eyes and know that I had spent a night with you in my dreams, even if I didn't remember it," I laughed, but it was really a half sob, half cry. "Seth, you have to know that you have *made me feel so loved.*"

He put his big hands on my hips and tugged me to him, not leaving any room between us. "Stop," he hissed against my temple. "You're killing me."

"It's the truth."

"That doesn't mean you're not killing me," he said softly and leaned down to kiss my lips, pressing there for a long time, not wanting to leave or just unable to. When he finally pulled away, I knew what was coming. He started to speak. "You have to know that I feel the same." He tilted his head and swallowed, smoothing my cheek with his thumb and licking his lip. "Ava, sometimes when you fall asleep, I watch you. I run my fingers across your cheek and down your nose and just…wonder how the hell you're mine." His hand on my hip gripped me almost painfully to him, bunching in my shirt and twisting, as he gained steam and began to speak quickly. "You have to know that I would do anything for you. And that if we never got to touch again after today, that I would die happy—"

I put my fingers on his lips, ending his speech in its tracks. He sighed against my fingers. "Seth, you have proven over and over again that you love me. I was the one that needed to make sure you knew." He shook his head a 'no' but I kept going. "For all the reasons I said, you make sure I know, now I hope you know. But I have a lot of catching up to do." I let my arms circle his neck and went on my tiptoes, loving how his arms automatically wound themselves around me in response, lifting my feet from the ground and bringing my face to his. He looked so sexy, heavy lidded, and ready to do anything in the world I would ask of him, burn down bridges and take down mountains if that's what I needed. I spoke softly against the corner of his mouth. "Thank you for fighting for me, from the very beginning, and making sure I knew that you wanted me—my last name be damned."

He sighed and kissed me before setting me to my feet, but kept me against him with a big, warm hand against my back. It's funny what just a hand and nothing else on you can do to give you chills and goosebumps. He turned back to Ashlyn as if he had known this whole time that she was waiting for us. I on the other hand flushed pink at remembering we had an audience.

She smiled at my blushing, a little deviously I thought and then it changed to something more soft as she looked away and said, "No, you aren't Richard and I reincarnated, re-embodied, or anything of the like." She looked back at us. I must have looked shocked. "Surprised?"

"Yes, actually. Especially since it seemed as if you were leading us that way." I knew I had some bite in my voice. Ashlyn seemed to like to play games sometimes, and I got it. She never got to see anyone in the palace except us when we were kids and my Mom because she was the previous Visionary. I might go a little bonkers and get a mean streak, too. That was a lot of years of walking though brick walls and talking to myself. Seth squeezed my hand and I sighed a little twisting my lips.

She smiled again, seeming to enjoy our back and forth. "Gosh, you two… even as kids you two were so dynamic together. Coming and seeing you was my absolute favorite thing to do. You fought in the cutest ways and were so protective of each other."

"Did you know back then?" Mom asked and there was no question she expected to be answered. "When you told me that Seth would come back into our lives, did you know that he would be her significant."

"Of course."

"Then why not just tell me th—"

"You wouldn't have let him be, you wouldn't have let him go, you wouldn't have let things take their course if you knew. And things had to happen the way they did. I already told you."

Seth cut in, "If we're not you and Richard then how do you explain everything? Us being drawn here, to this spot, in the way we were?"

"This was where we met and where Richard died. Of course you would come back here."

Seth huffed. "You understand you just contradicted yourself, right?"

She squinted. "What do you mean?"

He looked down, trying to calm himself for a second before looking back up at her. "Ava with the birds and liking old music. And me with my drawings."

"Oh, that," she replied nonchalantly. I rolled my eyes. "It's just an imprint."

"An imprint?"

"Of course. What do you think imprints are? Putting a piece of yourself on someone else. What happened here—it left an imprint on this world, on this spot, and in turn gave me an opportunity to use it. So I was able to imprint a small piece of myself on Ava. That's why when you saw me, you couldn't see me very clearly. That's why these past few years, you've only been able to see me in your dreams when Ava has been present with you. But what I hadn't expected was for Richard to have been imprinted on you, too. But when you were a little boy, I saw your eyes and knew. That's when I saw it all play out and knew what had to be done. And I knew that you two would be significants one day. I'm sorry that it had to happen this way."

"I'm not," Seth told her quickly and I looked at him, surprised, "but why did we need to see it?"

His hands constantly moved on me, and I didn't know if he was trying to comfort me more or if he was just as riled up about everything as I was.

"Don't you see?" she asked and looked us all in the eyes, even looking over at my parents. "What I've been trying to tell you all for years? I didn't lock myself in this prison for nothing," she groaned, agony on her face. "I did it for you. For all of you. He said I didn't have the power. Oh, but I did, didn't I?" She took a deep breath through her nose. "I let myself get snared in this prison of my own making, the palace taking me as the bounty, the price, the penalty, because someone had to. And I was willing to do that if that's what it took for them to pay," she ground out.

I opened my mouth, but I still wasn't getting it. I was afraid that if I didn't understand that she would go off the deep end.

"It was you," Mom said and took a step toward her, Dad on her heels, a hand wrapped around her wrist, "you were the one who took the Virtuoso power. You put the curse on everyone."

"It wasn't a curse," she sneered, but that turned to tears as she clutched her chest and her nightgown. "It was a price. It was a judgment. It was…something that everyone had to pay a price for because either they participated or they knew about it and did nothing. Everyone else was *sins of the father*. A mass cleansing."

"Mass cleansings?" Dad muttered and shook his head. "I can think of someone else who did crazy things like that."

Mom tried to stop him, shaking her head and putting her hand up, but it was too late. She must had understood something the rest of us didn't. Ashlyn's hands shook as she clawed at the front of her nightgown, her hands traveling her body in a way that suggested memories of....things. Horrible things. And then I got it, too.

"Oh, God. No," I whispered.

How long had they kept her a prisoner? How long had they kept her against her will in that library, how long had he done God knows what to her? And her, powerless to stop him, no one would listen to her, an entire people who revered her so much, but revered their rules and regulations so deeply, and everyone all so scared of one man...and hadn't saved her.

When I saw her yank the lapels of her nightgown to a close, as if she was in throes of a memory so violent she couldn't help herself—I couldn't help myself either.

I pulled from Seth, ran to the railing, and threw up, heaved over and over as I tried to picture that library I'd been to as a child as anything but her home—no. Her prison. I'd snuck up there, even though it was supposed to be off limits...

I peeked back at her just as I felt Seth's hand on my back, rubbing circles. I felt his other hand start to pull my hair back, but I kept looking at her.

"Tell me I'm wrong," I croaked. "Tell me that what I think happened to you didn't happen."

Seth's head jerked and he stood slowly. Daddy was just now starting to get the gist also and cocked his head slowly. Dad made a small noise in his throat and then said, "No."

"Caleb," Mom implored.

"No," Dad said louder and shook his head. He looked a little distraught in that moment and I didn't understand...until he spoke. "Because if what you're saying is true, then my great, great grandfather sat on that council with you knowing what was going on...and did nothing. And that can't be true," he said softly.

Ashlyn gulped. "He was a good man. His significant was a good woman. They were so new back then, and she…kept him busy having babies during my short stint as Visionary. And making them." She smiled and I was surprised that it was genuine. "I was always envious that I would never get to experience certain aspects of a relationship and those were certainly several of them."

Dad looked away from her to Mom. He looked so tired, worn down, just…done. She hugged him around his neck and then looked at Ashlyn.

"Ashlyn, I'm sorry. I'm sorry that this happened, that…our kind," Mom had to stop to compose herself, "wasn't kind enough to you. I'm sorry that one man seemed to rule your entire fate and in essence all our fates. The Watsons don't even know that they're the ones who caused this, that their uncle was the one who did this and they are the ones who are starting the process all over again by not stopping." She shook her head. "I'm so sorry for what happened to you."

"He is but one bastard is a sea of bastards," Ashlyn said, looking off to the side slowly and then clenching her fist on her nightgown again. "You'd think after all these years I'd have gotten over it, wouldn't you?" she smiled and laughed once.

"No one ever gets over that, Ashlyn."

"Never?" she asked in a whisper and swallowed loudly.

"Not completely. Can they defeat it? Yes. Can they make that person pay for what they did in a just form? Absolutely. But will they ever forget?" Mom whispered softly. "No. And they shouldn't."

Ashlyn nodded and then looked at me. Her eyes ticked to me, to Seth, and back to me. Then she walked over me slowly. She smiled at us. "I'll miss you two most of all."

"What do you—"

"You'll remember everything from your dreams now. Everything will be as it should." She looked at Seth. "Even when you're crumbling, you're this mountain, this strong thing that refuses to break or sway or give." She smiled and once again I was shocked that she was genuine. "Never lose that. Never stop being that unmovable rock. I wish I could stay here and watch you two grow to love each other because that's a love story I know will be epic." Her eyes drifted back to me. "And don't worry about your mind, child. It's wide open now." She winked. Winked! "It was the only way the dream you and Seth were going to be able to work together to make you fall for him. And work together against the Watsons. The real you had to be out of the loop." I opened my mouth, completely flabbergasted, but she went on. "Goodbye, little bird." When she reached for my face I opened my mouth again to—what. Stop her? I knew that nothing would be the same. I felt so bad for her and I just wanted more time with her or something. But she cupped my cheek, looking into my eyes and I gasped, feeling the cold of the last hour fade away completely.

I watched as the dreams I'd been having with Seth played out in front of my eyes in rapid speed. The palace, the birds, talking in my room... about me, the planning with the Watsons. It all made sense. We landed quite unceremoniously on my bed together. I heard Mom and Dad cursing somewhere else in my room, but I didn't care about them right then.

Seth leaned down to look at me, looking worried.

"Are you all right?" I nodded. "I've never ended up in a different place than where I went to sleep before."

I smirked. "I'm sure she thought that was funny. She has a weird sense of humor if you couldn't tell."

"Ashlyn—" he questioned.

"Is at peace now. Truly," I answered. I stared at him. He was laying on top of me on my bed, his elbows on either side of my head, his legs next to mine. I heard the door click shut and was grateful. My breaths got harder. "I remember now."

"Everything?" he asked hopefully, low. His breaths were hard, too.

"Yes. Everything." I bit into my lip for a second, gaining courage. He watched me do it. When his eyes met mine again I thought a small fire might start in the room because...daggum. Who knew blue the color of the ocean could be so hot.

He grinned all of a sudden, so entirely happy with that thought. He thought to himself that it was about time I caught up to speed on things, that he wasn't sure how much longer he could have kept my real life and dream life separate like that. Something had to give. I felt my lips part. "I heard you," I whispered.

"What?"

"I heard you."

"No, I heard you that you heard me." He chuckled at my raised eyebrow. "What do you mean you heard me? And be very specific."

"You said it was about time I caught up." He cocked his head. "And that you didn't know how long you could keep—" Before I had even finished, he was already grinning again. "I've never heard you before without going in your mind and trying to, and then you can feel it when I do that."

"This is the way it's supposed to be. This is how it is for me all the time, all day long, being in your head. I think Ashlyn opened the trapdoor in your mind." His brow creased. "Or maybe it was just a fluke."

He was thinking that maybe since I was so worked up from the dream stuff that I was more gullible—

"That's not what's happening."

Are you sure?

Yes, I'm sure.

He grinned again. *I'm just joking. Obviously if you could hear me, you'd kick my ass over that one.*

You're lucky you and your ass *are cute. Or else you'd get a beat down for that.*

I pushed him to roll off me and climbed over him as he laughed. "A beat down?" He watched me from the bed as I put toothpaste on my toothbrush.

"A beat down," I agreed with a nod of my head, but didn't look at him. I started to brush my teeth and realized he was watching my every move. I turned to look at him. He was all sprawled out on my bed sexily as I washed away where I'd lost my lunch. And still he looked at me as if it was the sexiest thing he'd ever seen. Now that I could hear him and tangibly knew that he could hear me, I could *hear* that he thought it was the sexiest thing. I shook my head at him and pushed the door shut slowly. I could still hear everything he was thinking on the other side of it. He was glad this was finally over, that he felt like he finally had me and us, that one day he was going to watch me brush my teeth and there was nothing I could do to stop him. I laughed quietly and rinsed my mouth.

He was right. Listening to his mind wasn't just information, it was beautiful and was the way it was always supposed to be. We'd been cheated. *I* had been cheated. I hated that all this time had been taken from us. Honestly it felt like the most important time—the beginning. I knew that Ashlyn has her reasons, it was for a purpose, but it didn't mean that it didn't suck. But it wasn't irreparable, it wasn't something that couldn't be undone. In fact, I was looking forward to the undoing.

I opened the door to find him directly on the other side, his arms up high in the doorframe.

He didn't say another word, he just moved in, cupping my face gently but firmly, and took my mouth because he owned it, groaning deep in his throat.

He tugged me to him, making our legs intersect. He turned us until my back was against the wall in my bedroom. I let my arms hang on his hips as his mouth devoured mine. He was thinking about how things were going to change now, about how good my mouth tasted from toothpaste and just *me*, how I always tasted good, and about how he couldn't wait to do an echoling with me where I could remember it the next day.

I sighed, tugging on his shirt, feeling lightheaded from so much at once. He pulled back a little, letting his forehead rest against mine.

We haven't even gotten started. Like I said, you've got a lot of catching up to do. You've been missing out on this and I think it's one of the reasons that it took you so long to...warm up to the idea of me. He chuckled once.

I didn't laugh with him because he was right. If I could have been in his head like this all the time, knowing how he really felt about me, not having to guess, not having to be a *true girl* about everything. If I could have been a real significant like I was supposed to, I'm sure our relationship would have been a lot different up to this point. I looked up at him.

He smiled. "You still fell for me even without it. How big of a compliment is that? It's almost like we were a human couple." I cocked my head with a smile. "Okay, that was a stretch."

One of his hands slid to the back of my neck before he kissed me again. He turned us, kissing me the whole time, and started to push me, directing us until I felt the bed at the backs of my legs. He let my mouth go for a few seconds, long enough to push me down on the bed gently by my stomach. He followed me down quickly and reclaimed my mouth, his arms on either side of the bed beside me, but this time, I tugged his hair in my hands and used that as leverage. His groan this time I knew was all my doing and I smiled against his lips.

So smug.

Yeah, I am.

He smiled, too. *I guess you earned it.*

One of his hands came down and gripped my thigh, coaxing it up against his side, gripping my jeans with his hard fingers, and forcing a puff of excited breath to leave my lips. He used my wide open mouth to dive even deeper, our tongues not only brushing against each other, but fighting each other for delicious space.

I was the one who moaned this time.

His fingers on my thigh squeezed tighter.

Seth.

Ava.

I pulled back just far enough to see his eyes. "I wouldn't want to be rescued if I was lost in them either."

And I got lost in them for a long time.

In the morning, I expected to wake up and remember all the places he had taken me, but I didn't. I only remembered the palace with Ashlyn and I wondered if I was broken again. I felt him shake his head behind me and turned to find him awake, which surprised me.

"You remember that echoling," he said, "so why do you think you wouldn't remember any of them anymore?"

Oh…right.

"I didn't take you into another echoling. I figured we'd had enough for one night. It was the first time that I didn't feel the pull like I had to come to you when you fell asleep."

"So it's truly over," I said and let a breath go through my lips, not really understanding what that meant until then. I hadn't even had time to process it. "And all that *stuff* with Ashlyn and Richard."

"I don't know what to make of all that," he said quietly, "and really I don't care. I don't love you because someone told me to and I don't love you because you like birds or old music or wax poetic sometimes or have brown eyes. I love you because you're you and honestly, I don't want to spend any more time worrying about it. I don't want you to look at me every time you bite your lip and wonder if Ashlyn bit hers, too, and that's the only reason."

His eyes were soft even as his words were hard. He was letting me know this went no further and he meant it.

"Agreed." I wouldn't want to sit here and think that every time he looked at me if he was thinking about Ashlyn. I would drive myself crazy. We both needed to just forget this. I knew he'd heard me though. He tilted his head.

"Why would I think about her when I'm looking at you?"

"We went through a lot, Seth. I mean…" I looked down, "when you looked at her and gripped her chin and said she was me, it was really convincing."

He brought my face back up. "Sweetheart, I'm sorry." His voice was gruff.

I shook my head. "No, I'm not trying to be jealous or anything, I just…."

"I know that. And when you were screaming Richard's name when he was dying…" he sighed, "God…it hurt in my guts, but I knew it wasn't you."

I cupped his face. "We were so naïve to think that we would just walk out of there and not have a scar left behind, huh." I thumbed the scar on his chin.

He looked me right in the eyes and said in a small voice, "They used to pit me and my cousins against each other."

My gasp got stuck in my throat. "What?" I wheezed.

He gulped. "When I was a little boy. It started when I was eight." When he was eight…

I knew I wanted to be a fireman since I was eight years old.

He took my fingers in his and ran them across the scar on his chin and then under his shirt to the long one on his stomach so I'd know what he was talking about. I shook my head 'no', but he kept going.

"That's when the training began. The *revenge* training. They said we had to know how to fight since all their powers had been taken. Then they started to give us these…" he gulped again, "energy drinks." He shook his head. "I know now that it was your mom's blood and I can't even believe they would do that to a bunch of kids. Though the rest of them probably knew. I was probably the only naïve one."

"You weren't naïve, you have a conscience."

He continued on as if I hadn't spoken. "They used to make us fight until one of us tapped out, passed out, or got knocked out. And that kid went to bed without food that night."

"Oh, God no…"

"They even made Harper fight." He looked up at me again and I got it. I finally got it. My sweet Seth had been protecting Harper all these years. "She was one of only two girl cousins and they never took it easy on them. They didn't want to miss a meal because of them. And they didn't want to get in trouble because of them. Our uncles said the Jacobsons would kill girls just the same. That they didn't care if she was a girl so why should we?" He shook his head, looking sick. "There were seven of us that used to train together. When we got older, they stopped making us fight, especially since it wasn't even organized, it was just throwing us together and saying 'Whoever comes out wins.'"

"So how did you get this?" I asked and rubbed my hand on his stomach.

"My cousin came at me with a mower blade." He clucked his tongue. "It was the first thing he could get his hands on."

"Seth," I hissed.

"Thirty-one stitches and a night in the hospital. One day you can see all my scars because there are lots of them."

My bottom lip quivered and I was afraid to ask. I could see that he wasn't going to tell me without my asking. I wondered if Harper had given it to him and that was why he was so upset and weirdly protective of it.

He sighed. "It wasn't Harper. My mom gave me this." He rubbed his thumb across his chin. "She had been fighting with Dad and it was the worst fight I'd ever seen from them. They were in the kitchen and I could hear them yelling. I couldn't even tell what it was about, but it was bad. I came in to act like I was getting something from the fridge and saw him reach back and hit her."

I gasped and covered my mouth, my eyes watering. I shook my head. How was that even possible! He waited for me, his eyes softening as he rubbed my arm.

"I ran and grabbed him by his collar. I caught him off guard because he hadn't seen me coming. I punched him in the jaw, Mamma screaming at me to stop the whole time. She grabbed me and slapped me." He chuckled, shaking his head. "When she grabbed my shirt, her wedding ring had turn around in the process so when she slapped me, her rock was on the underside and I got a nice scar. That was the night I moved out and got my own place. I just couldn't do it anymore. My mom picked her husband who had just hit her over her son who was trying to defend her. And I know you're confused because I fought so hard for them, but...I thought if anything and anyone could make them see that all this was stupid and we can change things if we wanted to, it was you and me. I wanted to give them one more chance..." he looked down, "to actually be my family. To not let everything I've been through be in vain." I was already crying before he was finished. He looked surprised. "Ah, sweetheart, I'm sorry—"

"No." I sniffed. "No, there is absolutely nothing for you to be sorry about. I'm crying because I'm sad for you. I'm mourning the life and childhood you never had. I'm crying because you're an amazing person who the Watsons got to spend their whole life with and they so didn't deserve it." I was full-blown sobbing now. Seth looked distraught as for what to do with me. "Those bastards just took advantage and tried to break you, but you just fought back and came out on the other side, finding me and doing what you were always destined to do. They didn't deserve you. I'm so sorry that they took you from your mom, and that you never got to know her. It's not fair. You're so amazing and it's *not fair* that you had to have such a crappy life."

He cupped my face. "Sweetheart, breathe," he ordered. "I already told you—I would do everything over a hundred times if it led me back to you. It was worth it."

"And then you say things like that."

He smiled. "It wasn't all bad. When I was little, there was this ghost that used to come and she'd have this little girl with her. Ava."

I smiled, too, and hiccuped. "Do you think we'll ever see Ashlyn again?"

"No. I think she's gone."

I took a deep breath. "I just want this day to be over." I squeezed my eyes shut. "I just want to forget it."

He pulled me to him even as he put his elbow on the other side of my head and hovered over me. "Ah, come on now." He smiled. Smirked, really. "It isn't all bad, is it? It's starting out pretty good."

I couldn't help myself and sighed as I let him settle over me, combing his short hair back. He closed his eyes, putting his head on my chest like that night he slept, enjoying my ministrations. "You always know just what to say to make me feel better."

"We're going to be okay, Ave. I'm going to figure out what my family is planning and we're going to stop it. And then you'll get your happily ever after."

After breakfast, which my mom insisted on cooking, Seth had an inquiry at the fire station he was called to that was apparently mandatory. When the police called you in for questioning, you didn't tell them that your soulmate had had a rough day and you needed to skip it. So I was determined not to mope and was taking my laundry downstairs when my cell dinged. I got the biggest grin on my face. It was Lilith. Problem solved.

So bored so I came out for some studies. At the school library. Here with a few others already. Get your cute chastity belt wearing butt here.

I rolled my eyes.

Coming. Maybe you can meet my BOYFRIEND Seth later too.

OHMYGOSH! You R N so much trouble missy!

We're taking things slow…

Oh I'm sure ;)

I laughed and tossed my basket in the laundry room. Mom eyed it from the kitchen and gave me a look. I bit my lip. "Um, I'll get it later?"

She laughed. "Seth is right." She pointed at me. "You *do* do that a lot."

"When and *why* did you talk about me biting my lip?" I said as I grabbed my keys and jacket, wrapping my scarf around me.

"Where are you going?"

"Study group."

Her eyes went wide, not expecting that answer. "Oh. Well, where are your books?"

"In the car, Mom." I went and hugged her. "Thanks for saving the world again, but I have to run."

"Ava…" she shook her head, "I really don't like you being alone. Besides, it's winter break. Don't you wanna take a break from school?"

"Seth said the Watsons are waiting for the reunification to do anything. And they'll be giving us pop quizzes left and right when we get back. No, I don't want to take a break."

"That doesn't mean that the Watsons are going to let you be…" She sighed. "I'm not saying I don't trust Seth, at all; I don't trust them."

I sighed. "What if I leave my phone on the entire ride there until I'm in

Lilith's care? Then you'll know I'm safe and sound in a boring study group. And I'll tell Seth where I am so he can come when he gets out of his inquisition and chauffer me home."

She sighed louder. "Okay. You better go before your dad gets out of the shower or you'll never leave."

"Thanks, Mom."

I practically ran. It wasn't that I was tired of my home or my family or Seth, at all, but school was my one normalcy. My one place to be completely normal and human.

I almost slipped on the ice in the driveway so I slowed down and walked more carefully, rolling my eyes at myself. I scrunched my nose and looked down at my cute little ballet slip-ons. My family was right about me and my shoes…

I dialed my Mom's cell number from my UConnect as soon as I got in and we talked all the way to school. She told me some stories about when she and Dad went to school. I shook my head. Those two were so freaking adorable, especially back then. The things that Dad used to do was so ridiculous on the sweet-o-meter.

"Okay, I'm here. And…Seth's here," I said, confusion in my voice as I looked at Seth leaning against his truck, relaxed and natural. He smiled when he saw me pulling in.

"I texted him. He must be done already."

"Thanks, Mom. I'm all safe now. I'll see you later."

"Okay," she said softly. "See you guys later. Be careful, okay?"

"We will. Promise."

I got out and shut my door gently, leaning against it. "Hey."

"Hey. Your mom—"

"Yeah, I was on the phone with her."

He smiled in a cutely, kind of embarrassed way as he stopped in front of me. "I just didn't want you to think I was following you around, couldn't be without you for five minutes, just, in essence, being a pathetic creature." He shook his head. "No, that's not what's going on here."

I smiled and bit my lip, but let it go, realizing I was doing it. "Sorry," I mumbled under my breath.

He scoffed. "Don't ever stop biting that lip." He leaned into me and lifted my chin. "What you and that lip do to me…"

I grinned and went on my toes to reach him, our arms winding around each other. It didn't matter that it was freaking freezing out there and the car window on my back was like a sheet of straight up ice. All that mattered was Seth and his lips that were warming me in more ways than one.

Seth pulled back, but stayed close. "All right, go on in. I'll wait for you. I told your mom I would."

"I'm not going inside to study and leaving you out here to wait for me."

"I interrupted your plans and I don't want you break them because I showed up."

"Come with me." He gave me a look. "I'm serious. It is a library. I'm sure there's something you can find to read in there."

"And what's going to be the reason for dragging me along?"

I scoffed and gave him my best doe-eyed look. "Baby, all they have to do is look at you."

I reached back up to kiss him as he laughed against my lips. I didn't know how long we stayed like that.

"I'll go get coffee and lunch. Deal?"

"Deal." But I didn't let him leave. I continued to keep him there so close, my hands going into his jacket pockets.

"This is taking things slow?" someone quipped from behind us. I looked behind Seth to see Lilith. She looked Seth up and down. She came forward and held out her hand. "Hi. I'm Lilith. You must be Seth."

"Lilith," Seth said, his arms around me tightened painfully as he growled, "what the hell are you doing here?"

My blood turned to ice in my veins. "You know her?" My voice shook.

"She's a Watson, Ava." He put me behind him and pushed me as Lilith came closer. We marched backward, her grinning at us the whole time, in between the cars, Seth pushing me harder and harder as I tried not to slip on the ice, until we were between two buildings.

Why are we running from her?

I'm not the only one who they did experiments on. She has abilities, too. She can shock you, but she can only do it once. When she puts me down, because she will—I'm the biggest—run like hell.

Seth—

Run like hell, Ava. I won't be here to protect you. Oh, God, I'm sorry. I didn't know they were planning this.

SHELLY CRANE

Lilith has been my friend since I started college here, Seth.

He looked back at me, shocked. *What?*

"Enough of the chatter." She smiled and it was so not the Lilith that I have grown to know. "Gosh, you two are freaking *adorable*." She blocked our way, but walked back and forth. "Listening to Ava talk about how she was saving herself all these years. I mean—I call it chastity belt chatter. Even tempting her with frat boys didn't work. And then you. You were the one all along. It couldn't have been more perfect. I was the *in* for the family. I was the one who was going to take her down by being her friend, but then you bonded with her. And then you went soft." She clucked her tongue. "She never even talked about you until today so—if that tells you what kind of an impact you've had on her—"

"Lilith," he growled and moved forward. I grabbed his arm. "I'm gonna—"

"Gonna what?" She lifted her hand and let the charge show. The little charges of lightning danced on her fingers. "Come on, Seth. I've wanted to do this to you at full charge all my life. Ever since we were kids and you used to make me look bad because you'd never fight me."

He scoffed. "Yeah. I'd go to bed without supper and let you have yours. I wouldn't hit a girl and that makes me a bad guy."

"It makes you weak," she hissed so close to his face. I tried to pull him back. "And it made me look weak in the process."

"You proved today more than any other day that I am not nor was I ever a Watson," he whispered.

"Truer words have never been spoken," she spat back and then reached up, letting her palm slam into his chest.

He tried to move back, but couldn't get away fast enough. I screamed as I watched him convulse. When he stopped moving, she leaned back against the wall, looking like she might pass out for a second. I remembered what I promised Seth. He was down for the count, but still.

Seth!

He never answered me. It was like he was asleep. But then I felt it. His heartbeat… He was alive.

I couldn't carry him. I had to get help. I pushed past her, slamming her into the wall as I passed. I heard her head slam into the snow-covered bricks and her calling me some colorful names as she tried to chase me, but it was like a baby chasing a puppy.

As soon as I reached my door, someone grabbed me by my hair and snatched me back against them.

"The fact that you thought it was going to be that easy is actually kind of sweet." Gaston pulled my hair harder, making me hiss. "No, no, sweet, stupid, naïve Ava, we're just getting started."

And then my head was smashed against the car door. Everything went black as I called my significant's name, begging him to get up, begging him to run.

I coughed. It was hard to breathe. I covered my mouth with my hand, but that didn't help. Maybe I was getting sick. Ugh, to get sick over winter break just blew...

I opened my eyes to see smoke. I sat up quickly but my heart beat so sluggishly. I didn't understand why. I could hear Seth's voice, but I didn't see him in the room. He was saying that he didn't know why Lilith attacked him, but his plans were the same. He wanted to use me until he got the info he wanted and then throw me away. I looked around until I found that my phone was on. It was calling a number I didn't know and the speakerphone was on so I could hear the conversation. What?

The smoke was getting worse. I pulled my shirt over my nose and mouth and ran to the nearest window to see if I could see anything.

We were at the school. This must be the library attic or something. The library was on the back of the property and the school was deserted for winter break. There had been no one else meeting me to study. I knew I wasn't getting out of this.

Seth and the Watsons stood out on the lawn and just watched as the placed burned. Seth couldn't know I was inside. He must have thought I ran off like he told me to, but he was fidgeting. Nervous. I wondered what they were doing. There had to be a point to this.

"So what are we doing here?" Seth asked. "This is Ava's school, but they're on winter break." He looked up. "Why are you...burning the library?"

"It's not the library burning that's important, Seth." Gaston grinned. "It's what inside it."

Seth didn't even try to keep his cover intact. He gripped Gaston's collar. "What the hell did you do? Where's Ava?"

Seth!

Ava, I'm coming.

Gaston laughed as a couple of Watsons pulled him off. "Wow. So disappointing. And after that laughably convincing speech you gave us the other day. It was Harper that gave you away, by the way. She told us to put a listening device in your phone. So we did. We heard it all as you told them everything." He sucked his lip. "A Watson woman scorned is a powerful thing, huh?"

"Let me go!" Seth yelled, not even listening to them.

"There's no way out. All the doors are sealed and nailed. All the windows, the same. We made sure of it. She's going to die in that fire. This is your last chance to prove to us—"

Seth groaned. "Then I'll die with her. I'd rather die with a Jacobson than live with a Watson. Let. Me. Go."

No, I begged him.

Gaston was so red. "We took you in. We raised you."

"You *trained* me. And you always made sure I knew I didn't belong! After you killed my mother!"

"Your mother is the woman who raised you."

"You mean the woman who faked a heart attack so I'd have to leave Ava? And the woman who texted me and lied, told me there was a family emergency when there wasn't any so Ava would be angry with me?"

He kept going as if Seth hadn't spoken at all. "The woman that gave birth to you was not your *mother*. She couldn't give you what we could. Power. We helped you become the man you are. And this is how you thank us? You betray us? For her? We can fix this for you, son. All you have to do is let her die. We're doing all the work. You don't have to do a thing."

"No!" Seth growled.

"There's no coming back from this. You will die in there. I will *not* open that door for you, no matter how much begging you do. Think about this. Just stop for a second and think." He put his hand on his shoulder. "This is your bond talking. You don't really want her. She's our enemy. That's just your body. Choose your family over that. Be stronger than that."

Seth jerked against them. "You are *not* my family. My family is in that library. Let me go, you evil bastard!"

Gaston nodded his head. "Do it, boys." They forced him to his knees, him fighting them the whole way, and held him down. One of them put Seth's arm across his knee and yanked his sleeve up. I understood exactly what they were about to do. I shook my head violently, but it all happened so fast. He pulled out his knife and sliced a viciously sloppy "X" through Seth's wrist tattoo. Seth tried to yank away, but it was no use. They wasted no time once the deed was done. Gaston gripped his jaw and got right in his face. "I knew you weren't going to pull this off from the beginning. We've always had a plan to move forward without you. You're more than a failure. You're such a disappointment. Let him go, boys."

Seth started running toward the building the second their hands were off of him.

No, Seth!

Gaston bellowed, "So he can die with his little Jacobson like he always should have! We should have let you die all those years ago! We wasted years on you, boy."

I yanked my phone down and tried to call 911, but they had disabled it. I tossed it to the side and ran to the hall to meet Seth. I heard the door slam below me and then saw him coming up the stairs, two at a time, that were usually restricted to students. I knew we were going to collide when he reached me, but I still wasn't prepared for it. He put his uninjured hand on my back to take some of the blow as my back was slammed into the wall and his mouth ascended on mine.

He didn't kiss me long, but it was long enough to get his message across. "I can't believe you came in here knowing there was no way out," I scolded.

"I can't believe you think I wouldn't come after you," he scolded back.

A sob climbed up my chest. "Seth." I pulled his head to mine. "I'm so sorry."

"What the hell are you sorry for?"

"I tried to run for help like you told me, but he got me before I made it."

He looked at me and gritted his teeth as his fingers swept over my cheekbone gently.

"I can see that," he growled. I hadn't even felt it until he said anything. I winced when I touched it. "Why can't I feel your heartbeat?"

"They gave me something. It's slow. Too slow."

He closed his eyes. "Those…bastards."

"Yeah," I sighed and pulled his wrist up since he didn't seem too worried about it. "Those bastards."

My heart ached to heal him and couldn't. They hadn't gone deep enough to worry about him bleeding out or anything, just enough to mangle the skin.

"It doesn't matter." He looked at it with disgust. "I was going to have it removed anyway. They just took care of it for me." He wiped the blood on his shirt and pushed off the wall, looking around. "There's not much smoke. Let's—"

We heard a commotion below us and looked over the railing to the bottom floor, three floors down. They were pouring gasoline everywhere on the carpet stairs and bookcases. One of them looked up and gave us a crooked wave with a smile before flipping out his lighter and tossing it on the liquid. It blew up in waves of flames up the stairs. We could hear them banging on the door and I could only guess they were nailing that door shut as well. So they hadn't been bluffing.

And I'm sure they've disabled all the alarms, too. By the time anyone sees the smoke, it'll be too late.

My heart was beginning to pick up speed and be normal again. *What do we do?*

He scoffed. *Burning a fireman. They are so daggum twisted.* He looked at me. *Come on. We need to get low. The fire will move up and if we need to jump, I don't want to do it from the fourth floor. Just stay with me. I'm getting you out of this.*

Okay. I'm with you.

He smiled. *You are so brave, sweetheart. You came into that burning building to get me without blinking an eye. And now, you're following me, without a shadow of doubt, that I'll get us out of here.*

I trust you. And I would do it again to save you.

I know. I love you, little bird. The first thing we're doing when we get out of here is getting married because I'm done waiting.

I felt my mouth open, but he took my hand and pulled me behind him. *Stay low,* he ordered.

Gosh, Seth ordering my safety and weddings was so sexy. I tried to remember we were in a deadly situation. He smiled back at me and shook his head.

"Okay," he said loudly over the roar of the fire that hadn't been there before, "that was the only stairway it seems. But the Watsons aren't as smart as they think they are." He called them 'the Watsons', not 'his family'. "That ship has sailed far, far away," he said loudly. He pointed to a small, waist-high door in the wall. It looked a little like Nana's laundry chute. He opened it, pulling up the door. There was nothing inside. "It's a dumb-waiter for taking books from one floor to the other," he explained. "In you go."

He hoisted me up and I squealed just a bit, but he climbed in right behind me. It was definitely tight. He lowered us down slowly and felt the panels with his hand before he opened them. The bottom floor was ablaze on the side near the stairs, but where we were hadn't been touched yet. The bookcases between there and us were steadily going up in flames though, the books being just the tinder it needed to feed the flames.

"All the windows have bars." I looked to see that Seth was right. It wasn't crazy for a college campus' windows to have bars on them. "Come on. I'm going to check the doors."

I followed him to the one door in the back that wasn't covered with fire and he tried to open it, and then kicked it. He got a chair and hit it with it. He beat on the handle and kicked at it some more. The door wouldn't budge. I pressed inside his head and heard in his mind that he was getting more scared by the minute, that he knew they had disabled the security measures in the building. The safety sprinklers never came on. Seth looked for an ax or an extinguisher, but they had both been removed from the hallway. They had taken his phone outside. We checked the desk phones and they were gone, too. No one was coming for us.

He tried to get near the front door which was ablaze, but we couldn't get anywhere near it. The entire hallway and stairwell was aflame.

He pulled me to the men's bathroom and took my coat off, soaking it in the sink before putting it back on me.

"The fire is all around us now." He soaked his jacket, too. "We're only going to have one shot at that door." He looked down at me. "No matter what happens, we keep going, no stopping 'til we're out that door. We worry about the cuts and bruises and burns later. We can handle that. We have to survive first."

I nodded and tried not to cry. "Okay."

316

He soaked my scarf and wrapped it around my head and hair before cupping my face. He looked so distraught, but determined.

"I love you, Ava. I'm getting you outta here."

I nodded again. "Okay. I love you more."

He smiled. "We'll get to fight about that for the rest of our lives."

"Deal," I whispered and reached up on my tiptoes to kiss him, my hands on his arms to steady me, but I didn't need that. He was holding me steady with his hands, never letting me go.

"Let's go, sweetheart." He took my hand, tugged me behind him, and even though I was scared, I knew that we either lived through this or we died together trying to get out. And there was a strange peace in that. Either way, we were together, and for some reason, I didn't feel like we'd gone through everything to get to this point just to not get our happily ever after. And for Richard and Ashlyn to not get their happily ever after again just couldn't happen.

We just had to make it.

When we reached the hallway to the door, the fire was so hot on my face, I turned into his chest. He spoke in my mind since the fire was raging so loudly.

We've got one chance. We can't stop. We can't turn back, we can't slow down, or we're done for. The door has been on fire long enough that it should be weakened enough for us to hit it and it go down. The fire will start to evaporate the water on our clothes as soon as we go, so go fast. Don't think, just keep running.

Okay.

We may be met with Watsons on the other side, but we'll deal with them then. Ready?

Ready.

He gave me one last look, not giving me time to overthink. *Go.*

We raced past the burning shelves and around the desk, now in flames. The stacks of burning books made me want to weep, truly, it was a pyre of literary genius and the sadness fell over me as I watched it all burn needlessly as we raced past. The stairway was ablaze and I felt it burn hot on my face and the backs of my legs as we ran by. I knew the hallway was next and tried not to look because I knew it was completely in flames from top to bottom. I didn't want to lose my nerve. So I just closed my eyes and let Seth guide me. All he needed was my body to help him ram through the door. I tensed when he tensed, but the door was so solid when we hit it, I knew there was no way it would budge, no matter how many times we hit it.

"No! No!" He yelled and shoved me in the corner by the door, blocking my body with his. It was the only little piece of the hall that wasn't consumed, but the fire was all around us. The fire was so hot, that it was all I could do not to yell out from the pain of it on my face. I knew he had to be feeling it on his back.

We have to go back.

There's no going back. He looked at me softly and cupped my face, though I knew he was in pain. I could feel it. *I love you.*

"No!" I yelled. "We can… We can…" I looked behind him and saw that the fire was across the hallway and there was no way to go back, just like he had said. That was our one chance. The whole library was going up because the books had caught on fire. If it hadn't been now, it would have been soon anyway. I sobbed as I looked back at him. *I'm sorry. If I hadn't gotten caught, you wouldn't—*

This was their plan all along. They knew I loved you. See, I was right. He hissed. I went to look, but he pulled my face back up so I couldn't see. *Look right here. Remember that night that I told you that there was no way they could look at me and not know I was in love with you? It was true. They knew.*

It's not supposed to be this way. I shook my head, feeling my pant legs start to heat. My face was so hot, I could no longer contain it and I started to cry out loud. But I kept talking, because I wanted him to know. *We were supposed to get our happily ever after. I wanted you to be happy. I just wanted you to finally be happy. You had such a crappy life. Not like this—*

Ah, Ava, I am so happy, he said the words in my mind and whispered them against my lips before he kissed me. *It doesn't matter what happened to me before I met you. You happened. Just close your eyes tight.*

We wrapped our arms around each other. He tried to tuck me into his chest, but I made sure to wrap my arms around his back, trying to take some of the brunt of the heat. He grunted, angry that I wouldn't let him protect me. Even in our final moments, he was adamant that he protect me.

I'd never felt anything so awful before. I could feel him, feel his pain as the heat began to burn his back, the water and moisture in our clothes long gone, but I could do nothing for him. He could feel me, as the licks of heat began to burn my hands so badly that I could no longer hold it in and started to scream. I tried to hold it in. I knew it would just make it worse for him, but he could do nothing for me.

I wondered if the Watsons were out there, listening, enjoying this, waiting to hear my screams, knowing they'd come eventually, knowing that I'd soon enough have to give in.

Seth yanked my hands from his back and tucked me into his chest, taking the brunt of all the heat. He covered me, putting his arms around me above my head on the wall and we both yelled as the heat became too much. I closed my eyes, my fingers twisted in his shirt and knew that when I opened them again, I'd be in a better place. I'd be with Seth again.

But Seth stopped yelling and my breath ran out, too, and something started to happen behind my eyelids. Sparks…

Then my body began to cool, my blood turning cold in my veins, jolts going through me that were too fast, a hazy fog rolled through me, too much like…imprinting. I felt my lips fall open as I looked up at him.

"The ascension," I whispered, but he didn't need to hear me to know what I meant.

He yelled again and leaned into me as far as he would go. "Just hold on, baby. Just hold on."

I could feel his back as he burned. It was too late. It happened too late. Why didn't it come sooner? He was thinking that if he could just protect me long enough, I'd be okay. Always thinking about me. I was so furious. I started to shake with it. He yelled over me, begging me to make it, just hold on. I did hold on. I held on to him and begged that if we got out of this alive I'd do anything God asked of me.

And then Seth's heart started to beat in my chest so hard, way harder than it already was because we were scared. My skin started to burn again, but I realized that it was just the blood in my veins. I was tingly, hot and cold chills running all over me, but it was the kind that made me stand up and take notice that something was happening. It was the kind that happened when we touched when we'd been away for a long time, it was the kind that happened when he touched me with purpose.

He opened his eyes above me and looked at me, blinking slowly, before he pulled his hand back and looked at it. I realized that I was no longer feeling the heat from the fire. And that's when we both noticed at the same time that his Watson wrist tattoo was gone. It was as if the fire had burned it away, took

it away to the ashes, and I had healed the wound from their knife.

Their hold over him was over the minute they turned him loose to come into this burning building, and it was final when the fire they meant to kill him with instead singed away the last thing tying him to them—their family crest on his skin.

How poetic.

I grabbed onto him, yanking him to me as I put my arms around his neck and held on, my fingers gripping his hair as I held on through the ascension.

He groaned in my ear, putting his hands on the backs on my thighs and lifted me, slamming me the tiniest bit closer to the wall at my back. I opened my eyes and then slammed them shut because I couldn't believe what I was seeing. The fire was all around us. We were *in* the fire. We should be dead. We would have been dead.

My heart began to beat out of control before I felt his fingers on my face.

Just be right here with me. Don't think about that. This is going to let me save you.

I gasped. *I don't want to have hope if it won't work—*

Ava, he chuckled, *look at us. We're standing in fire. I'm getting you out of here. I can feel it. My ability.*

But he already had an ability. I had wondered about that before—how it was going to work, if he was going to get another ability and have two or the new one would cancel out the old one. This was crazy. This whole thing. Our whole relationship was unconventional and I was in love with it. Keeping my eyes closed tight, I pulled his mouth to mine and just breathed, knowing that Ashlyn had been right. When there's so much evil in the world and in a situation, it's bound to leave a mark—leave an imprint. If the Watsons thought they were going to get away with this without repercussions, they were sorely mistaken.

He kissed me back with abandon, the hands on my thighs pulling and tugging me closer, pressing into me in all the places we were touching. I gasped into his mouth and he used that, diving deeper, plundering and taking all the little noises I was making for his own. I tugged his hair harder and that's when I felt it. All the tingles sizzled away in an instant and my body was just left feeling so right. He stopped kissing me, but just stayed there, close and touching.

Sweetheart?

I don't wanna open my eyes. I could still hear the fire raging around us.

Just keep your eyes closed. I'll get us out of here.

I could feel his hands as they slid from my legs and then took my hand in his. His hand buzzed in mine. I gasped, but couldn't look.

It's okay. Everything's okay, he soothed and kissed my forehead. He pulled me from the wall. I could feel us maneuvering a little and then he put me behind him.

Stay here.

No! Don't leave.

I would never. I just don't want you in the way of debris. I'm right here. Stay behind me. Keep touching me. Keep your eyes closed.

But I couldn't any longer.

I peeked them open to see Seth, red and orange flames of fire all around him from the fire, but he wasn't touched by them and neither was I. He had a little hazy quality to his skin, like a fog. So he wasn't affected by the fire. That was his ability. I had a feeling that it wasn't just fire that his ability could protect him from, but other elements, too. I looked over at the flames on the wall and felt this tingling start in my arms and go up my spine.

I held out my hand, not really knowing what I was doing, but just following my gut. The fire was...calling me. And then I called *it*. It came to me, all of it. I gasped as I sucked it to me like a hurricane, like a vacuum, in one fell swoop, and since there was no air, there was no fire. The place was almost completely burned up inside, all blackened and hollow. I gasped for air and turned to look up at Seth, who was smiling as he cupped my face.

"That's not keeping your eyes closed."

"I couldn't." I looked at his face as I put my hands on his arms. He was bigger, his muscles a little more defined. And his face was...

"Ava, you are so gorgeous," he said, beating me to it, his eyes searching my dirty face. His mind said he didn't care what I looked like, that the ascension honestly hadn't changed my looks that much, and honestly, they hadn't changed his much either. They just refined it. We were both just glad to be alive, glad to be able to look at each other at all.

He lifted me up, his arms circling my waist, as his face pressed to my chest. He sighed the sigh of a man who was so grateful. I hadn't known what was coming out of his mouth, though. Maybe he hadn't either or his mind was closed off.

"Will you marry me, little bird?" I didn't gasp. I had run out of those. I just stared down at him, my hand on his hair. "Marry me, sweetheart," he asked again, softly.

I smiled, feeling the tears coming up my throat. "I wish we were married already."

He grinned. "Is that a yes?"

I sobbed, "That's a yes."

He let me slide down just enough to kiss him and then he put me behind him again.

"Get back. We'll celebrate later. Believe me," he said low and threatening. I actually shivered as I move to stand against the wall.

He pressed his hand to the doorknob and I watched as his hand made the knob and door around it turn red and angry. Then he kicked it and the door gave way. I rushed to him. He stopped me, holding me behind him as he looked out the door first. He didn't see anyone. The cowards had left the scene of the crime.

Shaking his head, he pulled me forward and out the door. As soon as we were free, I grabbed onto his neck, pressing against him. He swung me around, chuckling happily in my ear.

"It's not possible." We stopped and Seth put me behind him again, but Lilith was behind us, coming for us slowly. His Uncle Gaston came around the building, looking impossibly angry as he bellowed his impossibly angry words. "How do the Jacobsons keep cheating death? It's not possible and it's not fair. There is no way that you two should be alive." He peeked back inside and back at us, shaking his head. "Of course. You ascended. Of course!" he yelled. "Lilith, take them out."

"I haven't charged," she said and backed away.

"What?" he growled.

"I thought they were going to die like you said they were. It takes a long time to charge, Uncle Gaston, you know that. I can't help it. I wasn't going to charge up on the off chance that your little plan fell through. You know how bad it sucks."

"You idiot," he yelled. "Now he's ascended and you have no idea what kind of power he has. He's going to hurt you, you little—"

"No. He's going to hurt you. I'm out."

"No, you're not. Get back here!"

She turned, but stopped. "I can't help it if I'm the only one the little experiments worked on. You all ran me into the ground using my ability. For what? You don't treat me any better. For family? Pfft. This isn't a family. This is an army. And this soldier sees that she's outnumbered in this battle. Have fun, Uncle Gaston."

"Come back here!"

Once she was gone, Gaston turned to Seth. And I knew from the look on his face, it was not going to be pretty.

"This is all your fault. The family started to fall apart when you bonded with her. Any one of us would have killed to have been given the privilege of the task that you were handed. Instead you fall in love with her." He spit in our direction. "You deserve to live with them. Their sentimental crap, their drivel. If only I could go back and not waste an entire lifetime on you. You disgust me. You may be ascended, but so am I." He came toward us. "And this ends today."

Seth pushed me with a hand on my stomach. "Get back, Ava."

"Oh, God," I moaned and prayed, and realized that Gaston was truly going to try to fight him. I didn't even know what his ability was, but I didn't even have my phone—

The words had barely left my mouth when a car pulled into the lot. Seth was looking, too, and Gaston was about to take advantage of it when he was nearing him.

Look out.

He ducked out of the swing and sighed. "Are you really going to fight me?"

"Are you really going to duck me the whole time?"

I could see in Seth's mind that his ability was that he could hit you with the force of two punches at once if he could get a hit on you. That was why Seth came at him from behind that night at my house. But that wasn't going to kill him, so why did he think he was going to be able to end it tonight?

Something wasn't right.

I looked to see Rodney getting out of the car. His eyes bulged as he looked at the scene.

"You never answered the texts. Mom was a little worried so she sent me to make sure you and Seth hadn't fallen in a pothole."

I turned back to watch and could feel Seth's pain and guilt over this already. His uncle's rage was just too much and he wasn't going to let it go. He didn't want to live with them, he didn't want to look over our shoulder forever, he wanted me to be safe, but that didn't mean he wanted to kill his uncle.

And his uncle, in his stupid rage, didn't even know what Seth's ability was. He didn't even care. He just stupidly thought he could take him if he could just get one swing on him.

"What happened to you?"

"I can't right now," I answered.

I could only guess what I looked like right then, but I couldn't worry about that, I had to focus on Seth. I watched as Seth ducked again, and was about to deck his uncle and leave him there when Gaston pulled a knife from his boot. Between blocking the knives and the fists, Seth took a hit to the stomach and got sliced on the arm. I tried not to scream as I bit into my fist. I felt Rodney holding me back so I didn't try to run forward. Seth gripped his uncle's arm and he hissed and slid backward. He raised his arm like he was going to throw the knife at him, but in its place was a poultice bottle. Like the one he had thrown at my father. Seth lifted his arm to block it, but there was nothing he could do. I yelled and threw my hands forward in frustration. There was no way I could have gotten there in time. A strand of fire came barreling out from my fingers in front of Gaston, obliterating the bottle.

He groaned and then threw the knife next. I blocked that one, too.

He looked at me angrily, knowing that my power was obviously more proactive than his. So he ran at Seth, knowing I wouldn't risk hitting Seth if they were so close together. They tumbled on the ground and Gaston wound up on top. I tried to break free, but Rodney held me back. "Wait."

Seth kept burning his uncle's hand, but he just kept yelling through the pain and pushing on, determined to put that dagger in his chest.

"Uncle, don't make me do this."

"It's over!" Gaston yelled. "Starting with you, and then every last Jacobson."

Seth reached up with his other hand and wrapped it around his uncle's neck. It began to burn. He screamed and Rodney turned me to make me look away. I could feel how badly Seth felt as he looked into his uncle's eyes, watched as he took his life, watched as he watched the man he thought had actually cared about him, even if it had been only because he was his protégé, die.

I heard the fire trucks in the distance. Someone had finally seen or heard something. And now we were going to have to come up with a story. I felt Seth's hand on my arm and swung around to hug him to me.

"I'm so sorry," I told him.

"We need to go," he told me, avoiding how guilty he felt, how ripped up inside he was.

"Too late." Rodney pointed at the cop pulling in.

"Daggumit. Now we'll have to come up with a story," he growled.

"We'll be okay." I walked back to the door before the cop could see inside and tried to figure out how to get the fire out of my hands again. Smoke was still everywhere, so it looked like there was still a fire. There was no way we were going to be able to explain how the fire got put out. When the place was sufficiently ablaze again, we went over to cop and began a concocted story that we made up between the two of us in our connected minds, that sadly, wasn't far from the truth.

And then the firemen showed up.

"You're trying to tell me that this guy set the place on fire with you inside it? And he's your uncle?" Seth nodded. "And I thought my family reunions were bad."

Trouble had been getting us blankets and coffee and trying to make us comfortable since he got there and the fire had been put out. We hadn't been allowed to leave, no matter how much Seth asked them to let us. Seth was a mess. His fingers never left me, always touching me or caressing, moving, down my arms or hands. Trouble had gotten us to take off what was left of our other jackets and put us in some blankets.

"I won't ask how these are practically burned to nothing and you don't have a scratch on you," he quipped and eyed me, obviously thinking I was the culprit. I guess I was in a sense. We had healed each other of anything that had happened to us. But he didn't know that Seth could do things, too. And it could stay that way. He could just keep thinking I was the freak.

"You're not a freak," Seth growled all of a sudden and then sighed when

Trouble and I both looked at him in shock. "Will you just stop with that?"

"I was half kidding," I said softly, trying to joke and lighten the mood. He didn't go for it.

"I'm the only one who's actually been a freak all my life."

Trouble's eyebrows lifted.

"Seth," I tried to stop him.

He looked at Trouble. "I've had an ability since I was eight. I can go into people's dreams." He gave him a pointed look that I didn't understand until…

Trouble gasped and pointed. "That *was* you." He let a breath go. "I'm actually kind of relieved. Now I don't have to feel weird about having a dream about you anymore." He cut his eyes at him. "I mean, really, what was with putting me in the tutu? And the zoo? I mean I get it was my birthday and all."

I smiled, not even wanting to know, but Seth stayed stoic and angry.

"This was all because of me," he said to the ground. "I should have been able to stop Lilith. I should have known they were using her to get to you. I should have been more convincing with them. I should have known they'd try something and not believe me. I…should have known," he groaned and looked at me, so angry. "And you almost died because of it. My one job on this earth is to keep you safe and I can't even do that right. Over and over I keep putting you in danger."

"Our families—"

"They are not my family," he growled in response.

"The Watsons and the Jacobsons," I answered softly, "have always hated each other. My mom took the Watson's power before we were born. This day was coming whether we were together or not. If it hadn't been me, it would have been Rodney." I looked at him and he knew I was right. He nodded and looked down. "You can't help what other people do. You can only react to their decisions and do the best you can. You told me Lilith was going to take you down, you knew, and you told me to run. I did. I would have made it if your uncle hadn't been here."

"I don't want to spend my whole life looking over my shoulder to see what the next thing is that's going to try to hurt you." He let his gaze swing up to meet mine. "And that's what this is going to be. You know that, right? Especially now that Gaston—" He gulped. "I've just fed the flame, made it so much worse. Once again, not protecting you like I should have."

"Did you not hear him?" I said a little too loudly and adjusted my tone. I could feel his guilt all around him. It was all around us, but he was so angry, too. It was so confusing to sift through. "He said he was starting with you and going down the line of Jacobsons. You don't think I was next as soon as he finished with you? You had no choice but to do what you did. This didn't just start, Seth. I know you're upset," I whispered, but heard a ruckus near the road and turned to see our parents trying to get through. They weren't letting them. I looked at Rodney with a glare.

"What? You really didn't think I'd call them?"

"We're not minors. They wouldn't have called them, Rodney. We could have taken care of this at home. Now Mom is going to—"

"Let me go through now! My kids are in there," Mom yelled.

"—blow up the place," I finished and winced. I sighed. "I better go over there before someone gets their head blown up." Trouble's eyes widened. "Kidding. Sort of." I shrugged.

I went to pull my hand from Seth's. He was so angry he didn't want me around anyway it seemed. But before the tips of my fingers could even leave his, he gripped my wrist. I looked back, confused. His eyes begged me not to go, not to leave his touch, not to leave his sight, not to leave him at all.

He was angry, yes, he was so guilty for what he had to do, yes, and he did feel like always let me down. And he was trying so hard not to lose it. The only way he knew how not to was to put up a front and act like he was the opposite. I knew if I tried to comfort him, it would open the flood gates, so I didn't. It would be the same for me, too. I was almost…numb at this point.

We hadn't even gotten to properly celebrate the fact that we had ascended. And given the fact that Rodney hadn't said anything, I must have looked pretty bad and he couldn't tell. I started to turn to Rodney and tell him to go handle Mom, but he was already looking at me. He must have seen it on Seth's face because he said, "I'll go," and smirked, shaking his head.

I didn't say anything else. I just turned, my blanket still wrapped tightly around me, and sat in between Seth's legs on the back of the truck, leaning back against his chest. He engulfed me in his arms, wrapping his blanket around me as well, pressing his cheek to mine so we'd be touching in more places than one.

"God, thank you," he whispered. "Thank you for saving her." He kissed my jaw and squeezed me to him. I felt the numbness start to drift away. "I love you, little bird. I'm sorry."

"Don't," I begged. Now I was the one not wanting to show and tell what we'd been through. He didn't say another word, just held me, kissing my jaw and neck every now and then, as we waited for the cops to come and get our final statement.

When they said we could go, I'd never been happier in my life. Trouble eyed us with something close to sadness, like he'd never see us again. I rolled my eyes and left Seth's embrace, but he kept my hand in his the whole time as I hugged Trouble to me.

"Thank you. For keeping our secret."

"You saved my life. The future Mrs. Trouble greatly thanks you. Because who wants to miss out on all this." He smirked.

I laughed while Seth brought him in for a brotherly hug. "You are ridiculous, man."

"It's why you love me."

"It's true," Seth agreed and sighed. "I don't know what I'm going to do with myself now. I'm going to miss it."

He looked at the burned building and I felt guilt pound into me once more. He looked over at me. "No. It's meant to be this way." He smiled a little and it was actually genuine. "I'll find something great to do. Let's get you home."

When we reached Mom and Dad, who were still stuck behind the line, and not happy about it mind you, Mom wrapped me in a tight hug. "Oh, my gosh. I never imagined this when I sent Rodney after you."

"It's fine now, Mom. Seth took care of everything."

I looked back at Seth to see Dad already hugging him. I wanted to cry. This whole day just made me want to cry.

"Thank you, son," he told him. "Rodney told us what you did."

Seth nodded, looking down at the ground, his fingers reached across, latched on to mine, because we still hadn't let go.

"We need to go to home," I told them, knowing Seth needed me. The breaking point was reaching the thin thread for both of us. "It's…been a long day. Please."

"Of course," Mom said and opened the back door of her car. "We'll come get your car later."

We climbed in and I put my head on his shoulder as we made the ride to my house, gripping his arm and hand so tight.

As soon as we reached my room and I pushed the door closed, he pulled me to him and pressed me to the door. Just pressed me there. I loved feeling of his mouth against my forehead, but he was still trying not to lose it, still holding it in with everything he had, and that wasn't what this was about anymore. This was the place you *could* lose it. This was the place you *should* lose it. I pulled him down to me and kissed him once.

"No more stalling," I told him, my eyes finding his in the dark. "This is the only place in the world you can fall apart, Seth." I cupped his face. "And I feel you. And I know," I started to feel the sob rising, "that I need to let tonight go for myself. So let it go."

I tossed off my blanket, and pulled his off as well. I kicked off my shoes, watching him do the same. Then I pulled him straight to the bed and it was so much like that night where we went to bed smelling like smoke and fire, but I just didn't care. I laid on the bed and he followed me, hovering, but he made sure to touch me this time. So different than before. Everything had changed.

"I watched him die by my hand," he whispered, his eyes closed as he remembered what he looked like.

"He was going to kill you."

"He was going to kill you next," he said and shook his head. "I just don't understand why. Why couldn't he stop and live to fight this another day? Why did he have to do it this way, this day?"

I pulled his face up from where he was staring at my shirt, numb. "Everything happens the way it should, and that's a hard lesson sometimes," I rushed to say. "I truly believe that your uncle just…" I shrugged. "Evil has its day at some point and they all will meet their day. His day was today. I'm sorry that it had to be you. I'm so sorry," I said, my voice catching.

His thumb rubbed my cheek. "They all will meet their day by me if they come after you. I'm sorry today was cut so close." His eyes squeezed as he remembered thinking we were going to die. He shuddered and shook his head.

"We're alive. You're alive and I get to wake up with you tomorrow. That's all that matters to me right now."

He pushed breath from his lips and then looked up at me. "And you said you'd marry me." He was still upset, but he managed a small smile. "Was that just the thrill of death talking?"

"I wanted to marry you before I even met you." I smiled and pulled him

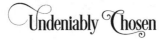

down to my lips. He sighed into our kiss. I then pulled his head to my chest just like before, letting him settle against my body, and began to comb his short hair with my fingers.

His mind ran with the thoughts of the Watsons, the way he grew up, the way the day unfolded, the way things could have gone down, the fact that we ascended, how proud of me he was, but mostly, he was just raw. He was always here for me, always protecting me, always making me feel better and making sure I was happy and safe. But that was my job, too.

I couldn't even imagine what I would feel if someone in my family had tried to kill me. So I stayed right there, being whatever he needed me to be, and held him to me tightly, kissing his forehead every few seconds just because I needed to, and combed his hair to let him know that I was still there and would always be there. No matter what. And I knew that when the tables were turned, he would be there for me.

Mom had been right about that. She didn't have to worry about me because Seth would be there.

Our lives weren't perfect, our lives weren't easy, our lives weren't simple or cookie-cutter, but who wanted that anyway?

The lives of significants were usually this spectacular fairytale. And ours hadn't started out that way by a long shot, but I was determined that we were going to get our happily ever after.

CHAPTER NINETEEN

When morning came, I was alone in my room. That was the first time that had happened in a long time. But I could hear him in the shower. His thoughts were a lot less somber than before. A stack of clothes were on the end of the bed, but they weren't Dad's. Mom had gone shopping.

Shopping for Seth.

I smiled, covering my lips with my fingers. I wondered what Seth was going to think about that. He was going to have to get used to it in this family. Mom was a mother hen and that wasn't going to change with him.

I heard the water turn off and got up quickly. I went to my closet to get some clothes for the day, but then went to bathroom door and knocked instead, "Seth?"

"I have clothes. I heard," he called back and chuckled. He opened the door with a towel wrapped around his waist. "You're not the only one with a gift, you know."

I could clearly see his face now. He hadn't changed *that* much, but gosh, he so daggum handsome. I let my eyes flick around his chest a little, noticing some changes there, and then back up to his eyes. He was thoroughly amused by the maneuver and my face apparently. "I didn't think you were listening. How are you?"

"Right now?" he asked low and came toward me. I backed up when my nose was against his chest, not wanting to back down, but having no other choice. "I'm great." He maneuvered me to the wall by the bathroom door. "How are you?"

"Seth," I whispered and put my hand on his chest to stop him when he kept coming.

He smiled. "Ava."

I smiled back and shook my head. "I'm amazing." That urge to cry came back so strong, but this time it was nothing but happiness. God, thank you, how did I get everything I ever wanted? I had gone to thinking my fairytale was ruined to thinking that I was the luckiest girl on the planet. Nobody could be this happy. I let my hand slide up around his neck, absolutely loving the way his lips parted and the harsh breath that came.

"I want to tell your parents today," he said, his eyes half-closed.

I knew what he meant. The wedding. "Are you sure? We can wait. We don't have to. They're going to go crazy and I want you to be ready—"

He stopped me, leaning in and kissing the words from my mouth. "I'm ready," he said as he leaned back. "I'm not going to let the Watsons stop me from moving on when it's the one thing I want to do. I promise you, if we could get married tomorrow, I'd do it."

I pressed into his mind a little, wanting to make sure he was certain and not just trying to make me happy. He had this barrier that surrounded his mind that was nothing but love and protectiveness for me. I groaned and little, gripping his neck tighter. I hadn't meant to open the floodgates or start something, but I had almost forgotten that we had ascended. It was a whole new ballgame. I knew what this led to now.

He leaned into me, his breath hitting my cheek, and I wrapped my arms around his neck because I would buckle otherwise. He wanted to stay. His mind told me so. We never got to do things like this. Our relationship was so rocky at times and so fast and slow, so different. And with whatever Ashlyn had done to my mind making it so I couldn't read his, we'd never really gotten to do much in each other's minds but that once.

I could see the way he saw me in the mornings when he'd take me to school. I'd be sitting way over there in my seat, being sullen, and he'd be thinking I was so beautiful and angry, like one of my robins.

I felt a tear fall free. His mind was beautiful. I could sit and swim in it all day. It was like my favorite warm blanket, a pool that was just the right temperature.

But this was really the first time we'd gotten to do this with each other, and I wasn't going to mutualize with him the day after we almost died, with my parents downstairs, me still smelling like smoke, and him in a towel.

We both pulled back at the same time, agreeing, and I was grateful. I thought he might want to mutualize now and not wait.

"Of course I do," he said, pulling my face up. "Everything in me wants to. And we will. Just not today." He took my mouth gently, but it quickly moved to passionate. I felt bad. He just took a shower and smelled delicious, and here I was smelling like smoke and—

He growled. *Trust me, the way you smell is not what interests me right now. Okay.*

He pulled back and licked his lip. "Okay what?" But he knew. He was grinning.

"Okay. Let's tell my parents." He grinned wider. "I just hope you know what you're getting into. The weddings aren't normal, but they are crazy."

"I just want to marry your cute behind." He kissed my forehead. "I don't care about the rest."

"It'll be a good way to bury the hatchet with the family, I guess," I mused, thinking he was in such a better mood.

"Thank you for yesterday," he said, distractedly. "I wouldn't have made it without you."

I tilted my head. "I wouldn't have made it without you either."

"No, I mean after. I'm sorry I was an ass." He pursed his lips. "But you saved me. I wouldn't have been okay without you." He sighed. "I'm still not, I just…need to move on."

I hugged him tighter. "I want nothing more than to move on with you. Truly."

He mentally tensed. "I guess we should talk about where we're going to live and all that?"

I laughed and looked up at him, putting my chin on his chest. "Why? We're going to live here, of course. I'm not going to leave my parents." He tried to keep a straight face, I'll give him that. "I'm completely kidding."

He whooshed a breath. "That was dirty."

I laughed harder. "Your. Face. Was. Priceless."

"Jacobsons and their jokes." He shook his head. "I guess I'll have to learn some, huh?" I squinted. "Well, I'm not going to be a Watson anymore, and I for daggum sure don't want their name any longer. Do you think your family would mind if I took their—"

"Are you kidding?" I wanted to cry again. "No, they won't mind!"

"We better ask," he said wryly. "We both know this family isn't exactly known for their enthusiasm for me. In fact, I bet you at least one has something to say about the wedding." He scoffed and looked down. "I somehow managed to piss off two entire families by just being born. That takes skill."

I cupped his face. "If anyone says anything, I will personally disown them. I am so over it. And where else would we live for our first place but your apartment. I like your apartment. It's close to school. It's the right size for us. Why wouldn't we live there?"

"It's a big step down for you, Ave."

He was smiling, but he was feeling the pressure. He lost his job because of our bond and had no idea what he was going to do now. He had no idea about the house buying tradition. He was still worrying about how to buy me a ring. I sighed. So the Watsons had apparently adopted some human traditions and kept some Virtuoso ones. I'd talk to him about that later. And I was sure he'd feel guilty about that, too. If anyone in my family made him feel bad about this, I would…

"Hey." I looked up. "What's the matter?"

I had been blocking him so he wouldn't see, but had apparently gotten a little worked up. "I'm just…everything. Nothing. All of it. I can't wait to tell my family and then…I don't even want to see them."

He rubbed my jaw with his thumb. "They were protecting you."

"And condemning you. It pisses me off."

He smirked. "Wow."

"What?"

"That will never lose its luster."

I scoffed and smiled. "My crazy side?"

"Your sexy, protective side." He kissed the corner of my mouth. "Go take a shower while I get dressed. Meet you downstairs and we'll tell them."

I slithered into the bathroom on jelly legs as he backed away. I showered quickly because I couldn't believe what was about to happen. I was still slicking on my lipgloss coming down the stairs when I yelled at Mom through her bathroom door and asked where Seth was. I could hear the shower running.

"He's at the side door. One of your friends from school came for you." My blood ran as thick as mud in my veins. "He answered the door, said he knew her. They're on the porch."

I walked quickly, ready to throw Lilith out on her behind. Why would he even be talking to her knowing what she did? Knowing that she could get to him or me at any moment? Or my family? I picked up the speed. They probably weren't talking; they were probably fighting. But his heartbeat was fine... I opened the door and...

Harper.

Seth was blocking the doorway, his arms crossed. He looked at me and I could tell how torn he was. He was checking to see if I was angry with him, but why would I be? Did he make her come here? Harper looked at me and her entire face changed. She had been pleading, half-smiling, looking sorry for something. Now she just looked peeved.

"You ruined everything," she said.

"You came to see me?" I asked politely. "Mom said?"

"Oh, bite me. I came for Seth. I knew he was here. I knew he was going to have to coddle you all night after my father almost killed you. You're alive so, I'm assuming he failed." Seth and I looked at her. She didn't know about her father yet. They hadn't called her?

"How did you know that he failed?"

"I didn't." She looked at Seth. "I hoped. I haven't been home. I didn't want to hear about it. Pfft." She looked away, shaking her head. "I'm so sick of Dad's agendas and plotting. And he's started to," she looked at me quickly, "*bring in* new people. He wants me to bond with one of them."

Bring in? For their experiments.

Yes, Seth confirmed.

"I don't want to bond to any of them. Dad doesn't care who I bond with as long as it's somebody so I get an ability for *his army*," she sneered.

"What are you doing here?" I asked, not caring about the pity party. I felt bad about her father, but she didn't seem to have much *like* for the guy. That didn't mean she wouldn't be upset about his death.

"I came for Seth." Her eyes never left him.

Well, this was just getting awkward. "You need to leave," he told her.

"You were promised to me," she said, like a toddler who didn't get her favorite toy on Christmas.

"That's not how it works, Harper."

"Stop calling me that!"

"I get it," I said softer. "Seth told me about what they did to you all as kids." She scoffed and looked at him as if he had betrayed her. "You're grateful for what he did, and he wasn't related to you so you thought you could actually do the bond with him and everything would be okay. I get it. But he doesn't belong to you."

"No, you don't get it," she said and sighed. "We had a thing, okay. It may not be a significant thing, but it was enough of a promise in my book."

Even though I knew it wasn't true, just hearing her say the words made my blood ice over.

"Being your friend is not *a thing*," he told her, his color rising.

"In a world where you have no true friends, yes it is!" she yelled back.

"When he went to do our imprint, I said no. I said it was disgusting." She glared. "I said we were family and it was never going to happen. How much clearer can it get than that?"

She looked away. "I thought you were just protecting my virtue or something."

Enough. I refused to feel sorry for this girl. "All right, Harper, it's time to go."

"I'm not leaving. Not until Seth agrees to keep seeing me. You're not just throwing me away. Not after all we've been through. And maybe we can... talk. Say that you'll at least think about pushing the imprint with me one day. It's only fair. We would have been great together if she hadn't come along."

I tried not to yell. "If you had forced the imprint, we still would have imprinted and it would have cancelled yours out. Don't you get it? We're soulmates. We were supposed to be together!"

She shook her head. "No. We could experiment and find out if you like. See if your bond is as strong as you think it is."

"Reverse psychology? Really? Get off my porch, Harper."

She looked at Seth, back at me, and then back at him. "But when will I see you again?"

He paused for only a moment. I knew it was my job to be the bad guy in this situation. It was *my* job to protect my significant. And boy, did I want to. My hands were shaking with the restraint of wanting to grip her jaw and throw her backwards from the porch in a good ol' *Tennessee see ya later.*

"I'm going to answer that one for him and say, nada." Her mouth opened. "Nope. Get going." She scoffed. "Bye." Her mouth opened again. "You're lucky that I'm letting you just *walk* away."

"Seth!" she yelled over me. "Do something!"

"What did you think was going to happen?" he asked, exasperated, but quiet. "A fairytale ending? I've already got one of those."

"You need to go home anyway," I told her, my voice softer. "Things didn't go that well last night."

She squinted. "What do you mean?"

"Just go home."

"Look, I don't care what happened to them. Seth could be my ticket out of all that. He *was* my ticket."

I stared in complete and utter, dubious silence and awe. "Seth isn't the only good guy in the world, Harper. Not that you deserve one; you have to earn a good guy. If you want to leave your family, then leave. That doesn't have anything to do with Seth."

"They'll just call me back with the blood bond."

"There are ways around that." Her eyes bugged. I smirked. "Well, a Jacobson knows something about blood and alchemy that a Watson doesn't. Who would have thought?"

"Whatever. I'm not leaving. I'm going to stay here and fight for what I want." Her eyes looked at Seth.

"Harper—"

"The family has been so calm the past few years until you showed up, *Ava*," she sneered. "That's why all this got started back up again. They had almost let it go with your family, given up, just let it fall to the back of their minds and moved on. But then you came and woke up the beast. And ruined my life."

She came the couple steps that were between us and I felt Seth's hand gripping my arm to swing me behind him. But this was my fight. I had to fight for my significant, just like if another guy came to the house for me Seth would take care of it. Oh, and I imagined he would.

And I was about to take care of this.

I planted my feet and held my hand out to her, turning my face to the side because I still wasn't exactly sure what was going to happen. When I heard her screech, I looked to see her moving aside as ice shards flung past her and slammed into the driveway. I felt the coolness under my fingertips. I looked under my feet to see the ice on the doormat. She gazed back at me like I was Beelzebub himself standing there in that doorway.

"You asked for it," I told her. "Get. Off. My. Porch. And stay away from Seth."

"You're a freak," she hissed.

"I'm ascended," I corrected and held out my hand again. She scooted backward off that porch so fast, almost tripping in the process, and didn't look back. I thought about that. If that had been me, she would have had to hurt me or worse to get me to leave Seth. She came here like it was going to be some big fight and at the first sign that she might actually have one, she turned tail and ran.

I felt Seth pulling me to look at him instead of watching her go. That in itself made my pulse race.

"That…" he sighed and licked his lip, "was the hottest thing I've ever seen."

"You're not upset with me?"

The corner of his mouth lifted just a smidge before he leaned in ever so slowly and captured my lips, his warm palm finding my side inside my open sweater, tugging me to him with a jolt. I gasped against his lips. He enjoyed that immensely, smiling into our kiss. His free hand found my other side and he gripped me to him tightly, his fingers spreading to cover more of me. The tingles that spread from his lips to mine were a full-on assault. I felt lightheaded, I felt on fire, I felt like he was practically swimming through my veins, I felt…so complete.

So he liked seeing my protective side, huh?

Ah, you have no idea, little bird…

So this was what it was like to be a real significant couple. I grinned and went up on my tiptoes, pressing closer, loving the way he groaned a little and picked my feet from the floor.

I was thinking about how good his hands felt on me, how his magic fingers could lull me into any reality he wanted me to believe in. Even though we had almost died when we ascended at the library, when he gripped my legs, pressing me to his chest, kissing me and slamming me to the wall…

I barely got my thought out when I felt his hand on the back of my thigh and in my hair. I opened my eyes a little, feeling how heavy they were, and pulled away just enough to see him. My lips were parted and my breaths were ragged as I saw his arms still tightly around me, not moving, but felt his mind's hands moving on me where he wanted them to go.

Oh…I wasn't going to survive being his significant.

He chuckled huskily and smugly, too. He pressed me to the door and kissed me hard once more. "Let's get you inside. It's too cold out here." His eyes darkened as his lips morphed into a smirk. "And you had to wear those tights today, didn't you?"

"They're a different color," I defended with a laugh.

"Oh, I know." I didn't think he even noticed with our *guest* that I was wearing tights again. I felt his actual hand just above my knee. He looked down and over at my leg. "I kinda like the grey ones myself." I felt my eyes bug. "What? You didn't think I had you pegged the second you came out that door with these on?" He tsked and then sighed long and hard looking over at my leg. "Man, these tights are going to be a problem for me."

I laughed and hit his chest with the side of my fist. "You are so crazy."

"And, no, I'm not mad," he said, his eyes staring into mine so deeply I feared I'd get lost in them forever. I knew exactly what Ashlyn had been talking about. He finished softly, "Why would I be? If the situation was reversed, you don't think I'd protect what's mine?"

My heart skipped and he smiled a little at feeling it, obviously enjoying that.

"I just felt like you had put her in her place and it was my turn. It's my right to if she won't stop," I said and bit my lip, feeling a little…I don't know. I didn't have to defend myself, I knew that.

"It's not jealousy," he told me with a smile. "Jealousy is when you want something that you can't have, something that doesn't belong to you. Being protective is defending what's yours." He leaned in, his hand closing around my jaw as his nose skimmed up to mine. "And you better believe that I'll be protecting what's mine. Against frat boys or anybody else. Or Paul…your little coffee *buddy*." He smirked.

I giggled and kissed him. "You're right. That is hot." I sighed as I leaned away. "Now what?"

"Now let's go tell your parents that you're all stuck with me forever."

I nodded and smiled happily. "Yeah. Let's do that."

Mom was just getting off the phone and got off quickly when she saw us coming. Dad and Rodney were sitting at the table and both of them stopped eating mid-bite and stared. It took me a second to catch on before I remembered.

The ascension.

I smiled. "Yep. That's how Seth got me out of the fire. Remember? We ascended." I looked over at Rodney. "Or did you leave that part out?"

"No, I told them, it's just…"

I wished I had Mom's mind-reading ability in that moment because this was getting ever so awkward. They all just continued to stare. Dad got that sad, faraway look that made me want to cry. Mom just looked proud. Rodney—who knew what he was thinking. I shuffled my feet and squeezed Seth's hand, turning into his side a little.

Do I have something on my face?

Yeah. I looked up at him. *You're so freaking gorgeous and you don't even know it.*

I rolled my eyes. "All right. Cut it out," I told everyone. "Geez. We ascended. I get it. We look a little different."

"You look beautiful," Dad said. I looked up to find him smiling. "You always have. Maybe now you'll believe it."

The goofy smiles had to stop. "Okay, seriously, enough. We have some news."

"What news?" Mom asked and pointed to the coffee maker to see if we wanted some. I shook my head.

"Um," I tried, but really I didn't know if I wanted to shout it or cry I was so happy.

"What's the matter?" Mom asked and stepped toward us a little. "What's happened?"

"Nothing," I laughed and looked down. "Um."

Seth lifted my chin and smiled as he looked at me. "Nothing but I'm marrying your daughter."

Mom's gasp made us both look over. Dad was standing and Mom was covering her mouth. It only took about one point seven seconds before she start to squeal, however.

My smile was so wide it hurt. I bit into my lip and Seth reached up with his thumb and tugged it loose.

"No more hiding it. You're going to have so many reasons to be happy,

Ava. I'm going to make sure of it."

"Take these to Dad," Mom ordered. "He's at the back patio."

"Mom, do we really have to have a cookout today?" I whined as she pushed me. She'd sent Seth and Rodney out right before me with handfuls of stuff. "With everything that happened yesterday, I'm not really in the mood. I just want to…" I looked at her and she was cocking her brow, "hang out."

"You still have to eat. March."

I barely kept my groan to myself. Visionary or not, she could be a pain in the tush—

"Ava!" Ember yelled and tackled me as I turned the corner of the garage. She took everything from my hands and handed them to the first person she saw, took my hand, and proceeded to drag me near the middle of the family where Seth was already being ambushed by Dawson and Maria.

"What is this?" I asked as I looked around at my entire family.

"A do-over," she said and pointed to Grandpa Jim, who was grilling sausage dogs. "It was his idea."

I squinted. So they found out that Seth saved my life yesterday and decided to throw together a party to thank him? Nice, but… I guess it was better than nothing. They were trying. I smiled just as Grandpa looked over. He waved his huge tongs in the air and gave me a sad smile. I smiled back.

Mom's hand landed on the tops of my arms from behind. "He's been telling people if they didn't come they weren't getting anything for Christmas." I chuckled. "He feels bad. He wasn't just protecting you, he was protecting everyone. When you have a gift, sometimes it can be a burden. Especially with his gift weakening, he let it go too far trying to keep everyone safe." She moved to the side and sighed. "What else do men do to make things right but feed you?"

I smiled.

I felt Seth's arm go around me lightly and my entire being sighed a little, inside out.

"We ask them to marry us," he said low, but Ember heard him. And if

Ember hears you, then the world may as well have heard you.

"Oh, my gosh!"

We spent the next four hours with my family as they congratulated us and tried—and they did try hard, I'll give them that—to make up for their misgivings and wrongs against Seth. Jordan and Drake even let him win at horseshoes and that is saying something. Even though it was *so* obvious.

Turned out that none of my family even knew about what had happened the day before until Rodney started telling everyone. Grandpa had planned the bar-b-que the day after the summit. But once everyone got wind of the attack, they all wanted to know what happened.

I didn't want to tell them exactly. If Mom and Dad knew how close it had come, I didn't know what they would do. But everyone felt so bad about what Seth had to do to his uncle to save us. And when Mom and Dad looked at me, I could tell they knew that I wasn't telling the whole truth. Mom watched the way Seth clutched me to his side, the way my fingers wrapped in his collar, and I could tell that she knew.

I looked away and stared at Seth's neck as Rodney told them about how Seth had saved me, but they didn't know the half of it.

"Your clothes were burned."

I closed my eyes for a second and then looked over at Dad. "Dad, don't."

"I saw the jackets you took off and tried to hide before you put on the blankets. How did you do it? How did you survive the fire when the entire inside of the building was burned out?"

Ember gasped and looked at me for explanation.

Seth tried not to think about it, but couldn't help himself. He closed his eyes and shook his head, groaning a little. I put my hand on his neck, his eyes snapping open to mine.

"Gah, what happened in there?" Daddy growled.

"You don't want to know," I finally said, letting them know that it was something bad, confirming it, but needing him to stop. I felt my eyes water as I remembered. Seth wiped under my eye with his thumb.

When the phone rang, it was, almost as if my body knew it wasn't good. I tensed and started to shake. I watched as Mom went to answer it. I just... knew...

Today of all days, while we were all together, who else would call us?

"What?" she said loudly after listening for a minute. "How did you even find out about it? I haven't informed the council of it y—" She listened and then the window began to rattle. Dad was already making his way over. Seth gripped me to his chest tightly. Whether it was protectiveness or because he understood just like I did that whatever was on that phone call wasn't good, it just didn't matter. I buried my face in his neck and breathed him in, wanting the world to disappear, wanting everything to go away but this man, my family, and his touch.

"You can't do this," she said so softly, Dad moving in to wrap his arms around her from behind. And that's when I knew exactly what it was about. They had heard about Seth killing his uncle and were going to hold a Tribune for him. I cupped his face, knowing he wouldn't know about it, once again getting the shaft from our people. He had been listening to my thoughts and got the gist, even if he didn't understand what it was exactly. He gripped my sides and gave me an everything-will-be-okay smile. "He's in the same clan as his uncle." She listened. "Nothing is official yet—" She listened, the glasses on the tables began to shake. "You can't pick and choose the rules you want to follow, councilor!" she yelled, and when the window behind her shattered, Dad raised his fist, borrowing Mom's ability and stopping all the shards mid-air, swinging his fist down and forcing them all to fall to the ground with it. She was breathing heavy as she listened.

Seth just watched in scared, awe-struck wonder. He knew this was all about him and he couldn't believe that one, people cared so much about him either way that it mattered and two, that my mom would defend him so strongly. He watched her like she was some avenging angel.

Mom shook her head. "Pablo…as long as you know that you just declared war against your Visionary." A few people gasped around me and started to whisper and chatter. She nodded and said softly, "So be it," and hung up.

Grandpa Peter stood. "Quiet." He looked around at them all. "Your whole life is about to change." He looked back at us. "And it's *not* because of Seth and Ava. This has been a long time coming, for generations. Don't for one second think this is your fault."

Seth gulped, but nodded. Grandpa looked back at Mom and Dad, who were still standing there, but Mom had moved from him and was pulling something up on the laptop.

"Maggie," Dad started.

"They said there was a video," Mom said without turning as she pulled up

her email. "The Watsons called the council to claim their right to a Tribune for their dead member." She found what she was looking for and then took the remote for the projector and turned on a video. "He said there was video from the library damning Seth and showing that they showed themselves to humans." Seth and I looked at each other.

Video? And we hadn't shown ourselves—

The video began and it showed us running through the burning library into the bathroom, Seth tugging me behind him. My family gasped at seeing us surrounded by flames, the entire library engulfed. A minute later, we emerged and it showed us running for it, just like we planned, all the way to the end—and not making it. I watched with horror in my veins as my family watched me almost die, watched as Seth cupped my face in a goodbye, forcing me to the wall, and surrounding me with his body. There was no sound, but the visual was enough of a nightmare.

"Mom, turn it off," I begged in a loud whisper that she definitely heard.

I could vaguely hear my family's groans and gasps around me.

Her eyes stayed glued to the screen as she watched Seth pull me to his chest, leaning over me, taking all the brunt of everything the fire had to offer. I looked away. I couldn't do it anymore. And now they were trying to hurt him even more and take him away from me.

Seth took my face in his hands.

We were literally forged in fire. We're made of steel. Nothing is going to happen to us. Nothing can take me away from you. Or vice versa.

He was right. I took a deep breath, knowing that no matter what, I was prepared to fight. Whether it be girls on my porch or councils in gold ballrooms. He smiled a little at my thought.

When Ember's loud gasp sounded, we both turned to see what it looked like when we ascended, when Seth realized that he was no longer going to burn but could control it, it was magical. He looked like Thor or some comic book character from a movie.

He chuckled as he kissed my forehead and tucked me under his chin. I hugged him so tight as we watched our story unfold.

When he pushed me behind him, and then I sucked all the air and fire out of the room, everyone was so quiet it was eerie. And then Ember said, "Holy…cannoli…did you see that!? She was all like *Oh, you think you're bad, well look what I can do!*"

I rolled my eyes. Then the camera switched to an outside view and it showed Seth and his uncle mid-fight. *Convenient.* When he pulled his knife and went to throw it at Seth and I stopped him, my family gasped again. And then he went for Seth and I knew what was next. I pulled from his embrace and ran to the laptop, pressing buttons until it stopped. When I turned back around, my family was looking at me with new eyes, but *my* eyes were at the back of the room with my significant…who was currently being engulfed by Dad, and Mom and Rodney were right behind him.

I could hear through Seth all the things Dad was saying to him and I was about to seriously burst wide open. I made my way back to them quickly, just as Dad was pulling back from Seth. Both of them looked so torn up.

"I just don't know how to…" Dad tried.

"You don't have to," Seth said and took my wrist, tugging me closer. "Ever."

"Thank you, son." He looked at me. "Thank you so much." He hugged me long and hard.

Once everyone hugged him and me and told him how thankful they were, I saw it in their eyes then—my family would never be the same after that. Seth was no longer the Watson who got added in to the mix, he was one of us now.

All this stuff between Seth and my family happened for a reason. Now they'd never doubt him ever again. They'd never wonder if he was a Watson ever again. They'd never look at him with suspicion ever again. And for that alone, I was grateful. He was one of us.

So when Mom started telling everyone about the council setting up the Tribune against Seth to vindicate Gaston's death for the next reunification, it did not go over well.

Then she told everyone about the vision Ashlyn had and about finding our names on the wall, about her own vision of seeing her and Dad fighting side by side in battle, about how she thought it meant for us to do what was needed. And what was needed might be to…break off from the council and start our own.

To say my family was shocked was an understatement, but it wasn't the first time my mother had shocked her people and I doubted it would be the last. She sat back and watched as they talked and bickered back and forth, already debating whether or not we should do this. Most were for it. The only reason a few were against it was because they knew what that meant. Exactly what she had said on the phone.

War.

She stood off to the side and shook her head. "It's already started. Our people, divided, not cooperating."

Dad looked at her over the table, leaning in. "We're just talking. Nobody is saying it's not what needs to be done."

Uncle Kyle crossed his arms. "You're saying we should break off and tell the council that we don't want anything to do with them?"

"It's step one." She sighed. "In a long line of things that will have to be done. Hard things."

He squinted. "And you had a vision that told you this is what we should do? Can we see it?"

She shook her head. "I didn't see a vision about this exact thing. We just saw our names on the wall, like I told you all before. It's just—it's just what I know we have to do."

He pressed his lips in a hard line. "You've never led us astray." He gulped and looked at Aunt Lynne. "We'll follow you. No matter what."

"And I love you for it." She smiled but it wasn't a happy smile. "But what about the ones who won't or are just too scared? What about the ones who I can't reach because they're under the thumb of the wrong people? I'm ripping our people apart," she whispered.

Dad slammed his fist on the table. "You're not ripping our people apart!" He stood and stalked over to her. "He saved our daughter from those monsters and they want to blame him for it, just like they tried to blame me all those years ago for saving their *Visionary*. I can't stand another second of the hypocrisy."

I hadn't seen Mom this upset in a really long time. Her arms were wrapped around herself as she looked at the floor. He lifted her face with his fingers under his chin like Seth did to me all the time and I wanted to cry, knowing everything was going to be different, and not in a good way.

"This is why you were brought here," he told her so softly, it made me ache and look away. "Ashlyn put all our names on that wall and I think this is why. She said war was coming. She hasn't been wrong so far, baby."

"I don't want to be known as the Visionary that brought down the Virtuoso," Mom said miserably.

"What about the one that built it back up?" he said louder. "Look at us. We're struggling. We're a sham. We are not what we used to be, we're not what we should be. The only reason we got our bonds back was because of you, and now it's time for the real work to begin." He gulped. "I don't want war any more than you do, but we have to do what you feel is the right thing, the right path. And what do you feel is the right path?"

She sighed long and hard before wrapping her arms around his stomach, accepting his hug and his kiss on her forehead. "We have to make them choose."

"The sad thing?" Dad said against her skin. "It won't even be a surprise who goes to what side."

"No," she said and sobbed a little before catching herself and steeling her back. She looked up and wiped her eye. "No, it won't. Pablo," Mom said and Dad nodded. "In the vision I had from Seth's phone." She looked over at us. "That's how your family knew about the summit."

"What?" Seth asked, his voice cracking. "How do you—"

"They've always held someone from the council in their pocket. I don't know how they got to him or what they promised him, but they did. He wanted you to be deunified and it didn't make any sense, unless he was trying to get out of a deal he'd made with the Watsons. And just now, he's trying to push this Tribune so hard." She shook her head angrily and looked at Seth. "I don't know if it's just Pablo or the whole clan, but he's definitely in the Watson's pocket, and he definitely has it in for you. He was the one who worked with Watsons to make the video of you two in the fire possible. I think he thinks this union will make some kind of alliance or make them soft or something, like they won't go on with whatever plans they've made." She scoffed. "He apparently doesn't know them as well as he thinks he does. He just wants to destroy our—"

"Okay, okay, okay," Dad soothed and smoothed his hands down her arms. "No more talk about this today. It's going to happen. We'll deal with it." He looked at the family. "But we do this like we do everything." He pulled out the cog and set it on the table. "If anyone isn't ready for this—"

Everyone stood that wasn't standing already. Mom didn't try to hide her tears this time. She and Dad hugged as they looked out at their people.

"First things first," Dad finally said and wiped under her eye. "We have a wedding to get ready for."

Everybody started whooping and clapping. Dad looked at me over the noise and expanse of our family, hugging my mother, knowing war was

coming, but he looked so happy in that moment and so utterly devastated. And I knew it had nothing to do with the council. I'd never fought tears so hard before and still lost. I looked away from him because it was seriously killing me.

Seth was in a bubble of his own, not really knowing how to process the fact that my family was willing to go to war to keep him. To *fight* for him.

"That's what family does for each other." I grinned a little and shook my head. "We fight, we make up, and then we start wars on your behalf." He chuckled a little, but it still wasn't right. "Seth, you heard them. This was a long time coming. You saw what they did to Ashlyn and Richard with your own eyes. That wasn't just the Watsons, though it was mostly them. The entire council sat back and let that happen, and they've been doing that forever. You're not the cause; you're just the catalyst. *We're* the catalyst. You didn't do this alone."

"I've never had anyone want to fight for me before." He put his arms around my back and pulled me against him. "And now it's happened twice in one day."

I let my hands rest on his chest over my heart and his that were picking up speed. "I think you better get used to it," I whispered.

When he leaned in to kiss me, I gasped at feeling how hot he was. It was fitting for my fireman to get that ability. It was *fair*. But it didn't burn me. It was like I was immune to it or…drawn to it. Like I was made for it. Because I was.

His fire could cancel out my ice, I could cool his burn, or we could both burn hot and be happy together in the ashes.

"Ava, get up," he whispered in my ear.

"Mmm?"

"Come on, little bird. You can't sleep the day away. Get up."

"The annoying part is supposed to come after we're married," I grumbled and tried to roll over.

He chuckled and straddled me as he held my arms over my head. "Well this is certainly new."

"What?"

"Having to coax you out of bed in an echo." My eyes popped open. "Usually, you're running to me, can't wait to see me," I surveyed the room to see we were at the palace, "but for some reason your mind wants to pretend it's asleep instead of spending time with me." He smirked. "I'm hurt."

"You can still do them?" I said in awe. He let my wrists go the first time I tried to move them. I cupped his neck. "I wondered…I mean, I thought when you got your other ability…"

"I did, too." He smiled. "And the thing is that they don't know." He laughed once. "The Watsons gave me this ability to destroy you with and now I'm going to turn around and use it on them. And they don't even know I have it. It's actually really poetic."

I pulled him down and hugged him around his neck. "Are you sure you're okay with everything? I don't want you to feel like you have to—"

He leaned up and captured my mouth in a kiss that ended all arguments, with suction that left no worries, licking at my lip in ways that made me know in *all ways* that I was wanted, and his hand just above my knee, gripping me to him so I was consumed, tingling in my veins. He pulled back, licking his lip, touching mine in the process. Ah, it was the sweetest, sexiest thing.

"This is the first time I've brought you here that you remembered me, you remembered our life, and you remembered that I asked you to marry me." I bit my lip and couldn't stop my smile or the goosebumps at the look he was giving me. "It's daylight outside, we've got about seven hours in London, and you promised me a tour. I have a feeling when we come here for real next time, there won't be much time for that."

He smoothed my cheek and tried to keep up the positivity, so I did, too. I was determined to. The Watsons and the council were about try to take a lot from us and ruin a lot of lives and change a lot of things. We had this time, we had now, and they were not taking this from us.

I held his collar and kissed him again, harder and longer, loving the way his groans carried down into my throat and body, down into my very heart and soul where he belonged. My heart was made of pieces of him, he was imprinted on me, and my soul carried him with me everywhere I went.

He pulled me to stand and it was then I noticed what I was wearing. I cocked my head. "Tights? Really?"

His grin was cocky, adorable, and all male. "What else would I have put you in?" He wrapped his arms around me from behind as we made our way out the door. "Ah…those tights," he groaned into my neck.

I laughed so loud into the empty hallway, loving the little bit of power I seemed to have of him, loving that he found me beautiful and sexy because I thought he was so sexy and gorgeous, loving that he wanted me to show him London, and loving him so much that my heart literally ached and burned with it.

I took him all over London and we did all the cheesy tourists things. We rode the boats, we took cab rides, we ate tons of food, we walked and talked and just…were. That was the point. It didn't matter what was coming for us because I wasn't about to step aside and let anyone take this away from me—my fairytale that I'd waited a lifetime for which had finally come true.

We talked it over with Mom and Dad and everyone wanted to have the wedding that weekend. Seth was all for it. I smiled remembering. It was only five days away. I didn't know what was going to happen after that. Honestly, I didn't even want to go back to school. It felt pointless and it felt unsafe. But I knew that wasn't going to fly with the Jacobson men.

So we'd have to be extra careful. We'd have to let the other clans that we knew were our allies know what was going on as soon as possible, and we'd have to hope beyond hope that all the misery Ashlyn went through wasn't in vain, and that she was put here for a purpose. To send us on the right path and lead Mom on the right course. Mom's purpose was just as bold and valiant as Ashlyn's and we all believed.

Now we just had to put the action behind that belief and if that meant war, then so be it.

I took Seth's hand and tugged him through all the people, how they even got here I didn't know, but they acted normal, and they pretended like they were happy to be in our dream and be in London. And that was good enough for me. When we got back to the palace terrace, I just stood there and looked at the city we had spent all day exploring. It was still daylight and the sun was still high in the sky. It was so neat how there were no rules there. Too bad it couldn't be that way for real life.

He engulfed me in his arms from behind and nibbled the side of my neck. I gripped his hair and leaned back against him.

"What's gotten into you today?" I whispered because that's all I could manage.

He was so…happy. And giddy. And something was different. Yesterday we told our family that we were getting married and then our people declared war on us. Two very different sides of a coin. But tonight, he was acting as if none of this bothered him at all.

"I can't just be happy to be here with you?" he asked into the skin under my ear.

I let my head fall back and closed my eyes. "Yes."

He laughed. "That's it? You're not going to pry any further, just stopping there?"

"As long as you keep biting my neck like that," I said, barely breathing any longer.

He turned me to face him, his smile so happy. That's when I realized that I was right. Something had happened. I fisted his collar. "What is it? What happened?"

"Everything." He tucked my hair behind my ear and let his fingers follow it down my shoulder. "You happened and I got everything I wanted all in one second. How does that happen?" he said quietly and I knew it was rhetorical, so I said nothing.

I let him talk and just listened, soaking in every word, every detail of our new life and story, loving his ministrations and touch, whether they calmed me or not. His fingers moved to smooth down my arms and back up, over and over, and it was then I realized that the weather had been perfect. I hadn't even thought about a sweater until that moment when I realized I was sleeveless. He gulped as he watched his fingers move over my skin.

He chuckled a little. "I was so scared before I came over to see you that first night. Scared out of my damn mind. I'd only ever been told that the Jacobsons were terrible people who had done awful things, with the sole purpose of destroying everything they were and everyone, right down to the children who had done nothing to them. And then you happened." He smiled, still watching his fingers caress my skin. The combination was so heady that I shivered as goosebumps raced across my shoulders and down my arms. His smile grew as he continued on. "I always thought that they were full of crap, that the stories were more fiction than non, and in that moment I knew— because there was no way in hell someone as sweet and beautiful as you were could be a villain. I realized I'd been playing the villain all along, right beside 'em. And when I realized that you were mine, that you'd been given to me to protect, to keep safe and happy," he shook his head, "I knew I had to do whatever it took to make sure you knew I understood that I'd never deserve you, but I would never stop trying to be worthy of you."

"Seth," I breathed.

"And then everything fell apart. You hated me." His face showed how painful that time was. He closed his eyes for a few seconds and then opened them, moving his hand up to my other side, letting his hand reach down and take mine, pulling it up between us where he stroked my tattoo with his thumb, still watching his movements. *That thumb*... I gulped. "And then we slowly started to get past that and it was...the best thing in the world to watch you let those pieces fall away. It might sound weird, but I think I actually preferred it this way to you just falling and trusting the bond." He laced our fingers and finally looked up to meet my eyes, blue colliding with brown, and sparks ignited. "We know that we earned this and it just makes me that much more appreciative of it. I know what I've got here and, yeah, it's magical. But it's *real*, too." I took a shuddering breath. He kept lacing and unlacing our fingers. "And now, I've got my girl, she's going to marry me, I've got this family that's willing to fight for me, and I've...almost got my dream job."

I tilted my head. "What..."

"When you were in the shower tonight, I got a call." He smiled and it was the one he'd been wearing all night. "I told them I can't be a firefighter. I told the chief I had to leave that night after the fire. He thought I was just being a pansy, afraid to get married and risk myself. So...he said I could take the fire investigator job at the station if I wanted it. It's not the same thing." He chuckled. "Not by a longshot. I won't be fighting fires, but I'll be with the guys and helping them. And that's as close as I could have imagined."

I still couldn't help the little slice of guilt that crept up. I tried to smile. "Is this what—"

"I can see it on your face, sweetheart. Have you not see how happy I've been tonight?" His smile really was ridiculous. "I never thought it would work out to the point where my life was almost perfect." Both of his warm hands came up and cupped my face. "You did this. You did this for me. If you hadn't been running late that day, I wouldn't be the happiest man in the world right now." I couldn't hold it in any longer after that. He wiped under my eyes with his thumbs, but continued his assault. "I love you more than I thought I'd ever love anyone." He put his forehead to mine. "I can't wait to be Mr. Jacobson."

I laughed through my tears and went on my tiptoes to reach him, grabbing his collar for leverage.

"Those sounds like wedding vows."

The London sun warmed us for another minute as he kissed me senseless before he took me home to my dark room where I knew I was safe with him. We'd be married in a few days. He would be mine.

I couldn't wait for him to be Mr. Jacobson either.

As we settled into the covers for the first time, because we were engaged now, he laid on his back and pulled me to him, putting my head on his chest. I sighed so contented, realizing this was how he'd slept on me before. Gosh, it was comfortable. He chuckled.

"The best part?" he whispered against my temple. "I got to listen to your heartbeat all night long." He tapped his chest. "Feeling it and hearing are two different things."

I turned my head a little and pressed my ear to his heart. I could hear his and mine beating together there, different rhythms, different patterns, but still always coming back around together every few beats. It was like beautiful music—our heartbeats. He was right.

"It's beautiful," I told him and let my eyes drift up to meet his. The room had enough light to make out his face in the dark. "The way we were chosen for each other, the way our worlds are woven, the way our hearts are beating in our chests together, so perfectly but still so out of synch." I smiled and wiped the one tear that fell. "I'm so scared of what's coming for our people and yet I'm so utterly happy in this moment and all the ones coming after it that I can barely breathe," I breathed the words.

He let his knuckles graze my cheek. "One day at a time, Ava. When we have to deal with war, then we will, and I'll be right there to protect you. Right now?" I heard a little growl come from his throat. "All I want to do is lie in this bed with you, listen to your heartbeat as you sleep, and dare someone to come through that door before we're ready to leave."

I found myself laughing softly. I bit my lip, seeing his eyes move to it.

"It's my turn," I told him and laid my head on his chest, settling in against him, my head right over his and my heart, letting my arm swing up to his neck.

He chuckled into my hair and tugged the covers around us. "Ah, I love you," he groaned as he gripped me to him.

"I love you more," I whispered.

"*This* again."

"Just give up."

He nuzzled my neck. "A lifetime of fighting about this sounds so enticing."

We had just drifted off when the door burst open. Seth's thoughts automatically assumed the worst and he threw me behind him, still on our knees. It was actually pretty impressive.

"Wha...Rodney? What the hell, man?"

I peeked around his arm, ready to strangle him. He held up his hands in defense.

"Dude, it's almost noon. Why are you still in bed?"

"I don't have school," I ticked off on my finger. Seth held me back with his arm around my waist. I think he knew I would commit murder if I reached my sibling. "I almost died. I got engaged and want to *be alone with my fiancé*," I ticked off with my finger again.

"Ew," Rodney said and rolled his eyes, "now you're just *trying* to gross me out."

"Yesterday we declared freaking war on our people," I finished softly, losing steam. I sagged and Seth took my wrist in his fingers. I was learning it was his customary move to comfort me.

"Yeah." He nodded. "So that makes you wanna sleep all day?"

"Seth took me to London last night," I explained and yawned. I swung my hand at him and laid back down. "So we're tired. We were there all night. Get out, cretin."

"You know, I've always wanted to go to Cabo San Lucas, Mexico, but Mom and Dad would never let me go." He sighed.

"Rodney, please."

"They said it wasn't safe or something. Which is just a bunch of bull. Kids go there for spring break and stuff all the time."

"Rodney," Seth tried. He laid down beside me and sighed. "Come on, man, have mercy."

"Was it fun? In London? What did you guys do? Was it your first time? Did you take him to see—"

"Rodney!" I yelled.

"I could be your tour guide next time if you obviously don't even remember if you have a good time."

Seth sat up. "I'll take you to Cabo. Out."

I couldn't see him, but I could hear that little grin. Cretin. "Thanks, bro!"

"Out!" Seth yelled and laid back down. "Wow," he said and chuckled as he pulled me back to his chest, the exact spot I had been before. "We just got hustled."

I sighed and rubbed my leg against Seth's. "I have a feeling it won't be the last time either."

Seth laughed as he kissed my forehead. "If this is our life and our problems? Then I don't think we have much to worry about."

But one day we would.

He reached down and raised my chin on his chest. "One day at a time, remember?"

I smiled, deciding he was right. The Watsons don't get to win. "One day at a time."

With my significant's heartbeat in my ear, his lips on mine, and his palm sending anything but calming tingles as it coasted down my arm to lace with my fingers, I knew that I was right where I was supposed to be. And how many people could say that and truly mean it?

His heart beat more loudly in my chest with every passing minute, and I knew that mine was as loud as a kick drum for him. Our hearts made music together, just like we made our way in this new Virtuoso world we didn't fit in. Oil and water were never supposed to mix and go together, and spoiler alert, Romeo and Juliet didn't live happily ever after in the end if you remember correctly, but somehow, we were making this work.

I knew I was going to get my happy ending, the one I always dreamed about, the one I was always promised.

But more than that?

I was forged in fire with the man who was literally of my dreams. This wasn't some fairytale, but it felt like one, and I couldn't wait to see how our story ended.

No matter what, I knew it would be happily…ever… after.

EPILOGUE

Our wedding day was ruined.

Completely, utterly, devastatingly, five ways to Sunday ruined.

Well, that's what Ember said anyway. I didn't look at her as I passed her on the way through my family to my significant because I knew I would cry before I even made it to him. In fact, I didn't look at any of them because they would all make me cry. I just focused on the way the freezing air felt so freeing and good on my bare legs. Daddy had turned on the porch heaters for the ceremony and everyone standing around was definitely helping to create body heat. He had wanted to have it inside, but I wanted it outside. It was our custom. They said we were shattering all the rules anyway and it didn't matter so we could protect my feet and legs from the snow.

No, I had said. Some things were sacred. Just because we were changing didn't mean that all our traditions and things we cherished had to go out the window.

Two days before our wedding, Grandpa Peter and Nana came with a lot of other family members and said they wanted to go on a gem expedition. They hadn't been in a while and wanted to take Seth and me with them.

They were getting older and needed the younger folks to help. So Dad, Mom, Rodney, and all of us packed up and we went into the mountains. Seth was so fascinated. I'd been on two of these in my lifetime and it was neat to watch. Grandpa didn't do too many of them anymore because his business did so well, he didn't need to.

But when the day was done, we camped out like we always did and they started to get weird, talking about life and love and all sorts of weird things around the fire. Seth and I remembered the last time we had a campfire and the ambush that ensued. But this time, Grandpa and the family had done something else entirely. Something that made me cry for a different reason. They took all the gems that Grandpa found in the dig that day and gave a third of the find's profits to Seth and me. The rest they saved for the family fund, for the fight coming, in case something happened. It made me think they were worried about their business or something. We had ways of getting money…but Grandpa wouldn't always be here.

That made me cry harder when I realized what Grandpa was doing. He was getting us ready in case something happened to him.

They all knew that Seth didn't have any money, coming from the Watsons, who had always spent and been bad with their investments, and he hadn't planned to use his degree, instead wanting to use his morals and brawn to save lives. They knew that he had given up his job because of what happened and were thrilled to hear that a new job had opened up for him. So the next surprise and the next "wedding ruiner", as Ember called it, was when, on the way home the next day, the family took us to a house in between the college and my parent's house. I didn't understand what was going on when we pulled in. I thought at first that Daddy was showing me a location for a new center or something. But the whole family came with us.

And Seth knew right away.

"It's for you," he whispered as we looked out his truck window at it.

"What?"

"The house." He gulped and looked over at me in the seat. "Rodney told me about the tradition." He smiled, but I could tell that he was feeling a little… inadequate stacked up against my family. They could do that sometimes. "I didn't know about it. We—the Watsons," he corrected and scolded himself for the mistake, "they didn't carry on that tradition. You could have told me that day when I was going on about getting you a ring and us living in my crappy apartment."

He scoffed a little laugh, but I could see it building. This was what I feared. This was *why* I hadn't said anything.

My college was already paid for, so that wasn't a problem. And honestly, I had no qualms about living in his apartment. I liked it. It was the perfect size for us. The tradition was all about making sure you could provide for your wife and honestly, in this day and age, asking a young guy like that to be able to buy his own house at such a young age was pretty unreasonable.

He tilted his head and smiled. "Doesn't take away the fact that I was supposed to buy you a house before I could marry you according to our people." He shook his head. "And by their standards, we'll never get married."

"Yeah," I whispered and nodded, "and look at all the wonderful things they've done lately. They've tried to deunify us, the leader of the council is a traitor with the Watsons, and they declared war on us just because you were defending yourself and me. That doesn't sound like a race of people that I want to listen to the letter on anymore. I think we should make our rules from now on. Follow the traditions we want and think are important and let everything else go."

He nodded and looked at the house again. "It's a gorgeous house. Nothing like I've ever lived in, that's for sure." He swung his eyes back to me. "As long as it makes you happy, that's all I care about. I don't care where we live or what we do. I just..." He licked his lip. "I just don't want your family to think that I can't take care of you. First the money we'll get from the gems, which is... insane. And now a house?"

"They don't think that," I assured him.

He smiled looking down. "Okay. Let's go before they think we're fighting about it or something and that's *all I need*."

He opened his door and got out, pulling me from his side, helping me down gently. He kissed my forehead before we turned and I jumped as everyone yelled, "Surprise!"

Seth's hand came out to rest on my wrist on instinct. He was right. I tried to smile, but I was so confused. Wouldn't they see how this would make a Virtuoso man feel weird about this? When it was his right to—

"Now before we go any further," Dad started and he and Grandpa Peter came and stood on either side of me and Seth, "Seth, we wanted to tell you that this is the first time we've ever done anything like this." Not helping,

Daddy. "We know that it's tradition for the man to buy his wife a house. It used to be the tradition for him to build the house back in the old days. In less prominent or wealthy clans, they've started to share duplexes and condos and I even heard of an old house boat a couple years back just so it qualifies as technically *buying her a house.* And this isn't the only tradition that needs to be changed. In the old days, it had its purpose for very good reason. But today, it hurts more than it helps. It's sad that we let it get this far. It's sad that we haven't done something before now. Like the other tradition where the wife leaves her family?" He shook his head. "I got lucky with Ava, but I watched her grow up thinking that I was only going to see her a handful of times after her marriage. Some of our traditions sounds so romantic and then some of them leave me scratching my head wondering what the council was thinking." He clapped Seth on the shoulder. "This is one of those things that we've decided to change. Our new tradition is that we're going to buy the couple their first home, the Jacobsons, as a family." He grinned. "They are under no obligation to keep it past a few years. It's a starter home. Then you sell it, move on, pick the home you truly want, or stay there forever, we don't care. Truly, it's yours." He looked at Seth. "I don't want you to think that we didn't think you could take care of Ava. This is just a landslide year of change. I have no doubt that she will be more than safe and happy with you. But I wanted to buy this house for you." He held the keys out to him. "So don't feel guilty about it. Just take them and let us do this. Not only is this a time for change, but you saved her—" He fisted the keys tightly, trying to get a rein on his emotions. I heard Maria sniffle beside me and turned to see her already crying as she watched.

If Daddy started to cry, I was going to lose it. I felt Grandpa's hand on my shoulder and smiled at him before looking back at Seth as Daddy tried to finish.

"You saved my Ava." He gripped his shoulder. "What I saw you do for her in that video—"

"I never meant for anyone to see that," Seth told him in a hurry and sighed, embarrassed at the attention. "I was just trying to..." He gritted his teeth. "Keep her from..." He shook his head. "It was an impossible situation."

I could tell this was just like when he'd been given those awards in his apartment. They wanted to award him for the good thing he'd done and he just wanted to brush it off. He glanced back at me and I knew I was right by the little bit of annoyance I saw there.

I smiled, maybe a little coyly, and held his arm tightly in my hands. He was losing this fight, he knew and I knew it.

"I know, son. I don't know that any of us could have done it better." Everybody shook their heads. I swear. *Everybody.*

Seth let a breath go from open lips. "Uh."

"Take it," Dad said, using his Champion voice. "Like I said, we are grateful to you for saving our Ava, so grateful, but this isn't charity or pity. This is the start of a new tradition." Daddy smiled. "And you're both just the first recipients. Take them."

Seth accepted the keys and everyone clapped. My cheesy family. "Thank you, sir," he whispered, letting his free hand slide down to take mine. He looked at our family. "Thank you," he said and I no longer wondered if he was thankful or embarrassed. It was obvious that Seth was caught in the moment, caught in the fact that a family would do something so big and wonderful for him. He looked up at that house and couldn't believe it was actually ours.

Let's go look inside.

He looked back at me. *Can we?*

It's ours now. I smiled.

"Who's next you think?" I heard Dad ask Mom behind us.

"I volunteer!" Ember yelled loudly, making me laugh so loud. "I volunteer as tribute!"

Everyone laughed and giggled, but I knew. Ember was beyond ready for her own story to begin. I couldn't think about that though because my significant picked me up in his arms, making me squeal, and carried me across the threshold. I didn't listen to my family's 'oohs' and 'awws' as we made our way inside, fighting with the lock as I tried to unlock it and he held me up, laughing the entire time.

When we finally made it inside, we just stood there on that hardwood floor and looked at each other. The house was gorgeous. It wasn't huge by any means, but it wasn't small. It had a small little backyard that I could imagine doing things with him in.

My family did good.

But in that moment, all I wanted to do was think about my life in it, starting with kissing him on every surface. He collided with me, his hand wrapping around my jaw as he moved me backward to the kitchen counter.

He lifted me easily and we made good use of it until we heard the door open.

Dawson and Maria laughed and stalled until we could get ourselves back together as everyone piled in. Maria later told me that she and Dawson had "christened" their house in a similar fashion.

I smiled thinking about it, biting my lip to stop it so no one would know.

"Imprinting isn't a life sentence," I heard and jolted back to the present. I looked up to Seth as he looked down at me, knowing what I was thinking about, and listened to Dad's words spoken, as they were spoken at every ceremony. "Our people thrive with our significant by our side. The proof of how destiny works and moves is right here in this circle, in this couple that will be joined together...today." I didn't look at Daddy as he got choked up. I couldn't. So I looked down at my new Chucks—the other "wedding ruiner" that Ember enjoyed so much, sarcasm not implied. How dare I not carry on the barefoot tradition and wear shoes on my feet instead? I wiggled each toe as if they each held some kind of little rebellion and smiled.

Seth has sprung them on me the night before our wedding. He redid the art on the tops of my Chucks just like he had done in the back of the truck that day. "At Last" on one side and "My Love" on the other. Such an amazingly sweet gesture when he knew how upset I was that they were ruined. And it was practically his vows, wasn't it? At last, my love.

"But more than destiny and purpose is love," Dad continued, his voice strong and ringing with conviction. "The love one feels for his significant is bigger than any ocean, deeper than any well, more powerful than any storm," I mouthed them with Dad and felt my eyes begin to well as I told them to Seth, believing them to my core. Seth took one of his hands from around my back and cupped my cheek, wiping my tears away. "When we join these significants today, they are telling us that they want no one else, they'll always be here for each other, and they will never part from their soulmate."

Ah, that dress...at least there are no tights.

I smirked. I was wearing Mom's dress that Gran had made for her. *No, just skin.*

His face changed as he thought about that. *Mean.*

After we said our vows, he kissed me so hard and long, his arms and hands reaching around me to press me to him so tightly. Truly it was as if the world around us didn't exist at all. People left us alone for a little while and eventually we danced. And no one did jigs; we just danced. All of us together.

There was no oil and water, no Watsons and Jacobsons, no Romeo and Juliet.

Just Seth and Ava.

Please continue on with me to the next book in the series,
UNDENIABLY FATED,
as the Jacobsons continue to fight for their family and their significants.

Information on release dates, these books and Shelly's other series,
giveaways, and all the ways to reach her on social media, on the author's site
www.shellycraneauthor.com

Now you can own the Significant song written for the first book in the series, *Significance*, by Kerrigan Brianne Arnold! A fan of the series and a songwriter and singer, she wrote and recorded this song for me and sent it to me. I fell in love with it and we decided to have it produced for you guys so YOU could enjoy this beautiful story in song that depicts Caleb and Maggie, or any significant's love story, so perfectly!

Go and get your copy of this single today!

iTunes: http://apple.co/109LfOU
Amazon: http://amzn.to/1A53Psk

Sunday Kind Of Love : Etta James

(Theme song) *Surround You* : Echosmith

Fire Escape : Sounds Under Radio

Looking For You : The Lone Bellow

Life Is Beautiful : Vega 4

Something I Need : One Republic

Black Bear : Andrew Belle

Movement And Location : Punch Brothers

Invented : Jimmy Eat World

Drown : Carolina Liar

Infinite : House of Heroes

Some Kind of Beautiful : Tyler Ward

The Funeral : Band of Horses

Thinking Out Loud : Ed Sheeran

The Fog : Biffy Clyro

Day Will Come : Keane

I Only Have Eyes For You : The Flamingos

Wings : Birdy

Miss America : Carolina Liar

Love Don't Die : The Fray

Photograph : Ed Sheeran

No Good In Goodbye : The Script

Shut The World : The Royal Concept

Rolling Waves : The Naked And Famous
New Love : Maroon 5
Pas de Deux : Graham Moseley Brown
At Last : Etta James

ABOUT THE AUTHOR

Shelly is a *NEW YORK TIMES & USA TODAY* bestselling author from a small town in Georgia and loves everything about the south. She is wife to a fantastical husband and stay-at-home mom to two boisterous and mischievous boys who keep her on her toes. She hoards paperbacks, devours sweet tea, searches year-round for candy corn, and loves to spend time with her family and friends, go out to eat at new restaurants, sight-see in the new areas they travel to, listen to music, and, of course, loves to read, but doesn't have much time to these days with all the characters filling her head begging to come out.

Her own books happen by accident and she revels in the writing and imagination process. She doesn't go anywhere without her notepad for fear of an idea creeping up and not being able to write it down immediately, even in the middle of the night, where her best ideas are born.

Please feel free to contact/follow Shelly at the following avenues.

www.facebook.com/shellycranefanpage
www.twitter.com/authshellycrane
www.shellycrane.blogspot.com
instagram.com/authshellycrane

CPSIA information can be obtained
at www.ICGtesting.com
Printed in the USA
LVHW081702131220
674080LV00044B/2839

9 781508 996392